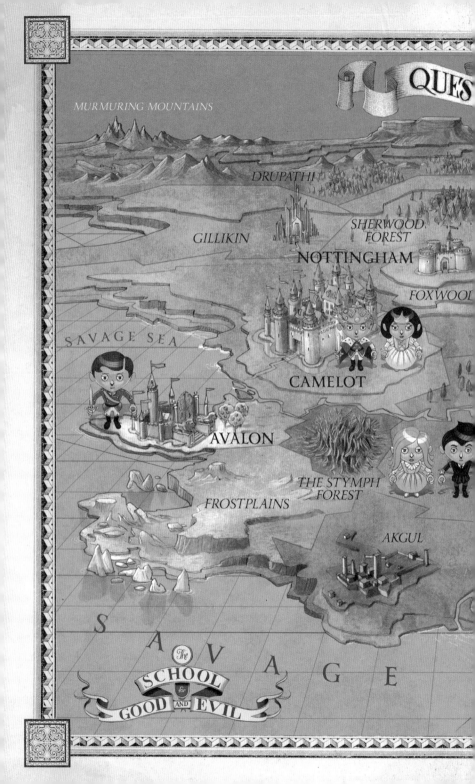

QUES[T]

MURMURING MOUNTAINS

DRUPATHI

GILLIKIN

SHERWOOD
FOREST

NOTTINGHAM

FOXWOO[D]

SAVAGE SEA

CAMELOT

AVALON

THE STYMPH
FOREST

FROSTPLAINS

AKGUL

S   A   V   A   G   E

The
SCHOOL *for*
GOOD *and* EVIL

SOMAN CHAINANI

The

SCHOOL

for

GOOD AND EVIL

QUESTS FOR GLORY

Illustrations by

IACOPO BRUNO

HARPER

An Imprint of HarperCollinsPublishers

The School for Good and Evil #4: Quests for Glory
Text copyright © 2017 by Soman Chainani
Illustration on page 190 by Michael Blank
Illustrations copyright © 2017 by Iacopo Bruno
All rights reserved. Printed in the United States of America.

Library of Congress Control Number: 2017942896
ISBN 978-0-06-265847-0 (trade bdg.) — ISBN 978-0-06-266768-7 (int.)
ISBN 978-0-06-267752-5 (special edition) — ISBN 978-0-06-268176-8 (special edition)
ISBN 978-0-06-274163-9 (special edition) — ISBN 978-0-06-274811-9 (special edition)

Typography by Amy Ryan
17 18 19 20 21   CG/LSCH   10 9 8 7 6 5 4 3 2 1
❖
First Edition

For Ally and Brendan

IN THE FOREST PRIMEVAL

A SCHOOL FOR GOOD AND EVIL

TWO TOWERS LIKE TWIN HEADS

ONE FOR THE PURE

ONE FOR THE WICKED

TRY TO ESCAPE YOU'LL ALWAYS FAIL

THE ONLY WAY OUT IS

THROUGH A FAIRY TALE

PART I

1

The Almost Queen

When you spend most of your life planning your Ever After with a girl, it feels strange to be planning your wedding to a boy.

A boy who'd been avoiding Agatha for months.

She couldn't sleep, dread brewing in her stomach. Her mind flurried with all the things left to do before the big day, but that wasn't the real reason she was still awake. No, it was something else: a memory of the boy she was about to marry . . . a memory she couldn't bear to think about. . . .

Tedros, stained with tears and slung over a man's shoulder. Tedros unleashing a primal scream, so pained and shattering that sometimes Agatha could hear nothing else—

She rolled over, burying her head under a pillow.

It had been six months since that day: the day of the coronation.

She hadn't slept well since.

Agatha felt Reaper tossing tetchily at the foot of the bed, her restlessness keeping him up. Agatha sighed, feeling sorry for him, and tried to focus on her breaths. Little by little, her mind began to ease. She was always better when she was doing something to help someone else, even if it was falling asleep to spare her bald, mashed-up cat. . . . If only she could do something to help her prince too, Agatha thought. Together they always managed to work things ou—

Click.

Her heart stopped.

The door.

She listened closely, hearing Reaper's soft snores and the sound of the latch creaking open.

Agatha pretended to sleep as her hand inched forward, probing for the knife on her night table.

She'd kept the knife there ever since she'd arrived at Camelot. She had to—Tedros earned enemies here long before he'd come to take his place as king. Even if these enemies were in jail now, they had spies everywhere, desperate to kill him and his future queen. . . .

And now the door to her chamber was opening.

No one was allowed in her hall at this hour. No one was allowed in her *wing*.

Moonlight spilled onto her back through the cracked-open door. Her breaths shallowed as she heard footsteps muffle against the marble floor. A shadow crept up her neck, stretching onto the bedsheets.

Agatha gripped the knife harder.

Slowly a weight sank into the mattress behind her.

Hold, she told herself.

The weight grew heavier. Closer.

Hold.

She could hear its breath.

Hold.

The shadow reached for her—

Now.

With a gasp, Agatha swiveled, swinging the knife for the intruder's neck before he seized her wrist and pinned her to the bed, the knife a millimeter from his throat.

Agatha panted with terror as she and the intruder stared into the wide whites of each other's eyes.

In the dark, it was all she could see of him, but now she felt the heat of his skin and smelled his fresh, dewy sweat, and all the fear seeped out of her body. Bit by bit, she let him pry the knife away before he exhaled and dropped into the pillow beside her. It all happened so fast, so softly, that Reaper never stirred.

She waited for him to speak or pull her to his chest or tell her why he'd been avoiding her all this time. Instead he just curled into a ball against her, whimpering like a tired dog.

Agatha stroked his silky hair, mopping up the sweat on his temples with her fingertips, and let him sniffle into her nightgown.

She'd never seen him cry. Not like this, so scared and defeated.

But as she held him, his breaths settled, his body surrendering to her touch, and he glanced up at her with the faintest of smiles. . . .

Then his smile vanished.

Someone was watching them. A tall, turbaned woman looming in the doorway, her gleaming teeth gnashed tight.

And just like that, Tedros was gone as quick as he came.

Splinters of August sun streamed through the window onto the chandelier, refracting light into Agatha's eyes.

Blinking groggily, she could see missing crystals in the chandelier, covered in cobwebs like an old gravestone.

She hugged her pillow to her chest. It still smelled like him. Reaper slithered up from the foot of the bed, sniffing at the pillow, poised to slash it to shreds, before Agatha shot him a look. Her cat slunk back to the foot of the bed. *He's improving at least*, Agatha thought; the first night in the castle, he'd peed in Tedros' shoe.

Voices echoed in her wing. She wouldn't be alone much longer.

Agatha sat up in her baggy black nightgown, peering at

her room. It was three times the size of her old house in Gavaldon, with dusty gem-crusted mirrors, a sagging settee, and a two-hundred-year-old desk of ivory and bone. Clutching her pillow like a life raft, she soaked in the quiet coming off the cracked marble tiles dyed robin's-egg blue and the matching walls inlaid with mottled gold flowers. The queen's chamber was like everything at Camelot: royal from afar, tarnished up close. This applied to her too—she was living in the queen's quarters but she wasn't even queen yet.

The wedding was still two months away.

A wedding that was making her uneasier each day.

Once upon a time, Agatha had imagined she'd live happily ever after with Sophie in Gavaldon. The two of them would be proud owners of a cottage in town, where they'd have tea and toast each morning, then jaunt off to Mr. Deauville's Storybook Shop, now the A&S Bookshop, since she and Sophie would take it over once the old man died. After work, she'd help pick herbs and flowers that Sophie would use to make her beauty creams, before they'd visit Agatha's mother on Graves Hill for dinners of lamb-brain stew and lizard quiche (steamed prunes and cucumbers for Sophie, of course). How ordinary their life would be together. How *happy*. Friendship was all they needed.

Agatha squeezed the pillow harder. *How things change.*

Now her mother was dead, Sophie was Dean of Evil at a magical school, and Agatha was marrying King Arthur's son.

No one was more excited about the wedding than Sophie, who'd sent letter after letter from her faraway castle with sketches of dresses and cakes and china that she insisted Agatha use for her big day. (*"Dear Aggie, I haven't heard back from you about the chiffon veil swatches I sent. Or the proposed canapés. Really, darling, if you don't want my help just tell me. . . ."*)

Agatha could see these letters piled on the desk, coated in spidery trails of dust. Every day she told herself she would answer them, but she never did. And the worst part was she didn't know why.

Footsteps grew louder outside her room.

Agatha's stomach churned.

It'd been this way for six months. She felt more and more anxious while Tedros grew more and more withdrawn. Last night was the closest they'd come to speaking about what happened on coronation day and neither of them had even said a word. She knew he was embarrassed . . . devastated . . . ashamed. . . . But she couldn't help him if he didn't talk to her. And he couldn't talk to her if he was never *with* her.

More voices now. More footsteps.

Mouth dry, Agatha snatched the glass of water from her night table. Empty. So was the pitcher.

Reaper slid off the bed, prowling towards the faded double doors.

She needed time alone with Tedros. Time where they weren't living separate lives. Time where they could be honest and intimate with each other like they used to be. Time where they could be *themselves* again—

The doors crashed open and four maids paraded in, each wearing the same draping robe in a different shade of pastel—peach, pistachio, grapefruit, rose—as if they were a box of mixed macarons. They were led by a tall, tan woman in lavender with dark, smoky eyes, shiny red lipstick, and wild black hair barely cooped by a turban. She carried a leather-bound notebook in one hand and in the other, a feather-pen so long it looked like a whip.

"Breakfast with the wedding florist at seven in the Blue Tower Dining Room; then meetings with tailor candidates in twenty-minute intervals to decide who should stitch the wedding linens; then an interview with the *Camelot Courier* for their Wedding Preview Edition. At nine, you'll visit the Camelot Zoo to pick the official wedding doves; they have several species, each a varying shade of white. . . ."

Agatha could barely listen, because Peach and Pistachio had hoisted her out of bed and were already scrubbing her with scalding towels, while Grapefruit shoved a toothbrush in her mouth and Rose smeared her face with an array of potions, like Sophie used to do, only without Sophie's charisma or humor.

"Then a signing of *The Tale of Sophie and Agatha* at Books & Crannies to raise funds for the castle's plumbing renovation," the lavender woman continued in a crisp, posh accent, "followed by a lunch fundraiser at the Spansel Club, where you'll read a storybook to children of rich patrons whose donations will repair the drawbridge . . ."

"Um, Lady Gremlaine? Is there time for me to see Tedros today?" muffled Agatha beneath a blue gown the women were tugging over her. "We haven't had a meal alone in ages—"

"After lunch, you'll begin waltz lessons to prepare for your wedding dance, then etiquette training so you don't make a mess of yourself at the wedding feast, and finally, history class about the triumphs and disasters of royal weddings past so that yours might end in the annals of the first rather than the last," Lady Gremlaine finished.

Agatha gritted her teeth as her maids fussed with her hair and makeup like the nymphs in the Groom Room used to. "Dancing, etiquette, history . . . it's the School for Good all over again. Only at school, I actually had time with my prince."

Lady Gremlaine raised her eyes to Agatha. She snapped her book shut so sharply a gemstone fell out of the mirror. "Well, since you have no further questions, your chambermaids here will see that you get to your breakfast on time," she said, turning for the door. "The king needs me by his side every possible moment—"

"I'd like to see Tedros today," Agatha insisted. "Please add it to my schedule."

Lady Gremlaine stopped cold and turned, her lips a tight red slash. The chambermaids subtly backed away from Agatha.

"I'd say you saw more than enough of him last night. Against the *rules*," said Lady Gremlaine. "A king cannot be alone in your room before the wedding."

"Tedros should have the right to see me whenever he wishes," said Agatha. "I am his queen."

"Not yet, Princess," said Lady Gremlaine coolly.

"I will be after the wedding," Agatha challenged, "which I spend all my time planning like some brainless biddy when I'd rather be with Tedros, helping him run the kingdom of which he is now king. And seeing that you're Chief Steward in service to the king *and* future queen, surely that's something you can arrange."

"I see," said Lady Gremlaine, moving towards Agatha. "The castle is crumbling, your king wears a crown still in dispute, you have spies plotting to kill you, the former queen and her traitorous knight have been in hiding since the coronation, and the *Royal Rot*, a rogue publication intent on overthrowing the monarchy, calls you, amongst other things, 'a gilded celebrity from an amateur fairy tale destined to bring more shame to Tedros than his own mother once did.'"

Lady Gremlaine smiled, lording over Agatha. "And here you are, still pining for your days at school and a little kissy-time in the hall with the Class Captain."

"No. That's not it at all. I want to *help* him," Agatha retorted, enduring the onslaught of her steward's perfume. "I'm fully aware of the problems we face, but Tedros and I are supposed to be a team—"

"Then why hasn't he ever asked to see *you?*" said Lady Gremlaine.

Agatha flinched.

"In fact, except for his momentary lapse last night, which he assured me will never happen again, the king hasn't mentioned your name once," Lady Gremlaine added.

Agatha said nothing.

"You see, I'm afraid King Tedros has better things to do, trying to bring Camelot out of *shame* in time for the wedding,"

Lady Gremlaine went on. "A wedding that must be so magnificent, so memorable, so *inspiring* that it will erase all doubts that rose from that humiliating coronation. And it is a wedding that, per thousands of years of tradition, is up to the future queen to plan. That's your job. That's how you can *help* your king." She leaned in, her nose almost touching Agatha's. "But if you would like me to tell King Tedros that you find your responsibilities beneath you and that you have questioned every one of our decisions, down to the colors of your wardrobe, the importance of baths, and your choice of footwear, and now, on top of that, would like him to interrupt his urgent efforts to prove his place as king so he can make you feel part of a *team* . . . then by all means, Princess. Let's see what he has to say."

Agatha swallowed, her neck rashing red. Her eyes drifted down to her clumps. "No . . . that's okay. I'm sure I'll see him tomorrow," she said softly, looking back up.

But Lady Gremlaine was gone and all that was left were her pastel minions, ready to whisk the princess to a breakfast she would have no time to eat.

Halfway through the day, Agatha was about to turn runaway bride.

She'd endured weeks of this with a forced smile—the same deadly dull routine of inspecting a thousand place-cards and cakes and candles and centerpieces, even though they all looked the same to her and she'd be happy marrying Tedros in a bat cave (she'd prefer it actually; no room for guests). Interspersed with all this tedium were appearances for "Camelot Beautiful," a queen-led campaign to raise funds for the broken-down castle that had been left to blight after King Arthur had died. Agatha believed in the cause wholeheartedly and had a high tolerance for nonsense—she was friends with Sophie after all—but Lady Gremlaine seemed determined to humiliate her with each day's schedule, whether making her sing the anthem at the Woods Rugby Cup (even the Camelot team covered their ears) or ride a bull at the Spring Fair (it bucked her into a mound of poo) or kiss the highest bidder in a Smooch-the-Princess auction (a toothless hoodlum who Lady Gremlaine insisted had won fair and square).

Guinevere had warned Agatha to expect resistance from her new warden. Lady Gremlaine had been Chief Steward when Guinevere was Arthur's wife, until she and Guinevere had a falling-out and Guinevere had her dismissed. But after Guinevere's disappearance and Arthur's death, his Council of Advisors took over Camelot since Tedros wasn't yet sixteen— and these advisors brought Lady Gremlaine *back*. Now with Guinevere returned to the castle, surely Gremlaine would be prickling to exert control over Guinevere's son and his new queen. Even worse, the old fusspot couldn't be fired until Tedros' coronation was sealed.

Knowing this, Agatha had tried to befriend her steward, but Lady Gremlaine hated her at first sight. Agatha had no idea why, but clearly the woman didn't want her marrying

Camelot's king. It was as if Lady Gremlaine thought if she just tried hard enough, Agatha would give up her groom before the wedding.

I'd sooner die, Agatha vowed.

So for the last six months, she'd woken up each morning ready for the fight.

But today was the day that broke her.

First there was the florist, who shoved Agatha's face in so many effluvious bouquets over the course of an hour that she'd left red-eyed and nose dripping. Next there were the six tailors who showed her dozens of linens that looked exactly the same. Then came the reporter from the *Camelot Courier*, a miserably cheerful young girl named Bettina, who arrived sucking a red lollipop.

"Lady Gremlaine already scripted all your answers, so let's have an off-the-record chat for *fun*," she diddled, before launching into an array of startlingly personal questions about Agatha's relationship with Tedros: "What does he wear when he sleeps?" "Does he have a nickname for you?" "Do you ever catch him looking at other girls?"

"*No*," Agatha said to the last, about to add, "especially not fart bubbles like you," but she held her tongue through nearly an hour of this before she'd had enough.

"So do you and Tedros want children?" Bettina wisped.

"Why? Are you looking for parents?" Agatha snapped.

The meeting was over after that.

She nearly lost her temper again at the Spansel Club fund-raiser when she had to read *The Lion and the Snake*, a famous

Camelot storybook, to rich, bratty children, who kept interrupting her because they already knew the story. Now in
her carriage after picking wedding doves at the zoo, Agatha
slumped over in her sweaty gown, thinking of the waltz and
etiquette lessons ahead, and sucked back tears.

"The king hasn't mentioned your name once," Lady Gremlaine echoed.

She'd tried to pretend that the meddling bat had lied. But
Agatha knew she hadn't.

Even when Agatha had run into Tedros in the castle
these past few months, he'd tell her how pretty she looked or
prattle something inane about the weather or ask her if she
was comfortable in her quarters before shuttling away like a
spooked squirrel. Last night in her room was the first time
she'd seen him without a flushed, plastic smile on his face
that told her not to ask how he was doing because he was
doing just fine.

But he wasn't fine, of course. And she didn't know how to
help him.

Agatha dabbed at her eyes. She had come to Camelot for
Tedros. To be *his* queen. To stand by him in his finest and
darkest hours. But instead they were both alone, fending for
themselves.

It was clear he needed her. That's why he'd crawled into
her arms last night. So why couldn't he just admit it? She knew
deep down it wasn't her fault. But she still couldn't help feeling
rejected and hurt.

Reaper curled up in her lap, reminding her he was there.

She rubbed his bald head. "If only we could go back to our graveyard before we ever thought about boys."

Reaper spat in agreement.

Agatha gazed out the window of her blue-and-gold carriage as it rolled into Maker's Market, the main thoroughfare of Camelot City. Given the conditions of its roads, her driver normally avoided it and took the longer route back to the castle, but they were already running late for her wedding waltz lesson and she didn't want to make a poor impression on her new teacher. Dirt kicked up around the carriage from unpaved streets, clouding her view of the bright-colored tents, each carrying a flag with Camelot's crest: two eagles, flanking the sword Excalibur on a blue shield.

But as the dust cleared, Agatha noticed a stark divide between the rich villagers in expensive coats and jewels as they shopped along the main street and the thousands of grimy, skeletal peasants living in crumbling shanties in the alley-ways adjoining the market. Royal guards patrolled these slums, forcefully blocking any peasants who drew too close to wealthy patrons entering or leaving the tents. Agatha slid down her window to get a better view, but her driver rapped his horsewhip on the glass—

"Lay low, milady," he said.

Agatha pushed the window back up. When she first rode into her new kingdom six months ago, she'd seen the same slum cities smack in the middle of Camelot. As Tedros explained then, his father had led Camelot to a golden age, where every citizen improved his or her fortune. But upon

Arthur's death, his advisors had allied with the rich, passing shady laws to reclaim land and wealth from the middle-class, plunging them into poverty. Tedros had vowed to undo these laws and resettle those without homes, but in the past half-year, the divide between rich and poor had only gotten worse. Why hadn't he succeeded? Had he not seen how far his father's legacy had fallen? How could he let his own kingdom languish like this? If *she* was king—

Agatha exhaled. But she wasn't, was she. She wasn't even queen yet. And from the way Tedros acted last night, he was clearly frustrated too. He was managing Camelot by himself and had no one to help him: not her, not his father, not his mother, not Lancelot, not even Merlin, the last three of who'd been gone for the past six months—

SPLAT! A black, mashed hunk of food hit the window. Agatha spun to see a filthy peasant yell, "SO-CALLED KING AND HIS ALMOST QUEEN!"

Suddenly, others in the slum cities spotted her carriage and globbed onto the chant—"SO-CALLED KING AND HIS ALMOST QUEEN!"—while pelting her vehicle with food, shoes, and handfuls of dirt. Her driver beat the horses harder, racing them out of the market.

Blood boiling, Agatha wanted to leap out of the carriage and tell those goons that none of this was her or Tedros' fault— not the slum cities, not the coronation, not a once-legendary kingdom gone to shambles—

How would that help anything? Agatha scolded herself. If she were starving in the streets, wouldn't she blame herself and

Tedros too? They were the ones in power now, even if they hadn't caused the kingdom's fall. The poor and suffering had no time for the past, only for progress. But this wasn't school anymore, where progress could be charted with rankings and a scoreboard. This was real life and despite the dismal results thus far, they were two teenagers trying to be good leaders.

Or Tedros was, surely.

She was on her way to dancing lessons.

Agatha sulked as the carriage rumbled up the hill towards the bone-white gates of Camelot, which the royal guards pulled open for their arrival. It didn't matter that the gates were streaked with rust or the towers ahead faded by weather and soot. Camelot Castle was still a magnificent sight, built into jagged gray cliffs over the Savage Sea. Under the August sun, the white spires took on a liquid sheen, capped with rounded blue turrets that speared through low-flying clouds.

The carriage stopped short of a gap in the cliffs, leading to the castle's entrance.

"Drawbridge is still broken from the coronation, milady," the driver sighed, pulling into a carriage house at the edge of the cliff. "We'll have to use the ropes to cross."

Agatha barreled out of the carriage herself before the driver could open her door. *Enough whining*, she thought, as she wobbled along the unsteady rope bridge that even honored guests had to use until the embarrassing drawbridge problem could be fixed. Tedros wasn't haggling over when they would have time alone. Tedros wasn't hounding her about being a team. Tedros was working for his *people*, like she should be.

Maybe Lady Gremlaine was right, Agatha confessed. Maybe she should stop obsessing over what she couldn't do as queen and start focusing on the one thing she could. Indeed, a wedding filled with love and beauty and intention might be just the way to restore the kingdom's faith in them after the coronation. A wedding could show everyone that Camelot's best days were to come . . . that her and Tedros' Ever After had brought them here for a reason . . . that they could find a happy ending not just as King and Queen, but for the people too, even those who'd lost hope. . . .

Head held high, Agatha marched back into the castle, eager for her wedding lessons now and determined to do her very best.

That is, until she found out who was teaching them.

How Not to Throw a Coronation

Though he had no time for himself, no time for Agatha, no time at all, Tedros refused to get soft.

In his knee-length black socks and cut-off breeches, he snuck through the dark, muggy halls of Gold Tower, a towel slung over his bare, tanned chest. He knew it was vain and obsessive, this getting up at half past four to exercise, but it felt like the only thing left he could actually control. Because at six on the dot, Lady Gremlaine and four male stewards would barge into his room and from that moment until he slogged back into bed at night, he was no longer in charge of his own life.

He passed Agatha's room, tempted to slip in and wake her up, but he'd gotten in trouble for that last night and he didn't need any more trouble. His kingdom was already on the verge of revolt. That's why he'd ceded Lady Gremlaine total control over the castle. As Arthur's once-steward, she was a known face and gave people faith that the new king would be well-managed. But there was another reason he'd let Gremlaine keep him on a tight leash, one he could never say out loud.

Tedros didn't trust himself as king.

He needed someone like Lady Gremlaine who could watch his every move, who would check his every decision. If he'd only listened to her at the coronation, none of this would have happened. But he was listening to her now. Because if there was one thing he knew, it was that there could be no more mistakes.

Last night had already been a serious blunder. Lady Gremlaine had warned him not to repeat his father's errors and let a girl interfere with his duties as king. Tedros took this warning seriously. Up until yesterday, he'd done well to concentrate on his tasks and let Agatha concentrate on hers, even if it meant he'd had more freedom to see Agatha at school than he did now as king in his own castle. But then he'd gone and snuck into her room dead-tired, defenses down, and acted like a sniveling child. Tedros cringed, replaying the moment in his head. He'd brought Agatha to Camelot away from everyone and everything she knew, and he wanted her to feel safe and taken care of. He couldn't let her see how weak and scared he was. He couldn't let her see that all he wanted to do was run away with her. To hold her tight and shut the world out.

But that's exactly what he had done last night.

And for the fleeting relief he'd found in her arms, he left his future queen anxious and worried for him and his steward angry and disappointed.

Stop acting like a boy, Tedros chastised himself. *Act like a king.*

So today he let Agatha sleep, even if it left a big black hole in his heart.

Tedros scuttled through the hall's colossal gold passage and soaring arches, sweat sopping his wavy blond hair, his breeches sticking to his thighs. He couldn't remember the castle ever feeling this stifling. Two mice darted past him into a hole in the plaster. A procession of ants wove around the friezes of famous knights on the wall, now damaged and missing limbs. When his father and mother were king and queen, this hall used to be minty clean, even in the August doldrums. Now it smelled like dead cat.

Down three flights he went, socks slippery on dull gold stone, before he hustled through the Gymnasium, a lavish collection of training equipment surrounded by weapons and armor from Camelot's history, enclosed in glass cases. One would assume this was Tedros' destination, but instead he scurried right through, his pure blue eyes pinned to the dusty floor, trying not to look at the large glass case in the center of

the room . . . the one case that happened to be empty. Its plac-
ard read:

He was still thinking about that large, empty case when he
arrived at King's Cove, a sunken bathing pool in the bowels of
the castle. When he was a young prince, this manmade grotto
had flowering vines around tall piles of rock and a steam-
ing-hot waterfall. The balmy water once shimmered with a
thousand purple and pink lights from fairies who tended the
pool in exchange for safe shelter at Camelot. Tedros remembered his mornings here as a child, racing the fairies around
his father's statue at the center of the pool, his tiny opponents
lighting up the water like fireworks.

King's Cove was different now. The pool was dark and
cold, the water algae-green. The plants were dead, the waterfall a drip, drip, drip. The fairies were gone too, banished from
the castle by Arthur after Guinevere and Merlin had both
abandoned him, destroying Arthur's faith in magic.

Tedros looked down at the kettlebells he'd stolen from the
gym and stashed by the pool, along with a sad, lowly rope he'd
tied to the ceiling to practice climbing.

He couldn't exercise in that other room. Not if he had to
be near that empty case and think about where the sword was
now.

Slowly, his eyes rose to his father's statue in the murky pool, caked with moss and dirt—King Arthur, Excalibur in hand, staring down at him.

Only he wasn't staring. At least not anymore. His eyes were gone, violently gouged out, leaving two big black holes.

Tedros endured a wave of guilt, more intense than the one he'd felt in the gym.

He'd done it.

He'd carved out his own father's eyes.

Because he couldn't bear the old king looking at him after what happened at the coronation.

I'll fix it, Father, he vowed. *I'll fix everything.*

Tedros tossed his towel onto the mildewed floor and dove into the pool, thoughts wiped out by the harsh, stabbing cold.

Six months before, the day of the coronation had been brilliant and warm.

Tedros was utterly spent after everything that had happened leading up to it—reconciling with his mother, fighting a war against an Evil School Master, and making an all-night ride from school to Camelot in time for him to be crowned king the next day.

And yet, despite feeling like a sore, sleepless zombie, he couldn't stop smiling. After so many false starts and twists and turns, he'd finally found his Ever After. He was the ruler of the most legendary kingdom in the Woods. He'd have Agatha by his side forever. His mother (and Lancelot) would live with them in the castle. For the first time since he was a child, he had a full family again—and soon a queen to share it with.

Any one of those would be a wonderful enough gift on this, his sixteenth birthday. But the best present of all? Sophie, his old friend-enemy-princess-witch, had been appointed Dean at the School for Evil far far away, where she'd remain at a safe distance from him and Agatha. Which meant no more Sophie thuggery, no more Sophie skullduggery for the rest of their lives. (He'd learned from experience that he and that girl couldn't be in the same place without killing each other, kissing each other, or a lot of people ending up dead.)

"Hmm, can't Merlin do a spell to make this smell better?" Tedros said in front of his bedroom mirror, sniffing at his father's old robes. "This thing is rancid."

"Whole *castle* is rancid," groused Lancelot, gnawing on a slab of dried beef. "And I haven't seen Merlin since he hopped out of the carriage in Maidenvale. Said he'd meet us at the castle. Should be here by now."

"Merlin runs on his own time," Guinevere sighed, sitting next to Lancelot on her son's bed.

"He'll be here soon. Can't possibly miss my coronation," Tedros said, holding his nose. "Maybe if we spritz this with a little cologne—"

"It's a coronation gown, Teddy. You only have to wear it once," said his mother. "Besides, I don't smell anything except whatever it is Lance raided from the pantry."

"Oh be serious, Gwen," Lancelot growled, smacking at the bedsheets and spawning a dust storm. "What *happened* to this place?"

"Don't worry. Agatha and I will fix everything," Tedros

declared, combing his hair. "We knew what we were coming back to. Dad's advisors let the castle go to waste and lined their pockets with the kingdom's taxes. Would've loved to have seen their faces when Lance threw them in the dungeons."

"Oddly calm, to be honest. As if they expected it—or at least knew better than to fight," Lance said, with a loud belch. "Insisted I don't have the authority to jail them until Tedros is king. Told them to sod off."

"They're right," Guinevere clipped. "And if you can't eat like a proper human, I'll have the kitchen put you on a vegetable diet."

Tedros and Lancelot gaped at her.

"They're *right*?" Tedros asked incredulously.

"*Vegetables?*" Lancelot blurted, mouth full.

"Until your coronation as king is official, the Council of Advisors appointed by Arthur has full authority to decide who runs Camelot," Guinevere explained. "But in a few hours you *will* be king and it's not like there's a rival with a claim to the throne they can summon out of thin air. That's why the guards didn't stop Lance from jailing them."

Reassured, Tedros went back to assessing his reflection.

"Darling, enough with the mirror. You look beautiful," his mother said. "Meanwhile, poor Agatha is getting ready by herself and surely needs a lady's help. Why don't I go to her and leave you here with Lan—"

"Agatha's fine," Tedros said, picking at an annoying pimple near his mouth. *God, I'm almost as bad as Sophie*, he thought.

But he was about to have an entire kingdom judging him. Who wouldn't be self-conscious? "Besides, it's my birthday," he added, "and I want to spend time with my mother."

He saw his mother blush, still unused to him being nice to her.

"Sounds more like Little King's afraid of being alone with me," Lancelot cracked.

"Call me 'little' again and I'll run you through," Tedros flared, tapping Excalibur on his waist. "No one on earth would choose to be alone with you anyway."

"Except your mother. Likes our alone time just fine," said Lancelot tartly.

"Oh good lord," Guinevere mumbled.

"In any case, Agatha has that strange steward woman helping her get ready, the one who greeted us when we arrived last night and reeks of perfume," said Tedros, checking his teeth. "Wanted to help me get ready but I said I had you two. Didn't seem happy about it."

"What's the story there, Gwen? Looked about as thrilled to see you as you did her," said Lancelot.

"There is no story. She was my steward until after Tedros was born. I had her dismissed. Now she's back," Guinevere said curtly.

"Well, clearly something happened between you two—"

"Nothing happened."

"Then why are you making the same face about her as you made around Millie?"

"Who's Millie?" Tedros asked.

"A horny goat that used to chase your mother around the farm," Lancelot said.

Guinevere kicked him.

"God, you two had a lot of free time out there," Tedros muttered into the mirror.

"Lady Gremlaine is irrelevant," said Guinevere, sobering. "A steward only has responsibility over a prince until his coronation. After you seal your coronation, you're in charge and can remove Lady Gremlaine from the castle once and for all."

"So what does that mean, 'seal my coronation'? I repeat a few vows and give a speech?" Tedros asked, finally tired of looking at himself. He plopped on a sooty armchair next to the bed.

His mother frowned. "You said you knew what happened at a coronation."

"That you didn't need a 'lecture' from us," sniped Lancelot.

"Well, is there something special about the speech I should know about?" Tedros said impatiently.

"There is no speech, you twit," Lancelot retorted.

Tedros blinked. "Then when do I introduce you two as part of my royal court?"

His mother and Lancelot exchanged looks. "Um, Teddy, I don't think that's a good move—"

"It's the right move and the right move *is* the Good move," said Tedros. "It's been years since what happened between you two and Dad. I'm sure the people have moved on."

Lancelot drew a breath. "Tedros, it's not that simple. You're not thinking about all the—"

"If we live in fear, we'll never get anything done," said Tedros, cutting him off. "I'll tell this Gremlaine woman to seat you on the stage next to me."

"I'm sure that will go over well," his mother said cryptically.

Lancelot gave her another curious look, but Guinevere didn't elaborate.

Tedros let the point go. From his one interaction with Lady Gremlaine, he was confident his new steward would abide by his wishes.

"So if there's no speech, then what is there?" he asked, reclining against the chair.

"The chaplain will swear you in and make you repeat your vows in front of the kingdom," his mother said. "Then you have to complete a ceremonial test."

Tedros' eyes widened. "Like those written tests we had in Good Deeds class?"

"You really are clueless," Lancelot grouched. "It's a test of your father's choosing, written in his will and revealed at the coronation."

"Pfft, Dad told me about that. That's not a 'test,'" Tedros scoffed. "It's a token gesture. Said he'd never pick something I couldn't do. That he'd pick something to make me look as strong and commanding before my people as possible."

"Make you look strong and commanding? That's a test in itself," Lancelot murmured.

Guinevere glared at him and moved next to her son.

"So I have to perform the test Dad left for me?" said Tedros. "And then . . . I'm king."

"Then you're king," his mother smiled, ruffling his hair.

Tedros smiled back, his heart light as a cloud (even though he'd have to comb his hair again).

"But first there's dancing monkeys," said Lancelot.

"Oh hush," said Guinevere, chortling.

Tedros glanced between them. "Very funny."

His mother was still laughing.

"Very *funny*," Tedros repeated.

"Presenting the Mahaba Monkeys of Malabar Hills!" the courtier shouted.

A cannon blew confetti on the crowd and the people cheered, at least 50,000 of them, packed onto the hills beneath the castle. Per tradition, the drawbridge had been lowered, inviting citizens of Camelot onto royal grounds. They'd been crossing over since the morning to witness the coronation of King Arthur's son and yet there were still thousands who wouldn't fit, leaving them stranded on the drawbridge or below the cliffs, peering up at the castle balcony and the beautiful stone stage built for the occasion.

Sitting onstage, however, Tedros knew full well it wasn't stone. It was cheap, rickety wood, masked with paint that made it look like stone and it creaked hideously under the weight of his father's throne. Even worse, hot wax dripped onto his sweltering robes from wobbly candelabras they'd nicked from the castle chapel to save on ceremonial torches. Still, he'd kept his mouth shut: Camelot was broke and splurging on a coronation would be irresponsible. But now, watching hapless performers from neighboring realms, he was beginning to lose patience. First there was a fire-eater from Jaunt Jolie who accidentally set her dress aflame; then a tone-deaf chanteuse from Foxwood who forgot the lyrics to "God Save the King"; then two portly young brothers from Avonlea who fell off a flying trapeze into the crowd . . .

And now apes.

"If they weren't trying so hard, I'd think they were mocking me," Tedros grumbled, itching under his robes.

"I'm afraid the more skilled acts were out of budget," Lady Gremlaine said from her seat beside him, sipping at a goblet of sparkling water. "We did pay for the monkeys, however. They were your father's favorite."

Tedros peered downstage at the six monkeys in red sequined fedoras, scratching their privates and wagging their bums out of synch.

"Was this before or after he started drinking," Tedros said.

Lady Gremlaine didn't laugh.

Agatha would have, he thought peevishly. Not only that, but for a woman who'd been determined to spend time with him, Lady Gremlaine didn't seem to like him much.

When they first met last night, he'd assumed she thought him handsome and charming and would do anything he asked. But now that they were seated together, she kept throwing him skeptical looks any time he spoke as if he had the brain of an oyster. It was undermining his confidence right when he needed it most.

"I don't understand why Agatha can't sit here with me," he said, squinting at the royal gallery below on the lawn where she was just a shadow, cooped up with the dukes, counts, and other titled nobles. "Or my mother for that matter."

Lady Gremlaine straightened her turban. "Agatha is not your queen yet. After you're married, she can join you at official events. As for your mother, given her and Lancelot's ignominious flight from the castle, I thought it best to keep them out of sight and withhold news of their return until a more appropriate time."

Tedros followed her eyes to a white scrim curtaining off the balcony behind them. Through the scrim, he could see his mother and Lancelot watching the ceremony with a few maids and kitchen boys.

"It's a wonder news hasn't leaked," Lady Gremlaine added. "Lancelot made a spectacle throwing those advisors into the castle jail last night."

"Who cares if it had leaked?" Tedros countered. "The sooner we tell the people my mother and Lance have returned the better."

"Once you are crowned king, you can make your own decisions."

"It's just stupid having my own mother confined like a leper while I sit here with you," Tedros badgered, glancing up at a cloud blocking the sun. "As if you're my queen or something."

Lady Gremlaine pursed her lips.

"When Merlin gets here, give him your seat, as he'll be my *real* advisor once I'm king," Tedros piled on.

"Merlin won't breach the gates of Camelot. After he deserted your father, Arthur had him banned from the kingdom," said Lady Gremlaine.

Tedros gave her a bewildered look. Neither Merlin nor his father had ever told him that.

"Well, Arthur also put a death warrant on my mother's head and she's very much alive," Tedros said brusquely. "I don't follow an ex-king's edict and neither does Merlin, even if it was my father's."

"Then why isn't Merlin *here*?" Lady Gremlaine challenged.

Tedros bristled, wondering the same thing. "He'll be here. You'll see."

He has to be, the prince thought. The idea of ruling Camelot without Merlin was unfathomable.

"I wouldn't bet on it. Defying banishment is punished by death," said Lady Gremlaine crisply.

Tedros snorted. "If you think you can execute Merlin while I'm king you're as clueless as those monkeys."

A sequined hat hit him in the face and he swiveled to see the chimps in a violent brawl, pummeling each other as the crowd tittered.

"Is this really the *best* we can do?" Tedros moaned. "Who planned this idiocy?"

"I did," said Lady Gremlaine.

"Well, let's hope you're not planning the wedding."

"The wedding is planned entirely by the future queen," Lady Gremlaine said, her face a cold mask. "I hope she is capable."

"That's a bet I'm willing to take," said Tedros defiantly, trying not to frown.

Agatha: the *wedding planner*? Hadn't she dressed as a bride for Halloween? If it were up to her, they'd marry at midnight in a boneyard, with that satanic cat presiding. . . .

She'll be fine, he thought. Agatha always found a way. She'd no doubt share his opinion of Lady Gremlaine and his determination to prove her wrong. Plus, once Agatha saw how he handled his coronation, with royal decorum and integrity, she'd follow his example for the wedding. Soon Lady Grimface would be eating her words.

A long while later, after the monkeys had been soothed with a vat of banana pudding and dragged from the stage, Tedros took his place before Camelot's chaplain, perilously old, with a bright red nose and wiry hair growing out of his ears. The chaplain put his hand on Tedros' back and guided him to the front of the stage, overlooking the teeming hills.

On cue, the sun broke out from behind the cloud, spilling onto the young prince.

An awed hush fell over the crowd.

Tedros could see the legions gazing up at him with wide-eyed hope: the boy who vanquished the School Master . . . the boy who saved the Ever kingdoms . . . the boy who would make Camelot great again.

"I'm king of *all* these people?" Tedros rasped, the weight of responsibility finally hitting him.

"Oh, oh, your father asked the same thing, lad! Fear is a very good sign," the old chaplain said, hacking a laugh. "And luckily, no one can hear us from way up here."

The chaplain turned to a skinny, red-haired altar boy, who carefully handed him a jeweled box. The chaplain opened it. Sunlight ricocheted through five spires like a web of gold, eliciting gasps from the mob. Tedros gazed down at King Arthur's crown, the five-pointed fleur-de-lis, each with a diamond in the center.

Once, when he was six, he'd stolen it from his father's bed table and worn it to his lessons with Merlin, insisting the wizard bow and call him King. He assumed Merlin would put an end to his mischief—but instead the wizard obeyed his command, bowing eminently and addressing him as Your Majesty, all the way through math and astronomy and vocabulary and history. Perhaps the old wizard would have let him be king forever . . . but soon the young prince removed his crown and sheepishly returned it to his father's table. For it was too heavy for his soft little head.

Now, ten years later, the chaplain held out the very same crown. "Repeat after me, young prince. The words might sound a bit funny, given it's an oath that harkens back two thousand years. But words aren't what make a king. That fear you feel is all you need. Fear means you know this crown has a history and future far bigger than you. Fear means you are ready, dear Tedros: ready to quest for glory."

Legs quivering, Tedros repeated the chaplain's oath.

"By thy Lord, on wrest that Godes doth place on my head, I swear to uphold the honor of Camelot against all foel. I swear to be a beacon in the darknell to thy enlightened realm . . ."

Like the old man warned, he tripped over the strange sylla-bles and sounds, without knowing what he was saying. And yet, somewhere in his heart he did. His eyes welled up, the moment getting to him. Just a few years ago, he was a first-year boy at the School for Good and Evil, full of bluster and insecurity.

Now the boy would be a king.

A husband.

And someday a father.

Tedros made a silent prayer: that he would do Good as all three, just like the man who had made him. A man who he loved and missed every single day of his life. A man he'd give anything to touch one last time.

The chaplain placed the crown upon Tedros' head and tears streamed down the young king's cheeks while the crowd roared a passionate ovation that lasted long after he'd managed to get his emotions under control.

The chaplain patted his shoulder. "And now to seal the coronation and officially make you king, you must complete the ceremonial tes—"

"Do you mind if I say a few words first?" he asked the chaplain. "To my people, I mean."

The chaplain furrowed. "It is a bit unusual to speak before the proceedings are complete, especially since no one will hear you."

Something fell from above, right into the folds of Tedros'

oversized robe: a small five-pointed white star, like the ones Merlin used to lay in tribute at his father's tomb in Avalon.

"Strange," Tedros said, studying it closely. "Why would one of these be . . ."

His voice instantly amplified for miles.

The crowd gaped in astonishment, as did the chaplain, but Tedros knew full well where such sorcery had come from.

He looked up into the big blue sky and smiled. "Thanks, M," he whispered.

Then he put the magic star on his shoulder so it would broadcast him far and wide.

"Felt funny looking down at all of you without saying hello," he spoke, his voice resounding over the cliffs. "So, um, hello! I'm Tedros. And welcome to the . . . show."

Crickets.

"Right. You know who I am. Same boy who used to stand here and fidget when my father gave speeches. Just older now. And hopefully a bit better looking."

A ripple of laughter.

Tedros smiled, feeling the warmth of the crowd. They *wanted* to hear from him. They wanted him to do well.

He searched for Agatha below, but the sun washed out the faces. He was so used to having his princess by his side when it mattered. But after all they'd been through, he could feel her inside him even when they were apart. What would she tell him to say?

The same thing she always told him to say: the truth about what he was feeling.

Only he was never very good at that.

Tedros took a deep breath.

"When I was a boy standing up here with my dad, Good and Evil seemed so black and white," he said, his voice steadying. "But of all the things I learned at school, one lesson proved the most important: no one knows what is good or bad until after the story is written. No one knows if a happy ending will last or if a happy ending is happy at all. The only thing we have is the moment we are in and what we choose to do with it.

"And so here we are at *this* moment. A moment where riding into Camelot doesn't feel the same as it used to when I was a boy. We aren't the shining kingdom by which all others are measured anymore. The streets are dirty, the people are hungry, and I can feel a rot at our core. Even the king's chamber smells a bit moldy.

"Part of it is neglect, of course," Tedros went on, "and those responsible have been removed from power and punished. But that won't fix our problems. Even if we could bring back my father, King Arthur couldn't make things the way they were. The Woods have been changed forever by an Evil School Master. And though he is dead now, the line between Good and Evil has blurred. Enemies disguise as friends and friends as enemies. Look at our own Camelot, decayed from the *inside*."

The masses were rapt as they listened, their bodies like trees in a windless forest.

"I may be young. I may be untested. But I trust my instincts," Tedros declared, confidence growing. "Instincts that helped me find my way back to you even when I had Evil's sword at my heart and an axe at my neck. Instincts that helped me choose the greatest of all princesses, soon to be your queen."

Everyone followed his eyes to the royal gallery, where the nobles stepped back, revealing Agatha in the sun's spotlight.

Tedros smiled, expecting applause.

He didn't get it.

The crowd took in her pallid, ghostly face, buggy brown eyes, and witchy black helmet of hair and then seemed to look around her, as if she was a stand-in for the great princess Tedros was speaking of, as if they couldn't believe that *this* was the Agatha whose fairy tale had grown so famous throughout the Endless Woods. . . . But then they saw the diadem on her head—the same tiara Arthur once bestowed upon his own wife—and their postures stiffened, a soft murmur building.

"Together, Agatha and I have faced down terrible villains and found our happy ending," said Tedros. "But after a fairy tale comes real life. This is no longer my and Agatha's story, written by the Storian. This is the story of our kingdom, which we must all write together. A history and future you are now a part of, even those who doubted my father, even those who doubt me. Today we turn the page."

He took a deep breath. "And to prove that this is indeed the beginning of a new Camelot, my first act as your king is to present two members of my royal court. Two people who know our kingdom better than anyone and will protect it with love and courage."

From the corner of his eye, he saw Lady Gremlaine leap out of her seat—

In a flash, Tedros tomahawked Excalibur across the stage, slashing open the scrim over the castle balcony, before the sword planted blade-first in the balcony's archway.

"Presenting my mother, Queen Guinevere, and our greatest knight, Sir Lancelot!"

Tedros beamed down at the crowd, believing full-heartedly that since he'd learned to forgive Guinevere and Lancelot, his people would do the same.

But now there was a collective wide-eyed gape as if they'd all stopped breathing, and a cold, deathly silence.

"Come, Mother. Come Lance," Tedros prodded, hurrying over to his mother and yanking at her hand—

Gobsmacked, Guinevere stumbled over the fallen scrim, losing a shoe and almost face-planting before Lancelot caught her and glared daggers at Tedros. "What the hell are you doing!"

"Sit down!" Tedros hissed, shoving his one-shoed mother into his throne and Lancelot into Lady Gremlaine's seat, while Lady Gremlaine gawped in horror.

Something in the crowd changed too. Tedros felt it in his gut: the way the once warm, hopeful air had turned wary upon his unveiling of Agatha and now had become menacing and tense. Sweat pooled beneath his crown.

His heart had told him welcoming back his mother and Lancelot was the right thing to do . . . the *Good* thing . . .

Did I make a mistake?

He swallowed his doubt. No going back now.

"Let's get to the test," Tedros pressured the chaplain, eager to seal this coronation and get his mother and Agatha inside.

"Yes—uh—of course," the chaplain stammered, his eyes darting to Guinevere and the knight as he fumbled a faded parchment card from his robes. "Uh, hear ye, hear ye. As all prior kings, King Arthur Pendragon conceived this test to prove his successor be worthy of—"

Tedros ripped the card from his hands and read it out loud, his voice booming through the magic star:

"To seal his coronation, the future King of Camelot must pull Excalibur from an ordinary stone, as I once did."

"Wow. That's easy," he blurted, voice echoing.

He hadn't meant for the crowd to hear that.

"CAN SOMEONE FIND ME A STONE?" Tedros puffed, glancing uselessly around the stage.

Lancelot shifted in his chair, which made the stage creak so loudly the audience's eyes went to him.

"Preferably one that isn't made out of wood," the knight said.

A ruckus echoed behind him and everyone turned to see the red-haired altar boy careen through the fallen scrim onto the stage, having tripped on Guinevere's shoe. "Sorry! That's my cue!" he squawked, dragging an iron anvil behind him. "Behold! The stone from which King Arthur once pulled Excali—"

The heavy anvil splintered the wooden platform. The edge of the stage imploded and the anvil plummeted straight through the hole like a cannonball, down to a cliff, where it bounced off the rock and fell into the ocean.

"This is going well," said Lancelot.

Tedros scorched pink.

His mother's eyes were glued to her one shoe. Lady Gremlaine wasn't on the stage anymore. And he couldn't even *look* in Agatha's direction. He'd wanted the coronation to show her what kind of king he'd be. Instead, she was probably as mortified as he was.

"Merlin . . . some help?" he peeped desperately, glancing upwards.

A pigeon pooed, just missing his head.

"*Enough*," Tedros boiled, jaw clenching. "To seal the coronation, I have to pull a sword from a stone? Well, the sword's in one right now!"

He stamped to the back of the stage and the once-curtained-off castle balcony, where Excalibur was still lodged blade-first into the stone archway.

"So if I pull my sword out of *this* stone, it's done, right? We can all go home," he barked at the chaplain.

"Well, I don't believe your father meant—"

"IS IT DONE OR IS IT NOT," Tedros bullied.

The chaplain quailed. "Oh, yes . . . I suppose. . . ."

Tedros grabbed the hilt, practically screeching into the star on his shoulder, deafening the crowd: "Then in the name of my father, my kingdom, and my people, I hereby accept my place as Leader, Protector, and King of Camelot!"

He pulled at the sword.

It didn't move.

"Huh?"

Tedros jerked harder. Still didn't budge.

He could hear the restless mob shifting.

Putting his foot on the wall, he pried at the blade with all of his strength, his biceps straining against his skin—

Nope. Nothing.

Tedros was sweating now. He pulled right, left, front, back, trying to make the sword slide, but with each pull it seemed to bury harder into the stone. It didn't make sense. Excalibur wasn't wedged that deep and the archway's stone was loamy and weak. Why wasn't it moving?

People in the crowd were clutching each other, pointing at him open-mouthed. They knew what was happening. They knew after promising to save them as king, he was failing the first test that would *make* him king, a test that shouldn't have been a test at all—

"Merlin . . . ," he pleaded, but the sky was clear overhead, the white star on his shoulder lost and gone.

He couldn't breathe, his wet grip on the hilt making his pulls shallow and frantic. His crown skewed on his head. His coronation gown ripped at the seams—

Please, he begged, heaving at the sword. *Please!*

Lancelot ran up. "Just yank the damn thing out!" he said, helping him jostle the hilt—

Tedros shoved him away. "It's *my* test—I have to do it—"

But he pushed Lancelot too hard, who knocked backwards straight into the chaplain, upending the old man over the balcony. His priestly gown caught on the railing, leaving him dangling upside down, robes over his head, exposed save for his saggy pantaloons. Gold coins showered out of his pockets onto the crowd, causing a stampede for them as the chaplain howled. The altar boy ran to help his master, only to plunge through the hole in the stage left by the lost anvil.

Paralyzed, Tedros scanned the scene: Lancelot hoisting the chaplain over a balcony; Guinevere lurching to rescue a squealing altar boy hanging off a beam; his kingdom's people punching each other for a handful of coins . . .

And six monkeys straddling a sword stuck in stone, slathering it with banana pudding, and sliding up and down the blade.

Tedros dropped to his knees.

"IT'S THEM!" a woman bellowed down below, pointing at Lancelot and Guinevere. "THEY'VE CURSED US! THEY'VE CURSED CAMELOT!"

"RIGHT FROM THE BEGINNING!" an old man yelled.

"WHY'D YOU THINK ARTHUR WANTED 'EM DEAD!" his wife shouted.

"TRAITORS!" a young boy heckled.

"FINKS!"

From the masses exploded a murderous mob, climbing up the stage's beams towards Guinevere and Lancelot—

"GET THEM!"

"*KILL* THEM!"

But the beams couldn't support their weight and shattered like sticks, sending the remainder of the stage timbering down over the crowd, the candles igniting the wood and pooled wax and detonating the stage like a fireball into the drawbridge. Shrieking villagers fled for their lives just as royal guards came smashing out the balcony windows, armed with swords and spears, led by Lady Gremlaine.

"TRAITORS!" the terrible cries echoed below. *"MON-STERS!"*

As people hurled things at the balcony, guards grabbed Guinevere and Lancelot and spirited them inside to safety, along with the others.

Only Tedros stayed behind, pulling and pulling at Excalibur, his bleeding hands slick with pudding, his face streaked with tears, before he suddenly felt the arms of men throw him over their shoulders—

"No! I can do it!" he choked, hands flailing for the sword. *"I can do it!"*

He screamed those words again and again, voice crumbling to rasps as they dragged him into the castle, until all that remained of Camelot's Great Hope was a sobbing little boy, crown slid down over his eyes, hands stabbing wildly into the dark.

3

Flah-sé-dah

"**S**o is he king or isn't he?" Dean Sophie asked, nose buried in the *Royal Rot*. "According to the *Camelot Courier*, he is, but according to the *Rot*, he *isn't*.
What both agree on, however, is that once Tedros finds a way to pull Excalibur out of that balcony, then it's settled and he's king once and for all. But if someone *else* were to pull Excalibur out before Teddy . . . well, it wouldn't matter, would it, since only the blood of Arthur can sit upon

the throne . . . which means Tedros *is* king, now and forever, though it sounds like he's only a 'half-king' without respect or support . . . or a sword."

Draped in a plushy black bathrobe, Sophie leaned back, picking at the curlers in her blond hair as she scanned more articles:

EXCLUSIVE INTERVIEW WITH CORONATION MONKEYS!

AGATHA: LOYAL PRINCESS . . . OR WITCH WHO CURSED THE CORONATION?

HORRO-NATION FALLOUT: IS LANCELOT PLOTTING TO STEAL THE CROWN?

"Six months later and it's all anyone still talks about," Sophie sighed, folding the newspaper and fingering a vial of gold liquid hanging from her necklace. "Poor, poor Teddy."

"If Teddy's so poor, why are you smiling," grunted Hort.

Sophie looked out at her shirtless, raven-haired friend and two first-year Neverboys in sleek black uniforms lugging a marble statue of her across newly refurbished Evil Hall. "Are you implying that I'm happy about my two best friends being the laughingstock of Camelot? Are you implying that I take secret *delight* in whatever strains this humiliation has put upon their relationship?"

"You stalked Tedros for three years, tried to marry a mur- derous sorcerer to make him jealous, then held the whole

Woods hostage when Tedros wouldn't kiss you," Hort said, rippled muscles shining as he slid Sophie's statue through the red-and-gold ballroom. Above him, a few Nevergirls teetered on ladders to hang a chandelier, each crystal shaped like an *S*. "Plus, you've been writing Agatha for months trying to hijack the wedding planning and she won't write you back and now you secretly want the wedding to bomb," he added. "So yeah, not really implying. More just saying it."

Sophie stared at him. "I want to be helpful to Aggie, Hort. She's far away in a whole new kingdom, preparing for the biggest day of her life, and I want to be there for her. Am I hurt she hasn't responded? A little, perhaps. But I'm not *mad*."

"When you're hurt, you *get* mad," said Hort. "You get so mad that you turn witchy and start wars and people die. Check the history textbook."

"Oh sweetie, that's the *past*," Sophie groaned, reclining against her glass throne, shaped like a five-pointed crown. "It's a new year now and I've moved on, just like our former classmates who are off in the Woods, pursuing their fairy-tale quests. Look . . ."

She slipped the lid off the vial attached to her necklace and turned the vial upside down, emptying the gold liquid. But instead of falling to the floor, the liquid suspended midair, creating the outline of a large square before it magically filled in with a magnificent three-dimensional map of the Endless Woods. Scattered across kingdoms near and far were dozens of brightly colored figurines, like an army of toy soldiers, each resembling a fourth-year student from the School for Good and Evil and labeled with their name.

"And from the Quest Map, it looks like our friends are doing quite well," said Sophie. "See, here's Beatrix in Jaunt Jolie, fighting with Reena and Millicent as her sidekicks. . . . Here's Ravan in Akgul, plundering the Iron Village with Drax as his henchman and Arachne as his mogrified newt. . . . Here's Hester, Dot, and Anadil in Kyrgios on some 'important' mission they won't tell me about, though it can't be that important if they're never in the same kingdom for more than a day. . . . And here's Chaddick, off on Avalon Island by himself—mmm, strange; I thought he'd gone to Camelot to be Tedros' knight. Why would he be in Avalon? Nothing but snow and tundra. No one even lives there. Well, except the Lady of the Lake, but she seals her castle's gates to everyone except Merlin and Camelot's king. . . . But it looks like Chaddick's figure is *inside* her gates, doesn't it? Maybe he's flying over the island on a stymph or something. . . ."

"Blue means they're winning their quest?" Hort asked.

"And red means they're losing. That's why *my* name is in blue," preened Sophie, pointing to her figurine by the miniature school towers on the map. "My quest as Dean was to bring Evil into a new age, and clearly I've succeeded."

"Well, my name's in blue too," said Hort, spotting his figure obscured by Sophie's. "My students love me, I work out every night, and I've even started getting fan mail. Just the other day I got a note in a girl's handwriting saying I was her favorite character from your story and that they didn't make boys like me in Woods Beyond. Must be a Reader from your old town—"

"Or Castor playing a prank," Sophie sniffed.

The puff went out of Hort's chest. "Hey, wait a second. Isn't it weird that every single name on this map is blue? Shouldn't *someone* be losing their quest?"

"Ever since Clarissa gave me this map, we've been nothing but winners," Sophie crowed. "So either I'm good luck or we're a *very* talented group."

"Or your map is broken, which would explain why it says Chaddick is inside the Lady of the Lake's gates when that's *impossible*," said Hort. "Look, even Tedros and Agatha are in blue, which means, according to the Quest Map, they're doing just fine."

Sophie peered at him, then at Agatha's and Tedros' names in Camelot, just as blue as the others.

"That can't be right," she murmured. "How can Tedros be winning? I read Camelot's papers every day. He's the town fool! He's a *disgrace*!"

She saw Hort smirking at her.

"Poor Teddy," he said.

Sophie rose from her throne and sashayed past Hort. "Oh please, for all we know, Clarissa hexed his name to make him look good. Fairy godmothers love to cheat." She swept her hand through the map, dispersing it to liquid and back into the vial on her neck. "And honestly, I can't worry about a failed king and a princess who isn't even queen and yet is somehow too busy to write her best *friend*. I have my school to run: 125 new Nevers who think Tedros and Agatha are old news and have their eyes on *me*. Plus, I have these pesky Readers we've accepted, who don't have a clue. Why, on the very first day, a girl from Gavaldon caved in an entire classroom. So my hands are quite full, thank you. And even if I could spare a thought for Tedros—or any boy, for that matter—it would be a wasted one. I'm completely happy on my own, unattached and untroubled by the vagaries of love. *Flah-sé-dah*, that's my new mantra: a blissful mélange of 'laissez-faire' and 'la-di-da.' Who needs the stress of love when there's important work to do? I prefer a *modest* life now, dedicated to my students."

"Um, throwing a Dean's Dance the second week of school with the theme 'Night of a Thousand Sophies' where people have to dress up in outfits inspired by your fairy tale doesn't seem *modest* to me," said Hort, his Neverboy helpers murmuring assent as they polished the statue of Sophie in hooded robes, a crown of flowers upon her head. "Nor does taking half the Evil students out of class to decorate for it serve anyone but *you*," Hort added, surveying the ballroom filled with Nevergirls in chic leather dresses and high black boots and Neverboys in stylish leather coats and skinny black pants, all hard at work: hanging tapestries of Sophie's best moments as a student, polishing stained glass windows of Sophie's face, and scrubbing the marble floor branded with a red *S* circled by olive leaves and topped with a gold crown.

"And yet here you are, helping them," Sophie said, simpering at Hort.

"Yeah, so you'll take me to the dance."

"A Dean doesn't need a date to her own dance," Sophie bristled.

"But maybe she *wants* one," said Hort, sweat dripping.

"What I want is for you to put on a shirt," said Sophie, eyeing his sculpted torso.

"I seem to have lost it," said Hort.

Sophie arched a brow. "Indeed."

"Um, Professor?" a voice peeped.

Hort and Sophie turned.

Fifty first years blinked at them. "Someone's knocking on the door," a vampiric-looking girl wisped.

A barrage of loud raps echoed through the Hall.

Sophie waited until the knocking stopped. "Really? I don't hear a thing."

"By the way, I liked the castle better how it was before, when it was crumbly and dirty," Hort said, rubbing out a stain on Sophie's statue with his hand. "Everything's too clean now. Like we're trying to hide something."

"Hogwash. How could anyone possibly prefer the *old* Evil," Sophie pooh-poohed, glancing out the window at the renovated towers of Malice, Mischief, and Vice, lit up with red-and-gold paper lanterns. "Evil was so *dark* before. So morose and unattractive. No wonder we were always the losers. We *acted* like losers!"

"So Evil's been around since the dawn of time, waiting for *you* to save it?" said Hort, stonefaced.

"Darling, if it wasn't for me, Evil would have kept playing second fiddle to Good, dying in every story for no other reason than it made a tidier ending for the sweet, pretty Ever to win. But now look at us: new uniforms, new classes, new castle. . . .

A new *brand* of Evil. Which is why I've invited the students from Good to join our dance tonight. I want them to see Evil is no longer the ugly stepsister. Evil is young and glamorous and *en vogue*. Tonight isn't just a celebration; it's a flag in the sand. A flag that says: it's Evil's time now. And if we happen to bring a few Evers into our ranks along the way . . . well, then, *flah-sé-dah*."

She snapped her fingers—a scrawny, brown, rat-faced boy ran in from the wings and handed her a glass of green juice.

"Isn't that right, Bogden?" Sophie smiled, sipping her juice.

"*Flah-sé-dah*," he squeaked, fanning her with a palm frond.

Hort glared at the rat boy. "Why is *he* here?"

More loud knocks assaulted the Hall.

"Bogden of Woods Beyond?" said Sophie innocently, ignoring the knocks. "Didn't you have him in class, *Professor* Hort? You are our school's teacher of Evil history, are you not? Or do you make it a habit of not paying attention to the students you teach?"

Hort clenched his teeth. "First of all, I'm here to teach history as a last-minute *favor* to you since no one wanted a job where everybody who takes it ends up dead. Second, I shouldn't even be here since Lady Lesso assigned me a normal quest like everyone else, which means my little soldier on your magic map should be in Maidenvale, fighting dragons and elves and maybe even getting my own fairy tale. But instead I left my quest to help *you*—"

"As Dean, I have the right to modify your quest as I see fit," said Sophie.

"—and third, I know perfectly well who Bogden is," Hort plowed on, "because he flunked my challenges and every other teacher's the first week, which means he should have been expelled, since by your new rules, anyone who fails three challenges in a row is sent packing."

"I know my rules, thank you. I just couldn't bring myself to fail a fellow Reader," Sophie sighed. "I too came from humble beginnings. I too craved a life better than Gavaldon's, where I would have to churn butter and wash clothes and marry an obese man who expected me to obey him and you know . . . *cook*. It's why I started accepting applications from Readers. They deserve to live out their fairy tales."

"Then why have you been complaining about Readers the past two weeks?" Hort asked.

"Just that one Gavaldon Girl who destroyed a classroom and gives me the Evil eye every time she sees me. And not in a Good way. Bogden, on the other hand, treats me like a goddess," Sophie said, beaming at the rat-faced boy. "So after his poor first week, I gave him the choice between being sent home or being my personal steward for the year. Looks a bit like the old you, doesn't he, Hort? Before you started lifting weights to look like Tedros, I mean."

Harder knocking now.

"If this is what you're like as Dean, I can't imagine what you'd have been like as Camelot's *queen*," said Hort.

"Psshh, no way," Sophie said, lounging against her throne. "Presiding at court while people present their problems . . . that's not me."

KNOCK! KNOCK! KNOCK!

"Oh, let them in, for heaven's sake!" Sophie moaned.

Instantly Bogden snatched a rolled-up red carpet from behind Sophie's throne and unfurled it across Evil Hall, shunting Nevers out of the way with catlike hisses before he flung open the doors with a courtier's bow—

A gaggle of adults flurried down the carpet, waving wild arms and shouting so loudly that Sophie peeked around for a window to jump out of.

"You can't yank students out of class willy-nilly!" Professor Bilious Manley yelled, pimply head flushing red.

"You can't invite Evers into Evil castle without School Master approval!" scolded Professor Sheeba Sheeks, shaking her fists.

"You can't turn the School Master's tower into your own private residence!" said Yuba the Gnome, white beard twitching.

"YOU THINK THAT'S BAD? SHE MADE BATHS MANDATORY!" Castor the Dog bellowed. "FOR *TEACHERS* TOO."

The others gasped.

Sophie cinched her bathrobe tighter, curlers bouncing like Christmas ornaments. "First of all, I can do whatever I want with our students since *I'm* Dean. Second, seeing there *is* no School Master, I could invite Evers to a tarheeled hootenanny if I felt like it and no one could stop me! Third, even if we have a fleet of new fairies watching the Storian, I felt more secure living beside it, given that the protection of the enchanted pen is our school's top priority—"

"And this protection includes renovating the tower to be a five-star hotel?" Manley barked, pointing out the window at scaffolding encasing the School Master's spire. "The stymphs' construction on the tower has been going on for months and nearly suffocated us all with dust! We've had enough!"

Sophie glared. "You expected me to live in that old stone cell like Rafal once did? Without silk carpeting or a proper bathtub or 360-degree lighting?"

The teachers were speechless.

Wolf howls echoed in the hallway.

"I believe that's your cue to get back to teaching and mine to get ready for a Dean's Dance," said Sophie, rising from her throne—

Evil Hall's doors flung open once more and Clarissa Dovey marched in, silver hair fraying from her high bun, beetle wings flapping on her green teacher's gown.

"If it is, in fact, a Dean's Dance, then one would assume I'm invited, since I am a *Dean*," she said, gliding down the red carpet, a gold vial identical to Sophie's dangling around her neck. "Only I received no such invitation."

"Tonight is a celebration of glamour, charisma, and hope. Despite the rather maleficent entrance, I'm afraid you'd feel quite out of place," said Sophie coolly.

"And yet you invited *my* students," said Dovey.

"Who have RSVPed in remarkable numbers," said Sophie. "I can assure you that none of *my* first years would attend a dance in your castle. And if they did, the fusty old smell would surely drive them away."

Dean Dovey's eyes flashed. "Oh, how the School Master will cook your goose."

"Too bad there *is* no School Master," Sophie purred.

Clarissa leaned in, eye to eye. "That will soon *change.*"

Sophie turned dead white.

The Dean of Good swept out of the Hall, Evil's teachers following her, until the doors slammed behind them, shaking the chandelier. A clump of *S* crystals fell and shattered against Sophie's glass throne.

She hardly noticed as Bogden picked shards out of her hair, her big, spooked pupils fixed on the door.

"New School M-M-Master?" she croaked.

She saw Hort, barechested against her statue, grinning like a weasel.

"*Flah-sé-dah,*" he sang.

4

THE COVEN

Mission Diverted

"Let's say a new Dean steps out of bounds—" started Hester.

"And becomes a menace to her own school," added Anadil.

"And throws parties in honor of herself and forces everyone to take baths and makes kids eat boiled asparagus and wheatgrass," said Dot.

"What would you do if you were School Master?" Hester finished.

The three witches each held a notebook open, feathered pen at the ready.

Seated in his

rickety hut at the top of a very tall pea-tree, the Grand Vizier of Kingdom Kyrgios scratched his long, curly black beard, speckled with gold flakes like the strands of his flowing black hair. "I'm assuming this new Dean is . . . young?"

"And blond," said Dot.

"I see," mulled the Vizier in a deep baritone. "I would encourage this Dean to think closely about what is going on in her personal life that is affecting her professional one. Sometimes a Dean thinks a life of service is enough to bring fulfillment. And when it isn't, they begin to push boundaries as a cry for help. A School Master can look that Dean in the eye and ask: 'What is it you *really* need?' Sometimes it's as simple as a vacation to the salt baths in Shazabah. But sometimes it's more than that. Much more. And it takes someone wise—*deeply* wise—to draw that out."

Hester saw Anadil's eyes flick to her before finding the Vizier's once more. "But why would a Dean of Evil listen to you if you were School Master?" the albino girl asked. "You're from an Ever kingdom, and no offense, even if you pledge to be 'impartial,' most Nevers think Evers are half-brained, milk-livered airtraps." (Three black rats poked out of her pocket and hissed agreement.)

"Well, having two School Masters, one Good and one Evil, didn't work out, did it?" the Vizier answered, glancing at the wooden clock on his mantel. "I suggest this time you focus on quality over quantity. Also, as I'd hope you'd have learned in your history classes, Kingdom Kyrgios was once a Never kingdom. Which means given my long life span, I've served both

Ever *and* Never kings with equal success."

Dot scribbled a few notes, her stomach burbling loudly. "Speaking of life spans, from our research, it seems you've been able to stay alive this long by using a variety of life-extending magic. Excuse my bluntness, but we don't want a School Master who will drop dead his second week on the job. How much longer do you expect to live?"

"Are the crisps stale? None of you have touched them," the Vizier said.

Hester followed his eyes to the green-colored chips stacked on a plate. Like everything else in Kyrgios, they smelled of peas, since peas were the lifeblood of the kingdom. The Kyrgians even slept inside the pea pods that hung off trees like the one they were in now. Luckily, the witches weren't staying the night since they had another interview scheduled in Pasha Dunes the next morning.

"Not hungry. Had a big breakfast," Hester snipped, though Dot's stomach was rumbling like a kettledrum now. "Now if you don't mind answering Dot's question . . ."

"I'm confused. When is Dean Dovey joining us?" the Vizier asked, frowning. "I need to get back to work. We've had strange attacks of late: a rogue carriage deliberately running over people, along with reports of pirates lurking near the Four Point, which is sacred land. I made the time to come here, assuming your Dean would be present."

"And we thank you for making that time. But as we informed you in our letter, Dean Dovey entrusted *us* with the task of researching, locating, and interviewing possible School

Master candidates as our fourth-year quest," Hester spouted, as if she'd had to say this many times before. "Though we check in with Dean Dovey regularly, she will only be meeting with our final nominees."

The Vizier smiled blandly. "So Dovey remains in her glass towers fussing over lunch menus and school dances while she leaves the crucial work of choosing a School Master, protecting the Storian, and defending the balance of our world to . . . *children*."

"Children who have spent the last six months meeting with some of the most illustrious heroes and villains in the Woods," said Anadil.

"Children who have sought out candidates in floating mountains, cloud forests, piranha lakes, active volcanoes, ice castles, mermaid lagoons, elephant graveyards, and the belly of a very large whale," said Dot.

"Children who will do whatever it takes to find the right person for the job, because this is *our* fairy-tale quest," said Hester, demon tattoo twitching on her neck.

"Wouldn't you rather be fighting a giant or elf-prince so you can get your name in a storybook?" the Vizier said, becoming serious. "This all feels like a leader sending their henchmen to get the job done. And that never turns out well."

"Unless the leader knows we are the *only* people who can get the job done," said Hester. "Because this is a quest that will shape Good and Evil for a long time to come and our coven cares more about that than having our names in a storybook, which is precisely why Professor Dovey picked us in the first place. And if she—the Dean of our enemy school—is willing to put the fate of the Woods in our hands rather than her own or anyone else's, then I suggest you stop worrying about our ages and start worrying about how to best respect the students you so *wisely* expect to lead."

The Vizier gaped at her.

"That's all," chimed Dot, turning a pea-crisp to chocolate and flouncing with her friends out of his hut.

A moment later Dot shuffled back in. "Can you help us get down from this tree?"

Dovey checked in with them each day at one o'clock, so the witches found a place to settle for lunch in Eternal Springs, a small jungle kingdom fifteen miles from Kyrgios. Eternal Springs was populated entirely by animals since it rained nearly every day of the year, and despite the abundance of greenery and food, no human or sentient creature wanted to live in a place that wet. As the witches waded through lush thickets and colorful flowers in their dumpy black dresses and boots, Hester could see deer, storks, and squirrels watching them as if they were an eclipse of the sun.

They'd been on foot most of these past six months, since the Flowerground had restored only limited service after being ravaged during the previous School Master's reign. Along the way, they'd seen wonderful, curious things: the kingdom of Kasatkina, ruled entirely by cats; the Night Pools in Netherwood, which brought your worst fears to life; the Living Library in Pifflepaff Hills, which had ancestry scrolls on every soul in the Woods, kept by a very large bat; and the Caves of Contempo in Borna Coric, where time ran backwards. They'd even taken a ride aboard the legendary Blue-Boned Stymph, from which they'd had a rare view of the Four Point: a small, square plot of land at the intersection of four kingdoms. It was the site of King Arthur's last battle, where he'd been mortally wounded, and was now considered a truce mark between Good and Evil, explained Hester, who'd read about it in *A Student's History of the Woods*. Camelot's flag flew high over the land, whose boundaries were guarded by four walls made of rushing waterfalls, enchanted by the Lady of the Lake. If anyone got close enough that even a drop of water touched their skin, the Lady would reach out and drown them. The girls had made sure to stay at a safe distance as they flew on to their next interview in Hamelin.

But that was back when they'd first started, when the search for a School Master was marvelous fun, no matter how tiring or dangerous. Endless travel in the summer heat had taken its toll: Dot had blisters and an aching lower back, Hester's demon had a perpetual frown, and even Anadil's albino-white skin had the hint of a tan. At least they were safe here in Eternal Springs, if a little damp, and after six months of crossing in and out of new kingdoms, all in pursuit of the best possible candidates they could take back to their Dean . . . well, safety was about as much as they could ask for.

Finding a spot under a well-canopied palm, Hester whipped up a lunch of avocados and custard-apples that she'd snapped off trees, while Anadil cracked open a few coconuts filled with sweet water and Dot spread out sheets of crumpled old newspaper she'd dug out of her bag so they wouldn't have to sit in wet dirt. For ten minutes, they ate silently as rain spritzed around them, the three witches lost in their own heads, before they came out of their fugue all at once, like best friends often do.

"I thought this last one was the most promising so far," Anadil said, watching her rats wrestle over a dead caterpillar.

"Pea-man?" Dot snarfled, mouth full.

"Calm, reasonable . . . I can see him in the School Master's tower," Anadil continued, slurping coconut water. "Even more than the Ice Giant from Frostplains, the fairy-rights activist from Gillikin, or that monkey king from Runyon Mills."

"None of them have been right," muttered Hester. "We can do better."

"At some point, we have to pick someone, Hester. It's been six *months*," said Anadil. "Without a School Master, the Storian is vulnerable. So are the Woods."

"I liked the Augur of Ladelflop," said Dot. "He told me I was pretty."

"He was blind," snapped Anadil.

"Oh. Pea-man was better, then," said Dot.

"We have to pick someone by the wedding," Anadil resolved, giving Hester a wary look. "We're not missing the wedding, right?"

Hester paused, picking at her food before looking up. "No. We're not missing the wedding."

Anadil sighed softly.

"No letters from Agatha in months, though," Dot said, sliding off her boots. "Not since the one where she pretended like everything at Camelot was peaches and roses. Hope the wedding's still on."

"Dovey would have told us if it wasn't," said Anadil.

"I knew we should have been at the coronation. Maybe we could have stopped everything from going belly-up," said Dot.

"Finding a new School Master was more important than watching Tedros make an ass of himself . . . *again*," said Hester, pulling back her red-and-black hair. "I'm sure he'll give a repeat performance in two months."

"The wedding's that soon?" Dot said.

"Here comes the 'wedding diet.' Let me guess: everything you touch will turn to kim-chi," Anadil cracked.

"Noooo ma'am. No more diets. I've been fat, I've been thin. Fat is better, no matter what Daddy says," Dot piped, digging into her chocolate-avocado pudding. "I just mean time is going fast and we haven't found a School Master yet."

They suddenly noticed Hester had gone quiet, squinting at her food.

"Hester?" Dot prodded.

Hester lifted her half-eaten avocado and studied the newspaper beneath the dish. "How old is this paper?"

"Um, got it in Gillikin . . . so like three weeks ago?" said Dot.

Hester leaned in, inspecting the headlines on the crusty parchment:

PIRATES TAKE OVER PORTS IN JAUNT JOLIE; NUMBERS GROWING

KIDNAPPING FOILED IN RAINBOW GALE

FIRE AT GLASS MOUNTAIN ORCHARD

Her stomach twisted. Every single headline involved one of their classmates' quests. Beatrix was leading the charge against vicious pirates in Jaunt Jolie; Vex and Mona were supposed to kidnap the Seer of Rainbow Gale who'd been helping Evers cheat their happy endings; Kiko was with the group tending the consecrated orchard atop Glass Mountain. . . .

And from the headlines, it didn't sound like any of it was going well.

"What's wrong?" Anadil asked, her rats peeking up from their meal.

Hester put her own food down, obscuring the parchment. No use worrying her friends over old news. Besides, was it her fault if her classmates were incompetent twits and failing their missions? Right now, she had her own quest to worry about.

She turned to her friends. "Are you sure we're asking the right questions?"

"You mean should we be asking candidates if they like candlelit dinners and walks on the beach?" said Anadil. "After six months, eighty interviews, and I don't know how many nights listening to Dot fart in her sleep, *now* you're wondering if we're asking the right questions?"

"It was those lentil cakes in Drupathi," Dot lamented.

"I just keep thinking about what Lady Lesso would do if she was here," Hester said, "because it feels like everyone we meet is saying exactly what we want to hear. Like how do we know Mr. Calm and Reasonable won't turn into psychotic Rafal the moment he gets near the Storian?"

Dot and Anadil had no defense.

"Look, I know some are definitely better than others," said Hester, "but this is the future School Master we're talking about—the protector of the pen that rules all our lives—and we can't make a mistake."

"But we also can't read their minds," pushed Anadil. "And the longer we wait, the more chance there is that someone swoops in and tries to fill the School Master's place on his own. Someone as bad as Rafal. Or *worse*. And then who are the Woods going to turn to for help? The King of Camelot, like they used do? *Tedros?* You think he can lead? You think he can unite Good *and* Evil? He couldn't even get through his own coronation!"

Hester watched her avocado turn black.

"Besides, it's not like we're making the final decision. We just have to give Dovey a shortlist. The final decision is up to her—" Anadil persisted.

"It's up to *both* Deans," Hester shot back. "Do you really want Sophie picking the next School Master? After she fell in *love* with the last one?"

"Mmm, he'd be pretty at least," Dot mused. "Sophie does have good taste in men."

Hester gave her a putrid look.

"What? It's true," Dot said. "She's probably sneaking gorgeous Everboys into Evil as we speak."

"Maybe the old Sophie would have," Anadil countered. "But she's Dean now. She's the face of Evil."

"Ani's right. She *has* changed," Hester admitted. "I mean we hated her as Dean those last months of school, but she really did seem happy without a boy."

"For now," said Dot.

"For now," Anadil conceded.

"And from what Dovey's told us, she's getting worse," said Dot. "Moving into the School Master's tower . . . adding beach cabanas to Halfway Bay . . . turning the Doom Room into a dance club on Saturday nights . . . morphing the castle into a living memorial to herself . . . Sounds like she's starting to 'push boundaries,' just like Pea-man said. I mean, how long before she decides she needs a date to Agatha's wedding?"

Hester and Anadil goggled at her.

"Um, helllllloo, you don't think Sophie would show up alone, do you? To her best friend's wedding to a *king*?" Dot asked.

Hester looked at Anadil. "Every once in a while, she says something worth thinking about."

"Not enough to keep her around," said Anadil.

"Next time I'm eating all the lentil cakes," Dot huffed.

Suddenly a tiny spray of white light appeared above them, as if the air had ripped open, giving them a peek into a new dimension. The light distended and wobbled like a sack of water before it slowly took the shape of a circle and Professor

Dovey's face appeared in the middle, blinking at them from inside a crystal ball.

"Girls, I have news," she said breathlessly.

Immediately Hester noticed something was wrong. Dovey's eyes were rimmed red, her hair frazzled and greasy, and the lines around her mouth rutted deep.

Her office was a mess, littered with newspapers and scrolls. The gold vial that Dovey had recently been wearing around her neck was now empty and there was a map floating in the air like a wandering balloon, covered in red lettering Hester couldn't make out. There was even a food stain on the Dean's green gown, which made Hester think the situation was dire indeed, since no one had ever seen Professor Dovey look anything but spotless.

"Uh, are you okay, Professor?" Hester asked, struggling to muster sympathy, an emotion she didn't really have. Though she had zero respect for fairy godmothers (and Dovey had been Cinderella's before becoming Good's Dean), the fact Dovey trusted them with this mission had softened Hester's opinion of her. She'd even begun to see Clarissa Dovey as a friend. "You look a little . . . um . . ."

"Girls, your quest is over for now," Professor Dovey declared. "I need you to return to school."

The witches gasped.

"You can't do that—" Dot started.

"After all we've—" Anadil overlapped.

Hester cut them off. "Professor, I know we haven't brought you a shortlist of candidates, but we're working like dogs to find someone we believe in and trust me when I say, we're all deeply grateful for this responsibility—"

"Hester," said Professor Dovey.

"You can trust us to finish the job. Please don't punish us by taking our quest away, not when we're finally starting to figure out—"

"*Hester*," Professor Dovey snapped. "This is not about punishing you. On the contrary, I have complete faith in your abilities. That's why I need your help on an urgent matter. A matter that supersedes all else."

Hester stared at her. "But what can be more urgent than finding a new School Mas—"

Behind Dovey, the door to her office swung open and Professor Emma Anemone peeked beneath the floating map, slathered in a green beauty mask. "Clarissa, do you mind if I attend Dean Sophie's Dance this evening? Given how many of our students are going and with Princess Uma still on leave, surely someone from Good should be—"

"Not now, Emma!" the Dean barked.

Professor Anemone fled.

"Professor Dovey—" Hester started.

"I don't have time for questions, Hester. I need you to return to the castle at once. The Peony line on the Flowerground is up and running from Eternal Springs and can get you back by nightfall."

"Of course. Anything to help," Hester said feebly, still upset their quest would be cut short. "But can I at least ask . . . Is this about Sophie?"

"And Everboys?" said Dot.

"Oh shut it, Dot," Hester ripped.

"Girls, our troubles are far bigger than the antics of a fellow Dean," Professor Dovey said, glancing up anxiously at the magic map. "But I will say this . . ."

She leaned in, glaring hard into the crystal ball. "I'm hoping you can take care of two birds with one *stone*."

5

Intervention

"One two three, one two three . . . Buttocks in, child! And head up! You're waltzing, not scouring the floor for lost coins!" Pollux barked at Agatha, his dog's head attached to a fat sheep's carcass. Wobbling around the Gold Tower ballroom, Pollux kept time with a willow stick as Agatha danced with the skeletal, red-haired altar boy who'd made a spectacle of himself at Tedros' coronation. "Don't rush, girl . . . one two three . . . and stop gripping Willam like he's the last lifeboat out of Ooty! And *smile*, Agatha. This isn't a devil's haunt.

Dance like this and you'll be egged at your own wedding!"

"How are you even here!" Agatha growled, exasperated by her clumsy feet, her hapless partner, and the return of a prissy, scant-furred, snub-nosed canine she thought she'd left behind at school. Pollux was one half of a two-headed Cerberus who taught at the School for Good and routinely lost the battle to use the body to his Evil brother Castor. Which meant that whenever the two siblings were apart, Pollux had to find dead animals to attach his own head to—in this case, a rotting ewe's.

"Clarissa Dovey and I had a falling out," Pollux sniffed. "After Sophie was appointed Dean of Evil, I encouraged Clarissa to consider her *own* succession plan just as her friend Lady Lesso did before her untimely death. As I explained to Dean Dovey, not only is she *ripe* in age, but it's time for Good to have a fresh face at the fore rather than one sagging past its prime. Of course I pointed this out in the most *tactful* manner, but Clarissa ignored my many missives. . . . Spine straight!" He swatted Willam with the stick and the boy yelped—

"So, I circulated a petition advocating for a mandatory retirement age, which Dean Dovey is *well* past. Naturally, I also nominated myself to replace her, but the shrew caught wind of the plan and had me fired—" Pollux jabbed Agatha with his stick. Agatha snapped it in two and handed it back to him.

"I see royal life has done nothing for your attitude," Pollux glowered. "Do you want your wedding to be as pathetic as the coronation? Imagine the *Royal Rot*: 'WORST BRIDE EVER!' Is that what you want, Agatha? *More* embarrassment?"

Agatha's anger fizzled. "No."

"Good, because when Lady Gremlaine heard of my travails at school, she brought me here to help *you*," said Pollux. "Specifically to teach dance, etiquette, and history in preparation for your wedding. She's even planning to make me your *permanent* steward, given your need for constant supervision."

"Stewards are for kids," Agatha frowned. "I won't need a steward once I'm officially queen—"

"Only you can't be officially queen until Tedros is officially king and right now there's a sword hanging over that prospect," Pollux said, gazing through the ballroom window at Excalibur, sticking out from a Blue Tower balcony across the catwalk. Two royal guards stood on either side.

Pollux met Agatha's eyes. "So until your dear unofficial king finds a way to pull that sword and seal his coronation, he has Lady Gremlaine watching his every move and you have *me*."

Agatha nearly retched.

Willam stepped hard on her toe.

"Ow!" Agatha blared, knocking Willam into Pollux.

"Who needs a wedding when you can have a circus?" Pollux scowled.

After two more insufferable hours, Agatha moved to etiquette training, where she had to learn the names of 1,600 wedding guests from fat albums of portraits, with Pollux spraying her with stinging lemon juice every time she missed one.

"For the last time, who is this?" Pollux crabbed, pointing

at a hook-nosed face.

"The Baron of Hajebaji," Agatha said confidently.

"Baroness! Baroness!" Pollux yelled.

Agatha goggled at him. "That's a *woman?*"

By then she was dripping in lemon juice, still distracted by the sight of the sword in the balcony and unable to focus on anything else. Thankfully the dog was interrupted by a courier crow (with a message from Castor), which gave Agatha time to think.

She'd always assumed that Tedros would pull Excalibur from the stone *eventually.*

Sooner or later he'd jolt the blade free or he'd figure out it was a clue to another puzzle or riddle and then he'd solve it. She'd yet to consider that Tedros might never complete his father's coronation test . . . that the sword might stubbornly hang in that balcony for the rest of their lives, an eternal reminder of his failure. In which case, Tedros would never feel like a true king. He'd be trapped in this cycle of shame and isolation, so different from the gallant, open-hearted boy who once looked to her as his partner.

But what can I do to help him? Agatha thought, gazing out the window at the rain. This wasn't like a Trial by Tale at school, where she could sneak in to save him. The sword was Tedros' test and his alone.

And yet, if she *could* help him somehow . . . wouldn't that fix everything?

Agatha watched the storm gust across the castle—

Something caught her eye through the rain.

Agatha leaned over the windowsill to get a closer look.

Across the catwalk, a boy had emerged onto the Blue Tower balcony in beige breeches and a gray hooded shirt with the hood pulled over his head. He dismissed the guards and stood there all alone, drenched clothes clinging to his muscular frame. He peeked around to make sure no one was watching—Agatha ducked out of sight—before he began stretching each of his arms and shaking the tension out of his legs.

Then, with a deep breath, he gripped Excalibur by the hilt and began to pull.

The past six months, she'd watched Tedros do this every night: the same skulking onto the balcony, the same dismissing of the guards, the same diligent warm-up before he did battle with his father's sword. In the beginning, there had been sword masters, blacksmiths, and ex-knights who coached him as he pulled, while Lady Gremlaine looked on with narrowed eyes. Back then, the kingdom had been on the verge of war, with half the people supporting Tedros as king and half calling for his deposal. Six months later, both sides had settled into a stagnant détente, the trapped sword a symbol of a king they were stuck with. Now there were no more coaches or watchful stewards, but still Tedros tried at the sword, again and again. This was the first time Agatha had ever seen him during the day, though, for he'd always waited until the sun was down, when no one beyond the castle would be able to spot him. Perhaps he thought the storm was camouflage enough or perhaps today he didn't care who saw him as he heaved and sweated, ripping at the blade from every angle. . . .

Excalibur didn't budge.

This too was part of the routine, and Tedros would react to defeat like he had every day these past six months: by getting up at dawn and working out even harder, as if it was his strength that was failing him and nothing else. Truth was Agatha had never seen him so strong, ripped muscles stretching his shirt, like he could shotput a ship out of the ocean. He tore at the hilt with this new strength, bright blood streaking his palms, dripping down steel, before he threw back his head and let out a single, futile cry—

Agatha closed her eyes and exhaled.

When she opened them, he was looking right at her.

She could hardly make out his face through the lashes of rain, but he was frozen still, gazing at her from beneath his hood. It was a dead, empty look, as if their shared past had been erased. As if this was the first time he'd ever seen her.

"You won't learn the Empress of Putsi's name by mooning into the rain," a voice said.

Agatha turned to see Pollux and his sheep corpse lording over her. He glared down at her soggy album, a mess of runny colors.

"I know you're not one for ceremony or celebration or nice things, Agatha. But this is your *wedding*," said Pollux.

"And I thought it was a Leprechaun's Ball," she said.

"If you're going to treat this as a joke, then maybe I should call Lady Gremlaine—"

"Run to mommy like you always do."

"You are a sad little girl," Pollux retorted.

"Says the dog puppeting a sheep."

Pollux sighed. "I'm not here to torture you, Agatha. I'm here to help you get married. You have to care."

"I care," Agatha said quietly.

"You have to care because it's a timeless tradition and because it's the first time your people will see you as a queen—"

"I care," Agatha repeated.

"You have to care because this is your legacy—"

"I *care*," Agatha said.

"Do you?" said Pollux incredulously. "Based on what I see, you don't. Tell me why I should believe you care about your wedding—"

Agatha looked at him. "Because I need to remind Tedros that we were happy once."

Sorrow softened Pollux's face.

Agatha turned back to the rain, hoping her prince was still there. . . .

But all she could see were two guards, wiping his blood off a sword.

Agatha ate dinner in the queen's bathroom, where no one could bother her.

She still had her Wedding History lesson, but Pollux let her eat before it without alerting her chambermaids—a clear breach in protocol, since they had to know where the princess was at all hours.

Instead, Agatha had barreled into the kitchen herself, sending ten cooks into coronary shock.

"Princess Agatha," Chef Silkima gasped, her rich brown skin flecked with flour. "What's happened? . . . Is everything all r—"

"Can I get spaghetti with cheese for dinner?" said Agatha. "Lots of cheese. Tons. Like enough to ruin the dish."

Chef Silkima and the cooks gaped down at their finished platters of cumin-spiced coconut soup, curried chicken in a green chili sauce, potato *tikki*s with peas and scallions, black-lentil salad with salmon crumbs, and a five-layer *kulfi* pistachio cake.

"Spaghetti with . . . cheese?" Chef Silkima croaked.

"To go, please," said Agatha.

One of the cooks dropped his spoon.

Now, as she sat dangling bare feet into a bathtub of hot water, surrounded by mirrors and peeling gold wallpaper, Agatha twirled creamy-white spaghetti from a porcelain bowl into her mouth, savoring the melted mozzarella.

Everyone had their comfort in times of stress: Sophie had sea-salt facials, juice fasts, yoga poses, and deep-tissue massages; Tedros had dumbbells and climbing ropes and anything to work up a sweat. . . .

Agatha had food.

More precisely: so much food that it induced a warm, velvety coma that dulled her senses and made her unable to think beyond the gurgles of her stomach.

Reaper moseyed into the bathroom and sniffed at a scrap of cheese. He gave Agatha a curdled look, as if he thought she'd outgrown all this, and shuffled away.

Agatha and Tedros had certainly had fights before. Fights that made Agatha doubt whether he loved her or she loved him or whether they even belonged together. But this wasn't a fight. She was sure Tedros loved her now—or at least as sure as she could be. . . .

Except relationships aren't just about love, Agatha realized. Relationships are about taking off the mask you wear to make someone like you and letting them see the real you. The one you hid all along. The one you never thought was good enough to find love in the first place.

Tedros had helped her peel off her mask in her years at school. He'd seen her at her most vulnerable and her absolute worst and loved her even more for it.

But now it was Tedros' turn to do the same and he was acting like most boys do when asked to face their feelings. . . .

They run.

There was another thing that also made this rift different than the others, Agatha thought, spotting the pile of letters on her desk. She could see the latest one, which she'd read so many times, yet left unanswered.

Darling,
I know you're not reading this. I know you're not reading any of my letters. You're in love and have a wedding to plan and have no time for silly old me, but if you do read this, just know that you are in my heart always. And living without you has been far harder

than I could ever admit out loud. So let me
say it here. I miss you.

Love,
Sophie

P.S. Did you know Hort has been getting
love letters from a *girl*?

Agatha wiped her eyes. Back at school, she'd always had
Sophie by her side, the third point in the triangle between her
and Tedros.

A hollow loneliness overwhelmed her and for the first
time she saw it wasn't just her old, chivalrous prince she was
yearning for, but her bold, beautiful best friend too. A best
friend she'd been avoiding, just like Tedros had been avoiding her.

Now she was all alone.

Outside, she heard wind and rain batter the ships in the
harbor. Glancing through a small window, she saw none of
these ships could sail; they were broken, neglected, and falling
apart, like the rest of Camelot. Well, not *all* the ships: there
was one that looked sturdy, with brilliant blue-and-gold finishes and milky white sails. Along the bow, she read the ship's
name . . . *IGRAINE*.

"Agatha?" Pollux's voice echoed outside. "Shall we resume
our—"

A loud hissing noise interrupted, followed by dog barks
and crashing furniture.

Pollux had met Reaper.

Twenty minutes later, Agatha was in the Library, a two-story collection in the Gold Tower that must have once been impressive, but was now a heap of cobwebs, moth-eaten books, and so much dust she could hardly breathe. There were colorful sheets slung over the bookcases and desks, as if someone had started renovating a decade ago and never got around to finishing. Agatha slouched at a desk shrouded in a purple sheet, trying to take notes as Pollux scrawled on a squeaky chalkboard, his face slashed with claw-marks, suggesting he'd lost the battle with her cat.

"You certainly don't want to be like Princess Kerber, who was so overwrought on her wedding day she ate an entire jar of peanut butter and vomited on her poor groom's shoes. Conversely, learn from the example of Princess Muguruza, who married a commoner, nearly prompting a revolt, until she revealed her bridal gown, made entirely out of pink pearls she'd dredged from the Savage Sea. No one dared attack a girl who'd braved such treacherous waters and in time, every last dissenter forgave her. . . ."

Agatha glazed over, her head drooping into the purple sheet. She tried to force herself awake, prying her eyes open—

That's when she saw the pattern stitched on the fabric.

Tiny, silver five-pointed stars in a purple night sky, like they'd been drawn by a child.

It wasn't a sheet at all.

It was a cape.

Agatha held in a smile, her eyes on Pollux's back. She put

her nose to the purple velvet and inhaled the scent of fresh cocoa, as if someone was brewing it right now. . . .

"Then there was Princess Mahalaxmi, whose father kidnapped her during the ceremony and sold her to a Never warlord in Ravenbow," Pollux rattled. "Which goes to show all family entanglements should be sorted *before* the wedding. . . ."

Agatha rose from her chair, careful not to make a sound, and slipped her palms into the cape, vanishing her hands like a magic trick . . . then her arms . . . then her shoulders. . . .

"I don't hear your pen, Agatha. This is for your own good," Pollux tutted—

But by the time he turned, all that remained of his student was a single clump, somehow left behind.

The moment Agatha put her face through the cape, she felt herself swaddled in velvet, then plummeting through darkness, pulses of blinding white light streaking by. She closed her eyes and let herself free-fall, her arms raised, her one-shoed feet splayed, her mind untethering from her thoughts, her fears . . . until at last she crashed face-first into something fluffy and soft and tasted sweet cloud in her mouth.

Agatha opened her eyes and craned up to a purple night sky lit by thousands of silvery five-pointed stars, as if the childish pattern on the cape in the Library had come to life in heavenly dimension.

"The Celestium," Tedros once called it. The place where wizards go to think.

Agatha rose to her knees and saw there was indeed a

wizard peering thinkingly at her, sitting cross-legged on the cloud with purple silk robes, a droopy cone hat, horn-rimmed spectacles, and soft-furred violet slippers.

"Merlin," she smiled.

"Sorry to interrupt your lessons, dear girl, but I'm afraid we have more important ones at the moment," the old wizard said, sipping at a mug of cream-topped cocoa. "First, tell me: Do you want whipped cream in your chocolate? Provided my hat complies. A third mug of cocoa might be too much to ask. He's been rather insubordinate of late, insisting on a minimum wage and a month of paid vacation—"

"A 'third'?" asked Agatha, confused. "But there's only you and me here."

"Goodness, you two really do have a hard time seeing eye to eye, don't you?" Merlin murmured.

He leaned back, revealing a boy sitting next to him, who'd been obscured by the wizard's profile.

Tedros didn't look at Agatha. He held his own undrunk mug of chocolate, heaped with cream and rainbow sprinkles, his bare legs dangling off the cloud. He wore a sleeveless white undershirt and pajama shorts, his gold king's crown sunken into his wet hair.

"Agatha and I have *work* to do, Merlin. Not that you would know since you've been gone for half a year, but we're in charge of a kingdom now," Tedros said, dumping his steaming mug over the cloud. "Our coffers are empty. We have no knights. Mother and Lance are missing. There's unrest all over the Woods. We don't have time for a wizard's games."

"You used to share your chocolate with Agatha. Now you're wasting it," Merlin upbraided him.

"I didn't *ask* for chocolate," said Tedros, yanking his crown tighter. "I'm too old to be bribed with sweets."

"But not too old to let your dear princess go hungry?" Merlin asked.

"I'm stuffed from dinner," said Agatha, trying to play both sides.

"Where's the girl's cocoa!" the wizard bellowed into his hat.

"You can't keep me here all night," Tedros scorned. "Air's too thin in the Celestium."

"I can keep you here until you're as white-haired as me. I'll just turn you into a goldfish and put you in a bowl. Agatha can feed you," said Merlin, giving his hat a good shake. "That is if she doesn't dump your food off a cloud."

The hat spat chocolate at Merlin, who promptly sat on the hat in return. "Now let's begin," the wizard harrumphed.

"Begin what?" asked Agatha.

"We don't need this, Merlin," Tedros hounded.

"Need what?" asked Agatha.

"You need this more than your obsessive workouts and overdeveloped stomach muscles," said Merlin, sitting harder on his squirming hat.

"You don't know anything about me anymore," Tedros snapped. "You disappeared when I needed you like you always do, haven't sent so much as a postcard in six months, and then drop in acting like you can help me when you don't have the faintest clue. Just go back to whatever hole you were hiding in."

"Because you were doing such a fine job as king without me," said the wizard.

Tedros snarled. "My father was right to banish you from the castle."

"Well, you're certainly seeming more and more like him each day," said Merlin.

"Stop it! You're like squabbling hens, the both of you!" Agatha yelled, echoing into the night. "What is this? What are we doing? Why are we here!"

The two men gaped at her sheepishly.

But it was the hat that spoke from beneath Merlin's rump, scowling at them all—

"Couples therapy!"

Two Theories

Somewhere inside, Tedros knew this would happen. He couldn't continue the way he'd been going, treating Agatha like a distant cousin while wrestling his own demons down down down into the basement of his soul.

These past six months, he'd told himself it was the only way forward—that Agatha was best left to the hopeful, happy duties of wedding planning while he reassured his castle staff that Camelot would return to glory. But he could only lie to himself for so long. There was nothing reassuring about his guards looking at him

with pity and doubt, their eyes darting to his sword jammed in a balcony. And there was nothing hopeful or happy about a princess planning a wedding to a boy who was doing everything he could to avoid her.

Someone had to intervene. Someone had to save him from himself. But now it was happening and he wasn't ready.

The worst part was that he'd been through this before—only *he'd* been the one ignored and abandoned. He'd been the one in Agatha's place.

He was nine years old. His mother had fled the castle with Lancelot, deserting both him and his father. But right when he needed his dad most, his father turned to drink instead, slowly poisoning himself rather than admit how much pain he was in. He'd begged his father to stop, but Arthur insisted it was Tedros' mother who needed help, not him. Yet in the end, it was his mother who'd been honest with herself, giving her a second chance at life, while his father numbed his feelings all the way to the grave.

Now, sitting with Agatha and Merlin, Tedros felt his own buried pain return. He didn't want Agatha to suffer the way he once did, shut out by someone she loved. And he didn't want to be like his father, refusing help until it was too late.

"I thought everything was going to be okay when we left school," he said finally, unable to look at his princess. "I didn't want her to worry for the rest of her life. She's been through enough. But then I saw her watching me this morning when I was on the balcony and I could see she was hurting—"

"'She' meaning . . . me?" Agatha asked.

Tedros saw Merlin squeeze Agatha's wrist, telling her this wasn't her turn to talk.

"Merlin, where were you all this time?" Tedros said, clearing his throat. "No one's seen you since the coronation. Not that I really 'saw' you then either."

"I'd hope not. It took a meticulous spell to turn me into a mosquito that could last a decent amount of time without sucking someone's blood," said Merlin.

"Too bad it couldn't be Lady Gremlaine's," Agatha offered.

The wizard frowned at her.

"You watched the coronation as a *mosquito*?" Tedros asked.

"I was hoping to avoid detection and have all attention be on you, my boy. If anyone saw me, they would have foolishly tried to execute me and it would have led to quite the spectacle indeed. But then you created your own spectacle by presenting your mother and Lancelot to the people against all reasonable advice. It was a stunning act of stubbornness, something a swaggering boy at school would do rather than a new king trying to build faith with his kingdom."

"And I'm sorry for it," said Tedros softly. "I thought it was the right thing at the time."

"I could have helped—" Agatha started.

Merlin's hat bit her bottom.

"Maybe I did do everything wrong and messed it all up. Maybe I am the worst king in the world. But isn't that punishment enough?" Tedros fought. "You didn't have to punish me too by disappearing for *six months*!"

"Punish you?" Merlin said, aghast. "Tedros, dear, I've been

gone keeping two people you love safe."

Tedros gaped, suddenly understanding. "You were with Mom and Lance! I've been going crazy trying to track them. . . . I got these mysterious cards from different parts of the Woods—"

"And she would have sent far more had I let her," said Merlin.

"I knew it! There wasn't anything written on them, but they smelled like honeysuckle, which she knows is my favorite. Where are they? When can I see them? I need to see them—"

"Patience, boy. Your mother and Lancelot still have Arthur's rich bounty on their heads: a bounty you can't rescind until you pull the sword and finish your test. Getting them to safety was difficult enough. As soon as they were dragged into the castle at the coronation, I turned them to fruit flies and hustled them into the Endless Woods. We couldn't return to the old safe house in Avalon; *The Tale of Sophie and Agatha* had revealed its existence to our whole world, which meant Avalon Island would be crawling with your mother's enemies. So to both hide your mother and Lancelot and distract them from worrying about you, I took them on a tour of kingdoms they'd never seen, given their years of exile. We traveled by enchanted ship: the *Igraine*, which obeys any 'lady' of Camelot, princess or queen, and can fly through the air or turn invisible on that lady's command. Soon news started spreading of what happened at the coronation, with WANTED posters for Guinevere and Lancelot tacked up everywhere we went. I had to be creative about disguising them. But that, as you know, is a specialty."

"So they're . . . safe?" Tedros asked anxiously.

"The *Igraine* is returned to Camelot harbor and your mother and Lance are hidden close by, rested and at ease. Except for the fact they're missing you. Well, your mother more than Lancelot," the wizard winked.

"Hope you disguised Lance as a girl," Tedros said, remembering his own time as a girl named Essa. All of a sudden he was craving his favorite hot cocoa and he wished he hadn't dumped out his mug. Why did he always act first and think later? He tried to catch Agatha's eye, wanting to somehow start a conversation, but he'd ignored her too long and now she was ignoring him.

"Merlin, if you were touring other kingdoms, surely you saw some of our classmates on their quests?" the princess asked.

"Indeed," the wizard said, finally acknowledging her.

Tedros' face fell. "And have they, um, you know . . . heard about me?"

The wizard paused. "Let's just say you're not the only one encountering obstacles on their quest."

"Huh? But I'm not even on a quest—" said Tedros.

"*Every* fourth-year Ever or Never from the School for Good and Evil is on a quest, Tedros," the wizard corrected. "A quest to discover if they have the strength, wit, and will to become a legend and have their name remembered for all time. It's just your classmates' quests for glory took them to faraway lands, while yours brought you back home."

"Doesn't feel like much of a quest to me," Tedros murmured. "I'm supposed to be king. It's what I was born to do."

Merlin peered at him as if he'd missed the point entirely. "You may have been born to do it, but that doesn't mean you'll do it *well*."

Tedros said nothing, two hot spots appearing on his cheeks.

"Tedros, have you thought about *why* your father's sword is stuck in the stone?" Merlin asked.

"Well, at first I thought it was caught at the wrong angle, then I thought maybe there was a riddle or a game that if I solved, the sword would pull loose."

"That was my theory too," said Agatha.

Tedros looked at her, wondering why she hadn't said something to him before, only to realize he'd never given her the chance.

"And now?" asked Merlin.

"I'm back to thinking it's caught at the wrong angle," Tedros sighed.

"What if we consider it from Excalibur's point of view?" Merlin asked.

"You think Excalibur doesn't want me to pull it out?" Tedros asked, surprised.

"More like it doesn't want you to be *king*," said Merlin.

"But I am king—"

"Only because someone else who has a rightful claim to the throne has yet to pull the sword. And no one does, since you are King Arthur's only child. So again: Why won't Excalibur let you complete your father's test?"

Tedros crossed his arms. "How should I know what a sword thinks?"

"Excalibur is a weapon of immense power, forged by the Lady of the Lake to fight Evil. It does not want to spend its days trapped in a balcony," said Merlin. "Perhaps the sword is trying to be sure you are ready to be king and is waiting for you to prove it. In which case, the question is . . . *how?*"

Merlin wiped his spectacles with his robes, making them even dustier. "That's theory #1."

"And theory #2?" Agatha asked.

"That it isn't the sword making these decisions at all," said Merlin. "That someone else has found a way to control it, like a master controls a puppet, preventing you from sealing your own coronation. In which case, the question is . . . *who?*"

"But no one is powerful enough to control Excalibur," Agatha rebutted. She slowly turned to Tedros. "Unless . . ."

"No way. The School Master is dead!" Tedros scoffed.

"Like forever dead," Agatha agreed.

"Like really forever dead," said Tedros.

They goggled at each other, then back at Merlin. *"Right?"*

"These are the same questions I have," said the wizard, looking troubled. "But it is up to Tedros to find the answers, since it is *his* test. The sooner he retrieves his sword and seals his coronation, the better. Not just for Camelot, but for the sake of the entire Woods."

"Entire *Woods?*" said Tedros. "What do you mea—"

"Are you talking about the attacks in the papers, Merlin?" Agatha cut in. "I've been reading about problems in Ever and Never kingdoms: pirate raids in Jaunt Jolie; a poisoned wishing well in Bremen; a band of werewolves looting families in Bloodbrook . . . but none of it seems connected."

"It isn't. Just a bunch of petty crime," said Tedros. "Leaders of neighboring kingdoms think it's more than that, but they just want Camelot to come in and clean up their problems like Dad used to. We have our own problems, thank you. But kings and queens keep writing me letters, demanding meetings."

"Which you clearly haven't answered," said Agatha. "I heard two chambermaids whispering about why you haven't investigated the fire on Glass Mountain."

Tedros turned to Merlin quickly. "Well, *are* the attacks connected? You said our classmates are having trouble on their quests. What's happening out there in the Woods?"

"Are they okay?" Agatha pressed.

"Dear girl, maybe you'd know the answer to that if you'd been answering *your* letters," the wizard replied. "Your best friend's included."

Tedros looked at Agatha, dumbfounded. "You haven't written Sophie?"

Agatha's big brown eyes turned wet.

"But *why?*" Tedros blurted against all better judgment. "I'm happily rid of that girl, but you two have so much history. You can't just cut her off—"

"She seems so excited about the wedding . . . and you don't," said Agatha, choking up. "Any time I tried to write her, all I could picture is me walking down the aisle to a boy I used to share everything with and now acts as if he barely knows me. But Sophie knows me: she'd see through anything I wrote . . . she'd see how I was feeling . . . and I didn't want anyone to know—"

She covered her face, muffling her sobs.

Tedros looked at Merlin, sitting between him and his future queen. "M, do you mind if I talk to Agatha alone?"

"Thought you'd never ask. Even wizards need the toilet," Merlin breezed. "Just jump off when you're finished and you'll find yourselves back where you started." He snatched his sleeping hat, which startled awake, spurting rainbow sprinkles, before the wizard dove off the cloud like a champion swimmer and vanished into the darkness.

Tedros scooted across the cloud, silky white fibers tickling his legs as he moved next to Agatha, who was crying into her palms. Gently he put his hand on her back.

"I love you, Agatha. No matter how stupid I can be, nothing will ever change that."

"I could only bring myself to write one letter—to Hester— and it was full of lies. I couldn't let anyone know how you were treating me," Agatha sniffled. "That's why I didn't write anyone else or ask about their quests. Six m-m-months. You made me feel so alone."

"I didn't want you to worry about me," Tedros said guiltily.

"Y-y-you made me worry more."

"I told you I was stupid."

"S-s-stupider than a tree s-s-stump," Agatha piled on.

"Stupider than a tree stump," Tedros conceded.

"Stupider than one of Rafal's zombie villains with no brains."

"I don't know if I'd go that—"

"It wasn't a question."

Tedros smiled and rolled back his eyes zombie-style, playfully sinking his teeth into her neck. Agatha yelped and shoved him away, but she was snickering now too.

She leaned against him and clasped his arm.

"You know, I'm surprised Sophie's still alive, let alone writing you letters," Tedros said. "Figured Dovey would have turned her into a pumpkin by now."

"Not sure fairy godmothers are allowed to be Evil," said Agatha.

"But wouldn't it be awesome if they could?"

Agatha laughed: that hissy, throaty laugh he'd missed for so long. He pulled her in closer.

"Though from Sophie's letters, it sounds like Dovey is out of sorts," said Agatha. "She insists it's because Dovey's threatened by her; Sophie claims she's turned Evil into the hot new thing and now all the first-year Evers want to go to her side."

"But you think it's something more sinister?"

"I'm sure Dovey wouldn't mind if a stymph dropped Sophie on her head, but I doubt she'd get too worked up over a former student's theatrics. Plus, you heard what Merlin said. If our classmates are having trouble on their quests, Dovey has her hands full. The Deans are responsible for all fourth years once they leave for their missions. Especially with no new School Master in place."

"Wouldn't Sophie have mentioned something in her letters? She's Dean too."

"It doesn't make sense, does it?" Agatha agreed. "What do you think is happening out there that has Dovey stressed?"

"And Merlin worried?" said Tedros.

"And why would it be connected to you not pulling your dad's sword?" said Agatha.

Tedros glanced away, tensing, and he could feel Agatha tighten too, knowing she'd said the wrong thing. He didn't want to talk about the sword with her. Not just because it made him feel inadequate, but because he didn't want her pity.

"I'm still imagining what Lance would look like if Merlin turned him into a girl," said Agatha, mercifully changing the subject.

"No way Merlin would go for it," said Tedros. "Lance would make such a beastly female that it would only call attention to itself."

"You were a pretty beastly female yourself, Essa."

"Wasn't I the one who had boys whistling at me in the halls?"

"Boys who like their girls hulking, hairy, and belligerent."

"Now you're just jealous."

"Well, if you want to be a girl so badly, maybe *you* should plan the wedding," Agatha teased.

"Honestly, I found it sexist too at first: the new king focuses on governance, his princess on the wedding," said Tedros. "But the more I thought about it, the more I realized traditions exist for a reason. I grew up in Camelot. The people have known me since I was a baby. You, on the other hand, are brand-new to them. The kingdom knows nothing about you. Planning the wedding is *your* coronation test."

"And I want to pass it with flying colors, not for me, but for the both of us," Agatha said earnestly. "But I'd rather be helping you."

Tedros exhaled. "Help me manage our debts to other kingdoms that will take centuries to repay? Or help me find out where all Camelot's gold went when the three advisors who handled this gold refuse to speak to me? Or help me fight rampant thieving by the poor, even though it helps them survive? Which would you like to help me with?"

"All of it. Any of it," Agatha said. "I know how hard it is—"

"No, you don't," he said. "You can't know how hard it is to watch your father's kingdom turn its back on Good."

"Just like you can't know how hard it is to watch your one true love turn his back on you," said Agatha.

Tedros didn't argue.

Finally he looked at her, tears gleaming. "You really want to help me, Agatha? Then tell me how to pull my sword out of that stone. Tell me how to pass my father's test." He wiped his nose. "Why do you think I've been avoiding you? I knew this would happen. I knew I'd break down and ask you for help. Can't even finish my coronation on my own. Maybe Merlin's right. Maybe the sword doesn't want me to be king." He slouched into a sealed-off ball. "Not now. Not ever."

He felt Agatha's hand slide across his back and wrap him into her. She tipped his face upwards.

"Who says a good king can't get help when he needs it most?"

His eyes met hers and a wall inside him crumbled, feelings rushing through. How had he gone this long without coming to her—she, the only person who ever truly understood him?

"I can see him looking at me in my dreams. My father," said Tedros. "Staring at me as if he knows why I've failed. He's part of this and I don't know how."

Agatha wasn't listening; she was deep in thought, already pouncing on his ask for help.

"Let's be smart about this," she said. "Merlin had two theories: either the sword wants you to prove you're king or the sword is being controlled by someone who doesn't want you to be king. In any case, grabbing at the sword day after day isn't going to get us anywhere."

"But loafing around on a cloud isn't going to solve the problem either," he said, sitting up.

"You're forgetting the most important thing Merlin said. He said it isn't only our quest that's run into trouble. It's our whole *class*."

"That would explain all those strange attacks in the Woods," said Tedros. "So you think whoever is messing up their quests is messing up ours too?"

"Maybe Merlin's two theories are actually one," Agatha nodded. "The King of Camelot is supposed to be the leader of the Woods. If something Evil is happening out there, you have to go and find it. You have to figure out what—or who—is disrupting our missions and set things right again. Maybe then you'll be able to pull the sword loose. Maybe that's your *real* quest."

Tedros' face glowed with hope . . . then dimmed. "Agatha, a king can't just desert his people and go questing in the Woods. Not when they already doubt me. Who knows how long I'd be out there? Look what became of this place while I was gone at school. Total chaos. Even if my reign has begun badly, if something happened to me, Camelot would end up in the wrong hands again. Maybe forever this time." He shook his head. "I can't go."

"But *I* can," Agatha jumped in, as if she'd known this would be their conclusion.

"Agatha, I asked you for help. Not to take over my test," said Tedros impatiently. "You heard Merlin. This isn't your quest. It's mine."

"And my quest is to be your queen. Helping seal your place as king is more worthy of a queen's attention than picking frosting for our cake. All I need is a few knights for the journey. Chaddick will be back any day with a new fleet for your Round Table—"

"He hasn't answered my letters in weeks," Tedros said. Then his face changed. "You don't think something went wrong on his quest too?"

"Even more reason for me to go, then, and to go right away," Agatha replied. "I need to find out what's stopping all of us from fulfilling our missions, Good *and* Evil. This is as much my test as it is yours, Tedros. You're not in this alone anymore."

Tedros saw the steely resolve in her big brown eyes and suddenly he knew that if he didn't let her go, she would go on her own.

"I shouldn't have asked you to butt in," he muttered.

"We're going to be married soon, Tedros," Agatha reminded him. "I'm *supposed* to butt in."

Tedros said nothing, picking at his shorts. "So how long would you be gone?"

"A few weeks. I'll send you letters each night."

"A few weeks in the Woods . . . *alone?*"

"But I'd see all our friends again," Agatha pressured. "And it would mean I can get away from Lady Gremlaine."

Tedros bit his lip, as if he couldn't deny her such a pleasure. "Even so, it's too dangerous," he said, shaking his head.

"I survived *Aric*. I can survive anything."

Tedros grimaced at the name of Lady Lesso's sadistic son. "Questing in the Woods alone is a death sentence, Agatha—"

"Then I'll take someone with me. Like . . . Willam."

"*Willam?* The altar boy? He can't even look me in the eye, let alone fight."

"Do you make it a habit of looking altar boys in the eye?"

"All I'm saying is—"

"The matter's settled. I'll leave tonight," Agatha declared. "And I suspect that's what Merlin wanted all along, because he dropped a clear hint of how I could escape the castle without anyone knowing. . . ."

Baffled, Tedros started to ask what this was, but Agatha

added: "The only question is who will take over wedding planning."

She looked at him hopefully.

"You're joking," said Tedros. "I have enough on my plate, thank you."

"I could hire someone."

"With what money?"

"Someone who would do it as a favor to the kingdom."

"And this someone would have good taste, be as invested in the wedding as you and me, manage all facets of a royal occasion that has to go off without a hitch, and also work for *free*?" said Tedros incredulously.

"I should think so."

"It will take months of searching to find such a person, Agatha. If such a person even exists."

"Mmm, not really."

Tedros cocked his head. "You have someone in mind?"

"Do you trust me?" Agatha asked, eyes twinkling.

"You know I do."

"And I can pick anyone I choose?"

"Of course. You'll be queen soon."

"Then promise me this is my choice and no one else's."

"I promise, but honestly—"

"Good," said Agatha, climbing into his lap, "then I'll pay her a visit on my first stop into the Woods."

Tedros peered at her, mystified. "Pay who a visit? Who's 'she'—"

He choked.

"HAVE YOU LOST YOUR DAMNED MIND!"

"You said it yourself. We can't just cut her off," Agatha replied, hands sliding up his chest.

"Not we! *You!*" Tedros shouted. "You think I'll let *her* plan our wedding? I'd rather eat glass for a month—I'd rather drown myself in hot lava—no no no no no—"

But now she was clasping his cheeks and kissing him, long and slow, and it'd been so long since she'd kissed him that suddenly he could think of nothing else . . . only her soft lips on his and his beautiful, brilliant bride-to-be . . .

"I love you, Tedros," she whispered.

"And I love you too," he breathed. "But *no.*"

"If only a king's promise wasn't stronger than a prince's," she said, smiling like a cat.

"A promise doesn't count if you tricked me!"

"And does that mean your trust doesn't count either?" Agatha asked intently.

Tedros gawped at her, knowing he'd been beaten. "But . . . but . . ."

He barked with frustration and kissed her again, hard and deep, because he couldn't possibly think about everything he'd just agreed to. He kissed her so long they ran out of air until Agatha pulled him backwards, dragging him off their perch, and they fell through clouds, the two of them still kissing, tangled in each other's limbs like interlocked stars.

7

CHADDICK

The Liege and the Lady

He had been stabbed twice in the back and once in the flank, but he was still alive.

Concealed behind a white wall, Chaddick listened for his attacker, but all he heard was a faint crashing of waves. Blood leaked through his shirt into his lap. He felt no pain, just cold, prickly shock.

It had happened so fast.

Five minutes ago, he'd been riding his horse on the snowy shores of Avalon, searching for the entrance to the Lady of the Lake's castle. He'd bought a map of the island from a nosy beaver, but the map only seemed to take him round in circles. At last, when he was frostbitten and ready to give up, he'd found it: towering iron doors as high as a mountain, guarded by two stone lions, concealed in shadow on either side.

He didn't expect the gates to open for him. They opened for no man except Merlin and the King of Camelot. The stone lions would devour anyone else who tried to enter.

But Chaddick hadn't come to enter the gates. He'd traveled long and hard across the Woods for only one reason: to make sure that these doors were still sealed tight. That no one had breached the Lady of the Lake's realm. That his fears were unfounded.

But as he'd approached, he'd seen his fears had come true.

The doors weren't sealed.

One was hanging off its hinges, the other splintered into pieces.

Who could splinter iron?

He'd gazed at the stone lions, motionless and piled with weeks of snow. If someone had broken in recently, they'd done so untouched.

Why would the lions let an intruder through?

Moving quicker, Chaddick had dug an iron shard into the snow and tied his horse to it before he'd cautiously stepped between the lions and onto castle grounds, scanning the towers and cliff rock for signs of Evil—

His attacker had come from behind.

Chaddick had tried to turn but his assailant jammed his cheek to a rock with one hand, the other on the boy's back. Even in his wrestling matches against Tedros, Chaddick had never felt such strength.

"Who—are—you—" Chaddick had choked.

But his attacker just hissed in his ear.

Dead calm, he'd slipped Chaddick's sword out of his belt and stabbed him in the back while Chaddick screamed with pain. As he'd stabbed again, Chaddick kicked with primal instinct, his boot connecting with bone. His attacker buckled and Chaddick broke free, limping past Avalon's towers until he'd found a place to hide.

It had all happened in five minutes.

Now he waited behind that white wall, listening to the echo of waves, stab wounds soaking his shirt red. Panic set in, his muscles slacking. He was losing too much blood.

Chaddick tensed.

Footsteps.

Coming down the path.

Crackle, crackle, crackle against the snow.

They stopped.

Chaddick held his breath.

He squinted up at the circle of pearl-white towers, coated in snow, for it was always winter in Avalon. The towers had no windows or doors to sneak through. The best he could do was dart from wall to wall like a hunted deer.

Rising from his crouch, he saw zigzagging staircases ahead leading from the towers down to a calm lake.

He had to get to the water.

The Lady of the Lake would hide him.

Just like she'd done for Guinevere and Lancelot.

Run for it?

He'd be in the open for his attacker to spot him. The stairs were slick with snow. His bloody shirt would be like a flag to a bull. And he didn't have his sword.

Chaddick stripped off his shirt. The frigid air flayed his skin as he tried to wipe clean. But the gash in his ribs kept gushing and he didn't even know where the blood on his back was coming from. Shock wore off, giving way to soul-crushing pain. Hands shaking, he scraped snow off the ground and packed it into the wounds to staunch them. It didn't work. Pain throttled from every direction now. He couldn't breathe—

Crackle, crackle, crackle.

The killer was coming.

Without thinking, Chaddick darted from his hiding spot and sprinted to the next tower, diving behind its wall.

For a moment, there was silence.

Then a soft, hissy laugh.

Crackle, crackle, crackle.

Tears stung Chaddick's eyes.

Two weeks earlier, he'd sent Dovey a note by crow: he'd been seeing strange things in the Woods. Ever and Never kingdoms attacked . . . unrest and fear spreading everywhere . . . classmates' quests sabotaged . . .

Something was happening.

He knew he was supposed to be collecting knights for Camelot. But he was Tedros' liege and a knight himself. If he could find out why things were going wrong in the Woods, maybe he could find out why Tedros' sword had gotten stuck too. . . . Maybe he could help Tedros free Excalibur and seal his crown. . . . Tedros would be so grateful to him. It would be Chaddick's first step to becoming a legendary knight, as precious to Tedros as Lancelot once was to Arthur . . . well, until a girl had come between them.

He'd be *better* than Lancelot, then.

Except Dovey had appeared via her crystal ball. *"I received your note, Chaddick. And I see from my Quest Map you're already deviating from your quest without my permission,"* she'd declared through a wobbly bubble in the sky. *"Go back to your quest. Do you understand? Leave the rest to me and Merlin."*

Chaddick had ignored her. It didn't matter that Dovey had assigned his quest. A knight's first loyalty is to his king. That's why he'd spent the last two weeks following clues in the Woods. That's how he came to discover everything.

It was all connected.

Tedros' trapped sword.

His friends' failed quests.

The attacks.

It was all the work of a new villain. More powerful than the School Master. More powerful than anything their world had ever seen.

Each new attack was part of a bigger plan.

A plan to destroy Camelot and its king.

A plan to take down Good *and* Evil.

A plan to rule the Endless Woods.

Chaddick heard footsteps get closer.

He'd tracked this villain all the way to Avalon.

He thought he could vanquish him on his own like a real knight.

He didn't know the villain was tracking him too.

Chaddick wiped his eyes. He couldn't go down like this. Not when his friends needed him. Not without a fight.

He focused on his fear . . . his loyalty to Tedros . . . his love for his fellow Evers and Nevers . . .

His fingertip glowed silver—

Now.

He leapt out of his hiding spot to face his attacker and shot him with a stun spell, not waiting to see if it hit before he dashed for a staircase thirty feet away. Chaddick hurtled down the steps towards the lake, slipping on snow and tumbling to the next landing, almost knocking himself out. Bleary with pain, he could hear his attacker's hissy laughter, his footsteps descending the stairs. . . .

Wheezing, Chaddick lurched to his feet, leaving a smear of blood in the snow, and continued to limp down. *The lake . . . I have to make it to the lake. . . .*

He staggered off the last steps and slid through icy mud on the shore—

"I need the Lady of the Lake!" he choked, dripping blood.

The clear, gray surface stayed still.

He looked back and saw a shadow moving down the stairs in no hurry at all.

Chaddick swiveled to the water. "I'm Camelot's knight!"

Now the lake changed. It spun into a whirlpool, mirroring the circle of towers above. The waters churned faster, faster . . . so fast that a thick foam spewed from the pool's eye, coalescing into human shape. . . .

A ghostly, silver-haired nymph in white robes floated out of the lake. She had pale skin, a long nose, and big black eyes that honed in on Chaddick.

Smiling with relief, he rushed towards the water, but the instant his foot touched it, it repelled him, flinging him to the ground.

The Lady of the Lake's expression didn't change.

"What are you waiting for!" he cried. "You have to protect me!"

"I protect those most loyal to Camelot," the Lady of the Lake replied.

"I *am* loyal! I'm Tedros' liege!"

Again he crawled for the water—

Again it repelled him.

"What . . . what are you doing . . . ," he gasped.

But the Lady of the Lake wasn't looking at him now. She was looking past him.

Slowly Chaddick turned to see his assailant coming off the stairs, dressed in black, his face covered by a scaly green mask. He was holding Chaddick's sword, coated with Chaddick's blood.

Chaddick dropped to his knees and clasped his hands towards the nymph. "Don't you see? He's going to kill me! Help! *Please!*"

But she didn't.

Instead she did something that made Chaddick sick.

She looked back into the eyes of his green-masked killer . . .

And smiled.

8

One Quest to Save Them All

"Where is the cake, Bogden? Where are the gift bags? Where is the *bouquet*?" Sophie berated, barreling towards Evil Hall in her white taffeta gown, crystal tiara, and spiked silver heels.

"Um, you need those things for a school *dance*?" Bogden asked, holding her train and stumbling behind.

"All Tedros had to do to seal his reign was host a coronation and now look where he is. You know why kingdoms fall, Bogden? Because of bad *parties*," Sophie flared. "How long until the doors open?"

"Five minutes. The Welcome Committee is almost done decorating—"

"Why don't I hear music, then? Why don't I smell cucumber-and-dill-butter canapés?

Bogden gaped at her.

"Were you taking notes when we went over this?" Sophie squawked, trundling towards the ballroom. "No wonder you failed all your classes!"

"Dean Sophie, I've been knocking on your bathroom door for five hours to ask questions—"

"As if anyone has time for questions! First Gavaldon Girl caves in a classroom and now you with your questions! Why did I bring Readers into this school at all?" Sophie moaned. "This is the first time a Dean has ever thrown an Evil party, the first time the Evers will see our castle, and the first time Clarissa Dovey will realize there's no need for a new School Master when the students already follow *me*. I've even invited the *Royal Rot* in case they want to write a story about Tedros' former flame, moved on to a life of staggering success and fawning fans, unlike her once-prince and now maligned king." She flung open the doors to Evil Hall with dramatic flourish—

The ballroom was lit dungeon-brown by two dying torches. The six first-year Nevers of the Welcome Committee beamed proudly at her as they hung wispy tinsel and laid out a cloudy punch bowl on a crooked wooden table along with a hunk of misshapen cheese. In the center of the room, under a dented mirror-ball, two bats perched on top of Sophie's statue, swiping and eating circling moths attracted by the weak, pulsing lights. A banner drooped between two walls—"DEAN SOPHIE WELCOMES U"—with the *U* looking more like a *V* since the painters had started their letters too big and run out of space. A wolf slumped on the floor beneath the banner, burping loudly and playing a dirge on a broken violin.

Sophie clutched her throat. "It's like one of Honora's garden parties!" She whirled to Bogden. "Where's Hort?"

"Um, Professor Hort said if he can't be your date, he's not coming."

Sophie curled her fists. "That whiny, mangy rodent . . ."

Through the windows, she saw the lights of fairies leading the Evers through Good's glass castle towards Halfway Bridge.

"Oh, I try to empower you fools like I'm supposed to and make you feel supported and involved and appreciated," Sophie seethed, shaking her fists. "But if you want something done right, you have to do it *yourself*."

In a flash, she whirled into action, pointing fingers at the Welcome Committee. "Fatima, fetch an enchanted pot from the kitchen! Barnaby, get a pouch of lizard tongues and a vial of cat tears from Professor Manley—if he won't give them to you, steal them! Vladimir, remember that putrid band you formed?"

"The one you sent us to the Doom Room for because you said we ruined your beauty sleep?" he peeped, blinking beneath his unibrow.

"It's legal for one night only," Sophie commanded. "Rex,

open up the windows! Bharthi, borrow Professor Sheeks'
spellbook (the password to her office is 'Ooty Queen'), and
someone tell Professor Hort if he doesn't get here in the next
ten seconds, I'll tell the whole school their history teacher sleeps
with a stuffed turtle!"

Her finger glowed pink and she thrust it at the mirror-ball,
which blinded all of them in an explosion of red.

Five minutes later, Sophie sat on the shoulders of Hort's
giant man-wolf, cheerily greeting awed Evers and Nevers as
they came through the doors. Towering seven feet tall, Hort
made sure to roar for each one and beat his hairy chest while
the first years moved into Evil Hall, glittering with magical
red and gold fireworks that ripped across the ceiling, spelling
"NIGHT OF A THOUSAND SOPHIES." On the walls,
scarlet shadows played scenes from Sophie's fairy tale, occasionally reaching out to spook passing kids. In the corner, Evers
and Nevers filled their cups with sparkly soda from a fountain
made out of two hundred crystal goblets; the glittering liquid
changed colors and flavors every minute: green apple, golden
honey, red raspberry, blue winter mint. . . . Nearby, a horde of
kids raided a table with trays that magically replenished with
wasabi shrimp, herbed biscuits, persimmon bruschetta, dill-
stuffed cucumbers, pork-wrapped mushrooms, baked potato
bites, salmon pinwheels, olive crostini, and vanilla-sage canapés.
But most of the revelers were jam-packed in the center around
Sophie's statue, headbanging to Vladimir's band ("VLADI-
MIR AND THE PLAGUE," the drums said), while Good's
fairies sprinkled fairy dust on band members, levitating them

over the crowd. (A few intrepid Nevers scooped fallen fairy dust off the floor and gobbed it under their tongues, sending them shooting across the dance floor like comets, earning raucous cheers.)

"And they've all dressed for the theme!" Sophie marveled, high atop Hort's shoulders, as both Evergirls and Nevergirls thronged in, flaunting Sophie's most famous looks from *The Tale of Sophie and Agatha*. There was a Kimono Sophie, with shimmering makeup and ruby-red hair; a Babydoll Sophie, in a black lacy dress and licking a pink lollipop; a No-Ball Sophie, complete with pink gown, bald cap, and stick-on warts; an Evil Queen Sophie in full-black leather and snakeskin cape; a Rebel Sophie, in a dazzling slit-back black dress, with red sequins that spelled "F is for *Fabulous*.". . . There were even a few Filips.

Not to be left out, several boys had dressed like Tedros, with some in his creamy white breeches and royal-blue lace-up shirt from the first-year Evers Ball, a few in his loose ivory shirt and black pants from his night with Sophie in an Avalon cave, and two tall Neverboys who'd worn the tightest of shorts and forgone shirts entirely.

"Hort, darling, there's even one of you!" Sophie said, pointing to a bone-thin, rabbit-faced boy in handmade frog pajamas, who'd just spilled his drink on a girl.

"Got the pajamas wrong," Hort's man-wolf grumped.

"Oh, don't be a louse. You know, they're all having so much fun I can't tell the Evers from the Nevers anymore," said Sophie, watching more of Good's students flood in with giddy smiles, as if they'd secretly been waiting their whole lives for an Evil party. "Even the teachers have stopped searching for a reason to shut it down."

Professor Manley and Professor Sheeks were snickering as they stealthily shot flames across the soda fountain every time an Ever reached for a glass. Nearby, Castor and Professor Anemone shook their rumps on the dance floor while students of both schools hooted them on.

"Listen, I can't last much longer like this. I'm hot, hairy, and hungry," Hort grouched, drool dripping from his snout. "Any second, I'm going to shrink back to human without any clothes on."

"You can't go *now*. The Room 46 boys are almost here!" Sophie said, squinting at a pack of Everboys crossing the bridge. "I knew Bodhi, Laithan, and the rest of their delicious little clan would come, even if they didn't RSVP. Handsome boys never RSVP. They just grace you with their presence like a balmy day in winter."

"What? Who's Bodhi? Who's Laithan?" Hort growled. "How do you know Everboys' names—"

"Don't be ridiculous. *Everybody* knows the boys of Honor Tower, Room 46. Besides, I'm sure you can last as a man-wolf for as long as you want. Think of first year when you could only do it for five seconds. Now you can go all night if you put your mind to it."

"I'm not lasting all night for a bunch of Everboys," Hort snapped.

"Don't be irrelevant, darling," Sophie wisped. "For six

months, I've been obsessing over Agatha and Tedros, wondering how they were doing in Camelot. I know I said I hadn't given them the slightest thought, but we both know that's a lie, so I might as well be honest. I couldn't bear the idea that they could be happy without me, even after that hellfire of a coronation. But tonight's the first night I haven't thought of them at all. Which goes to show: if Agatha doesn't want me to help her plan her wedding, then I'll happily throw a party for myself. And I assure you, mine will be far better."

She smiled as the fireworks over the dance floor arranged into a vision of her own face and students from both schools hollered their approval. Nearby, kids dug into a red velvet cake shaped as a giant *S* and flanked by piles of oat-ginger cookies frosted with sayings like "S is for Sublime," "S is for Succulent," "S is for Sophie." A pimply, sharp-toothed Neverboy climbed her statue and kissed it triumphantly, eliciting whistles and cheers, but Sophie didn't mind it in the least, soaking in the Ever-Never chants from the dance floor: "SOPHIE! SOPHIE! SOPHIE!"

"If you think about it, Aggie and I don't even have much in common anymore," Sophie added, waving back at the adoring crowd. "She has her life with Tedros, the two of them about to marry and become each other's family. And I have my own life: wedding-less, family-less, date-less, but so filled with possibilities. . . ."

"I thought I was your date," Hort said.

"Look at my little peaches. Aren't they scrumptious?" Sophie gushed, nodding at a few awkward Nevergirls in hip-hugging black leather talking to a shrimpy Everboy. "Spent all week teaching them how to fake self-esteem. What do you think? They're all your age. Any of them catch your fancy?"

"My *what*? Are you *insane*!" Hort retorted. "Not only are they first years, but I'm their *teach*—"

"Put me down!" Sophie gasped.

"What?"

"Down, Hort! Down!"

Hort quickly swung her to the floor and Sophie lunged in front of him—

"Bodhi, darling, welcome to *my* school," Sophie purred, holding out her hand to a tall, reedy boy in a royal-blue coat with dark-caramel skin and big black eyes, who gently took it and kissed it like a prince.

"And hello, Laithan, you're looking exceptionally handsome tonight," she said to his short, muscular friend with chestnut hair and freckles. Laithan smiled flirtily and kissed her on the cheek.

"Well, if that's how you're going to say hello, I'll say hello to all of you," Sophie cooed, presenting her cheek to the rest of their Everboy gang: swimmery, silver-haired Akiro; dark, wavy-haired Valentin; bald-headed, ghostly Devan. . . . "Save a dance for me," she whispered to each one.

"A *dance*!" Hort hissed in her ear, apoplectic. "You're a Dean, not a hostess at the Pig and Pepper! You can't dance with students!"

"I've combed *The Ever Never Handbook* thoroughly and see no rules against it. And besides, some of these boys look far older than I do," Sophie said, turning to greet the next boy—

Only it wasn't a boy at all.

It was a Dean.

And she wasn't alone.

Dean Dovey clacked past Sophie into Evil Hall, green gown sweeping behind her, as if this was her school and Sophie the intruder. The silver-haired professor was flanked by three witches, each of who glared at Sophie one by one.

"Everboys in our castle," said the tattooed witch.

"Everboys in our school," said the albino witch.

"Told you, told you, told you," huffed the jolly witch, turning Sophie's tiara into chocolate and gobbling it down in one bite.

"You *lied* to me?" Sophie mewled, gaping at Clarissa's Quest Map, floating over the sand on Evil's side of Halfway Bay. All her classmates' names were colored red beneath their moving figurines instead of blue like they were on her map. "But I'm supposed to know everything! I'm a Dean! I'm your *equal*! Instead, you give me a false map . . . you make me think all our quests are going well . . . you keep me in the dark on the fact my friends are failing miserably—"

"'Friends' is a loose term," Hester murmured.

"And you being 'equal' to Dovey is like Dot being 'equal' to me," said Anadil.

"We'll see who's equal when I turn your rats to fudge," said Dot.

"Oh be quiet, girls," Professor Dovey said, sitting gingerly in one of Evil's cabanas that Sophie had added when she turned the once-barren shores of Halfway Bay into a beach. Music and laughter from the party carried down the hill. With the August nights sultry and fresh, the elder Dean had recommended they speak outside, where students wouldn't overhear. But now Dovey was peering around at the torchlit huts decorated with glamorous portraits of Sophie . . . the golden sand speckled with S-shaped conchs . . . the once-sludgy black moat of Evil turned royal blue with a statue of Sophie astride a dragon spraying water from its mouth. . . .

"I honestly don't know where I am," she murmured.

Sophie cleared her throat harshly.

"I know you're upset, Sophie, and you have every right to be," Professor Dovey sighed, massaging her knees. "Fairy godmothers don't make it a habit of using magic to deceive. But fairy godmothers also have a duty to protect the greater Good. If you'd known what was happening, it was only a matter of time before word of the older students' struggles leaked through the school and distracted the first years. I know you'll say you can keep a secret, but frankly, you seem incapable of setting boundaries with your new charges at the moment."

Sophie put her hands on her hips. "What in heavens makes you say that?"

Dovey turned towards the castle's open windows. Inside Evil Hall, two Neverboys danced saucily on Sophie's statue, while an Everboy spotted Sophie watching and yelled: "DEAN SOPHIE, WILL YOU MARRY ME?"

Sophie stabbed out her glowing pink finger, shutting the

windows and drawing the curtains. "Well, if you were so scared of telling me about these failing quests, why are you telling me *now*?"

Professor Dovey turned to her. "Because I need you to lead a quest into the Woods and save your fellow classmates before any more of them die."

Every trace of defiance melted out of Sophie's face. She saw the three witches staring at Good's Dean the same way.

"Die?" Sophie rasped.

Professor Dovey looked away, mouth quivering.

Sophie could hardly get the word out. . . . "Who?"

The elder Dean watched the waters of the bay roll between Good and Evil, thin to thick, water to slime.

"The map," Dovey whispered.

Slowly Sophie and the witches raised their eyes to the Dean's Quest Map, its names in red-alarm red, so different from the cool, serene blues Sophie had seen across her doctored one.

But one name was different.

Its ink was darker red than the others and dripping off its label, as if seeping blood.

A thin black line ran through the name, scratching it out.

The name was CHADDICK.

Sophie's breath caught. In a single mark, a soul lost.

For a long while, no one spoke, the silence broken only by the festive buzz behind them and the snores of sleeping stymphs overhead, perched on the scaffolding shrouding the School Master's tower. Dot wiped her eyes while Anadil focused on the ground. Even Hester looked unsteady.

Gazing across the lake at Good's glass castle, Sophie thought of the burly, gray-eyed Everboy who'd once swaggered down those halls and been Tedros' most faithful liege, just like Agatha had been her own. But Agatha was still alive, of course, even if she was somewhere far away. . . .

Tedros' best friend was dead.

"H-h-how?" Sophie stammered.

"We don't know," said Professor Dovey emptily. "His body must be in Avalon. Otherwise his figure would have moved on the map."

Avalon, Sophie remembered. On her Quest Map, she'd seen Chaddick's figurine there when he should have been off seeking new knights for Tedros' kingdom. What was Chaddick doing alone in Avalon, which was perpetually cold and uninhabited? It's not like he could get into the Lady of the Lake's castle—only Merlin or the King of Camelot could do that. And yet, she distinctly remembered seeing Chaddick's figurine *inside* the castle gates. . . . Still, even if he did get in somehow, wouldn't the Lady of the Lake have protected him? Chaddick was Camelot's *knight*—

Dovey's voice severed her thoughts: "He sent me a note by crow a couple weeks ago. He'd been hearing reports of attacks in the Woods and wanted to find out who was behind them. I ordered him not to make a move. To stay on his original mission. Clearly he disobeyed."

Sophie looked at her.

"Whatever he found must have gotten him killed," the Dean said quietly.

"And now you want me to go and get killed too?" Sophie asked.

"Unlike Chaddick, you will have friends at your side," the Dean replied, eyeing the three witches.

"There's that word 'friends' again," Hester murmured.

Dovey ignored her. "I'd been looking into the news of attacks long before Chaddick wrote. The moment students' names started turning red on my map, I'd asked Merlin to investigate. It's common for students' quests to go badly at first—we've certainly dispatched rescue teams before—but for *all* to be failing was unprecedented. At the same time, we'd been hearing reports of unrest in the Woods, prompted by seemingly random crimes against Evers and Nevers alike. And then there was the matter of Tedros' sword, stuck in that stone. I thought Merlin could get to the bottom of all this. . . . Well, a few days ago, he finally returned to my chambers. He asked only one question: what fairy tale had the Storian been writing."

"Nothing of substance. I've told you that," Sophie said, glancing up at the School Master's tower, now her private quarters, which was connected to Evil's castle by a catwalk. She saw the Storian through the window, hovering over a stone table littered with crumpled paper. "Ever since it finished mine and Agatha's fairy tale, it's been starting and discarding tales of our classmates' quests."

"And whose story is it working on now?" said Dovey.

"It stopped writing completely last week, which after all that frantic scribbling and crumpling the past few months, is actually letting me sleep," Sophie puffed. "But you said that the

Storian often suspects a fairy tale will be a good one, only to scrap it midstory . . . that it's perfectly normal—"

"To a point," Professor Dovey replied. "The Storian only writes tales that we *need*: stories that will redress a balance between Good and Evil that is constantly in flux. But six months is a long time for the Storian not to put a new tale into the Woods. Perhaps it sees no story in your classmates' failing quests worth telling. Merlin, however, believes all these failures are connected and that there is a bigger quest waiting to be undertaken. That this is the fairy tale the Storian needs to tell."

"Yet you have no proof of this bigger quest or fairy tale?" said Sophie.

"And yet we still have to go with *her*?" Hester said, leering at Sophie.

"A student is dead, girls. I'd think at the very least you'd want to bury his body, let alone find out what killed him," said Professor Dovey frostily. "I do."

Sophie and the witches fell silent.

"There is also the fact that according to the map, you are all failing your quests too," Professor Dovey said.

Sophie and the coven gawked at her before swiveling to the map.

They'd been so focused on their classmates that they hadn't noticed their own names were in red.

"How can I be failing?" Sophie protested. "My quest is to be Dean of Evil. That's the quest Lady Lesso gave me—"

"And how could *we* be failing?" said Hester, looking at her witch friends. "We didn't do anything wrong on our quest—"

"Unless, of course, your quests no longer apply," said Professor Dovey.

Sophie and the witches exchanged confused looks.

"You see, your names only turned red on my map *yesterday*. Within minutes of Chaddick's death," said Professor Dovey. "I highly doubt it's a coincidence. The Storian creates a Quest Map every three years once the new class goes into the Woods. The fact the pen has stopped writing combined with your names turning red only strengthened Merlin's and my conclusion: that a new, more important quest awaits each of you. Only then will the Storian begin its next tale."

She paused, expecting questions, but Sophie and the witches still looked dazed.

"If it was up to me, Merlin and I would go into the Woods ourselves," Dovey went on. "But teachers cannot directly interfere in a student's quest just as we cannot interfere in a fairy tale. Which means *you* will represent the Nevers on this new quest, and Merlin will be sending an Ever contingent tonight to join your team. Given Chaddick's demise, all of this was too sensitive to be transmitted in any way other than in person, so that's why I brought you back to school. You must leave as soon as possible to prevent more casualties. But you're not just a rescue team. You're a detective team. Something out there is hurting our students and your new quest is to find it. . . . One quest to save them all."

Sophie couldn't focus, a single thought haunting her. "Has anyone told Tedros about . . ."

"No," Professor Dovey answered, rising from her seat.

"Telling Tedros will surely lead to him doing something rash, especially since we've yet to learn how his friend died. The island of Avalon, then, should be the first stop on your new quest. Even if you can't get through the castle's gates, you might find clues as to what Chaddick was doing there."

Sophie's mind went gauzy, as if she was trying to wake from a dream. Dead friends . . . bodies to be buried . . . a mysterious threat . . .

How quickly things change in a fairy tale.

A few minutes ago she was the host of a rollicking party that finally helped her turn the page and begin a new chapter. But now she was facing a new quest far away from school, where her life would be as much at risk as the friends' lives she had to save.

Only she wasn't *ready* to leave this place. After three years, she'd found her way out of a fairy tale and wouldn't let herself be dragged back into one. And the best part about being Evil was that she could admit this without guilt. The new and improved Sophie could accept the selfish shades of her soul as much as the generous ones. Which meant that no matter how terrible she felt for Chaddick and the rest of her old friends out there in the dark Endless Woods . . . Sophie wouldn't be the one to help them.

"I'm afraid I'm Dean of a school just like you, Professor Dovey, entrusted with more than a hundred students. I can't just abandon them," Sophie decided. "I don't care what your map says. Hester, Anadil, and Dot will do just fine on their own."

The three witches blinked at each other, as if they'd tele-pathically made a wish and had it granted.

Professor Dovey tightened her silvery bun. "Sophie, you might be a Dean, but you are *also* a fourth-year student, which means I can change your quest just like *you* changed Hort's. And once a Dean assigns your quest, you must accept it or be sent to the Brig of Betrayers—"

"Don't you threaten me, Clarissa," Sophie retorted, watching Dovey wince at her first name. "You can't tell me what to do. I know you want to get rid of me, given how fond of Evil your 'Good' students are, and this gives you the perfect excuse."

"You think this is about you. I should have known. Every time it seems you've changed, I'm reminded how selfish you can be," said Professor Dovey. "Your first three years you trampled on students of both schools to further your own arrogant, often cowardly, goals. You punished them, tor-mented them, betrayed them . . . and yet they forgave you and even obeyed you as their Dean in the remaining months of their third year. They showed you the loyalty you never once showed them. Now these same classmates are in peril and need your help. Which means the story isn't about you anymore, Sophie. It's about *them*. But if you would like to make it about you, then think of it this way. This is no longer a tale about whether you will find fame or fortune or your perfect little happy ending. This is a tale about whether you are capable of growing from the snake of your own story into the hero of someone else's. That is your *new* quest. That is the tale the Storian is waiting to write."

Sophie went quiet, her emerald eyes fixed on the elder Dean. A dark crimson spread into her cheeks and for a moment, she looked less like Evil's leader and more like a chastened child.

"She's coming, isn't she," Hester mumbled, her demon making faces.

"Please tell me you can turn a person to chocolate," Anadil asked Dot.

"I have enough trouble with lentil cakes, thank you," Dot nipped.

Sophie wasn't listening, her focus drifting to the party uphill. "But who will take over as Evil's Dean?" she asked weakly.

"Professor Manley," said the elder Dean, adding before Sophie could object, "and I suspect his unpopularity will only increase your status once you return."

"*If* I return, you mean," Sophie corrected.

She expected Professor Dovey to reassure her, but the Dean said nothing.

"And what about the new School Master?" asked Hester. "We spent the last six months combing the Woods for someone who would best serve the school—"

"New School Master? *That* was your quest? To find a School Master?" Sophie asked, whirling to Professor Dovey. "You left the choosing of the one person who has control over you and me to *them*?"

"And I still would," Professor Dovey said. "But that's not to say that part of their assignment is over. You may very well come across the right candidate on your new quest, girls. And if you do, I expect a full report so I can interview them myself."

This seemed to appease both the coven, who wanted to see the job through, and Sophie, who fully intended to supervise the School Master's selection now that she was along for the trip.

"In the meantime, I'll keep tabs on the Storian with the rest of the faculty," said Professor Dovey. "Though as Merlin pointed out, if there was one lesson in *The Tale of Sophie and Agatha*, it's that the Storian does a rather remarkable job of protecting itself."

"Speaking of Merlin, which Evers is he sending to be on our quest?" Hester asked.

"It better not be Beatrix and her rancid minions," Sophie griped. "And how do you expect us to travel? On *foot*? I'm famous now; the whole world knows my fairy tale. I can't be traipsing from kingdom to kingdom in a dirty dress—"

The clocks in both castles tolled midnight, drowning her out, while Professor Dovey peered at the bay. "Merlin assured me his Ever team would be here by now. Do you see them?"

Sophie and the witches exchanged glances, as if the old Dean had stayed up too long past her bedtime.

"Um, wouldn't they be arriving at the South Gate?" Sophie said delicately.

Suddenly, a ripple burped at the midpoint of the bay, right in front of the School Master's tower. The sound it made was low and croaky like a dyspeptic toad's. Then more ripples formed, faster and faster, spewing bubbles of clear water and blue sludge into the sky, each burp more violent than the last, as if the bay was trying to expel something it'd swallowed. Then, in one willful spurt, the hull of a ship popped through the surface, only upside down, with the rest of the ship buried beneath the bay. It took a final cacophonous belch to send the hull toppling over and turn the ship right-side up, a glorious blue and gold, billowing with creamy white sails and the name *"IGRAINE"* painted along the bow near a masthead statue of a young, dark-haired woman dangling a lantern over the sea.

For a moment, as water and slime drained off the vessel and it propelled towards the shore, Sophie thought it must be a ghost ship, for there didn't seem to be a captain. But then she saw a shadowy figure at the prow in a dark leather jacket and cut-off breeches, hair tied up in a bandana. And from what she could see, he was sharp-jawed, fine-featured, and hand-some. . . .

Yet as the boat slid onto torchlit banks and stuttered to a stop, Sophie saw for the second time in one evening that the boy she'd been expecting was not a boy at all.

"Agatha?" she choked.

Her friend was already throwing a rope over the side of the ship and sliding down—

The two girls dashed towards each other and collided in a breathless hug, falling into the bay. Sophie's white dress was slopped in sludge, but she didn't care, gripping Agatha like she might never let go, both of them caught between giggles and tears.

On the shore, Professor Dovey was dabbing her eyes, as

were Dot and Anadil, each of who knew what it meant to have a best friend. Even Hester was biting her lip.

"I missed you, Aggie," Sophie whispered.

"Not as much as I missed you. They made Pollux give me wedding lessons," Agatha said breathlessly.

"That little weenie? In Camelot?" Sophie squeaked. "Giving *wedding* advice?"

"A wedding you're now in charge of planning," said Agatha.

Sophie burst into laughter. "Good heavens, we have a lot to catch up on." She kissed her dearest friend and nuzzled against her. "But now that I have you, I'm not letting you go. Even if you didn't write me. Even if I thought you'd forgotten all about me. I love you, Agatha. I always will."

Her friend held her close. "I love you too. And I never forgot about you, Sophie. I never could."

Sophie hugged her tighter.

"I'm here!" a voice shouted.

The girls turned to see Hort bounding around the side of the bay, naked except for a tablecloth from the party wrapped around his waist. "I tried to follow you, but then my man-wolf started shrinking and it got really bad and then it took me forever to find you guys, so yeah . . ." He bent over, panting. "What'd I miss?"

He took one look at Professor Dovey and three witches goggling at him. Then at two girls embraced in the sand, gaping at him too, Sophie's red lipstick on Agatha's cheek.

"Not again!" Hort gasped.

Only the girls weren't looking at Hort at all.

They were looking past him at a tall, silver tower rising out of the bay . . . an open window lit by the moon . . . a sharp, steel pen sweeping ink across a page . . .

The Storian.

Writing.

A new fairy tale had begun.

9

Who Would Want a Hort?

"Come, girls! We need to see what the pen is writing before it turns the page!" Professor Dovey said, leading the group towards Evil's castle. "Once it moves on, it won't let us flip back—"

Hort was desperate to take a bath and put pants on, but he couldn't let Agatha run off with Sophie unsupervised, so he followed them up the shore.

Every time he was free of rivals for Sophie's attention, they always returned, more meddling than ever. Why couldn't these toads mind their own business? Or die like Rafal did? True, he'd had Sophie to himself these past six months, but most of that was spent waiting out her I'm-an-Independent-Woman phase, which consisted of her doing a lot of yoga, reading poetry in her study, and hosting girls' nights in the Common Room. But after what he just saw at the party, it was clear Sophie was slobbering after boys again. And not just boys.

Everboys.

Uggggh.

Did those preening stallions have any idea what it was like to be *normal*? Because that's what being a Never was. "Normal" as in you woke up with smelly armpits and you broke out in pimples if you ate too many fried pig's feet and you had to slave in the Groom Room gym for every ounce of muscle—time that you would rather spend learning spells or catching lizards or doing something useful; but if you *didn't* waste half your day pumping Norse hammers and swinging kettlebells and doing one-handed pushups, then you'd be a skinny, oily loser for the rest of your life.

And yet, in the end, it didn't matter how much work Hort did to improve himself. He still couldn't find love. At least not the love he wanted. Not Sophie.

He thought about the anonymous fan letters he'd been getting these past few months. (*"Dear Hort, I don't know why you chase girls who don't appreciate you. There are girls like me who've read* The Tale of Sophie and Agatha *and think you're the real hero. . . ."*) At first, he thought they were from a Reader in Sophie's old town, but then he'd noticed that the letters were written on school parchment. Which meant Sophie was right all along. They were just a prank to embarrass him. Hort felt ashamed for getting suckered yet again. It was so obvious the letters were fakes. Who would want a Hort when there were Bodhis and Laithans running around?

That's what he resented most about Everboys. Girls liked them for their looks, when they'd done *nothing* to earn those looks. The stupid idiots were born like sculpted gods out of sheer dumb luck, the way other people are born with crooked faces or clubbed legs, and instead of being thankful or humble about this luck, they acted like they'd deserved it!

But even if Sophie was smart enough to see through these arrogant gasbags, she *still* fell for them, like a mouse who couldn't tell the trap from the cheese.

Why did he want her then? Why care about a girl who couldn't see he was better than those soft-headed lumps? Why idolize someone who would rather kiss the hot blond boy with the charm of a pineapple over a thinking, feeling boy like him?

Maybe I'm broken, Hort thought to himself. Maybe he was drawn to mean girls the way a girl like Agatha was drawn to Good boys.

Then again, Agatha was about to marry *Tedros*. A boil on the backside of humanity.

Whatever. The point was that he should be free of Sophie by now.

Instead, he was her employee.

Hort had no business being professor of history in the first place, since he didn't know the slightest thing about history and was pretty sure his students knew it too but they never complained because he gave them high ranks and passed out candy every Friday. And he was also sure his students knew he was in love with Sophie, since any time she sat in on his class, they made fawning comments about his teaching, as if they'd collectively decided to be wingmen in helping him earn the Dean's heart. It made him like his students more than he thought possible, and he'd convinced himself that his crusade to marry Sophie wasn't just for him anymore, but for all Evil-kind.

Except now Agatha was back.

Bug-eyed, skinny-legged, helmet-haired Agatha, who made Sophie smile the way he wished he could. Agatha, who had the gall to tell him last year that Sophie would never love him.

Since then, all he'd wanted was to prove her wrong. To prove to himself . . . to his students . . . to whoever was sending those fake love letters . . . that a boy like Hort could finally get the girl.

But now none of it would happen. Because when Agatha was around, Sophie didn't even notice him, and he always ended up running after them in some wild-goose chase like he was right now.

"Will . . . you two . . . slow down," he wheezed, tripping over his toga, his bare feet punished by the pebbly floor as he followed them into Evil's castle.

"So Merlin set this whole thing up? That sly dog . . . ," Agatha was saying to Sophie while Hort scrambled to eavesdrop. "First he mentions the *Igraine* . . . then he chastises me for not talking to you. . . . He did it all so I'd steal the ship and come here! I thought I'd be taking on this quest alone when all the while he planned for us to do it together."

"But why a *ship*, Aggie?" Sophie moaned, magically dissolving blue sludge off her and Agatha with her glowing pink finger. "I despise boats. They smell like toilets, the beds are stiff, there's never any fresh vegetables, and it's impossible to do yoga without falling overboard any time there's a swell—"

"Wait until you see *this* ship, though. The *Igraine* magically steers on my command. It can turn invisible, it can fly—"

"Throw on a bandana and a pair of breeches and now you're Whiskey Woo, the Pirate Queen," Sophie grumped as they followed Dovey and the witches upstairs, bypassing the party in Evil Hall. "The *Igraine*. Good lord. Sounds like a prehistoric bird. Or a splitting headache. Well, if we're together, I suppose I'll muddle through. Speaking of which, where's the other Evers? Merlin said you'd have a crew."

"Crew?" Agatha said. "No crew. I mean, Willam's on board, but he's been in his cabin seasick ever since we left."

"Willam?" Sophie asked with keen interest.

Hort scowled. He had enough boys at school to compete with, let alone boys lurking in boats. (Also, what kind of name was Willam? Sounded like the noise frogs made when they sucked down flies.)

"Hold on. No crew?" Sophie asked. "But Merlin told Dovey he was sending a *team* of Evers tonight to join me and the coven. That together, we'd be in charge of saving our classmates' failing quests."

"Well, we could certainly use the help on board," Agatha

mulled, "especially since we're overloaded with Nevers. Maybe Dovey can give us a couple of her best first years. . . . Perhaps that's what Merlin wanted us to do for a crew. . . ."

"Then why not just tell us as much?" Sophie grouched. "Why is everything a riddle with that old prat?"

"Because these are *our* quests, Sophie, not his," said Agatha.

"I still think the man's a nosy, musty loon," said Sophie. "But do tell me about Willam. Is he gorgeous and strong? A strapping swabbie of the high seas?"

Behind them, Hort went apoplectic red—

"I don't think he's your type," Agatha chuckled.

Hort exhaled, relieved.

"To be fair, no one thought Rafal was my type either," said Sophie as they reached the highest floor and followed Dovey and the witches onto an outdoor catwalk. Two wolf guards patrolled the walk, which stretched between the highest floor of Evil's castle and the School Master's tower. As she passed, Sophie gave the guards an imperious smile and flicked dust off the red-and-gold SOPHIE'S WAY sign, lit up and pointing towards the silver spire that divided the bay between Good and Evil. "Now, Aggie, for the most important question of all: What do we do about this *wedding* of yours?"

"Can't be worrying about a wedding when we have to save the Woods," Agatha said. "It would have been a challenge anyway. You'd have had to plan the whole wedding from here at school. Camelot's castle is already a mess and Tedros doesn't want you there romping around and causing more upheaval—"

"I see," Sophie said archly. "Afraid I might steal his crown?"

"Um, right. I think it's well established that you two should stay as far from each other as possible. We'll get someone else to plan the wedding."

"Nonsense. I'll do it while we travel. I just need two assistants on board, a fleet of courier crows, and an unlimited budget—"

"Camelot is bankrupt, Sophie."

"—and naturally I'll bring Bogden as one of my assistants, so perhaps we can include another Ever to balance out our crew . . . a handsome boy like Bodhi or Laithan. . . ."

"*Wedding?*" Hort cried, interloping between the girls. "Twenty minutes ago, you said you were done with Agatha's wedding. That you never wanted to think about her and Tedros again. That you were throwing your own party because you were totally over—"

Sophie thrust out her glowing finger and zipped his mouth with a spell. Stunned, Hort tried to yell through sealed lips to no avail.

"One of Lesso's best hexes," Sophie told Agatha. "I've been reading her old spellbooks during my nightly baths."

Agatha took a deep breath. "Sorry I didn't write you all these months, Sophie," she said, nearing the School Master's tower. "So much has happened since I left school."

"The *Royal Rot* certainly agrees," Sophie replied.

"*Sophie!*"

"Darling, you weren't writing me and I needed news of my best friends. You didn't expect me to read the *Camelot Courier*, did you? Nothing but propaganda."

"And the *Rot* is any better? A tabloid that said I cursed Tedros to fall in love with me and plan to slit his throat on our wedding night, once I'm officially queen?"

Sophie snickered.

"And here I was feeling guilty I hadn't written you," Agatha said.

Sophie threw an arm around her. "Well, it doesn't matter now, does it? We're together again and this time without a prince in our hair as we head off on the biggest adventure of our lives."

Hort was grinding his teeth so loudly that the two girls glanced at each other.

"Is he really still there," Sophie murmured.

"Poor little weasel," Agatha said, pointing her glowing gold finger and unzipping his mouth.

Hort exploded at Sophie: "Adventure? *Adventure?* If you think you're going into the Woods with . . . with . . . *her,* then you have another thing coming! You reassigned my quest and made me a teacher and I didn't complain because you made it sound like you'd be my girlfriend and we'd go on dates and eat ice cream and kiss like normal couples do! And instead you treat me like a servant and now you're trying to abandon me at school and take skinny, stinky *Bogden?* Are you *kidding?* Just because Agatha deserted her stupid boyfriend to go gallivanting around the Woods doesn't mean you can! I spend every day teaching kids about Elf Wars and Wizard Summits and things I don't care a lick about to spend time with you and you think you can *leave?* Kiss my big, blooming arse! I'll set that ship on fire if you even get close!"

Sophie blinked at him, speechless.

"You know, sometimes I wonder what he sees in you," said Agatha.

Sophie laughed and took her hand. "Everything, darling. *Everything.*"

As the two girls continued towards the School Master's tower, Hort watched them go.

He knew what he saw in her. The same thing he'd always seen, no matter how badly she treated him. He saw a girl as soft and vulnerable as he was, if only she'd let herself feel it instead of distracting herself with the next best thing.

Don't follow her, Hort begged himself.

Please.

Don't. Follow. Her.

He followed.

As he scrambled to keep up with the girls, Hort told himself it was only because he'd never entered the School Master's tower before. But that wasn't the real reason, of course. The real reason was because the tower was now Sophie's private chamber. And he wanted to see the inside.

The scaffolding shrouding the spire was dotted with sleeping stymphs, slumbering after a long day of renovations. Stymphs detested Hort, so he held his breath as he passed. Skirting between two more watchful wolf guards, he followed Dovey and the girls through a gap in the silky black scaffold.

Don't act like it's a big deal, Hort thought as he climbed through the open window. *Don't be creepy.*

But he *was* creepy. He was *always* creepy. Creepiness was an inalienable, undeniable part of his essential Hortness—

His bare feet touched the carpet and Hort snapped out of his thoughts. Every inch of the floor of Sophie's chamber was blanketed in lush white threads, so soft and deep they swallowed his feet like warm milk. His eyes roamed the sky-blue walls, studded with thousands of tiny silver balls like congealed drops of rain. The stone ceiling had been knocked out and replaced with a shallow aquarium, filled with water that changed color every ten seconds, and glittery, floating glass flowers. In one corner, Sophie's king-sized bed was veiled in a gold lace canopy, and beyond it, he could see inside the all-mirrored bathroom, teeming with vials and bottles of potions and creams. Nearby was a walk-in closet with racks of magically suspended dresses, organized by color and theme, and presided over by a grim-faced black mongoose with the name BOOBESHWAR on a tag around his neck, who was in the process of steaming one of Sophie's kimonos.

"Crikey. All I got in my closet is moths and soggy breeches," Hort murmured.

He turned, expecting Dovey and the witches to be as surprised by all this as he was—

But the six of them were circled around the Storian as it wrote in a storybook, its gold-hued cover spread open on the white stone table.

Hort moved in closer and saw the pen's sharp nib sweeping

colors across a painting of a boy lying by a lake, his eyes closed. Blood leaked from a wound in the boy's ribs, framing him in a crimson puddle.

Hort and Agatha looked up at Professor Dovey. But neither she, nor the witches, nor Sophie seemed as frozen with shock.

"Chaddick?" Agatha rasped. "He's . . . he's . . ."

"We don't know who killed him or why," Sophie said softly, studying the storybook. "But if this is right, his body is by the lake that took us to Guinevere and Lancelot's safe house."

"That's where the Lady of the Lake lives," Hester added. "How did Chaddick get through her castle's gates? Maybe there's a part of the story we're missing. . . ."

Quickly Hester slipped her fingernail under the storybook's page to see the pages that came before. The Storian scorched red with fury and stabbed at her finger—

Hester withdrew it before it impaled her. "It's the first page."

"*What?*" Sophie blurted. "'Once upon a time a handsome boy died?'"

"Under other circumstances, I'd be enthralled," said Anadil.

"This proves that Chaddick was onto something," said Professor Dovey, giving her a look. "His death is part of a larger story, just as Merlin thought."

Hort could see Agatha staring at the storybook, tears on her cheeks. Even though Agatha was a nagging goat, the fact she was crying made Hort's eyes mist up too. Chaddick had been a boy at school, just like him. A boy who'd been on a quest in the Endless Woods and had now died for it. And here Hort was, a spineless sap confined to the castle because he'd given up his real quest to chase a *girl*. Guilt and determination flushed through him, two crisscrossing rivers. Like Chaddick, Hort's own father had been killed on a quest: a lifelong mission to serve Captain Hook in the fight against Peter Pan. Hort had come to the School for Evil to be better than his father. But what would his father think of him now? Still at school, pretending to be a teacher, puttering after someone who wouldn't give him the time of day. . . .

For the first time, he felt the death grip Sophie had on his soul weaken.

This wasn't about her anymore. This was about making something of his life.

Even Peter Pan had learned to grow up.

Hort gazed out the window at the *Igraine* in Evil's harbor, sails flapping in the wind.

Wherever that ship was going, he would be on it.

Suddenly the girls tensed all at once and huddled closer to the storybook—

"What is it?" he asked.

But now he saw for himself.

The Storian was writing its first words of the story.

Beneath the painting of Chaddick's body, the pen etched its bold, beautiful script:

Once upon a time, a Snake made its way into the Woods. Its plan was simple: take down the Lion.

The Storian turned the page and began to paint once more.

"A *snake*?" Hester asked, baffled.

"A *lion*?" Anadil echoed.

"So this is about, uh, disgruntled animals?" Dot said.

"No," Agatha replied, peering at the storybook. "It's not about animals at all."

Everyone watched her, waiting for her to elaborate.

"Um, then what's it about?" Hort prodded.

Agatha raised her eyes. "It's about getting to Avalon *now*."

There was panic in her face, as if she'd put a puzzle together the rest of them hadn't.

"How soon can you leave?" Professor Dovey pressed.

"We need food and weapons," said Agatha.

"I'll make sure you have both," said the Dean.

"Aggie, what is it?" Sophie asked, glancing between them.

But the Storian had finished its second painting now, a magnificent rendering of the twin-sailed *Igraine* sinking back under Halfway Bay, with Agatha at the stern, commanding the ship onwards. The pen wrote beneath:

Soon, a team of students from the School for Good and Evil set out to find the Snake, led by two best friends, Sophie and Agatha, along with a crew of three witches, an altar boy named Willam, and a first-year Never named Bogden.

The Storian halted.

"What about me!" Hort protested.

But no one was paying the slightest attention, because

Professor Dovey was rounding up the girls towards the window: "Come; there's provisions in the kitchen and weapons in the Armory—"

"*Boobeshwar!*" Sophie yelped at her startled mongoose: "Start packing my suitcase. . . ."

"Wait a second," Hort piped up.

"You'll need food and water for a week before you can reload in the Ever Lands," Dovey was saying.

"Enough clothes for two months, Boobeshwar!" Sophie hollered over her. "I'll send Bogden to fetch the luggage—"

"I SAID *WAIT A SECOND!*" Hort bellowed.

Six pairs of eyes went to him.

"Look," he said.

They followed his gaze to the long, white table.

The Storian was writing again.

There was one more member of their crew, however.
Someone they hadn't expected.
Someone who they'd need on their dangerous quest.

Hort raised his fist. "See! *See!* I told you! It saved the best for—"

Someone named Nicola.

"Nicola?" Agatha said, mystified.

Everyone stared at the page.

"Who in tarnation is *Nicola!*" Hort barked.

But only Dovey and Sophie seemed to know, for they both eyed each other with strange looks, before Sophie slowly turned to Agatha.

"Well, darling, it seems we've found the missing Ever for your team."

10

NICOLA

The Perks of Being a Reader

Sophie might be a Dean, but that didn't mean Nicola had respect for the girl or would join her ranks of fawning students.

For one thing, she'd met Sophie back when they lived in Gavaldon, but Sophie was acting as if she'd never seen Nicola in her life. For another, Nicola had read *The Tale of Sophie and Agatha* and thought Sophie was a class-A brat. And then on Nicola's first day, Sophie had blamed her for caving in a classroom when it wasn't her fault at all!

For these reasons (and

more), she'd been giving Sophie hostile looks ever since she got to school two weeks ago and Sophie had been giving them right back.

So imagine Nicola's surprise when it was Sophie herself who barged into her room tonight and dragged her onto this boat, helped by Hester, Dot, and Anadil, three witches she'd only seen in a storybook.

No one told her why. They'd just acted like she was their prisoner and gave her thirty seconds to pack before they flung her aboard and dumped her in the worst room. She didn't even know who else was on the crew, since no one had bothered to come check on her once they'd set sail.

It hurt her feelings, to be honest. Hester was one of her favorite characters in *The Tale of Sophie and Agatha* and being treated like a stray dog by your favorite characters is worse than never meeting them at all. Even Dot, who seemed so jolly and sweet on the page, hadn't managed a proper "hello."

I should have known, she thought. *Girls like me are always left out of fairy tales.*

Nicola steeled herself. Well, if this crew couldn't show her the most basic manners, then she wasn't going to make an effort either. Instead, she would handle them the way she'd handled rude customers at Pa's pub in Gavaldon: with grace, dignity, and pity for their poor souls.

Thunder blasted outside and a slash of lightning lit up her window.

Nicola unpacked her toothbrush, soap, and comb in her tiny bathroom. The boat had been swerving and lurching through this storm for the past hour.

Whoever was steering had no idea what they were doing.

"Man the sails!" Agatha cried, soaked to the bone as she gripped the captain's wheel—

Nicola snuck closer to the galley door so she could peer through the crack and survey the whole deck.

Lightning ripped through a sail and the *Igraine* lurched off-course, rain flooding over the rails. The storm had exploded only a few hours after they left, caging them into whirling winds they couldn't escape. Hester and the witches were siphoning water off the deck using their fingerglows—

"Lady of the Lake controls these waters! Should be giving us easy passage!" Hester was shouting at Anadil and Dot.

Meanwhile, Nicola's classmate Bogden was clutching a red-haired boy as he puked overboard; Sophie was crawling on all fours up the deck; and another boy was batting down the hatches, which kept coming loose—

Hort! Nicola gasped, recognizing him. Her whole body went hot. . . .

Wind slammed against the boat, spinning it like a pinwheel, knocking Sophie into a railing. The broken sail flapped over her, lashing against the mast. A huge shard of wood snapped under the rogue sail and came shearing down, about to spear the deck—

Instantly, Dot turned the shard to chocolate chips, which scattered into the rain. Hester's demon flew off her neck and hoisted up the heavy sail; Anadil's three rats secured its ropes (all the while catching chocolate in their mouths).

"What did I . . . say . . . about . . . *boats*!" Sophie mewled, makeup smeared, soggy hair caught around her neck like a noose. Blown side to side, she scooted on her stomach up the steps to the captain's level—

"The wind is sending us everywhere but Avalon," Agatha growled, wrangling the wheel. "We should be there by now!"

"You said the ship listens to you!" Sophie squawked behind her.

"The ship, not the *weather*! The faster I tell it to go, the more the wind hits us!"

Sophie lunged off the top step and grabbed hold of Agatha's ankle. "Isn't it a magic ship? Make it fly or turn invisible!"

"What good is being invisible in a storm! Or flying higher into it!" Agatha said, squinting into the rain. "We must be fifty miles off-course!"

There were clearer skies to the east, which would give them a chance to regroup. She just needed to steer the boat out of this wind-cage—

"SAIL EAST!" she shouted at the wheel.

The *Igraine* bounded eastwards but bashed into headwinds, making it swing back and forth like one of those sickening pirate-ship rides at the Gavaldon Fair. Sophie lost grip of Agatha's shoe and went rolling down the stairs.

"AGATHA!" she shrieked, hanging off the staircase banister.

Hort ran to save her, but tripped and plunged down a hatch. Bogden was now retching alongside the red-haired boy, while the witches tumbled across the deck like marbles. As the ship bobbed, water surged over the rail. The *Igraine* started to sink—

"Mind if I help?" a voice said behind Agatha.

Agatha turned to see a short, buxom black girl her age leaning against a rail, arms folded. She had a catlike face with thin eyes and sloping brows, along with springy black curls immune to the rain and a pink first-year's Ever uniform at odds with her cold expression.

"Nicola?" Agatha said, shouting over the storm. "That's your name, isn't it?"

"And yours is Agatha, though the Agatha I've read about would have come and said hello so maybe that's not your name after all," Nicola replied. Agatha winced, but Nicola didn't give her a chance to respond. "Steer like it's a riptide. The wheel's spinning left because you're trying to go right. If you want to go right, turn the ship left."

"AGGIE! HELP!" Sophie howled below, a seagull on her head.

Nicola narrowed her eyes. "Seagulls love the smell of hot decay. Wonder what that says about your friend."

She turned to find Agatha gaping at her.

"I just told you how to get us out of this storm," Nicola said.

Agatha shook her head. "Sailing in the opposite direction doesn't make sense—"

Nicola glared harder. "Listen, I may be a first-year Reader who no one on this boat cares about, but that also means I've read *your* fairy tale and know you're a smart girl. Smart enough to realize you've been trying to get us out of this storm for the past hour and have instead put us on the verge of a very watery death."

Another tidal wave detonated onto the deck, drenching Agatha.

"One more and we'll get to see who can hold their breath the longest," said Nicola.

Agatha swiveled towards the wheel. "SAIL WEST!" she commanded—

The *Igraine* pivoted smoothly to the west for just a moment. Then the current took over, counterposing the ship east. The wooden girl on the masthead swept her lantern towards the dawn-lit clearing. In a single move, the boat broke free of the wind-trap and glided towards Avalon.

Sophie dropped like a stone to the deck, her gown blown over her head like a broken umbrella. The rest of the crew peeked up, no longer thrashing or scrambling or retching. All of their eyes honed in on the new girl, who'd just saved their necks.

Sophie was the only one who didn't smile at her.

Nicola sauntered towards the galley in her sheepskin boots. "Is breakfast ready? Or should I take care of that too?"

"Wait! If you're a Reader, how'd you know how to do that!" Agatha called out behind her.

"The same way I know everything," the girl replied, without breaking stride. "I *read*."

"If you're from Gavaldon, how did we never meet?" quizzed Agatha.

"Didn't I see you in a Never's uniform the first day of school?" asked Hort, spooning his oatmeal.

"Why did the Storian write you into our crew?" said Willam.

"Do you even know what a fourth-year quest *is*?" asked Hester.

Sitting across the galley dining table painted with Camelot's crest, Nicola picked at a soggy tower of egg and cheese. "The real question is why an enchanted pot can't make an omelet when I was making them at six years old."

"Think Dovey gave us a broken pot," Bogden said, snacking on potato skins. "I asked for pancakes and it made these instead."

"Broken pot, broken map . . . Dovey's house certainly isn't in order," Dot murmured.

Nicola was midbite when she saw the ragtag Inquisition still gawking at her. "Oh, so I've been on this boat for hours and *now* I exist?"

("*BOOBESHWAR!*" Sophie screeched from her cabin.)

Nicola's lips tightened. "Well, let me answer your questions, then. Agatha, we never met in Gavaldon because you spent your time on Graves Hill and I spent mine at Papa Pipp's Pub, helping my father cook for his customers. I knew your mother, though, since she treated Pa for his bad back. As for your friend, Sophie, she met me a few times in Gavaldon, but she doesn't seem to remember, since girls like her only notice you if you're useful or a threat."

Nicola turned to Willam. "I haven't the faintest clue why

the Storian put me on your crew, though from what I can tell, maybe it's to keep you all alive."

Nicola turned to Hort, blushing hard. "As for why I'm now in an Ever's uniform, that's a long story. But I've read *The Tale of Sophie and Agatha* and you're a lot more handsome in person than on the page—except to be honest, I'd prefer the old you before you buffed up to look like Tedros, who's about as enticing as vanilla pudding. But even if you're deluded about your own self-image and are hooked on blond, skinny girls, the fact I'm talking to the real Hort instead of reading about you is the only nice part of being on this boat. Especially since you didn't answer *any* of my letters."

Hort dropped his spoon.

Nicola turned to Hester. "What do I know? I know we're on a quest to find out why your classmates' quests are failing and prevent any more from dying. I know that the Storian says a 'Snake' has made its way into the Woods and is determined to take down a 'Lion.' And I know only Agatha seems to know what those words mean. Which is why I'm curious as to why everyone is asking *me* questions instead of *her*."

Everyone stared at Nicola.

"Oh, this little fella told me everything," Nicola explained, as Boobeshwar hopped from her lap, where he'd been hidden, and perched on her shoulder. "Mongooses are chatty if you rub their heads. Learned that from reading *The Brave Maharajah*."

She zeroed in on Agatha. "But enough about me. Since this is now a quest that belongs to us all, I think it's time you told us what you know about lions and snakes."

Everyone turned to Agatha.

"There you are, Boobeshwar!" a voice rang out.

Sophie paraded in wearing a crystal-studded blue-and-white sailor's dress and towering heels. "Sorry, I needed to freshen up and—" She tripped over a mound of weapons they'd taken from school: swords, daggers, axes, spears. "Hort, for heaven's sakes, put these somewhere else. Can't have warmongering in the kitchen. Shall we start breakfast? I'm famish—"

Sophie bit her lip.

The crew was already eating.

And no one was even glancing in her direction, including Hort, who was ogling Nicola as if she'd shot an arrow through his heart.

Sophie cleared her throat. "Surely it's proper form to wait for a Dean before—"

Nicola whirled and shot her a withering look, Sophie's mongoose on her shoulder. Then she turned back to Agatha.

"You were saying, Captain?"

Nicola wasn't supposed to be here. Not on this ship, not at this school, not in the Woods. She should be in Gavaldon right now, working at the pub with Pa.

But her two older brothers, Gus and Gagan, had thrown a wrench in all that.

They wanted Papa Pipp's Pub for themselves, but Pa had no intention of leaving his legacy to two boys who would sell the place off the second he died. Instead, he decreed that Nicola would inherit the pub. With her in charge, Gus and Gagan could be kept at bay, continuing to pass plates and scrub pots to make a wage for the rest of their lives. (To make matters worse, Nicola beat them at every sport they played.)

Day after day, her brothers wished: *If only she wasn't around.*

Then one day they made their wish come true.

When Nicola was younger, the whole town was petrified of the School for Good and Evil. Every four years, two children were kidnapped from Gavaldon—the best-behaved kid for Good, the worst-behaved kid for Evil—and neither would ever see their family or friends again. Instead, they'd disappear into the Woods and reappear years later in illustrated tales that magically arrived at Mr. Deauville's Storybook Shop. Any child not taken would sigh with relief, knowing they were safe for four more years.

But that was before Sophie and Agatha.

Now a school of horrors had become every child's dream.

Statues of scenes from Sophie and Agatha's tale were built all over Gavaldon. Thousands of fan letters were left at these monuments, along with pleas to be kidnapped and taken to the school. For Halloween, children dressed as Sophie (pink dresses, blond wigs), Agatha (black sack dresses), and Tedros (no shirt, a sword). At Gavaldon Primary School, teachers used *The Tale of Sophie and Agatha* to explain everything from grammar ("Is 'stymph' a noun or proper noun?") to math ("If there are 10 kids from each school in the Trial by Tale and 6 kids die during it, how many make it out alive?") The annual Gavaldon Fair became a School for Good and Evil theme park, with a Wish Fish Fortune-Telling Pool, Flowerground

Roller Coaster, Trial by Tale Corn Maze, Princess Uma's Animal Merry-Go-Round, and Halfway Bay Wave Pool.

But it wasn't just children who were captivated by Sophie and Agatha. Stefan, Sophie's father, had become the most popular man in Gavaldon after the girls' tale revealed the Elders to be corrupt villains. Soon, the Council was replaced by a Mayor's Office, to which Stefan was elected by unanimous vote. Stefan's first act as Mayor was to tack a note for his daughter on his door demanding that a) she and Agatha visit home immediately and b) to satisfy Gavaldon's clamoring children, the School should start accepting applications from Readers, provided new students could return home on holidays to see their families.

Nothing came of the first request.

But a week later, the citizens of Gavaldon woke to a proclamation on their doors, announcing open applications to the School for Good and Evil, which would now host a new class of Evers and Nevers each year, beginning in August, instead of every four years. In addition, each household received a shiny new copy of *The Ever Never Handbook*, a guide to the School for Good and Evil with rules, classes, uniforms, and most importantly, formal applications to the school itself, with questions such as: *If you were marooned on a deserted island, what three things would you like to have?* and *If I were an animal, I'd like to be a* . . . Children eagerly filled out these forms and left them in sealed envelopes near the girls' statues, the envelopes piling up week after week like parchment mountains . . . until one night all the applications magically disappeared.

Nicola had been tempted to apply, of course. She'd read thousands of storybooks and knew she was smarter and stronger than any of the Readers that had been taken before.

Who needs Agatha and Sophie when they can have me? she'd thought. Those girls had made for a lively story, but their tale was over. It was time for a new hero.

And yet, as much as she wanted it to be her . . . it couldn't be.

She had an aging Pa to care for, customers to manage, and a business to run. If she left, everything her father had worked for—and his father and his father and his father—would be wasted by her brothers.

So it was a complete shock when two weeks ago, in the middle of a hot August night, she was magically sucked out of her bed, flung onto a bony bird, whisked on a harrowing ride through a dark forest, and dropped into the School for Evil's sludgy moat with more than a hundred villainous Nevers-to-be.

Her stupid, no-good, nasty brothers! Gus and Gagan must have filled out an application under her name. But there was no time to stew about it. The wolves were already whipping children onto shore. . . .

She had to get home. Pa was surely worried sick. But as she was shoved into a saggy black uniform and thrust books and a schedule, Nicola felt a sense of déjà vu. She'd read *The Tale of Sophie and Agatha* so many times that she couldn't help but enjoy being in this world she knew so much about.

Staying one day wouldn't hurt, would it? she wondered. If she stayed, she could explore places she'd only known in a book . . . participate in challenges she already knew how to beat . . . Imagine: she might even get a glimpse of beautiful, perfect *Hort*. . . .

But she never got the chance.

Evil didn't want her.

The dorm locked her out; hallways ejected her into the bay; doors slammed in her face and spellbooks on her hand. Everywhere she went the castle rebelled, until rooms started caving in the moment she entered. She had no idea why any of this was happening, yet Dean Sophie held her personally responsible for the mess and marched her across the bridge to Professor Dovey in the School for Good. But seeing the chaos Nicola had caused in Evil's castle, Dovey didn't want her either. She told Sophie that since Nicola had been delivered to Evil's door, she was Sophie's problem.

So there was nothing Dean Sophie could do except drag Nicola back across the bridge, grumbling about Readers and the burdens of being a Dean and why she'd been sentimental enough to listen to her father's idea of accepting Readers in the first place. . . .

That's when Nicola smashed into the invisible barrier.

The bridge had let her go from Evil to Good but wouldn't let her go from Good to Evil. She was trapped, no matter how much she tried to ram through. And unlike Evil, the Good towers had no allergy to her, welcoming Nicola without a tremor.

So the decision was made for her.

She would spend the next few months as an Ever. At

Christmas, she'd go back home with the other Readers and would stay with Pa forever, while the rest returned to school.

But until then . . . Nicola would wear *pink*.

"*The Lion and the Snake* is a fairy tale," said Agatha, sipping ginger tea.

"Not one I've heard of," said Nicola as she cleared the breakfast plates.

"Nor I," said Hort, magically erasing stains off the Camelot crest on the table.

"Nor I," chorused Bogden and Willam as they washed salt off portholes.

"Nor I," said Hester as the witches took dishes from Nicola and cleaned them with their fingerglows.

"Well, I've certainly heard of it," Sophie preened, cozying up to Agatha.

"No, you haven't," Agatha snapped to Nicola's delight. "No one here knows *The Lion and the Snake* because it's a fairy tale about Camelot and one mainly told inside its walls. I read it out loud to spoiled children yesterday to raise money for our broken drawbridge."

"How plebeian," murmured Sophie.

Says a girl whose father worked at the mill, Nicola thought, rolling her eyes.

"Apparently it's the only story that every child in Camelot knows," Agatha was saying. "Luckily, when you read a story out loud, you remember most of it. It went something like this."

She raised her glowing finger and tendrils of gold magically streamed from its tip, dispersing like threads over Nicola's head. . . .

"Once upon a time, a beautiful new kingdom appeared at the edge of the sea," said Agatha. "Only it had no king."

The golden threads morphed into majestic spires with rounded turrets. . . .

"Every kingdom must have a king, so it waited for some-one to take the throne. But to be king requires strength and cleverness, values rarely found in the same being. In the end, only two came forward to claim the crown. The Lion. And the Snake."

Each of the two rivals appeared out of Agatha's glow, strik-ing and slashing at each other.

"No one knew how to decide between them, so a vote was held. Those who believed the new kingdom should be ruled with strength chose the Lion. Those who believed the new kingdom should be ruled with cleverness chose the Snake. Both drew an equal number of votes, the kingdom in perfect balance."

Between the Lion and the Snake, a third glowing outline appeared. . . .

"And so the Eagle was brought in to make the final choice, since he flew high above and saw the world in a way no one else could. The Eagle asked each rival a single question: 'If you were king, would the Eagle be subject to your rule?'

"The Lion said yes. As long as the Eagle flew over his kingdom, he would receive his protection, but also be bound by his rule. The Snake said no. If he were king, the Eagle would be as free as he was before."

Slowly, the Lion's phantom disappeared.

"So the Eagle chose the Snake."

In a flash of glow, an army of hooded snakes descended on the Eagle—

"That night, without protection, the eagles were attacked. The Snake and his minions hid in the trees, decimating the eagles before the Lion and his friends came to their rescue. Soon, the Lion caught the murderous Snake. As he prepared to kill it, however, the Snake warned him. . . ."

The glowing serpent now had a voice:

"You dare not kill a king. The Eagle chosssse me because he wanted freedom. He got that freedom. What happened after doesn't change the Truth. The throne is mine. I am your king. Just because you do not like the Truth does not mean you can replacccce it with a Lie. And if you kill me, your new king will be a Lie. Kill me and I ssssshall return to take my crown. . . ."

The Lion paused, glowing brighter, seemingly taking this in. . . .

Then it tore apart the Snake.

"The Snake's warning was ignored. The Lion became King of Camelot and defender of all creatures. And to atone for his earlier mistake in choosing the Snake, the Eagle became the Lion's loyal advisor from that day forward, defending the realm in case the Snake should ever return."

The shadows dissolved as Agatha's fingerglow cooled.

"And that's how the kingdom of Camelot came to be," Agatha finished.

Nicola followed Agatha's eyes to the Camelot crest painted on the table: Excalibur, flanked by two eagles.

Only as she looked closer at the famous crest, Nicola saw something she hadn't seen before. . . .

The eagles had the bodies of lions.

"Wouldn't have ever thought of it again but clearly the Storian wants us to," said Agatha. "The pen said the Snake has come to take down the Lion—"

"Which means the Lion is the King of Camelot," Sophie proclaimed proudly.

Duh, thought Nicola.

"And the Snake wants his crown back," said Sophie. "And to take down the king."

Duhhhhh, Nicola scowled, seeing Agatha grow increasingly anxious.

"Tedros is definitely the Lion," said Sophie.

"Yes, we *know*," said Nicola impatiently. "What we don't know is: *Who is the Snake?* And how do we catch him before he gets to Tedros?"

"There's another question. And it's the reason we're going to Avalon first," said Agatha, meeting Nicola's eyes. "If the Lion is Tedros and the Snake wants to take him down . . . then why hasn't he gone after Tedros already? Why is he going after Tedros' *friends?*"

This time, even Nicola was quiet.

Standing at the captain's wheel, Nicola gazed out at the pink-and-gold sky, thin clouds knitted across it like snake scales.

Agatha had gone to take a brief nap after commanding the *Igraine* to forge southeast and leaving Nicola on watch. But it'd been smooth sailing for the past few hours and Nicola was about to fall asleep too. Even Sophie's mad mongoose had passed out, curled luxuriously around her ankle.

Perhaps I should wake Agatha, Nicola thought.

But the girl had sailed all night from Camelot, and from what the mongoose had told her, Agatha and Tedros had been having a rough time. Plus, Agatha had asked her to watch the ship—not Hester, not Anadil, not Willam—and Nicola felt honored. The other crew silently nodded when Agatha had made this decision, as if the first year had already earned her place.

Just like that, Nicola's bitterness about being on this boat was gone. Part of this was getting to meet Hort, of course. He'd even smiled at her in the galley. *Maybe my letters didn't put him off after all. . . .*

Suddenly she wasn't tired anymore. She could sleep for the rest of her life when she made it back home.

If she made it back, that is.

In a fairy tale, someone always dies so the others can live, she worried, thinking of Tristan, Nicholas, Cinderella, and others brutally killed in the last fairy tale that the Storian wrote. Is that why the pen added her to *this* story? To sacrifice her?

No way. She wasn't going to die here. No matter what the Storian had planned, she'd get back home to Pa and they'd celebrate Christmas together. If only she could let him know she was safe in the meantime. Then she could make the most of her stay here without worry or guilt. But how to get a letter to Gavaldon? Sophie would know, wouldn't she. . . . The one person she didn't want to ask for favors.

A flash of gold caught her attention and Nicola leaned over the wheel to see a chain hanging off it, carrying a small gold vial.

The Quest Map.

She'd seen Agatha and Sophie examining it earlier. Sophie had said something about Dovey fixing the map so it tracked quests accurately, before Agatha had borrowed it from Sophie to study it closer. She must have left the necklace here when she'd gone to nap. . . .

Nicola glanced back towards the galley. Through the windows, she could see Willam and Bogden huddling over what looked like tarot cards, while the three witches were still in a secret meeting about how to find a School Master on this quest (she'd eavesdropped in the bathroom). No one was on the deck with her. And no one could see her if she inched behind one of the masts. . . .

Remembering how Sophie and Agatha conjured the Quest Map, Nicola emptied the vial and watched the liquid gold suspend and congeal. Leaning into the map, she peered at a three-dimensional toy ship sailing towards Avalon, with Hester's, Agatha's, Sophie's, Anadil's, Hort's, and Dot's figurines aboard. There wasn't one for Willam since he wasn't a student, but there was one for Bogden and one for her, complete with a pink Ever's dress and curly black hair. The crew's names were bright blue, unlike the names in red scattered around the map.

Was the Snake tampering with these red-lettered quests? And hadn't the mongoose mentioned something about unrest in the kingdoms? Did the Snake have something to do with that too?

The answers were waiting in Avalon.

Instead of feeling scared, Nicola felt charged. There was danger ahead. But the idea that she was in a realm of adventure and magic and might meet more characters like Kiko, Merlin, or Guinevere . . . Her chest thumped faster. She wasn't just some observer anymore, reading a book while she stirred chowder at the pub. She was *inside* the book. And unlike other stories she'd read, this time she'd only find the ending by living through it.

Nicola's eyes shifted back to the toy *Igraine*, gliding across the map. It was millimeters away from Avalon. If the map was right, she would sight land any moment.

"Barely a first year and they've made you Captain," a voice said behind her.

Nicola's stomach dropped. *Hort!*

She turned. "Barely a fourth year and they made you a professor," she said, acting nonchalant.

"It could be worse. I was supposed to teach Evers too," said Hort. "But Professor Dovey put a stop to that."

He was in short black breeches, high black socks, and a long-sleeved white cotton shirt, the laces untied to reveal his muscular chest. His cheeks had a rosy glow as if he'd just scrubbed them and his black hair was wet and spiky. He smelled like clean laundry, which surprised her—from reading about him, she assumed he'd smell like wet rat or dead flowers. But instead, he smelled lovely . . . so either books got things wrong or Hort had cleaned up to talk to her. Both ideas were alarming.

"You're looking at me funny," said Hort.

"Oh, uh—" Nicola turned from him and collided loudly with the Quest Map, waking up Boobeshwar, who darted around as if he'd been fired out of a cannon. "Um, you had a fly in your hair. Shouldn't you be checking on Sophie?"

"Shouldn't you be giving her back her Quest Map?" said Hort.

"I found it like this," said Nicola.

"Spoken like a first year."

"Yet the Storian wrote me into this quest and not you," said Nicola.

"A *feisty* first year," said Hort.

"You have no idea," said Nicola.

Hort raised his brows.

Nicola stared into his beautiful, velvet-brown eyes.

"I would have answered your letters," said Hort.

"You read them? For real?" Nicola asked.

"Yeah, but I thought they were pranks."

"Oh."

"I liked them, though."

"Everything you just said… you could have written back to me," said Nicola.

Hort blinked at her. "You're not much of an Ever."

"Because I don't look like a princess?" Nicola asked, hurt. "I mean, I know they all look a certain way—"

"Because you're better than a princess," said Hort, moving closer to her. "And that uniform."

Nicola turned the color of her dress. "Well, seeing this is the only outfit I own at the moment and that I'm not going to be in the Woods very long . . ."

Hort cocked his head.

"I need to get home to my father," Nicola explained, wishing she could lay her head on his shoulder. "Even if I wanted to stay . . . even if I had good reason . . ."

"Your dad comes first," said Hort definitively.

Nicola sighed. *He understands.* Not just because Hort was a sensitive soul, but because from what Nicola had read, he'd been close to his dad too.

"Is it weird meeting people you've read about?" he asked, as if sensing her thoughts. "Do you feel like you know me because you've read about me?"

Nicola gazed at him. "I thought I did."

Hort went quiet for a moment.

Then he said: "I don't only like blond, skinny girls, you know."

Nicola's legs turned to jelly.

"That's not for a *student's* eyes," a voice said—

Sophie cut between Nicola and Hort, instantly shrinking the Quest Map into the vial and clasping it around her own neck. "Agatha should be more careful leaving a Dean's property around. Hort, will you go wake her up?"

"Actually, me and Nicola were—"

"Thank you, darling," Sophie said, giving him a peck on the cheek. "Hurry off now."

Hort frowned and walked towards the galley, touching his kissed cheek. "Whole world's gone mad . . . ," Nicola heard him murmur.

"I feel like we've started badly, Nicola," said Sophie, facing her. "We're going to have to work together and right now you and I are . . ." Sophie stopped because her mongoose had hopped onto Nicola's shoulder. Sophie glared at him slit-eyed. "I don't know whether it's because you've read stories about me or because you keep insisting that we've met before—"

"We *have* met," Nicola said. "You wrote a review of my father's pub in the town paper and said 'if the nut crumble is any indication, it's time Gavaldon moved on to more sophisticated cuisine.'"

Sophie waved dismissively. "Well, I'm sorry if I insulted your father's nuts—"

"It was *my* nut crumble," said Nicola. "I made it."

"And had I known that, I would have said it was delightful," Sophie chimed. "In any case, you can return home as soon as our quest is finished and you'll bake all the crumbles you like. But until then, I really *do* want us to be friends."

Nicola was stupefied. Whenever she'd read about Sophie, she'd always been frustrated that no one in the story stood up to her. But here she was in front of the girl, who was brazenly insulting her to her face, and all she could do was laugh.

"See, that's better," Sophie cooed cozily. "And don't think I haven't noticed that Professor Hort's taken a liking to you. You two seem to be quite fond of each other. Naughty girl."

"Well, if you're not interested in him, I certainly am," said Nicola.

"I see," Sophie chuckled. Then like a switch had flipped, her face clouded over. "See, that's the thing. To say something like that, and to a Dean no less, is highly inappropriate. Hort is a teacher and you are a student. It doesn't matter that he's hardly older than you and is as much of a 'teacher' as I am a horned troll. Anyone knows teachers can't be *chummy* with students. Besides, Hort already chose his true love long ago and it's not like she's going anywhere, is she? So if I were you, I'd focus on helping us complete our quest and getting home to your dear father as soon as you can."

Nicola felt as if she'd been slapped.

Sophie was already walking away. "Come, Boobeshwar. Mother has fresh nuts for you. . . ."

This time the mongoose followed, its loyalty easily bought.

Nicola watched them go, flurrying with emotions. For one thing, she knew from reading that the girl was a master manipulator. And yet, as much as she hated to admit it, Sophie was right: Nicola couldn't stay in this world much longer, even if she wanted to . . . so despite the fact her dreamy fantasy hunk had just flirted with her, keeping her distance from Hort seemed both prudent *and* practical. . . .

But there were bigger things to worry about right now. Because through the darkening sky, she heard the shriek of birds and saw the outline of tall, gray cliffs. . . .

"Land ho!" she cried.

The galley door flung open and she heard the crew running onto the deck—

Nicola turned to them, framed by the foaming spray of waves, like a captain in a storybook. "Man your stations! *Avalon ahead!*"

Stay with the Group

It's hard not to think of your true love when you're wearing his clothes.

But if Agatha thought about Tedros, she also had to think of a Snake who wanted to take him down . . . a Snake who didn't yet have a name. . . .

She could hear the crew crunching through snow—Sophie, Hort, Nicola, Bogden, Willam, the three witches—each armed with a weapon and following her dutifully even though Agatha didn't have a clue where she was going.

She'd been to Avalon Island before, but that was months ago, when Merlin was guiding them, the only person besides the King of Camelot to whom the Lady of the Lake's castle would open. But now Agatha had no Merlin to open those castle gates nor the slightest idea how to even *find* the castle, since last time she'd been so busy fretting about Tedros dumping her for Sophie that she hadn't noticed the route.

Not that there was a route to find anymore. Powdery snow matted the desolate shrubland and was still falling fast. There was no sun to guide them either, its afternoon light trapped behind a wall of gray. Shivering in her bandana, Agatha shoved her chapped hands deeper in Tedros' brown leather jacket, which she'd worn over his cut-off breeches. *Stupid me*, she thought. She'd packed for summer even though her teacher Yuba had told them in Forest Groups that it was *always* winter in Avalon.

Agatha plodded ahead gloomily. First she'd almost drowned her crew and now she was freezing them to death. Her quest was off to a rousing start.

A whiff of Tedros' minty scent came off her shirt.

"*This isn't your quest. It's mine,*" his voice echoed.

Maybe he'd been right. *He* was the one whose best friend was dead. *He* was the Lion in the Storian's tale.

So why am I here without him? Agatha thought.

Because he'd insisted that a king couldn't abandon his people. But that wasn't the whole truth, of course. The truth was that she *wanted* him to stay behind. She wanted to keep him out of danger.

Little had she known that a Snake might be coming for him.

Agatha gritted her teeth. No matter what—or who—was ahead, she'd save her prince.

This isn't right, said a voice inside her. *No one can save Tedros but himself.*

Agatha rolled her eyes. Didn't princes save princesses all the time?

This isn't about boys and girls, the voice said. *This is about destiny. This is about the truth. You're only making his problems worse—*

Agatha squashed the voice down.

She glanced over her shoulder at the *Igraine*, peeking behind the cliff rock where they'd anchored a couple miles off. Instinct told her she was going the right way. She plowed forward, snow coating her lashes, a dagger strapped to her back.

Sophie accosted her in a voluminous white fur coat. "At first I was thinking a 'Nanook of the North' theme for your wedding, with faux tundra, penguin caterers, and Teddy in an ice-blue leotard. Now not so much."

Agatha didn't smile.

"You're worried about him, aren't you?" Sophie sighed.

"Not because of whatever you read in the *Royal Rot*."

"You're worried about him because you love him, Aggie. Just like I worry about you."

Agatha looked at her.

"Don't be so shocked, darling. I know I'm wicked and petty and call Teddy a boob to anyone who will listen, but he loves you as much as you love him and you two *will* get married on October 14th come hell or high water," said Sophie.

"When Dovey first enlisted me for this quest, I tossed it off, thinking it had nothing to do with me. But I'm starting to see why it *is* my quest. Because I won't let any 'Snake' get in the way of my best friend's Ever After, especially after I played that role myself for far too long. And if it means risking my life to get you and Teddy to that altar safe and sound . . . well, even the villain can play the hero sometimes."

Agatha's eyes grew wide. "Did you really turn the Doom Room into a dance club on Saturday nights?"

"Complete with lava pit and monthly foam parties," said Sophie. "Why?"

"Just making sure you're the same girl," Agatha said.

"Well, if you go on ignoring my letters, I'll buy every last dungbomb in the Endless Woods and stymph-raid your castle."

"*Definitely* the same girl."

Sophie brushed snow off Agatha's face. "You know, if the Storian is referencing that fairy tale, it means the Snake wants Teddy's crown. So why doesn't he just storm Camelot and kill him? Why go after other kingdoms? Why go after our friends? Only that got me thinking . . . The Snake *can't* storm Camelot and kill Tedros. Killing Teddy won't make him king. It would lead to war with the whole Woods. So he must have some other plan."

"But what other plan could he have?" said Agatha. "Tedros is Arthur's blood and the only rightful king by royal law. No matter what he does, nothing will ever change that."

They pondered this silently, listening to Agatha's teeth chatter.

"Do you want to huddle under my coat?" Sophie asked. "We'll look like conjoined twins, but we can't have you dying. You're the only one who knows where we're going."

"Um, right," Agatha said as Sophie draped white fur over her. "Listen, I thought I knew the route, but—"

Dot shoved in under the fur. "Oooh, *toasty*," she gushed, hogging the coat. "Hester and Anadil have ice in their veins, but I've had enough, thank you. Tried eating chocolate snow but that just made me colder. How far are we from the gates? We aren't going to be there by the time Dovey checks in!"

"I don't understand why Dovey can't see us in her crystal ball whenever she wants," said Sophie, snatching back the fur.

"Because her ball is broken," grunted Anadil, shoving under the coat.

Everyone looked at her.

"I have limits to bodily pain. Not like Hester," Anadil soured, her frozen rats nuzzling the fur. "That girl took a knife in the stomach from Aric and didn't cry."

"Aric. What a *creep*," Dot shuddered.

"But why is Dovey using a broken ball?" Sophie pressed.

"When we interviewed a fairy godmother in Foxwood for School Master, she said that to make a crystal ball, a seer has to take a piece of a fairy godmother's soul and meld it with a piece of their own," Anadil explained. "That means every fairy godmother can only use the crystal ball made for her. Dovey told us hers was broken for years, but apparently Merlin helped her fix it."

"Useless pots, broken balls, and wasn't her wand a bit musty too?" said Dot. "Maybe Pollux was right to petition for a new Dean."

"I have 100% confidence in Dovey as Dean," Agatha refuted. "Besides, this is *our* quest. It's not like she can save us through a crystal *ball*."

"She could at least tell us if we're going the right way," Anadil said, giving Agatha a dubious look.

"Well, snowstorm or not, those lovebirds are doing just fine," Dot chimed.

Sophie leered back at Hort, deep in conversation with Nicola. "If that's love, then I'm a pink leopard. She's a first year who hasn't had her fingerglow unlocked, thinks she knows everything because she's read a few books, and wants to spend her life making casseroles at a pub. And she's wearing sheepskin booties. They're not even *shoes*."

Agatha frowned. "What happened to not being a snake?"

"With *you*, darling. With everyone else, I'm still me," Sophie breezed.

"In any case, they aren't the lovebirds I was talking about," said Dot.

The girls followed her eyes to Bogden and Willam, far behind. Bogden was short and dark; Willam, tall and fair. They weren't conversing. They weren't even looking at each other.

"Such a joker, Dot," Anadil snorted.

Dot just whistled merrily.

"All right, enough's enough," Hester snarled, shoving under the coat too, lips blue and cheeks frozen, glaring daggers at Agatha. "The Storian is writing our fairy tale, our lives are on the line, and instead of winning that tale, we're lost in a blizzard—"

"TOURS! AVALON TOURS! RIGHT HERE!"

For a moment, the girls blinked dumbly, each thinking they'd imagined the voice they'd just heard.

"DISCOVER AVALON AND ITS SECRETS! BEST TOURS IN TOWN!"

Sophie pulled the coat off them and the girls squinted through snow at a tiny hut fifty yards ahead with a dome of dead palm fronds over a lumpy white table. As they approached, they read the sign:

AJUBAJU TOURS
Now serving over 50 Kingdoms, from Avalon to Zagazig!
Maps: 1 silver piece
Guided Tours by Ajubaju: 3 silver pieces
* No weapons Allowed on Tours

Ajubaju, it turned out, was a blubbery balding beaver, sweating like a spigot even though it was below freezing.

"Cold? Lost? Confused? Then you have come to right place! I am Ajubaju, otherwise known as #1 best top tour guide in all the Woods!" he tooted in a clipped voice. "Many famous people love Ajubaju: Aladdin, Robin Hood, Peter Pan. . . . See my reviews!" He grabbed a scroll from his stand littered with newspapers, held it open for a half-second, teeming with unreadable script, then stashed it, scattering newspapers to the snow. Agatha glimpsed a few headlines:

MORE TROLL ATTACKS IN FOXWOOD
Council Appeals to Camelot for Help

BLOODBROOK KING KIDNAPPED
Nevers Petition Camelot for Good–Evil Alliance

TERROR IN NUPUR LALA!
Locals Demand King Tedros Intervene!

The beaver kicked these under his hut. "Ajubaju knows all about Avalon! Do you know you are near home of Lady of the Lake? Do you know she is maker of Excalibur? Do you know she hides King Arthur's body in her lake and not only that, she is most pretty lady in the Woods? I wish my wife look like her but my wife look like me."

Hester nudged Agatha. "It's like Dot turned into a beaver."

Dot spun to her: "You know what you've turned into? One of those tiny yapping dogs who thinks it's scary when all the other dogs think it's pathetic."

Hester gasped.

". . . Ajubaju can offer you hand-drawn map with gold leaf and ink of hummingbird that shows best parts of Avalon and is exclusive souvenir for you and your family!" the beaver gibbered. "But may I recommend for such beautiful ladies and gentlemen the full five-star guided tour experience, complete with buffet lunch and 50% off your next booking, rules and restrictions apply. Guided tours are available at 11:00 a.m., 1:00 p.m., 3:00 p.m., 5:00 p.m., and oh, lucky for you—" He glanced up at the sky unconvincingly. "It is one of those times. Mmm, if there's three witch girls, then blond girl with girlfriend in bandana, then two sweet boys, then boy who looks like weasel with lovely lady in pink . . . so 9 total at 3 pieces each . . ." Ajubaju pulled out a broken abacus and jangled colorful beads around, losing a few along the way—

"Can't you just tell us which way it is to the castle?" Agatha said, exasperated.

"That would be the same as giving you map, which is 1 silver piece, so 9 silver pieces since 9 of you will benefit," Ajubaju replied.

Sophie shunted in front of Agatha, scowling at the beaver. "Listen, Abracadabra. We don't have silver pieces. And even if we did, how do we know you won't just take our money and run? I don't remember you here the *last* time we were in Avalon."

The beaver didn't flinch. "Ajubaju in demand all over Woods. Surprised students of School for Good and Evil do not know, but I hear there is new Dean not as good as before."

Sophie's eyes darkened.

"With bounty on Guinevere and Lancelot, many people came after coronation to find them, since this is where fugitives hid last time. Except Avalon Island is very big! Bounty hunters need directions to Lady of the Lake castle. Prime opportunity for business," the beaver barreled on. "But now not so many as before. Will go to my family in Eternal Springs. Warmer there."

He paused, staring at Sophie. "If you don't have silver pieces for guided tour, I'll take fur coat."

"Over my dead body!" Sophie spat.

"And for the map?" Agatha jumped in.

The beaver looked at Nicola. "One of her shoes."

"What do you want my shoe for?" Nicola asked, startled.

Ajubaju bit his lip. "To put something inside."

He didn't explain further.

Moments later, Nicola was leaning against the beaver's hut, trying to yank off a snow-crusted bootie with Hort's help, while Ajubaju showed Agatha a dirty, crude map covered in food stains.

"Gold leaf and hummingbird ink, mmm?" Sophie said, glaring.

"Wore away in snow," Ajubaju snipped. "Gates are straight ahead, see. Keep walking and you'll be there soon."

"So we were going the right way to begin with?" Agatha asked angrily.

The beaver beamed yellow buckteeth.

"Give him the blasted shoe and let's go," Sophie growled, grabbing Agatha. "We've wasted enough time with this fool."

As she walked away, followed by the crew, they could hear Ajubaju still talking.

"Another student came few days ago speaking of Evers and

Nevers. Asked lots of questions. Handsome boy. Gray eyes. Wanted to find Lady of the Lake's castle. You must be knowing him."

The whole group stopped in their tracks, staring at each other.

But it was Agatha who finally turned around.

"We'll take the guided tour, please."

"Aggie, that coat was a *gift* from the Baroness of Hajebaji," Sophie hissed, stripped to her skimpy sailor's dress, snow chilling her bare arms and legs. "One-of-a-kind, custom-made in my size after she begged me to accept her daughter, Agnieszka, who is as charmless as a toenail, into my school. Now, thanks to you, I still have abominable Agnieszka but *no coat*—"

"You care about a coat? I care that we have no weapons," said Agatha, for the beaver had made them leave them at the hut, per "tour rules."

Ajubaju was ahead now, cocooned in Sophie's fur, leading the crew towards the edge of the island.

"I gave your friend map and told him how to get to castle, but I haven't seen him since. Hope he did not get lost. Should have taken full guided tour," he was saying. "No one lives in Avalon except Lady of the Lake because it is too cold. Even colder than Frostplains. Avalon means 'Paradise of Apples.' Easy to remember because apples are the only food here. They are special apples, of course, growing only in snow. . . ."

"Look," Agatha heard Anadil say. "Isn't that the Camelot seal?"

In the middle of the endless snowfield, a gray horse dappled with white spots was tied to a wooden stake. On its back was a leather saddle and blanket embroidered with the crest of two eagles flanking a sword. The horse paid them no mind, noshing on a bucket of bright green apples.

"Must have been Chaddick's horse," Dot said.

"Thank you, Lady Obvious," Hester sneered, clearly smarting over their earlier exchange. "But if that's Chaddick's, then who's feeding him? Bucket's full. And those apples look freshly picked."

Agatha was thinking the same thing. Chaddick couldn't have picked apples for his horse this morning because Chaddick wasn't alive this morning.

Her chest squeezed, the moment hitting her. Soon they'd see the Lady of the Lake's gates. And if they found a way inside, soon they'd see Chaddick's body too.

In the distance, she finally made out the bone-white castle built upon a bluff above stormy gray seas. The crash of waves echoed with deafening booms as colossal iron doors covered in snow swung open hard against the rock, lashed by the wind.

Crack! Crack!

"The gates are open?" Agatha asked, surprised.

"Lady opens gates for Ajubaju. Gave shelter to my family once. Knows me well," the beaver said quickly. "See the rock around castle? It is no ordinary rock. This is Rakkari Rock. No magic can be done inside its boundaries. Only by Lady of the Lake—"

"Doesn't make sense," Agatha whispered to Sophie. "Her

castle is supposed to be sealed. It's King Arthur's resting place. It's Good's most sacred hallows. Why would she open her gates for a *beaver*?"

"Maybe she has a soft spot for vermin. She does let Merlin in, after all," said Sophie.

But Agatha was looking closely now at the snow-piled doors ahead as they bashed open against the rock. One of them was sunken, like it'd been hit by a cannonball, and the other was . . . *crumpled*. Iron fragments lay half-buried in the snow.

"You said our friend asked lots of questions," Agatha prompted, turning to the beaver. "What did he ask?"

Ajubaju stopped midsentence, frowning. "Said he was here for school quest on behalf of Camelot. Wanted to know if anyone had broken into the Lady of the Lake castle. I said clearly they must not teach about Lady of the Lake at school. No one can break into Lady of the Lake castle. I will talk about Lady later in tour—"

"Talk about her now," Agatha demanded.

The beaver puffed loudly and waddled ahead. "Lady of Lake is Good's #1 most special top defender. She was born with beauty, immortality, and infinite magic . . . but she is *cursed*. If she ever kisses a boy—even once!—she will lose everything. So she hid in Avalon, free from temptation," he explained. "Lady of the Lake will always be Camelot's guardian, because Camelot is Good's oldest kingdom. Even from afar Lady protects Camelot by giving king her sword of power and her waters as shelter. Even more important, she protects the Four Point, most sacred land in Woods. Four Point is site of King Arthur's last battle, where he received mortal wound protecting balance between Good and Evil. As long as Lady of the Lake alive, Four Point is safe and Camelot is safe. That is why Lady must be secured. No one allowed here except Merlin and the king."

"And you and your tours," said Agatha sharply.

"Which I explained already," said Ajubaju, even sharper. "Come. I show you what your friend was looking for."

Agatha watched the beaver carefully as they moved through the gates.

He's lying, she thought, peering at the splintered iron. Someone *had* broken in.

And yet, the beaver had clearly met Chaddick and earned his trust. . . . How else would he know so much about him?

Warily, Agatha followed the group as they walked the path around Avalon's towers. These white spires were all connected into one circular palace with no windows or doors, overlooking a maze of zigzagging staircases. She could see the entrance to the stairs ahead, leading down to the lake, where the Lady lived. Agatha's stomach knotted. It's where Chaddick's body would be. Luckily most of the crew was listening to Ajubaju babble about the history of Avalon and hadn't noticed the stairs.

But Sophie had. "Aggie," she whispered, clutching her arm. "Is Chaddick . . . you know . . ."

Agatha subtly leaned over the edge of the path. Through the crisscrossing stairs, she started to get a glimpse of the gray-watered lake and its snow-heaped shore far below. Agatha held her breath, her gut twisting harder. . . .

Her eyes flared.

Chaddick's body wasn't there.

"Where is he?" Sophie breathed, sidling next to her. "That's where the Storian drew him . . . right by the water. . . . Aggie, we should look for him—"

"No," Agatha ordered. "Stay with the group."

Not that Agatha had any intention of staying with the group herself. The Storian had told them Chaddick would be here and the Storian was *never* wrong. Chills rippled down Agatha's spine. She needed to get to the Lady of the Lake. Surely she would have answers. But Agatha didn't want Sophie or the others to come. Not when she didn't know what else might be down there. It was too dangerous.

"All the storybooks I've read say the Lady of the Lake is immortal," she heard Nicola telling the beaver. "Don't say anything about losing powers if she kisses a boy."

"'Cause she's been around thousands of years and never *is* gonna kiss a boy," Willam chipped in. "Storybooks don't waste ink on something that'll never happen."

"Like you not puking every time the boat moves," Bogden cracked. Willam kicked him.

"Or like the Lady of the Lake becoming *School Master*," Hester said, glaring at Dot.

"We should at least ask," Dot said, appealing to Anadil.

"She's the Lady of the Lake, you lump," Anadil scorned.

"Lady or not, it sounds like she needs a kiss," said Hort, puckering his lips, to which Nicola made a farting noise and Hort poked her playfully (Sophie gagged).

"This is what your friend was looking for," Ajubaju said, stopping abruptly.

The crew stopped joshing around. Agatha gazed up at the fortress of white towers.

"Said he'd been following the attacks in Woods," the beaver went on. "Lots of kingdoms having trouble lately. Attacks on both Evers and Nevers. Your friend thought whoever was doing attacks might be hiding in Lady of Lake's castle."

"How could someone hide here? There's no doors or windows to get inside," said Nicola, knocking on the tower's solid walls.

"Ah," the beaver grinned. "That's where pretty lady needs tour guide."

Out of his pocket, Ajubaju drew a white, five-pointed star the size of a sand dollar. Sophie instantly recognized it as the same kind of star that Merlin had once laid in honor at King Arthur's tomb.

"Hey, how'd you get that . . . ," she said as the beaver pressed the star against the wall—

But the star was already glowing, as if burning from within. Little by little, the outline of a door whittled into the stone around the star. The beaver pressed hard and a door creaked open where there'd been no door before, just wide enough to let someone through.

"Lady of Lake must have let your friend inside," the beaver said. "We can go inside too, if you like. Maybe your friend still there."

Agatha was hardly listening. She was staring off towards

the stairs. Horse . . . apples . . . no body . . .

Is Chaddick still alive?

But the Quest Map said he was dead . . . and so did the Storian's painting. . . .

Had there been a mistake?

Eyes wide, she glanced back at the newly opened door into the tower.

Is the beaver right?

Is Chaddick inside?

"Agatha?"

She looked up and saw her crew watching her.

"Come on. We have to trace his steps," she said quickly, waving them in.

One by one, the crew followed the beaver into the towers.

Agatha hurried in last, cramming through the stone door—

She stopped short.

Out of the corner of her eye, she saw a drop of blood in the snow behind her, near one of the beaver's webbed pawprints. Sliding out the door, she dug her clump into the soft whiteness and swept off the top layer.

Crimson soaked the path below.

As she watched the others move into the tower, Agatha followed the trail, chipping away snow with her clump and uncovering a streak of red down the stairs.

There was so much blood.

Chest pounding, she descended the stairs. . . .

"What happened to 'stay with the group'?" Sophie snapped, bumping next to her.

Then Sophie saw the blood.

"Go with the others," Agatha said tensely.

But Sophie ignored her, rushing down the icy steps and slipping hard—

Agatha seized her arm before she could fall. Sophie gave her a sheepish glance, then charged ahead. Agatha held on, stumbling after her. Like it or not, this was a team effort now.

Coming down the jagged staircase, Agatha could see the mist of their twin breaths. Avalon was dead quiet, save the few pigeons on the staircase banister and the ripples of water below. Beneath the drab skies and white towers, the only flashes of color were the shiny green apples growing off rocks and the trail of blood down the snow-slicked stairs. Together, the two girls followed the stream of red, step by step, until they reached the bottom.

"The Storian painted him right here," Agatha said, rushing to the water's edge. She cleared away the mound of fresh snow on the shore—

"Sophie . . . ," she whispered.

The outline of a boy was framed in blood next to the lake. Only there was no boy.

"He was here," said Agatha. "He was definitely here—"

"He still is."

Agatha looked up and saw Sophie was a sick shade of white. Sophie raised her finger, pointing behind Agatha.

Agatha turned.

Deep in the corner against the staircase wall, Chaddick sat in the shadows. He had his knees to his bare, broad chest, his back flat against the stone, his eyes wide open.

He was holding something between his hands.

"Chaddick?" Agatha gasped.

She rushed forward, diving into the snow and grabbing him—

He was stone cold.

His skin looked waxy and colorless, the gash in his flank turned rusty-brown. He gazed right at them, his pupils big and glassy.

"He's dead, isn't he?" Sophie said softly.

Agatha's heart caved in. Of course he was dead. The Storian was right. . . . The Storian was always right. . . .

Except—

"How did his body move?" Agatha asked. "He died over there. The Storian said so. Someone must have moved him . . . *after* he was dead. . . ."

"But why?" Sophie asked. "It doesn't make any sense—"

Then Agatha saw what Chaddick was holding.

A folded piece of parchment.

She pried it out of his stiff fingers and held it to the light. Someone had drawn on it.

"It's the Camelot seal," said Agatha. "But around the sword . . . now there's . . ."

"The Snake knows we're looking for him," Sophie said, ashen.

Fingers quivering, Agatha turned the page over.

It was one of the beaver's maps of Avalon, streaked with Chaddick's blood, fingerprints smeared through it.

Only as they looked closer, they saw they weren't fingerprints.

They were pawprints.

Pawprints that looked a lot like the ones belonging to a beaver they'd just left with their friends.

The two girls locked eyes, faces dawning with horror. . . .

Then they heard someone scream.

First Loyalty

"Sophie, hurry!" Agatha called, far up the steps in front of her.

"It's these blasted shoes!" Sophie moaned, slipping on stairs like a cow on ice.

"Who told you to wear heels!"

More screams rang out from inside the tower.

"Sounds like Nicola!" cried Agatha, speeding up.

Sophie frowned, slowing down. "Well, in that case—"

"Move, you fool!" Agatha berated.

Sophie scurried after

her, resorting to crawling on her hands and knees, wondering how she was huffing like a hog while Agatha, who ate every cookie in a 50-mile radius, was sprinting up the stairs with ease. But soon she reached the top and was hustling behind her friend towards the stone door, still open a sliver. Both girls threw their weight against it, barely shoving it ajar, before Sophie's heels lost traction in the snow and she face-planted with a shriek. By the time she staggered up, Agatha was already inside. Sophie squeezed through behind her—

It was pitch dark.

"Aggie?" Sophie wisped.

"My fingerglow won't light," Agatha said nearby.

"Magic doesn't work here, remember? Raccoon rock or whatever he called it. Doesn't allow magic inside its bounds. Aggie, I can't see anything. Where are y—"

A cold hand seized her wrist.

"*Listen*," Agatha's voice said.

Then Sophie heard it.

A hissing sound somewhere far away. Or was it buzzing? Like a set of pipes leaking air . . .

Another scream echoed. This time a boy's.

"Come on," Agatha said, yanking Sophie down the tunnel.

"I hate it when you treat me like your sidekick," Sophie said, stumbling behind. "I'm a Dean and you're not even queen yet. If anyone's a sidekick here, it's—"

They slammed into a wall and careened to the ground.

In her haze of pain, Sophie thought they were back at school, foiled by the invisible barrier on Halfway Bridge that had set their original fairy tale into motion. But as the pain wore off, she could feel Agatha lumber up next to her, hands on the wall.

Sophie heard that strange hissing behind it, along with muffled voices—

"They're inside! I hear them!" she said.

She thrust her ear to the stone, trying to hear more, and felt it creak under her weight.

"It's another door," said Sophie, surprised.

"But there's no handle," said Agatha. "On the count of three, push as hard as you can. One . . . two . . ."

"On three or after three?"

"After three, you dolt."

"So on four, really."

"NO! After *three*!"

"Let me count, then," said Sophie.

"Hurry, you idiot!"

"One . . . two . . . three!"

They shoved the door as hard as they could and plunged through into a blitz of daylight—

"Watch out!" Hort's voice cried.

Toppling forward, Sophie snagged Agatha by the waist, trapping her in place. The two girls froze like mannequins, muscles clenched, breaths held.

Their bodies were an inch from being impaled on a blood-stained sword, planted handle-first into the dirt of a stone cave that opened into gray skies and a view of Avalon's coastline below.

The sword had Camelot's seal on the hilt.

Chaddick's sword.

Curled around it were two king cobras, hissing with forked tongues, mimicking the warped Camelot seal they'd seen on the map in Chaddick's dead hands. Behind the sword were dozens of treasure chests, hanging open and empty, with black velvet lining inside and the same snake-and-sword emblem carved on the outside. But that wasn't the most ominous sight. Because as Sophie peered closer, she saw now that the chests weren't empty at all. . . .

The black velvet was moving.

Snakes.

Hundreds of them.

Thin black ribbons, slowly slithering out of the chests and slipping into the sand.

"Don't *move*," said Nicola's voice above her.

Slowly Sophie's eyes lifted and saw the crew clinging to icicles on the ceiling of the cave.

"They're asps. They only see motion," warned Nicola, hanging on the same icicle as Hort. "I read about them in *The Brahman and the Jackal*—"

"No one cares," Sophie retorted. "All we care about is are they deadly?"

"Why do you think we're up here, you oaf!" Hort lashed. "Beaver trapped us while you two were off kissing somewhere!"

Sophie's eyes bulged—not just because Hort had never been so rude, but because even if the asps hadn't spotted her and Agatha, the *cobras* had. The two bigger snakes flicked off the sword, coiled in the dirt, and slithered towards the two girls.

"Aggie . . . ," Sophie hissed, watching their hoods spread with fiery red-and-orange patterns. She and Agatha stepped back, but the cobras accelerated, fangs gleaming.

"Agatha . . ."

The two snakes split paths, each heading for a different girl, faster, faster, like eels gliding through sea.

"Agatha!"

The cobras launched for their throats, jaws wide—

Agatha threw Sophie out the door and heaved it closed, hearing the cobras' bodies smack against stone.

Sweating hard, Agatha shouted through a slit in the door, "Where's the beaver?"

"Escaped, the sleazy trash-ball," Hester spat back. "Managed to get him by the neck with my legs for a second. Long enough to squeeze him into confessing that he got paid to kill us. Someone in a green mask. Didn't have the faintest clue who the guy was. Said they all get paid for the attacks."

"Who's 'they'?" Sophie asked.

"Everyone who's been attacking our friends' quests and terrorizing the kingdoms! Snake's behind all of it!" said Hester, still in disbelief. "Snake recruited this army of goons to throw the Woods into chaos. Forget that we spent three years trying to keep the balance between Good and Evil. Apparently there's a whole lot of creeps out there who don't have any loyalty to either side if you pay them enough. You thought Aric was bad?

At least he had a cause. This lot can be *bought*—"

The echo of hoofbeats cut her off. Inside the cave, the crew turned, looking out the opening. From outside the door, Sophie could see through the cave opening too, down to the faint outline of a beaver astride a gray horse galloping along the coast and out of view.

"Guess that answers the question of who's been feeding the horse," said Dot.

"I'm losing grip!" Anadil yelped.

Hester swiveled to her best friend slipping off a melting icicle, her three rats hanging by each other's tails. Hester spun to Dot. "Turn it to chocolate—something she can hold—"

"First, it'll melt, and second, magic doesn't work here!" Dot railed.

"I'm gonna fall!" Anadil gasped.

Without thinking, Agatha pulled at the door, about to rush in, but Sophie yanked her back. "You'll get killed!"

Agatha kicked the wall in frustration. "In storybooks, what kills snakes?"

"Handsome princes with swords?" said Sophie.

"WHAT KILLS SNAKES," Agatha shouted into the cave.

"Lions!" Dot replied. "That's what *The Lion and the Snake* said!"

"No lions here," clipped Bogden, wrapped around Willam's icicle.

"What about cats!" said Agatha. "Reaper hates snakes!"

"No cats," said Bogden.

"Demons!" said Hort. "In Bloodbrook, that's how we get rid of—"

"Magic doesn't work," said Bogden, nodding at Hester's dormant tattoo.

"Instead of telling us what doesn't work, why don't you tell us what does!" Sophie yelled through the door.

"Look, any moron knows only one thing kills snakes in fairy tales!" Nicola exploded, as if she couldn't take it anymore.

All eyes shifted to her.

"*Well?*" Sophie bellowed.

"MONGOOSES, for God's sake," Nicola blared. "It's always the mongoose that kills a snake at the end of the tale! Haven't you heard of 'Rikki-Tikki–Tavi' or *Indira and the Mongoose* or *The Tales of Panchatantra*? Don't any of you know anything besides *Snow White* and *Rapunzel* and stories about creamy fair princesses?"

"No mongoose," Bogden quipped.

"Wait! Yes, mongoose!" Agatha said, spinning to Sophie. "Where is he!"

"On the boat, obviously. He's steam-cleaning my boudoir. After the storm, it smelt of fish," Sophie said.

The whole crew groaned.

"So we have no weapons, no mongoose, and no plan. What *do* we have?" said Agatha.

"Hello, little chickadees!" a singsong voice called.

Jolted, Agatha and Sophie put their eyes to the door crack and saw a vision of Princess Uma's olive-skinned face floating in the cave.

"Professor Dovey asked me to let you know she's running late," said Uma, framed by the Dean's alarmingly messy office. "She's dealing with a few Neverboys who tried to feed Professor Manley to a stymph. I only just got back to school myself. Had to miss the first weeks of class because . . . well, it's personal. But I'm here now and . . . Why do you all look so grim? And why are you hanging from lanterns? And is that licorice under your feet? Sorry, it's quite blurry from my side. . . . This crystal ball is *ancient*. . . ." Her face distorted, turning upside down. "Sometimes if you give it a good joggle—"

She was flung out of the way by Professor Dovey, more disheveled than ever. "Those are snakes!" she squawked, peering through the rip in the air. "And the children are hanging from—dear God! Uma, you speak reptile! Put them to sleep or something!"

"Princesses don't speak *snake*, Clarissa," Uma huffed, tugging at her smooth black hair. "But I do speak a great many other animal languages, including—"

"I don't need your résumé, Uma! And please get out of my way!" Professor Dovey scolded, clawing spellbooks off her shelf. "Surely there's a sleeping hex in here that will work on snakes!"

Uma started to wail loudly. Sophie could see Agatha gnashing her teeth. If there's one thing they both hated, it was thin-skinned princesses.

"I can't hold on!" Dot howled, backside sagging two inches above the snakes.

"Hurry, Professor!" Agatha shouted into the cave.

"What's that, Agatha?" Dovey said, hand to ear.

But Uma was mewling more than ever.

"It has my pants!" Dot shrieked, an asp's fangs digging into her breeches.

"HURRY, PROFESSOR!" Sophie hollered.

"Uma, I can't hear a word!" Dovey yelled. "If you don't stop your crying—"

"Crying?" Uma scoffed. "I'm not crying. I'm calling a friend."

"Friend!" Dovey wheeled to her. "Our students are about to die, you ninny, and you're calling a *friend*—"

Suddenly, behind Dovey's bubble, a fleet of tiny furry heads poked over the cave hole in a perfect circle like synchronized swimmers, echoing Uma's wailful call. A white one with beady eyes took in the scene.

"Hardeep," he squeaked. "Uma friend."

"Moti-Lal," said the next. "Uma friend."

"Ganeshanathan. Uma friend."

"Pushpa. Uma friend."

"Ramanujan. Uma friend."

"Gutloo. Uma friend."

"Santanam. Uma friend."

And finally, one black as night, smiling pearly sharp teeth . . .

"Boobeshwar. Uma friend."

Princess Uma smiled into the crystal ball. "Close your eyes, children. This could get messy."

The snakes unleashed a panicked hiss—

Like cyclones, eight mongooses swung into the cave, screeching so loudly that Sophie and the crew not only closed their eyes, but also plugged their ears.

Five minutes later, Hort and Willam swept bloody asp and cobra carcasses out of the cave while Bogden sliced fresh apples with the tip of an icicle and fed them to the exhausted mongooses. Princess Uma thanked her friends with a few short wails (and promised to officiate Boobeshwar's wedding to Pushpa later that month).

Then Professor Dovey's face, already beginning to fade, looked down at Sophie and Agatha, who had finished explaining everything they'd faced in Avalon.

"Girls, our connection will end soon," said the Dean quickly. "From what you've told me, this Snake has trespassed into Avalon, killed one of our own, and wants Tedros' crown. And he's throwing the entire Woods into upheaval along the way. He's attacking kingdoms. He's attacking our students. Just this morning, Kiko's team didn't appear for its check-in with me, nor did Ravan's team in Akgul, and I'm quite sure the Snake has something to do with it. Luckily, both teams are still alive on my map in their respective kingdoms, so they could just be hiding. I'm looking into it. But whoever this Snake is, he's the worst kind of villain: he's a *terrorist*." She took a deep breath. "And all you know is we're searching for a man in a green mask?"

"Or a woman," Sophie ventured.

"And you're sure they've left Avalon?" Dovey pressed.

Agatha and Sophie exchanged looks. "Can't be sure of

anything anymore," said Agatha. "But the beaver made it sound like he was long gone."

"The Lady of the Lake would have never let him or the Snake in," said Dovey, dismayed. "Have you gone to her—"

"Wait a second," said Hester.

She was crouching near one of the chests. Inside it was a single, ragged gold coin. Hester held it up to the daylight.

A skull with crossbones glimmered on its face.

"Pirate gold," said Anadil. Her rats sniffed at the chests and tittered at her. "They say *all* of these were filled with pirate gold. Those asps must have been protecting it."

"Pirate numbers are growing in Jaunt Jolie," Hester said, remembering the newspaper she'd seen in Eternal Springs. "Snake has to be paying them."

Anadil swiveled to Hester. "Jaunt Jolie is one of the kingdoms bordering the Four Point. Didn't the Vizier in Kyrgios mention pirates lurking about sacred land?"

"If the Snake is planning something at the Four Point, you need to head him off at once," said Professor Dovey urgently. "The Four Point is where Arthur intervened to end a war between four kingdoms over a small piece of land. He gave his life to bring peace. Since then, the land belongs to Camelot as a symbol of its leadership of the Woods, beyond Good and Evil. Any breach would be a declaration of war on Camelot, not to mention a shattering of the truce. The Lady of the Lake vigilantly protects the Four Point, but it sounds like the Snake has his eyes on it. You must find out what these pirates are up to."

"Then we're off to Jaunt Jolie," Agatha said, eyeing the vial on Sophie's necklace. "Whose quest is stationed there?"

"Oh no," Sophie croaked. *"Beatrix."*

"And judging from the fact that some of our quest teams aren't communicating with me, Beatrix's team may be in danger too," said Professor Dovey. "Make haste to your next kingdom and find her. I won't be able to check in with you for a few days. My crystal ball only lets me use it a certain amount of time each day and tomorrow I have to use it for . . ." She didn't finish.

"Professor, is there no way to get a new ball?" Dot prodded respectfully.

"Along with a new cooking pot, new wand, and new maid for your office," Sophie murmured.

Professor Dovey was fading faster. "Listen, my children. Every second you spend in that cave is one more second a steadfast Ever of Good lies unburied in the cold. All I ask is that before you leave Avalon, you give him a worthy goodbye. Go to the Lady of the Lake. Find out how a boy of our own came to lie on her shores. At the very least, she must help you bury him." Professor Dovey choked up, her face translucent. "He is worthy of a home in the same grove as King Arthur, for he was a devoted friend to his son. Chaddick was an honorable boy. He didn't deserve to die alone. I should be there with you to pay my respects. . . . I wish I could, but I'm doing the best I can. . . ."

Tears filled the Dean's eyes, as if she could say no more.

Then she was gone.

"Lady of the Lake? Are you there?" Sophie asked a third time, her foot dipped in the glacial gray waters.

But again the Lady didn't answer.

A few minutes earlier, the crew had each taken a private moment with Chaddick to honor him. When it was her turn, Sophie had kneeled down and taken his rigid, chilled hands in hers.

"Thank you for being such a faithful, valiant friend to Teddy. A better friend than I've ever been, that's for sure. We'll protect him for you now, okay? And in the end, you'll be the reason we were able to save him."

She kissed his cheek. "Wherever you are, you'll have no pain or bad memories anymore. Only love. And one day, me, Teddy, and all the rest of your friends will be with you again. Not too soon, of course . . . but one day. So wait for us and watch over us if you can."

When she was finished, Agatha kneeled in front of Chaddick, then Hort kneeled, then Hester, then the others, one by one, even those who hadn't known him. They washed Chaddick's body clean with lake water and fitted him into Hort's clothes, leaving the weasel pink-skinned and shivering in his underpants. ("Always lose my clothes anyway, so might as well be for a good cause," he'd said.) The boys lifted Chaddick's body and lay him gently on the lakeshore, the water lapping up to his side. Without the use of magic, they could do little else to adorn him, but Nicola combed his hair and Bogden smoothed his shirt as the rest watched Agatha step into the water and call out for the Lady of the Lake to help bury their friend.

The Lady didn't answer.

And now, she wasn't responding to Sophie either.

"Maybe if we go farther in?" Anadil offered.

"Come on," Hester said, grabbing her and Dot and hauling them into the lake. Dot squealed, arctic water up to her thighs, but she gritted her teeth and plowed forward.

Sophie remained with Agatha, watching the witches wade deeper.

"What do you think Dovey meant when she said she's doing the best she can?" Agatha asked.

"Before you arrived at school, she told me she couldn't come on this quest because it was our fairy tale, not hers. But I'm starting to suspect there was another reason she had to stay behind," said Sophie.

"Is she sick?"

"Can fairy godmothers *get* sick? Besides, she doesn't look ill. She looks . . . *chaotic.* As if her mind is elsewhere," Sophie said. "But what could be more important for a Dean than protecting her students? Lady Lesso lied to a deadly School Master to keep her Nevers safe. She betrayed Evil itself, a cause she'd worked for her whole life. She betrayed her own *son.* And though I hate saying this, Dovey is just as good a Dean as Lady Lesso. Which means there's something else wrong with her. Something she isn't telling us. Do you think it might have to do with that crystal ball?"

"Even if it's broken, a crystal ball should *help* her, not leave her frazzled and overwhelmed." Agatha shook her head. "I'm scared, Sophie. You heard Dovey—she's never seen a villain

like this before. And if she's not at full strength to guide us . . ."
She paused. "The Woods is under siege. Our friend is dead.
Quest teams are missing. And Tedros is alone at Camelot,
with this Snake plotting to destroy him. We don't know who
the Snake is. We don't know what his plan is. All we know is
we're in a fairy tale again and this time the villain is playing
games with us." She gazed at her friend. "It's as if there's no
such thing as a happy ending anymore."

"Or perhaps we've traded in Good and Evil, black and
white, happy and unhappy for a thousand shades of gray," said
Sophie.

"Hey, guys?" Hester's voice called.

The two girls turned and saw the three witches looking
back at them, chest-deep.

"There's someone out there," said Hester.

Sophie stepped forward, squinting past the witches across
the lake. Then she saw it: a hundred yards away, a silhouette
hunched on top of the water. She couldn't see whose it was. She
couldn't even tell if it was man . . . animal . . . monster.

But whatever it was gave her a dark feeling.

"I'll go—" Agatha started.

"I'll go too," Sophie said without thinking, clasping
Agatha's wrist and dragging her past the witches and Hort,
who'd rushed to follow. The icy water knifed through Sophie's
dress as she swam, but she didn't make a sound nor stop swimming, her breaths achy and shallow.

But then something curious happened.

As the two girls swam farther, Agatha sank like the others,

down to her neck. But Sophie didn't sink at all. Her body started floating, higher, higher, magically sloughing off water, until suddenly she was walking on top of the lake as if it were solid ground.

She looked down at Agatha, dumbfounded.

Agatha seemed equally stunned, as did the rest of the crew, but there was no time to ask questions.

"Go," said Agatha quickly. "But be careful."

Sophie swallowed hard. Then she kept walking.

The lake felt rubbery under her heels and baffled fish ogled her from beneath the surface. Under dreary skies, the figure ahead remained cloaked in shadow as Sophie grew closer, closer. She could see its stooped back, wrapped in soaked gray robes.

The ominous churning in her stomach deepened.

"Hello?" she called out, inching nearer.

No answer.

From behind, the figure had scanty knots of white hair, a shiny skull gleaming through.

"Can you hear me?" Sophie asked.

Still nothing.

"I'm here on behalf of King Tedros of Camelot," Sophie rasped, mouth dry. "We're looking for the Lady of the Lake. We need her help burying our friend in King Arthur's grov—"

An old hag spun to face her, milk-white flesh hanging over bones and ruined with warts. Her teeth were rotted away and her coal-black eyes and thick peeling lips hung open in a foul, empty gape.

Sophie ate her own scream and stumbled back, bracing to run—

"Wait," the hag said.

Sophie froze.

The voice was low and husky . . . and beautiful.

It was a voice she knew.

Sophie inched back around. "It's . . . *you*. You're the Lady of the Lake—"

"I'm sorry for not letting the others see me like this, but they wouldn't understand," the Lady of the Lake said softly. "You are the only one who knows what it's like to lose who you are. Except you found your way back to your true self. I never will."

"This is *permanent*?" Sophie said, staggered. "But—but I saw you! Merlin brought us here to hide us in your waters. You were beautiful and magical and powerful! You didn't look like . . . like *this*. . . ."

The Lady sagged deeper, glancing away. "He said he loved me . . . that if I protected him, he would save me from my eternal loneliness . . . and I believed him."

"Chaddick?" Sophie said. "But he—"

"No," said the Lady, her voice catching. "Not him."

"Who, then? And what does love have to do with—"

But then Sophie remembered what the beaver had said when they started their tour . . . a tale of how the Lady of the Lake came to be. . . .

"You kissed someone," Sophie breathed. "You lost your powers. . . . It's why the gates to Avalon are open. . . ."

The Lady's eyes were bloodshot and wet. "I thought he'd take me away from here. That's why I gave him shelter."

Sophie's heart started hammering. "You kissed the *Snake*? You gave up your immortality . . . your magic . . . to kiss a *monster*? Do you know what he's doing in the Woods? Do you know what he did to our *friend*—" She caught herself. "Wait a second. If you kissed him, that means you saw him. Without a mask. You know who he is—you saw his face—"

"And it was beautiful," the Lady said, beginning to cry. "I know you won't forgive me. For letting your friend die. But I had no choice."

Sophie stared in horror. "You watched Chaddick get killed . . . and you didn't help him?"

The Lady sobbed harder.

Blood scorched through Sophie's veins. Once upon a time, she too had been willing to commit any Evil for love. But this was Excalibur's maker! This was Good's great defender!

"You *watched* him die! For a stupid *kiss*?" Sophie seethed. "You vowed to protect Camelot forever! You vowed to protect its king!"

"It's not that simple," the Lady stammered into her hands. "I—I—I had to protect him. Even Merlin would understand. I had no *choice*."

"You keep saying that! I had a choice. *You* had a choice. We all have choices! And you let a boy be murdered inside Avalon! Why? Because the Snake was *pretty*?" Sophie snarled. "Chaddick was the liege of King Arthur's son. Chaddick was Tedros' knight. That is your first loyalty—"

"No," said the Lady. "My first loyalty is to the king."

"And Chaddick was the king's best friend," Sophie spat. "A king you promised to defend until the end of time. Chaddick had Tedros' trust! Chaddick had Tedros' faith! What does a Snake have?"

The Lady of the Lake slowly lifted her head. The light had gone out of her eyes, replaced by a cold, dead glare.

"He has Arthur's blood," she said.

Sophie bleached white, the voice ripped out of her. "Wh-wh-what?"

"I'll take care of your friend as you ask," the Lady said stonily, turning back around. "It's the only power I still have."

Sophie couldn't breathe. "But—but—"

The Lady of the Lake vanished.

Shaking, Sophie whirled to the shore and saw Chaddick's body vanish too. And all that was left in her blurred, darkening vision was Agatha in the water, flailing towards her as if her friend knew something had gone terribly, terribly wrong.

Like Father, Like Son

Tedros was dripping blood all over the castle and he had no idea how to stop it.

It wouldn't have happened if he'd just stuck to the routine.

He'd gotten up at half past four to exercise in King's Cove, but as he'd snuck his way to the basement pool, he sensed that festering dread in his stomach: the dread he'd felt ever since Agatha left a week ago.

He'd lied to Lady Gremlaine and anyone who'd asked about the future queen, saying she'd suffered a bout of homesickness and taken the *Igraine* to Woods Beyond to see some old friends. Luckily, the

newspapers hadn't reported any sightings of her, so he'd held firm to his story, insisting she'd return any day. He couldn't admit the truth: that Agatha was on a quest to save his kingship, while he stayed behind like a lady-in-waiting.

On their last night together, Merlin had told them their friends' quests were all failing and that Tedros' own failed coronation might be part of a bigger story. Any real leader would have instantly set sail for the Woods to find this story . . . to find the villain behind it . . . but Agatha had insisted she take his place and he'd gone along with it because he was afraid to leave Camelot without a king.

At the time, he was sure that remaining at the castle was the right decision. But ever since Agatha had left, he'd been having dreams about his father again, silently glaring at him with those harsh blue eyes, eyes that Tedros had gouged out of his statue in order to *stop* these dreams. So why did he keep having them? Was it because his father would have never let Guinevere hijack his quest the way Tedros had let Agatha? No matter how dicey the situation at home, his father would have forcefully addressed the masses, explained the threat that faced them all, and convinced his kingdom to await his return.

Tedros had done none of those things. Instead, he'd helped Agatha escape like some piddling sidekick, distracting two guards on the bridge while Agatha boarded the *Igraine* with Willam, silently turned it invisible, and went off to sea.

First he'd almost gotten his mother and Lancelot killed at his coronation by ignoring everyone's advice. And now he'd put his future queen in danger by passing off his own quest to her. Both times he'd thought it was the Good thing to do. But why did Good things keep turning bad?

Tedros' mood spiraled as he padded down the Gold Tower stairs in his black socks. For the last few days, he'd hardly been able to focus on his royal duties and kept hounding guards to see if any letters had arrived. The guards already had little respect for him, given his botched coronation and constant deference to Lady Gremlaine, but now he'd been hearing them gossip that instead of a real king they'd gotten a love-whipped pup. (That idiot Pollux had encouraged them before Tedros had him fired.) This was his comeuppance, of course: he'd spent the last six months ignoring Agatha while she was with him and now that she was gone, all he could think about was when she'd be back.

He quickened his pace towards the basement, vowing to lift extra heavy today. He always felt better about himself after a punishing workout. . . .

Except now he was obsessing over why he hadn't received any letters from her. It took a day or two at most for a courier crow to deliver a note and Agatha had taken the new crow that Camelot had finally saved enough to buy. So why hadn't she written?

Magic was no use in finding her either. He'd been crap at spells at school, preferring to win battles with a sword, so he'd plundered Merlin's chamber, searching for a crystal ball or something that might help him pinpoint Agatha in the Woods. No luck. He'd even cast a locating spell out of the only one of Merlin's spellbooks he could actually read, but the first time he tried it he'd summoned a bowl of grapefruits from the kitchen and the second time he'd made all of Agatha's undergarments float around the castle for hours before guards had to shoot them down with bows and arrows.

Tedros stopped outside the Gymnasium in full panic. Where was she? Was she safe? Was she even *alive?* He pressed his forehead to the wall and struggled to breathe. First his mother and Lance sent off. Now his princess too. Even Merlin had disappeared again—though according to the *Royal Rot,* there'd been a sighting of him near the School for Good by an Ingertroll who insisted Merlin was having secret trysts with Professor Dovey in her office. (Tedros was so desperate for news of Agatha he'd succumbed to reading trash, only to stop when he saw the *Rot* had started labeling him "the so-called 'King.'")

He'd felt so alone after the coronation.

But now he had no one he trusted in this castle anymore.

Now he was *truly* alone.

Even worse, as he scoured the newspapers, Tedros saw it wasn't just Camelot or his friends' quests that were in trouble. All the kingdoms in the Woods were plagued by mysterious attacks, just as the letters he'd received from the leaders of these realms had attested. The selfish part of him was comforted that other leaders were having just as hard a time as he was. But these kings and queens from both Ever and Never lands were calling upon Camelot—on *him*—to take the lead in building a Woods-wide coalition and rooting out those responsible for the violence. It's what Tedros' father had done when wars between Good and Evil had raged out of control, threatening the Woods. And it's what ultimately killed him: sapped and impaired by his drunken spells, Arthur had still ridden into battle at the Four Point to forge peace between warring sides and paid for it with his life. Despite Tedros pleading with his father not to go. Despite Tedros begging him to stay home as the king put on his armor.

Perhaps this was one of the reasons why Tedros now ignored these calls for help from other kingdoms and refused meetings with any of its leaders. But the new king also had no help to offer them. Camelot had no money, no knights (Chaddick was still missing), and no army. Plus, Camelot had yet to be attacked like the rest of the kingdoms and its people didn't seem to care about what was happening in realms beyond its own. Camelot could no longer be the Woods' policeman. They were too busy with their own problems. Like growing poverty and a bankrupt treasury and rising crime—

And a so-called king.

Tedros' eyes opened. Looking past the wall, he could see Excalibur's empty case lit up by gem-blue moonlight.

That sword.

Everything, everything, everything was going wrong because of that sword.

Tedros never made it to King's Cove. He'd turned back and gone straight to the Blue Tower balcony, dismissed a listless guard, and launched himself at Excalibur once more with no other strategy than beating out his own fury . . . until he wrenched the hilt so brutally he split open a blister on his left hand.

Now blood was spurting off his palm, trailing him everywhere like a shadow.

He hustled through the Blue Tower, past the famous Map Room, where the Round Table had once met, but now lay cobwebbed and dormant. He could hear worried stewards calling to each other, having seen his blood. He didn't want to talk to them. He didn't care if they thought he was wounded or dead. He wanted it to be like school, where he could lock himself in a dorm room or bathroom to be alone and if he missed class, he'd be punished with detention or kitchen duties, neither with any real consequence.

His father had been like this after his mother left. Arthur would slip off without a word and shut himself in the White Tower guest room, to which the king had the only key.

It was where Tedros was headed now.

Merlin was right. Maybe I'm more like Dad than I thought, Tedros thought mordantly.

He could hear his stewards filing into the White Tower, but he was already upstairs, gliding in his socks towards the door at the end of the hall. He pulled out his cramped key ring, finding the gold-toothed key next to a small black one, slipped it into the lock, and swung into the room, latching the door behind him.

The room was dark.

He slid down and plopped on the warm marble, feet splayed in front of him. Blood leaked from his hand onto the skin of his thigh. He stripped off his shirt and wrapped it around his palm like a tourniquet, but that only seemed to make it bleed more. Out of ideas, he thrust his hand in the pocket of his gym shorts and leaned against the door.

The room smelled like musk and earth and sweat. His father had it built as a private guest suite that he could invite his most personal friends to stay in, but Arthur had never used it for guests as far as Tedros knew. His father didn't even allow maids in this room when he was alive, let alone his wife or his son—though Tedros had broken in once as a child, having picked the lock during a game of hide-and-seek with the fairies. When the king found out, it was the one and only time his dad had given him a thrashing.

It's why Tedros hadn't come back to this place before today.

It reminded him of his father's disappointment in him.

Using his good hand, Tedros lit his fingerglow like a torch, suffusing the room with soft gold. It still looked the same as it had then: a patterned brown-and-orange rug, a sunken leather sofa, and a modest bed in the corner. It didn't seem royal at all, let alone fitting for a "guest suite." Felt more like something you'd find at a seedy Netherwood inn, Tedros thought, scanning the bare beige walls with his glow. Why had his father built a private room so common and far away from the better parts of the castle? A guest room that guests never used—

Two green eyes speared through the torchlight. Tedros lurched back, bashing his head against the door.

Reaper moseyed out of the shadows, batting at fleas.

"Oh, it's you," Tedros grumped, rubbing his skull. He felt woozy, though he didn't know whether it was because of the head bump or his hand, which was still spewing a profuse amount of blood. "How'd you even get in here?"

Before Agatha left, he'd told her to take her unholy cat with her, but she'd brushed him off. "Someone has to watch over you," she'd quipped.

He'd assumed it was a joke. This was the cat that had bitten him, spat at him, peed in his shoes, and once carved heathen symbols into his bathroom mirror. But now that Agatha was gone, the heinous little imp had been following Tedros everywhere he went and even sleeping outside his chambers.

Reaper prowled closer and poked at Tedros' injured hand with his paw, nudging it out of his pocket. Grunting ominously, the cat sniffed the blood-soaked bandage. Then he climbed on Tedros' thigh and slashed the cloth open with his claw.

"Hey!" Tedros said.

But now Reaper seized Tedros' hand in his mouth, tongue to his skin, teeth starting to sink in—

Tedros kicked him hard, sending the cat flying into the wall.

"You little cretin," he gasped.

Reaper hobbled away whimpering and slunk under the bed in the corner.

Shaken, Tedros studied his hand to see the damage—

"Huh?"

He lit it up with his glow.

His hand wasn't bleeding anymore. And the wound looked . . . smaller.

Slowly, he lifted his head and saw Reaper's dim, wet pupils under the bed frame.

"You were trying to help me, weren't you?" Tedros asked. "That's why you've been following me all week. You're watching over me. Just like Agatha said."

Reaper hissed weakly and receded into darkness.

Tedros lay on his bare stomach at the foot of the bed and peeked underneath. "I'm sorry, little fella. I'm the cretin, not you. I can't do anything these days without hurting someone. Not even a cat."

He rolled onto his back. "I can't do this anymore. I can't be a half-king. My *people* don't deserve a half-king. But how can there be order and progress when I can't prove I'm fully king?" He roared in frustration and slung his keys at the ceiling, cracking the plaster. "I'm Arthur's *son*! It doesn't matter what Agatha finds in the Woods. It doesn't matter what's happening to my classmates. This is Camelot! The crown is mine. It's always been mine. So why won't that cursed sword *move*?"

"I never did think that girl was the homesick type," a voice said.

Tedros sprung up to see Lady Gremlaine's shadow in the open doorway.

"But then again, I never took you for a liar," she said, glaring at him.

"I came here to be alone," he retorted, eyeing his keys on the floor. "I thought the king had the only key."

"He does," Lady Gremlaine replied. "Only he forgot to lock the door."

Tedros stared at her. "But I did lock it—"

"Shall we walk?" his steward said, holding open the door. "The Treasury Master wants to see you, you're hardly dressed and bleeding, and to be honest . . . I'm not particularly fond of this *room*."

"I don't make it a habit of lying, but where Agatha went is between me, her, and Merlin," Tedros asserted.

"So you met Merlin too?" frowned Lady Gremlaine, clacking ahead into a big, circular white hall.

"I told you. I don't care who my father banished—"

"Your caring is irrelevant. Until your coronation is sealed, you cannot withdraw your father's decrees. Not Merlin's banishment, not the bounty on your mother's head."

"Look, there are things happening you wouldn't understand," said Tedros, shirtless and shoeless as he chased her lavender silhouette. "You're my steward and here to help me with whatever I ask. Anything outside of that is my domain."

"I see," Lady Gremlaine said, facing him. "So what you're telling me is even though I was your father's right hand, even though you've asked me to supervise your every decision, and even though I'm the only reason this kingdom is in one piece . . . you still don't *trust* me."

Tedros couldn't meet her eyes.

They were standing on a floor of cracked mosaic that depicted the Camelot seal. (Given his crap morning, Tedros found it fitting he was straddling Excalibur's blade.) The circular walls were covered in dozens of framed paintings, reminding him of the Legends Obelisk at the School for

Good, decorated with portraits of famous alumni. He'd been in this hall only a few times as a child, since the White Tower was far away from the others and used mostly for knights' meetings, arms-making, and staff quarters. Tedros had never paid much attention to the walls back then, but now one of the paintings caught his attention, since unlike the others, it had no other paintings near it. He stepped towards it, eyes wide. . . .

"It's me."

He was wearing his father's coronation robes, though most of the portrait was a close-up of his face. His hair was angelic blond, his eyes unnaturally blue, his skin as pure as gold dust. Everything about the Tedros in the painting seemed more Tedros than the real him, including his piercing, omniscient gaze. This Tedros was strong, mature, unflappable. . . . This Tedros looked like a king.

"Who drew it? I didn't sit for a royal portrait—"

"That's because it was painted sixteen years ago," Lady Gremlaine answered, cinching her turban. "Your father commissioned it from a seer after you were born. In his will, he said it was to be put up on your coronation day in the Hall of Kings."

Looking around, Tedros noticed the art was arranged in chronological columns, with each king's coronation portrait surrounded by smaller paintings of triumphant moments.

"One day your wall will be complete too," said Lady Gremlaine.

Tedros honed in on his father's column. While Tedros'

coronation painting was beautiful and inspiring, Arthur's portrayed him as a scrawny, timorous, red-faced teenager who didn't look capable of brushing his own teeth, let alone running Camelot.

"This is *Dad*?" Tedros said.

"Painted by the Palace Artist on the morning of his coronation, per tradition," Lady Gremlaine confirmed. "Given the result, your father fired the artist. And to ensure your coronation painting would be to his liking, he solicited the seer to imagine yours upon your birth. A portrait that would capture the essence of your soul and future."

"But if Dad hated his so much, why would he leave it up?"

"Oh, he made us take it down again and again. But in time, it would always mysteriously return, most likely by his own hand. It became quite clear that though your father loathed the painting, he also couldn't part with it. Perhaps it reminded him of the 'real' Arthur, before his time at the School for Good and Evil changed him."

Tedros looked at her, puzzled. "He was crowned before he went to school? But he wouldn't have been old enough—"

"How little you know of your father," his steward said drolly. "Back then, Camelot was so in need of a leader that they crowned Arthur even though he wasn't yet sixteen. Which meant he attended school as a legitimate king and an instant celebrity. No doubt you endured this yourself as a famous prince, with girls desperate to be your queen. . . ."

"You have no idea," Tedros murmured, thinking of Sophie.

"The difference is that you spent your whole life knowing you would be king, while Arthur was an ordinary boy who accidentally found himself the most powerful ruler in the Woods. One morning he'd gone out feverishly seeking a new sword for his master—Arthur had been punished for losing the old one—and he stumbled upon Excalibur, trapped in an anvil in the village square. He pulled the sword easily, without a second thought, intending to return it to the stone at a later date. What he didn't know was that Excalibur had been placed in that stone by the Lady of the Lake to settle the question of who would rule Camelot after a violent period of chaos and anarchy. Thousands had come from all over the Woods to try their hand at the sword before Arthur freed it from the stone without any knowledge of the consequences. So when he sat for this portrait, he was still very much a scared young boy. But also sensitive and whip smart. It's why Merlin took so strongly to him. As did I. Perhaps it's the only area where the wizard and I ever agreed."

Tedros looked back at his father's face, so lost and overwhelmed . . . and for a moment, it felt like Tedros was looking at his own. Unnerved, he shifted to another painting: this one of his mother and Arthur playing with their baby son, while a young, dark-haired female stood in the shadows. His father was holding the baby up in the air as his mother tickled the boy's stomach. Tedros found himself smiling before he remembered everything that happened between his parents once that baby grew up.

"Did your father really never mention my name to you?" Lady Gremlaine asked.

"Not even once."

Lady Gremlaine took this in with a wry grin. "Like father, like son."

Tedros furrowed, not understanding.

"When Agatha was pressing to see you, I pointed out that you too never mentioned her name to me. Not even once," said Lady Gremlaine. "Taking the women in your life for granted seems a shared trait."

"Well, Agatha and I are very different from you and my father, obviously," Tedros snorted. "How long did you even know him?"

His steward paused before answering. "Arthur and I grew up together. I'm not so much older than he was. We met because I was a housemaid to Sir Ector, Arthur's master, when Arthur was brought from the orphanage. Arthur and I soon became friends, for we were both treated quite poorly as children. So when he was crowned and needed a steward, he brought me to Camelot even though I was hardly capable of managing a king. But somehow we muddled through together, bucking his Council of Advisors and forging our own path, until he went off to school. I almost felt like his queen. . . ." Lady Gremlaine seemed off in another land now. "I remained his steward until after you were born. See, that's me right there."

She was looking at the painting of Arthur and Guinevere with baby Tedros.

Tedros stared closer at the young female in the corner, with wild black hair, nut-brown skin, and deep red lips.

"But—but—you were beautiful," Tedros blurted.

Lady Gremlaine burst into laughter. "Don't act so surprised!"

It was the first time he'd ever heard her laugh.

"I loved being with your father," she said, smiling at the painting. "I only wish I'd been here to help him raise his child. Perhaps you would have trusted me more if you'd known me the way he did."

Tedros peered at her. "So why did he let my mother fire you?"

Lady Gremlaine's smile vanished, her eyes still on the painting. "When it comes to women, men can be quite weak." She turned to him, a chill settling in. "In any case, when she returns, you'll no longer have use for me. Your mother will make sure of that."

"Well, *I'm* the king, not her," said Tedros. "And though I hate to admit it, I need your help like you helped Dad when he first started. Especially with Agatha gone now. My mother will respect my wishes."

"Your father promised the same thing once," Lady Gremlaine returned. "But when the time came to stand up to his wife, he stayed silent. I left the castle without him even noticing."

"I'm not like my father," Tedros said. "For worse and for better."

"And yet you break the same promises and tell the same white lies," said Lady Gremlaine.

The words hit Tedros hard.

He looked down at the Camelot shield on the floor. Out of the corner of his eye, he saw his steward's shoes inch closer. He could smell her powdered rose perfume.

"You know why I've been so harsh with you and Agatha?" Lady Gremlaine said quietly.

Tedros lifted his head.

"You reminded me of Arthur and Guinevere when he brought her here from school," she confessed. "We were all so naïve then, blinded by youth. We had no idea of what was to come. And then all these years later, to be steward to his son and his new princess . . . perhaps I let old feelings get the best of me."

Tedros felt a twinge of guilt; this wasn't the frigid dragon lady that he and Agatha had made her out to be. She was a real human with real emotions.

"I'll stand up for you. No matter what my mother says," Tedros vowed. "You have my word."

His steward searched his face. Slowly her pose softened as if she saw she could trust him even if he didn't trust her.

"I'm sorry," said Tedros.

"It was a long time ago," Lady Gremlaine sighed.

"No, I mean for being so rude when you came to find me. You were trying to take me to our Treasury meeting. You were doing your job."

Lady Gremlaine's face clouded.

"What is it?" Tedros asked.

"That wasn't the only reason I was trying to find you," she said.

From her pocket, she pulled a folded piece of newsprint. When he took it, her skin was clammy.

Tedros opened it.

It was a clipping from the *Camelot Courier.*

DECEASED: CHADDICK OF FOXWOOD

LOVING SON and brother and fourth-year student in the School for Good. While on a quest to serve King Tedros of Camelot, Chaddick was killed on Avalon Island, as reported by an unnamed mongoose. He was 16 years of age and is survived by his mother, father, and two brothers, aged 12 and 17.

"Professor Dovey contacted me this morning through her crystal ball," said Lady Gremlaine hastily. "She's despondent that the *Courier* printed it without contacting her first. She wanted to tell you in person, but I said I would handle it—"

Tedros buckled. "But . . . but how . . ."

"I pressed her, but she wouldn't give details—"

"Wouldn't give *details*? My best friend's dead and Agatha's gone and so is everyone else and the dumb bat won't give details!" Tedros cried, grabbing and kicking at the wall. Frames fell around him, cracking against the floor. "He didn't send me a note. . . . He shouldn't have even been in Avalon. . . . I—I—I don't understand—"

Lady Gremlaine touched him. Tedros fell into her, panting softly. He stayed in her arms a long time.

"He was my friend," Tedros rasped.

"And he always will be," Lady Gremlaine said.

"*You can't be here!*" a voice cried in the hall.

"*Well, I am here, so clearly I can be,*" said a hoary male voice.

"*But there's a warrant for your—*"

The doors to the hall flung open and Merlin, Professor Dovey, and Lancelot all marched in, chased by a phalanx of stewards, both Tedros' and Agatha's, Reaper biting at their heels. Guinevere swept in last, regal and coiffed in a rich purple gown—

She froze.

The once-queen gazed at her son, covered in blood and in Lady Gremlaine's arms.

"Lady Guinevere!" said Lady Gremlaine, letting go of Tedros. "They'll arrest you! How'd you even get—"

"We'll take it from here, Lady Gremlaine," said Guinevere.

Lady Gremlaine straightened. "The king and I have a meeting. You best leave the castle at on—"

"*We'll take it from here,*" Guinevere thundered.

The hall was dead silent.

Lady Gremlaine turned to Tedros, waiting for him to say something . . . to stand up in her defense . . .

But Tedros wasn't looking at her anymore.

"Mother—" he gasped.

He rushed into Guinevere's arms, wiping his eyes, before he moved on to embrace Professor Dovey, Merlin, and Lancelot, so thankful to have a family again just when he needed one most.

By the time Tedros even remembered his steward, Lady Gremlaine was already gone.

What It Feels Like for a King

The Treasury Master was put off until after lunch.

Chef Silkima nearly passed out when she saw there were five to feed instead of just the king and scampered back to the kitchens, which erupted in shrieks and a clatter of pans.

"I'd offer my hat to help, but it's on strike until I give it a pension plan," Merlin sighed, taking a seat in the Blue Tower dining room. "Says it wants 'security.'"

"And I thought fairies were a challenge," Professor Dovey murmured, sitting beside him.

"It's Lance's fault," said Guinevere across the table. "Couldn't leave the hat alone, demanding food night and day:

turkey legs and beef bourguignon and enough bacon to rid the world of pigs . . . Wore the poor thing out."

Lancelot shrugged. "A man needs to eat."

Sitting quietly at the head of the table, Tedros listened to the group banter: first about how they'd snuck into the castle (they'd mogrified into dung beetles beneath Merlin's hat and shoved it around like a dung ball) and then how'd they'd taken turns changing under Agatha's bed into clothes they'd hidden in the hat as royal guards made their rounds—

"But won't Lady Gremlaine tell everyone you're here?" Tedros cut in, wringing his hands. "Won't they kill you for the bounty?"

The group went quiet. Merlin met Tedros' eyes.

"I'm afraid the time has come to endure such risks, Tedros. Given recent events, we need your mother and Lance to be at your side from here on out. That said, if anyone gets too close, I've reminded your mother and Lance how to use their spells from school to defend themselves."

Under Merlin's stern glare, Guinevere and Lancelot quickly lit their fingers. Guinevere's flickered feebly. Lance's burnt hot red, then snuffed out spectacularly with a loud fart sound and burp of smoke.

"Or at least, confound their attackers," Merlin piffed.

Tedros managed a smile. "You don't know how much I've missed you. All of you."

His mother smiled back, her eyes glistening.

"If only this were a social call," said Merlin.

Tedros tensed. He knew there had to be a reason that

Merlin would risk his mother's and Lance's safety and Professor Dovey would leave her students to come here. But hearing it out loud made his stomach hollow.

"I've had my fill of bad news today," he said.

"No news, good or bad, should be discussed on an empty stomach," Merlin assured. *"Silkima!"*

More pots clanged in the kitchen.

Lunch was meatballs with yellow curry, spaghetti squash with smoked paprika, and peppered radish patties, all of which had been violently spiced, as if the cooks had taken out their angst on the food. By the end, Tedros had sweated through his shirt and the whole table spent as much time sniffling and gulping iced water as they did eating.

"Dessert is chili-spiced truffles," Chef Silkima announced, stonefaced.

"Perhaps we'll skip it," the wizard told the chef, waiting until she was gone before he turned to the rest. "Shall we talk?"

A short while later, they were all on one side of the table, some sitting, some standing, as they studied the Quest Map floating over them and listened to Professor Dovey finish recounting what she and Merlin knew about Chaddick's death and Sophie's and Agatha's adventures in Avalon.

"After I spoke to them in my crystal ball, Agatha and Sophie started tracking the Snake," she said, pointing at a miniature white-sailed ship inching across the Savage Sea. "The Storian painted them last night aboard the *Igraine*, which should reach Jaunt Jolie later today judging from its movements here. But four quest teams are missing that I haven't been able to reach

via crow or crystal ball—Ravan's, Kiko's, Vex's, and now Beatrix's in Jaunt Jolie. All their teams appear safe, given their
names haven't been crossed out on my map. But each of the
four teams seem to be moving away from their assigned kingdoms, which seems a rather ominous coincidence."

Tedros could see his mother and Lance as shocked by all
this as he was.

"This Snake killed Chaddick and is going after our quest
teams because of . . . *me?*" he said to the wizard and Dean.
"So *The Lion and the Snake* . . . that story we learned growing
up . . . It's *real?*"

"As a point of fact, no," said Merlin. "*The Lion and the
Snake* isn't a real tale at all. And whoever this Snake is likely
knows that."

"What do you mean it isn't real?" Lancelot asked.

"The Storian didn't write it," said the wizard. "By all
accounts, *The Lion and the Snake* was invented by an early
king of Camelot a thousand years ago. He and his brother both
laid claim to the throne, so he made up this tale and spread
it through the kingdom as if it were real. He portrayed his
brother as the Snake and himself as the Lion, suggesting the
kingdom would be in grave danger if his brother were picked
to rule instead of him. The people listened and crowned him
king."

"So we grew up learning a fake fairy tale?" Tedros said.

"But is it fake if people believe in it?" asked Merlin. "You
assume that it is truth that makes a story valuable, because the
tales that come from the Storian are true. The Storian writes

history. But man is capable of writing stories too and man has no obligation to truth or to history. Indeed, the Storian wrote its own honest version of *The Lion and the Snake* at the time, recounting the tale of the king who spread falsehoods to win his crown, but it is a story no one remembers or tells. Instead, the story that lasted is the *fraudulent* one. Even the *Royal Rot* stopped reminding its readers long ago that the founding tale of Camelot is fabricated, because no one seems to care. Something about the false story resonates with people. Something that makes the story endure. Even if it's based in a lie."

"And this Snake," said Tedros, "he believes the story is true?"

"You're not listening, Tedros. The story is a thousand years old. Clearly the Snake has no ties to the brothers in the tale," Merlin said, voice hardening. "What matters is how the Snake chooses to *interpret* the story. What matters is whether the Snake believes he can *use* the tale to take your throne."

"But the Snake *dies* in the story—" said Tedros.

"Wrongly, in this Snake's view," said the wizard. "In the story, the Snake believes the Lion has stolen a throne that is his. The Snake out there in the Woods must believe the same thing about you. It's why he's chosen to live out this story again and see it through to its just end. In his mind, you've taken his throne. Now he wants it back. And it is up to you, as the true king, to stop him."

Tedros' head was pounding. "I don't understand. No one else has a claim to the throne—"

"And yet your father's sword remains trapped in a stone. So your claim too remains in doubt," the wizard hectored. "And if the Snake comes for you, you've done nothing to show anyone that you are indeed the Lion in this story."

"What are you saying, Merlin?" Guinevere asked, sharing her son's confusion.

Merlin glared back at her. "His friend is dead, Guinevere. The rest of his friends might be next, along with his queen. Kingdoms everywhere are under threat and begging Camelot for help, only to get no response from its king. A king who someone out there believes shouldn't be king at all. So instead of jerking Excalibur day after day, which clearly isn't going to work, I'm saying he should be trying to find out why it's stuck there in the first place."

"I am King Arthur's *son*," Tedros declared, leveling Merlin with a stare. "I am the Lion by birthright and if a Snake dares challenge that, I will kill him. With or without my *sword*."

The room was quiet.

Merlin exhaled. "Clarissa. Show him."

Professor Dovey didn't move, grimacing. "Merlin, I don't think we—"

The wizard turned to her. "Show him or I will."

Professor Dovey took a deep breath and pulled a folded piece of paper from her pocket. She placed it on the table. "This was the Storian's last page before I left for Camelot. I had one of the fairies copy it as best they could."

Tedros pulled it open.

"You betrayed Chaddick for a Snake?" Sophie cried.
"Chaddick had Tedros' trust! Chaddick had Tedros' faith!
What does a Snake have?"
Slowly the Lady of the Lake raised her eyes.
"He has Arthur's blood," she said.

Tedros, his mother, and Lancelot all turned to Merlin, white as milk.

"Arthur's blood?" Guinevere breathed.

Lancelot shook his head. "That's . . . that's . . ."

"*Impossible,*" finished Tedros.

"Not necessarily," said Merlin, glancing at Professor Dovey as if they'd already thought this through. "There are a number of explanations for what the Lady of the Lake said to Sophie. The Snake may be a relative of Arthur: a half-brother or nephew or blood cousin we are unaware of. The Snake could be referring to having Arthur's physical blood in his possession, even to suggest that *he* killed Arthur, meaning he inflicted the mortal wound at the Battle of the Four Point almost seven years ago. He could even mean it figuratively: that he has Arthur's blood 'on his hands' and holds Arthur responsible for a crime he's committed. Whatever the Snake's meaning, it made the Lady of the Lake let him into her kingdom and protect him over Tedros' knight. Even more, this Snake must be quite the charmer, because it appears from the Storian's painting that the Lady of the Lake has lost her powers. . . . Which means the Lady likely *kissed* him as well."

"The Lady of the Lake? Sorceress eternal? Kiss a *boy*?" Lancelot said, agape.

"My reaction, precisely," said Professor Dovey.

"To seduce the Lady of the Lake into giving up her powers is a staggering feat—one that should strike fear into all of us," said Merlin gravely. "But that isn't the only thing that's troubling. The Lady of the Lake *is* capable of mistakes; she has human emotions after all. Excalibur, on the other hand, does not make mistakes. And it remains trapped in the stone at the same time that a Snake has made its way into the Woods, claiming to have King Arthur's blood."

Everyone was quiet, a thick unease filling the room.

For the first time, Tedros finally understood what Merlin had been trying to tell him.

"So there's two possibilities," Tedros said. "One is the Snake has no claim to the throne and Excalibur wants me to prove I'm the true king, not him. Only then can I pull the sword."

"Correct," said Merlin.

"And the second possibility?" asked Guinevere.

"The second possibility isn't a possibility," said Tedros.

"The second possibility is that Excalibur is waiting for the Snake to pull the sword and prove he's king, not Tedros," said Merlin.

Tedros felt nauseous, hearing the wizard say it out loud.

"The Snake can't have Dad's actual blood," he said, breathless. "Dad had no brothers or sisters."

"Unless there was one he didn't know about," said Guinevere. "He called Sir Ector his father, the man who adopted him. I never met his real parents. I don't even know who they were."

"Did *Dad* know who they were?" Tedros asked his mother.

Guinevere blushed and stared at her hands. "I feel so stupid. I should have asked more about his family. But Arthur had a way of closing off certain avenues of conversation. There were many things we just didn't talk about. It's why it was so easy for the two of us to keep secrets from each other."

An uncomfortable silence fell.

"After Lance and I left . . . ," Guinevere started. "Is it possible Arthur—"

"*No,*" said Tedros. "Dad never touched another woman after you abandoned him. He was faithful to you, even if you weren't to him."

Guinevere nodded, unable to look at him.

Tedros' head was hammering. *Chaddick dead . . . Lady of the Lake kissed . . . Dad's blood . . .*

"What do we do, Merlin?" he asked shakily.

The wizard looked him straight in the eyes. "My king, I am asking *you* that question."

Tedros saw the whole table turn to him.

"When you were in peril at school, Clarissa and I did our best to intervene," said Merlin. "We knew what we were up against with the School Master. But this time Clarissa and I are of little help. This is no ordinary villain. Not if he made the Lady of the Lake betray you and drained her powers. The Snake could surely waltz into Camelot and try his hand at Excalibur any moment he chooses. But he hasn't. *Why?* Because he wants to make you look weak first. He wants the people of the Woods to see they're behind the *wrong* king. Only then will he come for Excalibur—when they no longer have a Lion to believe in. And as that Lion, you must stop him. So now, my dear king, you must tell *us* what to do."

Tedros swallowed, every muscle in his body rigid.

He'd been king for more than six months. But this was the first time he felt like one.

"I'll lead an army against him," he said finally. "An army of Good *and* Evil, like my father would. The Snake won't stand a chance."

"Thank you, my king. Then that is what we will do," said Merlin, turning to the others. "But we must build this army *quickly*."

"Merlin, we have no soldiers, no knights, and no funds," said Tedros, feeling powerless again. "We don't even know the Snake's plan—"

"I said Clarissa and I would be of 'little help.' Not 'no help,'" said the wizard. "Look closer at this map."

Tedros leaned in, as did his mother and Lancelot.

"Or rather: look *bigger*," the wizard said.

He swished his hand and the floating Quest Map extended at both ends, showing more and more three-dimensional kingdoms far beyond the scope of the students' quests—kingdoms Tedros had never heard of: Dannamorah, Sing-Sing, Hisa Hassan, Shangri-La . . . The map kept stretching across the length of the dining room until it jammed against the walls and started curling in, reaching around Tedros like a python. . . .

"The Woods are endless. That we know, since fools like me keep trying to find the end of them," said the wizard, stopping the map's advance before it mummified the young king. "And yet, the Deans of the School for Good and Evil only assign students' quests in the kingdoms nearest to the school. A perfect little orbit . . ." He swept his hand, lighting up the fourth years in a fluorescent circle around the twin castles. "Why? To keep students at close distance, should there be a need to dispatch a rescue team."

He erased the glow along with all the figurines and names. "Now let's look at the terror attacks in the Woods. Terror that is supposedly random and assaulting kingdoms without warning. But is it so random? Look at where the attacks have happened—"

Merlin pointed a finger and instantly dozens of kingdoms on the map were plagued by shadows of magical terror: a raging fire in Glass Mountain; looting werewolves in Bloodbrook; clouds of bees in Gillikin; yogurt mudslides in Altazarra. . . .

"If the terror were random, then one would expect it to appear everywhere. Even in kingdoms at the farthest ends of the Woods. But as you can see . . ." He nodded towards the extended regions of the map, blissfully clear of attacks. "They seem to have been miraculously spared. Instead, all the terror is concentrated right here at the center of the map. And if we're even more precise . . ." He waved his hand, lighting up the afflicted kingdoms with fluorescent glow—

"They're all in a perfect orbit right around Camelot. Just as your classmates' quests are all circled around the School for Good and Evil."

Tedros stared at the illuminated sphere circling his kingdom. "Um, okay. I know I'm supposed to know what this means, but I wasn't as good a student as Agatha—"

"It means the unrest in the Woods is as carefully planned as the quest assignments are," Professor Dovey cut in, sounding as teacherly as when she'd taught his Good Deeds class. "The Snake doesn't want the entire Woods in upheaval. He only wants the kingdoms closest to Camelot to suffer and he's paying his minions to target these kingdoms specifically."

"But why the kingdoms *around* Camelot instead of Camelot?" Lancelot asked. "And why these small-time attacks? Fires? Looting? *Bees?* Why not just come for Tedros?"

"Oh, he's coming for Tedros. And soon. That is a certainty," said Merlin.

"Let him come for me," Tedros retorted, fists clenched. "I'll kill him—"

"And that is precisely the Snake's plan. To bait you into a

fight you are not ready for," said Merlin sternly. "You have no army yet. The people of Camelot doubt your place and fitness as king. The kingdoms around Camelot are plagued by chaos and fear, their rulers desperately calling on Camelot to save them as it has always done before. Only this time, Camelot's king has done *nothing* to help them. And yet . . . you still think you're ready to fight?"

"I'm King Arthur's *son*—" Tedros defended.

"A king is only as strong as his kingdom. A king is only as strong as his allies. A king is only as strong as his army. You are not strong, Tedros, and the Snake knows it," said Merlin, bearing down. "You are as weak now as your father was in the last year of his reign. And his weakness led not only to his death, but to the fall of the kingdom into *enemy* hands."

Tedros went quiet.

"The Snake is well aware of your father's history," said the wizard. "He will not give you the time to build an army or get stronger. Soon he'll reveal himself to the Woods as the mastermind behind all these attacks and dare you to battle him on a grand stage. And it's quite clear what this stage will be."

Tedros paled. "The Four Point," he said, meeting the wizard's eyes. "Where Dad was wounded."

"It's surely why he tricked the Lady of the Lake into kissing him. So the Four Point would no longer be protected," said the wizard. He pointed towards a tiny territory on the map not far from Camelot, where two Ever kingdoms and two Never kingdoms met: Jaunt Jolie, Kingdom Kyrgios, Ravenbow, and Bloodbrook. "The Four Point isn't just a symbol of

King Arthur's reign. It is the only reason there is lasting peace between Good and Evil—a truce point that reminds king-doms Camelot will fight to protect the balance. The people of the Woods are terrified right now. If the Snake murders you on the same spot your father suffered a fatal blow, it means he is not just more powerful than King Arthur, but more power-ful than his *legacy*. With that kind of power, I assure you, no one will stop him from walking into Camelot and taking your crown. Regardless of what becomes of Excalibur."

"Which is why I should ride out there right now," Tedros returned, rising from his seat—

"No, it's why you shouldn't ride out there at all," said Mer-lin. "Did you hear anything I just said? The Four Point will be a *trap*. And to fight the Snake there is to fall right into it."

The young king stared at him, still on his feet. "So I should let him violate Camelot's land? My father's sacred memorial? I have to stop him—"

"With no Excalibur and no Lady of the Lake?" Professor Dovey said, echoing the wizard. "On land that he's been scout-ing for weeks? Stay the course, Tedros, just like you planned. Build alliances. Build your army for the bigger war to come."

"I don't need Excalibur. I don't need the Lady of the Lake," Tedros persisted. "I have to fight for my people. I'm their leader, Merlin. I'm their defender. If he even gets *near* the Four Point, I'll slit this reptile's throat and prove I'm king once and for all."

"Tedros is right," Lancelot jumped in. "He can't let the Four Point go undefended. I'll ride with him and fight by his side."

"It's too dangerous!" said Guinevere, clearly distressed now that her love's life was at risk.

"Arthur and I always took on the most dangerous enemies ourselves. You know that, Gwen," Lancelot growled. "That was his duty as king. That was my duty as his knight. That's how we kept this kingdom *safe*."

"But this is Tedros, *not* Arthur," Guinevere came back. "Last time you and Tedros fought together, you ended up impaled to a tree by the School Master and nearly bled to death. Even you said that your shoulder isn't the same since. And now you want to ride into battle again? Listen to Merlin and Professor Dovey. Both of you. Don't do anything rash."

"Mother, I know I am not my father. Thank you for reminding me of that," Tedros said coldly. "But Agatha and my friends are out there in the Woods fighting *my* quest. I can't let them risk their lives for me any longer." He turned to Merlin. "This is my destiny as king. No one else's. You can't stop me from fighting—"

"I'm not trying to stop you from fighting, Tedros," said the wizard. "I'm trying to stop you from fighting before you are *ready*. This is a Snake who duped Good's greatest sorceress. A Snake who thinks *he's* the rightful king. He will not fight fairly and you must be prepared. If you fight him on his terms, he will kill you and your queen, just like he already killed your best friend."

Tedros fell silent.

"Four Point is only a three-hour ride from here. We should leave now, Tedros," Lancelot forced, ignoring Merlin. "Don't listen to the wizard. You and I beat the School Master, after all."

"Only because *I* had a plan and brought *you* an army," Merlin said sharply.

Lancelot opened his mouth to argue, then closed it.

Tedros looked between the wizard, the Dean, his mother, and the knight, thinking carefully.

Then he turned to Merlin.

"Let's get back to building our army," said the king.

Guinevere exhaled. Lancelot sank back in his chair and glowered out the window, rubbing at his shoulder.

The wizard continued: "If we are to build an army to fight the Snake, then we will need allies. Tedros must immediately convene a summit of Ever and Never leaders from the affected kingdoms. Despite the fact that you've ignored their pleas for help, you must assure them that Camelot is still on their side—and that you are the *only* ruler who still has all of their interests at heart."

Tedros nodded, trying to look confident.

"Until that summit occurs and while Agatha's crew tracks the Snake's movements, the five of us must be our own crew with our own task. . . ." Merlin looked around the table. "We need to find out *who* this Snake might be. And more importantly, where he gets his power."

Merlin turned to Professor Dovey. "On that note, perhaps it's best if I visit the Lady of the Lake myself."

"You can't go now, Merlin. I need you," the Dean breathed, quickly and tight-lipped as if she didn't want the others to hear.

"You're more than ready to do it on your own," the wizard murmured.

"Something's still bothering me, Merlin," said Guinevere, interrupting them. "Even if the Snake is Arthur's family, Tedros has the throne by *birthright*. He is Arthur's first and only son. No amount of Arthur's blood can challenge that."

The wizard gazed at her thoughtfully. "Quite right, Guinevere. Unless, of course, by 'Arthur's blood,' the Snake meant—"

He paused.

"Unless he meant . . . what," Tedros pushed.

Merlin turned to the Dean. "I'm afraid I need to depart at once, Clarissa. I'll see you at school in a few days' time."

He stood and gathered his cape and hat, leaving the Dean dismayed.

"But, Merlin—" Dovey pleaded.

"You'll do quite fine without me, Clarissa. Just *stay vigilant*," he said cryptically as he headed for the door. "As for the rest of you, I'll leave you to your afternoon meeting, which Clarissa would be wise to avoid as well, since it concerns the only thing in the world wizards and fairy godmothers are deathly allergic to."

"What's that?" Tedros asked.

"*Money*," said Merlin, without looking back.

"The advisors want to *talk* to me?" Tedros said, eyes wide. "Lady Gremlaine has been trying to arrange a meeting between me and them for six months and their only response has been to urinate in their food and throw it in her direction."

"Well, apparently, they've changed their minds," said the Treasury Master, not looking up from his ledger. "Sent a scrap of paper through a guard named Kei. He couldn't find Lady Gremlaine so he brought it to me."

The Treasury Master was an egg-shaped, fleshy figure, no taller than a baby Christmas tree, with a bald pate, floppy ears, and enormous gold glasses that took up most of his pug-nosed, pink-skinned face. Tedros couldn't tell if he was human or ogre.

"They'll see you after supper and they made it clear you're to be alone," said the Treasury Master. He lifted his head and looked at Lancelot and Guinevere, seated beside Tedros, then went back to his ledger. "I summoned you to give you the message, so now that it's delivered, I assume our meeting is at an end—"

"Not so fast," said Lancelot. "We have more questions, Treasury Master."

As the knight interrogated him, Tedros lapsed into his thoughts. After six months, his father's advisors had agreed to see him. The advisors who'd driven Camelot into debt. The advisors who'd done something with its gold. Finally he would get answers.

"I'm afraid I don't understand the question," the Treasury Master was saying, perched between stacks of soggy ledgers and chewing the end of his red pencil.

"You don't understand the question? Or do you not understand words in general?" Lancelot bullied, still pent up from the lunch meeting.

"*Lance*," Guinevere said, before simpering at the Treasury Master. "All we're asking is how are we still losing money now that the advisors are in jail? Since Tedros took the throne, the kingdom has been collecting taxes fairly and he's cut spending to the bone. Camelot should be bringing in more gold than before. Not falling deeper and deeper into debt—"

"Accounting is a complicated field, Lady Guinevere," said the Treasury Master vacantly. "Best left to the likes of men."

Guinevere's face changed. She glanced at Lancelot.

The knight cracked his knuckles. "Who appointed you Treasury Master, kind sir?"

"The Council of Advisors brought me in after Arthur's death, given my sterling reputation. And I have a contract for a twelve-year term, so my position is secure," said the Treasury Master, holding his gaze. "Speaking of security, isn't there still a bounty on both of your heads?"

Lancelot leaned in. "You're welcome to try to collect."

Tedros couldn't concentrate.

His mind was on Excalibur.

Was the sword waiting for him to kill the Snake?

Or was it waiting for the Snake to kill Tedros?

Tedros gritted his teeth. He could feel his fingers twitching. . . . How could he hold back for an army? . . . He wanted to fight the Snake right now. . . .

He took a deep breath.

Merlin and Professor Dovey were right. His father had ridden into the Battle of the Four Point weak and without a plan and lost everything. Tedros couldn't make the same mistake.

Not just for him, but for Agatha too.

Agatha.

His heart clenched thinking of his true love out in the Woods with her crew, tracking a deadly villain. He wished he could have spoken to Professor Dovey before she left. She was the last person to talk to Agatha and he wanted to know how she was and why she hadn't written when she promised she would. But now Tedros was thinking about the Storian's last page. . . . *"Arthur's blood . . ."* Why had Merlin gone just as he seemed to figure out what the words meant? Was there someone in Arthur's family who wanted the crown? Someone willing to kill his son for it? Someone Merlin *knew?* Tedros thought back to what Lady Gremlaine had said in the Hall of Kings. . . . *"How little you know of your father . . ."* And yet, deep inside, he had the sinking feeling that they were all wrong . . . that they had missed the real meaning of the Lady of the Lake's words. . . .

But now Tedros was thinking of the summit he had to call to build an army. He'd put off answering the urgent letters from neighboring kingdoms because Camelot had zero to offer them. If he went ahead with a summit, he'd have to face them all in person. . . .

"Tedros?" his mother's voice said.

He looked up to see her, Lance, and the Treasury Master staring at him.

"Oh. Um, what was the question?" Tedros asked.

Lance glowered. "I told Humpty Dumpty here to show me Camelot's accounts and he said no and I said show me or I'll give you the beating of your life and he said only the king can order him to show the kingdom's books—"

"And he isn't officially king," said the Treasury Master, barely looking at Tedros. "Which means maybe I should call some guards and see if they're interested in splitting a bounty." He grinned at Guinevere and Lancelot. "Think there's just enough gold in the kingdom left for *that*."

Maybe it was the way the fat little twit said it. Or the way he ignored Tedros like he was a kitchen maid. Or maybe now that a Snake wanted his crown, Tedros finally felt like a Lion. Whatever it was, it made Tedros stand up.

"I'm the only king you have at the moment, my friend. So as long as you plan to remain at Camelot, you and everyone else in this castle are under my command. Which means you'll hand over the kingdom's books without another word and you'll never threaten my mother and Lancelot again. First things first, though."

Tedros turned to Lance. "You have a beating to give."

The Treasury Master gasped.

Tedros knew from experience that Lancelot could inflict remarkable pain in a short time. The Treasury Master didn't fare well, then. Bruised and whimpering behind the desk like a dying cat, he quiveringly handed over all of Camelot's ledgers, which Lance, Tedros, and his mother lugged into a Blue Tower sitting room and spread out over the tattered mohair carpet.

The palm plant in the corner of the room was dead, the powder-blue wallpaper had water bubbles in it, and the cracked ceiling leaked onto the fireplace mantel, *drip, drip, drip*. A few mosquitoes buzzed around their heads. But the three of them stayed hunched on the carpet for hours, barely speaking as they scoured the Treasury Master's books. Soon the sky dimmed through the windows and stewards put down plates of chicken tikka and saffron rice, which were eaten hastily and shoved aside so they could get back to work.

Finally Lancelot looked up. "They taxed the poor and the middle class at double the rates Arthur did and cut the taxes of the wealthiest landowners. That's obvious. But it still looks like we have plenty of money coming into the accounts. More than enough to build an army."

"But if revenues are up, how can we be bankrupt? That's what I don't understand," said Guinevere. "Who has the expense books—"

"I do and they all look fine too," said Tedros, peering at a ledger. "Well, except the expenses for CB. Those numbers are astronomical. Must be where all the extra money went. But that's to be expected after Dad died."

"What's CB?" Guinevere asked.

"'Camelot Beautiful,'" Tedros answered. "Advisors started the fund after Dad died to help maintain and refurbish the castle. Agatha's been raising money for it the past six months—"

He stopped talking.

Slowly they took in the room around them . . . the warped wallpaper . . . dripping ceiling . . . molting plant . . .

"Well, one thing's for sure," said Lancelot. "Whatever money's in that fund isn't going to Camelot Beautiful."

Guinevere shook her head. "Where is it going, then? Where is all of Camelot's gold?"

"Only one way to find out," said Tedros, snapping his book shut. He stood and straightened his crown, his eyes crystal blue, his face regal, looking like the Tedros in the Hall of Kings.

"It's time for me to *meet* these advisors."

15

AGATHA

Pirate Pavilion

"Arthur's *blood*? What do you mean the Snake has Arthur's blood!" Nicola blurted.

"Shh! They'll hear us!" Sophie snapped. "Agatha and I were having a private conversation—"

"Your voice is so screechy there's nothing private about it."

"You moldy little *toadstool*—"

"Is this *really* the time to be bickering?" Agatha hissed between them. The three girls were chained by the hands, one behind the other, with Bogden, Willam, Hort,

Dot, Anadil, and Hester fixed to the same chain in lockstep ahead of them. Four teenage pirates in black leather, wielding curved swords, rode on horseback, two ahead, two behind, marshaling the prisoners through Jaunt Jolie, paved with yellow and pink brick, hot under their feet from the broiling summer sun. Agatha could see townspeople peeping from houses, many with black eyes or gashed cheeks.

"This is an Ever kingdom. Why aren't they helping us?" Sophie whispered, tripping over her long, ruffly blue dress. "Aren't Evers supposed to rescue Good from the clutches of Evil?"

"You're not Good," Agatha grumbled, dripping sweat. "Plus, they're probably relieved it's not them. Also, don't you have any *questing* clothes?"

"Like *your* tomboy getup? You look like a mill worker, while I look like Wendy from *Peter Pan,* only not as helpless or dull. I told Boobeshwar to hem it, but the fool's run off with his fiancée—"

Sophie stumbled on her dress again and a shirtless pirate smacked her hard with his horse reins. He couldn't have been more than sixteen, with a bony torso, a peeling sunburnt face, and a nose broken in two places.

"Izzis what lasses look like atta School for Evil? Pity I aint creepin' the halls, then," he chuckled, leering down at her. "School Master passed my house by on kidnappin' night. Musta thought little ol' Wesley wouldn't turn out Evil enough. Too bad. We coulda been friends." He curled towards Sophie, flashing snaggly teeth. "Bet ye smell like warm cherry pie."

"Well, you'll never know since that's the closest you'll ever get to me. Or any female, I suspect," Sophie snipped.

Wesley reddened and spat at her. "Wait 'til the Snake gets his hands on ye." He rode to join his fellow pirates ahead.

Agatha saw Sophie's finger glow hot pink. "Steady, Sophie."

"Dirty thugs. I could kill them all," Sophie fumed. "Though I'm a little out of practice."

"They're taking us to the Snake. That's what matters," said Agatha.

The original plan had been to fight the pirates and rescue Beatrix's quest team, wherever they were. Given reports that the pirates had taken over Jaunt Jolie's ports, Agatha had expected them to attack the moment the *Igraine* docked—and they did in startling numbers, surfacing from the water in scaly black cloaks and silver-tipped black boots, scrambling up the boat like lizards. From storybooks, Agatha had expected the pirates to be gnarly old men, with curly beards and stinking of rum, not a band of wild young alley cats. But after two days of sailing from Avalon back into balmy waters, two days that they filled with strategy meetings and spell practice, Agatha's crew had been prepared for anything. Sophie unleashed a chilling witch's scream that sent the young rogues diving underwater; Hester's demon flung them overboard; Anadil's rats sank teeth into necks; Dot rained steaming hot chocolate on their heads; Hort's man-wolf pitched boys to the horizon while Willam and Bogden beat them off rails with the only weapons they had left (the beaver had stolen the rest); even Nicola, who had no fingerglow yet, smacked a pirate with her shoe. . . .

Except Agatha had been so focused on her crew that she hadn't seen the cretin coming up behind *her*: a young pirate with bloodred tattoos around his eyes who shoved a knife against her throat. He recognized her hideous little face, he'd said, pulling a wet wad of parchment from his pocket—

"Snake said you lot'd be comin' our way," the boy cooed, smelling like rancid meat. "Won't pay us if we don't bring ye to him alive, though. Wants to kill ye all 'imself. Much as I'd like to cut yer neck and claim the bounty inna name of Thiago of Netherwood. Git my name in a fairy tale the ol'-fashion way. By *earnin'* it." He scowled murderously at the group. "Yellow-bellied cream puffs. Think 'cause you went to that hoity-toity school yer better than the lot of us? Pissin' Evers and Nevers, questin' for glory! We'll see what yer books 'n teachers are worth when yer squealin' like pigs—"

Hester's demon launched for him. So did Hort's man-wolf and the rest of the crew—

Agatha ordered them to stand down. Not because she was scared; she was quite sure she could take out this Thiago twerp with a stun spell and a knee to his groin. But after what happened in Avalon, this was their one chance to meet the Snake. They had to find out who this villain was.

But now squired in chains with her crew, Agatha could feel her nerves shredding as they neared the town square. If Tedros could see her right now, he'd be on the next ship out of Camelot to rescue her. It's why she hadn't written him, letting her new courier crow idle about the ship instead. She'd come on this quest to ease his problems, not add to them.

A fool's errand, her soul's voice said. *He can't be king without going through the fire.*

I'm his queen. My duty is to protect him, Agatha fought back.

You can't protect him from the truth.

"Good lord," Sophie said, distracting her. "Beasts didn't

take long to put their stink on the place."

Agatha looked past her and blanched. The main thorough-fare of Jaunt Jolie was once an airy yellow-and-pink pavilion of shops, marble arches, and fountains filled with Wish Fish that painted beautiful water-paintings of people's deepest wishes. Now it was a steamy pirates' den with more than fifty sweat-soaked boys lounging on stone benches, spray-painting graffiti, barbecuing beef over open flames, drinking cider out of bar-rels, and tormenting Wish Fish to draw lewd images. WANTED posters littered the foul-smelling pavilion, featuring different members of Agatha's crew with varying bounties (there was even one for Bogden at a meager 10 pennies).

"Four hundred gold coins?" Sophie said, spotting her own face on a poster. "Aren't you at 500, Aggie? Surely a Dean is worth more than a princess—"

"Forget that. How did the Snake know we were coming here?" Agatha asked, scanning posters of Hester . . . Hort . . . Dot. . . .

"Forget that too," Nicola butted in, staring at a poster of herself. "How does he know my *face*?"

"Wait a second," said Agatha, squinting ahead. "Isn't that . . . Beatrix?"

A portrait of their blond, doe-eyed classmate gazed back at them from one of three WANTED posters on a shop window. The other two posters were of ravishing, brown-skinned Reena and freckly, red-haired Millicent, both assigned by Professor Dovey as helpers to Beatrix in their quest against the pirates.

"Means the Snake hasn't caught them yet," Sophie surmised. "Pity."

"I thought Millicent had been mogrified," said Agatha.

"No wonder he can't find her, then—" said Sophie.

"Hey, guys?" Nicola interjected.

Agatha and Sophie followed her eyes to a tattered poster on the ground.

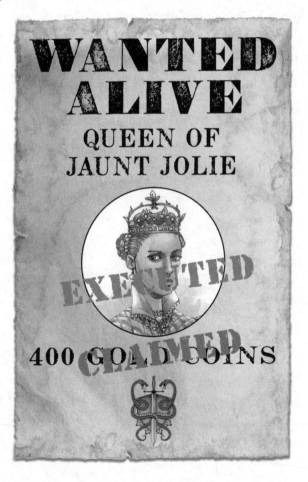

"He killed a queen?" Sophie breathed.

Agatha knew she should feel scared for her own fate, but looking at the queen's face, she only felt fury. "What kind of *boys* would help a masked murderer? They're just like that scummy beaver. Willing to do anything for a bundle of gold."

And yet scores of gold coins were littered across the pavilion, as if the scoundrels had earned so much booty that this was merely loose change. Nearby, a young pirate urinated on a wall beneath shops graffitied with new names: "DAMSEL IN 'DIS DRESS," "YO HO HOME FURNISHINGS," "THE PEG LEG PUB," "PLUNDER'S PLUMBING." And all the while, they sang shanties off-key as they waved cider jugs and stomped their silver-tipped boots—

> *Underneath me pirate hat,*
> *That's where I hide me treasure map!*

> *On the deck where floorboards creak,*
> *That's where I keep me wooden teeth!*

> *In lovely maidens' open hearts—*
> *That's where I'm storin' all me farts!*

"No wonder the School Master didn't take them for Evil," said Agatha. "Pirates in storybooks are bold and clever. These are just horrible."

"Wonder if Hort feels the same way," said Nicola.

"Hort, Hort, Hort. Is that all you talk about?" Sophie moaned.

"Hort's father was a pirate, which means Hort grew up *around* pirates," said Nicola. "He might very well know these boys."

"Good point," said Agatha.

Sophie muttered something under her breath.

Agatha wished she could talk to Hort, but he was at the front of the chain, sweaty and shirtless after reverting from a man-wolf (the pirates had thankfully let him put on breeches). The witches were with him too, whispering to each other and giving Agatha nervous looks.

Agatha's stomach sank. Had she really thought this through? Or had she unwittingly put her crew in danger like she had in Avalon? While sailing from there, they'd all been so busy preparing for the battle against the pirates that Agatha had never prepared for what would happen if they were captured (the pirates had even chained up Hester's demon). Nor had she or Sophie revealed to the witches what the Lady of the Lake had said. Agatha herself had barely processed what Sophie told her. . . .

Arthur's blood? How could the Snake have Arthur's blood? Was there another relative they didn't know about? Or did "Arthur's blood" mean something else? She needed to talk to Professor Dovey about it, but because of that cruddy crystal ball, Dovey wouldn't check in with them until tomorrow—

Wait. Wouldn't the Storian have written about it? They

were in a fairy tale, after all, where the pen recorded every key moment. Dovey was on watch in the School Master's tower. . . . She would have seen the scene unfold between Sophie and the Lady of the Lake . . . which meant Dovey surely knew what the Lady had said to Sophie before she vanished. And if Dovey knew, so would Merlin . . . perhaps even Tedros by now. . . .

Agatha tensed up. Did Tedros know, then, that his best friend was dead? Did he know that his princess was hunting the killer? All her efforts to insulate him from worry suddenly seemed foolish.

And yet, beneath it all, Agatha also felt an odd relief. If anyone could make sense of what the Lady of the Lake had said, it'd be Dovey and Arthur's own family. She'd leave the mystery in the Dean's hands for now, then. She *had* to. Because every part of her had to focus on how she and her crew could meet a murderous villain and still come out alive—

"Aggie, look," Sophie said, pointing to the royal castle ahead, with two pink-and-gold towers now flying black crossbones flags. It's where the pirates were leading them.

"Izzat the 'princess of Camelot'? I've seen prettier mole rats," a handsome young pirate heckled as the prisoners crossed into the pavilion.

"Don't care if they look like a horse's arse as long as I git me gold," a shaved-headed one said. "Tally those bounties, divide by us, and what's that make?"

"A whole lotta beef," said a fat pirate, firing up the barbecue to a resounding cheer.

"Blimey. A couple fine ones in there, innit?" grunted a swarthy one, swinging his arm around Nicola.

"And lookie here! The new Dean of Evil!" a runty one hooted, grabbing at Sophie. "Saw her portrait in my sis's school handbook! Wonder if she'll let me in for a kiss. . . ."

Agatha could see Sophie's finger glowing so pink it was starting to melt the gold vial on her necklace. But even with her cheeks hot with humiliation, Sophie knew full well they shouldn't fight these thugs. They'd be face-to-face with the Snake soon. . . .

"Hi-ho! Fair maidens! Sing us a shanty!" the fat pirate yelled.

"Shanty! Shanty!" the boys demanded.

"We need a plan for the Snake," Agatha whispered to Sophie.

"I have an idea," Nicola said, eavesdropping.

"We don't need anything from you, first year," Sophie grouched.

"A first year who's saved your life *twice*," said Nicola.

"Luck," Sophie poohed.

"I'll take any luck we can get," Agatha trumped to Nicola. "What do you have in mind?"

A spray of gold coins flew over their heads.

"Sing us a *shanty*!" the fat boy badgered, flinging more gold at them.

"Snake wears a mask, right?" said Nicola, ducking the coins. "He's not going to want to reveal his identity."

"Aren't you glad she's here, Aggie? So helpful," Sophie sniped.

"But that's how we find out who he is," said Nicola, looking squarely at her. "Sophie, we need you to—"

Someone yanked the line to a stop and the three girls crashed into Willam, who was right in front of them. Sunburnt Wesley glowered down from the horse, his sword blade hooked through the chain. "When a pirate gives ye an order, ye best obey it. Don't think the Snake would flinch if we delivered yer lot without noses." He tapped Sophie's and Nicola's noses with his sword. "Which means we ain't movin' another inch until these two lassies pucker up and *sing*."

Sophie and Nicola swallowed.

So did Agatha, Hester, Anadil, Dot, Hort, Bogden, and Willam, finally all able to look at each other again. This wasn't like the battle on the boat; here they were outnumbered by pirates twenty to one, they couldn't direct their finger-glows with their hands cuffed behind their backs (Anadil's rats included), and their best weapon, Hester's demon, was wrapped in chains, uselessly trapped on her neck. Meaning the future of the crew's noses depended on the song that was about to come out of the two girls' mouths.

"I'll start," Sophie announced—

"No, I will," Nicola cut in. She eyed Agatha intently and sang in a clear voice:

> *"There once was a boy named Ito*
> *Whose tale was in my storybook.*
> *He had a face of perfect beauty*
> *And all day in mirrors he looked.*

But Ito loved his face so much
He didn't want others to enjoy
So he put on a mask
And pretended to be coy

He wore the mask for days and years
Until he fell for a lovely girl
Who confided to a friend,
'He must be ugly and hiding from the world.'

So Ito finally removed his mask
To prove her wrong and be bold
Only to find that in time
His face had grown very old."

Agatha lit up with understanding. Looking miffed, Sophie glared at Nicola, then opened her mouth to sing, but Agatha jumped in and sang back to Nicola in a husky, barbarous croak:

"I know a boy like Ito
Who wears a mask of green
We need a pretty girl to tempt his pride
And make him want to be seen.
A girl like a prize or a trophy,
A girl whose name is . . ."

Agatha and Nicola turned and stared at Sophie.
Sophie blinked back at them, baffled.

Silence hung over the pavilion.

"THAT AIN'T A SHANTY!" a pirate cried.

"Boo!" the others shouted.

Beef bits and fistfuls of coins spewed violently in their direction. Someone threw a parrot and hit Hort in the groin—

"Poke out their eyes!" one ordered.

"Cut off their arms!" commanded another.

Young pirates with swords advanced. Agatha and Nicola recoiled, dragging the rest of the crew with them. There was nowhere to go. All nine members of the group backed up against a wall, shadows of pirate blades rising over them. Fingerglows burnt bright behind the kids' backs as they tried to melt each other's cuffs. . . . Hester's demon screeched and tore at his chains. . . . But it was too late. Swords slashed down—

"Yoo-hoo! Boys!"

Hands behind her back, Sophie shimmied her ruffly blue dress and started high-kicking—

> *"I'm Whiskey Woo, the pirate queen!*
> *Whiskey Woo!*
> *Whiskey Woo!*
>
> *I'm Whiskey Woo, the pirate queen!*
> *Whiskey Woo!*
> *Whiskey Woo!"*

Pirates held their swords, eyes big as gold coins.

Sophie kicked higher, flashing her bloomers and a pearly

white smile. *"I'm Whiskey Woo, the pirate queen! Whiskey Woo!*
Whiskey W—"

She saw the pirates' faces and slowly stopped singing.

The pavilion went silent as a tomb.

Somewhere a parrot squawked.

"Blimey. That's a worst shanty I ever 'eard," Wesley spat.

"Bottom of the barrel," said tattooed Thiago.

"Don't deserve the word 'barrel,'" said the fat pirate.

Agatha's palms dripped. She could see Sophie flush-faced,
knowing she'd just doomed them all—

Then like a sun ripping through clouds, the boys exploded
into laughter.

"Might be pretty, but she's stupid as a nut!" the handsome
pirate howled.

"Don't git too close or you might turn stupid too!" the
runty one whooped. "Put that inna school handbook!"

"Feel sorry for 'er students! Their Dean's a dope!" the fat
one sniggered.

Sophie gaped at them, red as a beet.

"Get these clods to the Snake," Wesley snarled, shaking his
head. "Faster ye get 'em out of our sight, the faster we're rid of
'em for good."

"Whiskey Woo! Whiskey Woo!" his mates mocked.

Eager to deliver their bounties, the horsebound pirates
whipped the kids on towards the castle. Agatha stared at
Sophie, speechless.

"I saved us, didn't I?" Sophie retorted.

As they filed out of the pavilion, they could hear pirates still jeering: "*Whiskey Woo! Whiskey Woo!*"

"A good laugh is worth its weight in gold!" Sophie called back at them angrily. "Better up that bounty on me now! A solid thousand, I'd say, wouldn't you?"

"*Whiskey Woo! Whiskey Woo!*" the pirates ragged.

Nicola whispered to Agatha. "At least we have our noses."

"She can't outsmart the Snake by being a fool, Nicola!" Agatha hissed, straining against her cuffs. "Your shanty was right. Sophie can get him to take off his mask, but only if he *likes* her. How is she going to make him like her? With a limerick and a cha-cha?"

"Leave it to me. I'll help her," Nicola whispered.

"Yeah, right. You don't know Sophie like I do—"

"This isn't just your fairy tale anymore, Agatha," Nicola said sharply.

Agatha was quiet.

"Listen," said Nicola. "Ever since I got to the Woods, I've thought my real life was back in Gavaldon. But the Storian wrote all of us into this quest for a reason, including me. And the only way I'll find out why I'm on this quest is if you let me be a part of it." Her dark eyes softened. "Maybe you already have a best friend, Agatha. Maybe you don't have room in your story for any more. But I have room in mine. Let me help you."

Agatha searched the first year's face. All this time, she thought she was the captain of this fairy tale. The only one who could steer them to a new happy ending, as if it were a mappable port on the shore. That's another reason she'd left Tedros behind. Because in her toughest moments, Agatha trusted herself and herself alone.

And yet . . . maybe that's why she could never find a happy ending that lasted.

She looked into Nicola's eyes.

"Friends?" the first year asked.

"Friends," said Agatha, a warm feeling spreading through her.

Together, the two girls raised their gaze to the castle, the chain pulling them towards its doors.

The warmth inside Agatha went cold.

A Snake was waiting.

16

TEDROS

Riddles and Mistrals

As Tedros swept through the White Tower, veering into dead ends and going round in circles, he kept passing the same square-jawed guard, smirking in his blue-and-gold uniform, daring him to ask for directions.

Tedros insisted to Lancelot he could meet the advisors without Lance taking him there. The knight demanded to come along, wary of a king treading into the dungeons on his own, but Tedros shoved past him, ordering him to stay behind. First of all, the advisors had made it clear they wanted to see him alone. Second, he didn't want to admit he hadn't a clue where the prison was after a lifetime of living in Camelot and six months of ruling it. And third, he was done passing the buck to others. On his first night in the castle, when the advisors had refused to see him, he'd let Lancelot throw them in jail instead of doing it himself.

But tonight he'd right that wrong. When it came to these advisors, this coming meeting felt *personal.*

He'd been roaming the White Tower for nearly an hour now, but the reddish torchlight made every hall look the same. Any time he opened a door it went wrong: a storage space filled with broken weapons . . . a steward undressing in his quarters . . . a laundry maid in the midst of ironing, so spooked at the sight of him she burnt through his shirt. . . . It was futile guesswork: the only part of White Tower that Tedros knew was the strange guest room his father had built on the second floor, which he kept returning to every few minutes like a rat restarting a maze.

Reaper could have shown me the way, Tedros thought, aware he was longing for a creature he'd often imagined falling into a lit fireplace. The cat seemed to know every nook and cranny of this castle. But after he'd kicked him in the guest room this morning, Reaper had vanished, no longer compelled to protect the king.

"Lost, Your Highness?" said the square-jawed guard as he passed.

"If I was, I'd ask," said Tedros. "Especially since guards don't speak to kings unless they're spoken to first."

The guard bolted to attention, spear to his chest.

One day these guards will look at me the way they looked at my father, Tedros thought, prowling through the empty staff dining room into a carpeted corridor. *One day no one will question my place as king—*

He tripped over a hole in a carpet and toppled through an open door, his crown flying off him, his body splaying onto a wet floor. He stood up gingerly, his chest and legs drenched. He lit his fingerglow and saw he was in a spacious bathroom, almost as big as his master bath in the Gold Tower. The floor was flooded an inch deep with water. Tedros scanned the bath with his glow until he found the source: a severed toilet hose that had dumped out the entire water tank. Tedros groaned and picked up his dripping crown, smushing it back on his head. He was about to trudge back into the hall and fetch one of the maids . . . but then something caught his eye.

Farther in, the bathroom had two side doors across from each other, each leading into opposing rooms. Which meant this bathroom was shared between whoever occupied those two rooms.

No wonder it's so big, Tedros thought.

Curious as to why neither of the rooms' inhabitants had noticed the leak, Tedros opened one of the side doors and stepped through—

He raised his brows.

It was the strange guest room, with the brown-and-orange rug, bare beige walls, and lonely bed in the corner. The one his father used to hide in during his drunken hazes.

But Tedros hadn't used this door earlier today. He'd entered through the front door across the room, which still had his bloody handprint on it. And he'd used a *key*.

He turned and examined the door he'd just come in, with no doorknob on the inside and deftly concealed within the pattern of the wallpaper. It's why he hadn't seen it when he was in here this morning.

A secret door? To a guest room?

It didn't make sense. Then again, many things in this castle didn't make sense. Especially in the middle of the night, when he could feel his brain deadening and his eyes starting to close. But then another thought struck him—

Who shared the bathroom with this room?

He stepped through the secret door back into the bathroom and waded across the wet floor to the opposite side door.

He opened it—

A blast of perfume hit him, smelling of powdered rose. The small room had lavender wallpaper, a dark purple carpet, and a crisply made bed. A plate of half-eaten biscuits and an empty glass were on the nightstand, a dried-out lemon on the glass's rim. Next to the glass was a leather-bound notebook. Tedros peeled it open and saw pages filled with Lady Gremlaine's clear, graceful handwriting: schedules, to-do lists, addresses, notes to self. . . .

Tedros looked around the deserted room.

Shouldn't she be sleeping?

There was nothing on the desk cabinets or mantel. He glanced back into the bathroom. There were no face creams or perfume bottles or even a toothbrush.

Tedros' chest tingled.

He pulled the closet door. Empty. He yanked open the drawers and cabinets. Empty.

He rushed through the room's main door into the hall and saw the square-jawed guard, reappeared.

Tedros frowned. "Weren't you in the other . . . Never mind. Where's Lady Gremlaine?"

The guard didn't look at him, his narrow, hooded brown eyes fixed ahead. "Gone, Your Highness."

"Yes, but gone *where*?"

"Packed up before lunch. Took all of her belongings and left the castle," the guard said. "Said she was no longer needed."

"What? Why would she—"

Tedros' eyes widened. When they were in the Hall of Kings, he'd promised to stand up for her. To vouch for her after she'd helped him these past six months. He'd given Lady Gremlaine his word. But instead, he'd forgotten all about her and let his mother dismiss her, just like his dad once had.

"*Like father, like son,*" her words echoed.

Tedros hadn't just been selfish. He'd been cruel.

The young king stiffened, heat coloring his cheeks.

It was time to swallow his pride.

Slowly he looked up at the guard.

"I seem to be lost after all," Tedros said.

The dungeon wasn't in the White Tower.

It was in the Gold Tower and to get there, they had to go through King's Cove. Turns out Tedros had been working out right over the prison every morning and he hadn't a clue. He followed the guard through the Gymnasium, tensing up as they passed Excalibur's empty case, then tightening even more as the guard spotted King Arthur's statue inside King's Cove, the eyes gouged out.

"Your Highness," he gasped, nostrils flaring, "someone has desecrated the—"

"I am aware, guard."

"I'll make sure to inform the other men—"

"I'm handling it," Tedros clipped. "It's one o'clock. I'd like to sleep tonight. Where is the prison?"

Still looking concerned, the guard stepped into the muggy grotto, the broad frame of his blue-and-gold uniform glowing in the pool's ghostly light. The weak torches lit up the surface of the fungus-filled water and the slow, leaky cascade over the tall pile of rocks. The guard reached up to the statue of King Arthur holding Excalibur and twisted the sword's hilt, the stone turning easily under his fingers.

All of a sudden the waterfall stopped running and the rocks parted, revealing a white stone door.

"I believe you have the key, Your Highness," said the guard.

"Key?" said Tedros.

"Only you and Lady Gremlaine have keys to the door. Lady Gremlaine let us in each day to feed the prisoners. But if she didn't leave her keys behind when she departed the castle, then only you can let us in now."

Tedros took out his key ring. "But I don't have the key to—"

He stopped. There was a coal-colored key scrunched between the many others on his ring—the one he always

assumed opened a far-flung lockbox or weapons case. Skirting the edge of the pool, Tedros slipped through the gap in the
rocks to reach the door and fit the black key into the lock. He
pushed the door open, revealing a steep staircase down into
darkness.

The guard lifted a torch off the wall and started descending the steps.

"This way, Your Highness."

The young king followed quickly, trying not to breathe in
the wet, fetid stench. Lancelot was right: the rest of the castle
might be crumbling, but the real Royal Rot was hidden down
beneath. Tedros was glad he hadn't come alone.

"Has the prison always been here?" he asked the guard.

"Far as I know, Your Highness. Suppose the old kings
enjoyed the thought of swimming idly while their prisoners
festered below them. I'm not much older than you, so don't
take my word for it. Started my duties here only a few months
after they packed you off to school."

"How does one even become a guard at Camelot?" Tedros
asked, guilty that he didn't know the answer. In fact, he hadn't
ever remembered talking to a guard before. Growing up, he'd
treated them like wallpaper.

"We go to school for it, Your Highness. Not all children
get to attend the School for Good and Evil. Though I certainly
wrote many a letter to the School Master, begging him to make
me an Ever," said the guard, starting to defrost.

"What kind of school did you go to?" Tedros prodded.

"An ordinary one, Your Highness. The Foxwood Boys

School for Conservative Education," the guard answered. "No magic or wizardry or fingerglows for us. No princess or king will ever ask our names. Storian won't write 'em in a storybook. Unless we stumble into one. My mate from school almost got his name in *The Tale of Sophie and Agatha*—served breakfast at his inn to the League of Thirteen before the war against the School Master. But most of us go on to be blacksmiths and bricklayers, far away from any real adventure. I was a lucky one. Kingdoms come to the schools looking for the toughest boys for their royal guards. Had to undergo a whole lot of tests to prove my loyalty to Good. In the end, Camelot and Foxwood both wanted me. Foxwood's home, but I couldn't turn down a chance to serve King Arthur's kingdom."

His expression changed. "Foxwood's been under attack by a band of trolls, though. Dad's a footman for the king; troll set fire to his carriage and snapped his arm in two. Can't work anymore, so I've been sending my wages home so he can feed my mum and sisters. No one knows who these trolls work for. Mum wrote, asking if Camelot was going to intervene. Lots of kingdoms asking the same question, she says." He glanced hopefully at the young king.

Tedros stood straighter. "I'm calling a summit."

The guard stared at him. "A summit?"

"Get all our allies together and build an army," Tedros said authoritatively. "That's what kings do."

"Oh." The hope went out of the guard's eyes. "And here I grew up with legends that your dad stormed into battle bare-chested and slayed villains himself," he said. "Made-up stories,

I bet. He must have called summits too. Can't always trust a pen to tell the truth, can you?"

Tedros looked at him. But they were at the end of the stairway now. The guard pointed down a long dark hall. "Prison's this way, Your Highness."

"I'll go on my own," said Tedros.

"But I should take you—"

"My meeting with the prisoners is a private one, guard," said Tedros, eager to be alone again. "You may return to your post."

The guard hesitated. "Are you sur—"

"*Go,*" said Tedros sharply. "Close the door behind you. That's an order."

The guard didn't flinch. "As you wish."

Tedros watched him go—

"Guard?"

The man turned.

"What's your name?" Tedros asked.

The guard looked surprised. "It's Kei, Your Highness."

Tedros gazed right at him. "I promise to make your home safe again, Kei."

Kei smiled. "I'll tell my mum, Your Highness. Kings don't often make promises they can't keep."

Tedros watched him hustle back upstairs. He waited until he heard the echo of a heavy door closing and the *thud* of stone.

Then the young king stepped off the staircase and moved into the hall, the glint of his crown fading into darkness.

Tedros thought the advisors might be dead.

Moving through the stale dungeon, he'd cast his gold fin-gerglow on empty cell after empty cell, seeing nothing but mold-speckled walls, desiccated roaches, and rows of thick iron bars. Rulers didn't make a habit of trapping criminals inside the bowels of their own castles, but in most kingdoms, Good or Evil, town jails were overcrowded, unsecured, and rife with corruption. (Indeed, the one and only time the Sher-iff of Nottingham caught Robin Hood, the rogue escaped the Sheriff's prison.) Kings and queens had learned to house their most significant enemies under their own roofs. But as Tedros approached the last cell, he couldn't hear a peep from the advisors, not a word or a breath or a snore. Had something happened to—

"Long live the So-Called King," sang a low, smoky voice.

"Long live the Cowardly Lion," sang a high, jingly voice.

"Long live the Worthless Son," sang a hissy third.

Tedros took a deep breath, pausing in front of the pitch-dark cell.

Not dead after all.

He lifted his glow, lighting up the inside.

Three old women leered back at him, each an identical replica of the other. Bristly salt-and-pepper hair hung down to their waists, their stick-thin legs jutting out of tattered gray tunics. Their skin was shriveled and coppery, their necks and faces elongated with high foreheads, slim noses, match-thin lips, and almond-shaped eyes. Tedros thought they looked like pale versions of the mandrill monkeys that defiled his coronation.

"A few more wrinkles since the last time you saw us," said the low-voiced one. "Alpa, especially."

"If anyone's lost their looks, it's you, Bethna," said the high-voiced one. "Besides, we didn't see much of the young prince before he went off to school. Avoided us like poison once we became his father's advisors. Omeida, especially."

"Maybe because I'm the prettiest," said the hissy one. "Our little Tedros doesn't like pretty girls. Just look at his princess. Got a good peek at her when she came to the castle."

"We all did," said Bethna.

"Before we were *illegally* jailed by that hideous knight," Alpa scorned.

"Proof Tedros is his mother's son, at least," rasped Omeida. "They share poor taste in mates."

The three hags cackled.

Tedros kept his cool. He'd had experience with covens trying to rile him up.

"Reason I avoided you when I was younger is because I didn't trust you," he said glacially. "For years, you'd been standing on stoops in Camelot's square, preaching against my father. You called him Merlin's puppet. You called my mother a two-faced tramp. You demanded Excalibur be returned to the stone and a new test held to find the 'one true king.' The king so strong and powerful he would reign forever. The king who would make Camelot great again." Heat seared Tedros' cheeks. "No one listened to you. Everyone knew Camelot was already great because of its king. Because of my *father*. No one thought of the three Mistral Sisters as anything other than demented, delusional *freaks*."

Bethna gripped the bars, gnashing uneven teeth. "Then why did your father bring us *here?*"

"Because after my mother and Merlin left him, he became a paranoid drunk," Tedros retorted. "He started to trust the *Royal Rot*. And you. He fired all his old counselors, thinking they were spies for my mother. And he brought you into his castle as his advisors because some of the things you'd preached on your stoop had come true. He began to think that you could help him become that one true king you'd spoken of. A king of infinite power who could live forever. But instead, you used him and his kingdom and watched both die. Well, now it's my turn to watch *you* do the same."

Alpa exhaled, looking bored. "Just like his mother, isn't he?"

"Only sees what he wants to see," said Bethna.

"Never sees the whole picture," said Omeida.

"If only he'd listened more closely to our stoop talks," said Alpa.

"Like his father did," said Bethna.

"Then he wouldn't be in this predicament, would he?" said Omeida.

Tedros had enough. "I've seen the ledgers. The 'Camelot Beautiful' funds are a fraud. You took all our gold and hid it somewhere."

"Check our pockets," Alpa quipped.

"Give us a good frisk," Bethna said.

"Tee hee," Omeida giggled.

Tedros felt his ears smoldering. "If you don't tell me where you hid it, I'll—"

"Shouldn't you be asking Lady Gremlaine?" Alpa mused. "She's the one up there while we've been down here minding our own business. Ask her."

"If you can find her," said Bethna.

Her sisters snickered.

Tedros furrowed. They knew his steward had left the castle? How? She'd only been gone a few hours—

Unless . . .

Kei had said Lady Gremlaine had the only other key to the prison. Had she been secretly in cahoots with these three this whole time? Had she deliberately been stonewalling Tedros meeting them? It was such an obvious idea—the advisors were the ones who'd brought her back to the castle—yet he'd never considered it until now. Lady Gremlaine had been so loyal to Camelot these past six months. Had his mother been right to mistrust Lady Gremlaine all this time? He had to find out what happened between his mother and his steward when his father was alive. . . .

"See that, Bethna? He's *thinking*," Alpa said.

"Like a candle without a flame," Bethna piped.

"Should stick to what he's good at," Omeida chipped in.

"What's that?" said Alpa quizzically.

"Nothing," said Omeida.

The trio tittered.

"Shut up," Tedros barked. "You set up the Camelot Beautiful fund long before Lady Gremlaine returned to the castle. You gave the orders to hide Camelot's money in that fund. And you know exactly where that money went."

"Indeed," said Alpa, slouched against the bars, biting her blackened nails. "To an endeavor far beyond the comprehension of your puny pea brain."

Tedros grabbed her by the throat through the bars, his fingers pressing into her larynx. "Tell me or I'll kill you."

"Touchy touchy," Alpa wheezed.

"Even that ugly knight behaved better," sneered Bethna, sidling beside her.

"Go ahead. Kill all of us," said Omeida, flanking Alpa's other side. "But it would be a very poor decision. Things are just beginning, little boy."

"At the Four Point, the *real* story begins," said Alpa.

"Four Point?" Tedros said urgently. "What about the Four Point—"

"You'll need us when he comes," said Bethna.

"Who? Your White Knight?" Tedros mocked. "In six months, no one has tried to rescue you. No loyal spies have tried to kill me. No one has made a peep over your arrest. So tell me, Sisters Freaks, who is coming that will make me need you?"

The sisters leaned in, grinning. "*The Snake*," they hissed.

It hit Tedros like a blow to the chest. He let go of Alpa's throat, fumbling for words: "Y-y-you know who he is—"

"Your father did too," Alpa offered.

"That's why he gave you your test," said Bethna.

"A test you failed," Omeida cracked.

They hewed together, like a three-headed serpent.

"War is coming, little boy," Alpa crowed.

"War between the Lion and the Snake," said Bethna.

"The winner will be the one true king," Omeida added.

They jammed their faces between bars: "The one with *Arthur's blood*."

Tedros felt nauseous, his heart sucked into his throat. It was what the Lady of the Lake had told Sophie. The same two words.

"I don't believe you," he said, faking calm. "No one has Arthur's blood besides me."

"The Snake does," Alpa corrected.

"You're lying," Tedros attacked.

Bethna yawned. "Only a half-wit confuses lying with the withholding of information."

"Tell me, then," Tedros pressured. "Tell me who the Snake is."

"Tell you where the money is. Tell you who the Snake is. Tell tell tell tell," Alpa mimicked.

"Besides, it's obvious," Bethna taunted.

"Staring at you right in the face," said Alpa.

"Only you don't want to see it," said Omeida.

"Should we spoonfeed the poor boy?" Bethna simpered to her sisters.

"Only if he feeds *us* better food," Alpa proposed, picking up a brass cup of murky water off a rusty tray in the corner of the cell. She shunted the tray towards Tedros under the cell door. It had a bowl of gruel crawling with ants.

"Done," said Tedros.

"Ham and mashed potatoes?" said Alpa, wide-eyed.

"Done."

"Chicken livers and wine?" said Bethna, hopefully.

"Done."

"Caviar and rampion salad?" said Omeida, breathless.

"Done, done, done. You have my word," Tedros hurried, his face glowing red. "Tell me who the Snake is. *Now.*"

"Tell him, Alpa," Bethna sighed.

Alpa sipped her water, eyes on Tedros. Then she stalked towards him, step by step. "Should have just asked your mousy old mum. She knows everything no matter how dumb she plays," she crooned, glaring hard. "But a deal is a deal, little boy. You want to know who has Arthur's blood? Then listen closely. . . ."

She slipped her face through the cell bars, her nose almost touching his. "The Snake's name is . . ."

She splashed her dirty water in his face. *"Ring a king a bees will sting so dance a timba tumba!"*

Her sisters screeched laughter.

"Fools," Tedros spat, wiping his face. "You're as crackbrained

as you were when you were raving on your stoops for coins. Let's see how you do with no food for a week!" He kicked the tray back under the bars, sending bowl and gruel flying and the women cowering. Vibrating with anger, Tedros turned for the stairs. "No one in this world has my father's blood but me. You hear me? No one! No uncle or brother or sister—"

"Or son?"

Tedros stopped dead in his tracks. He whirled back towards the cell, staring into its dark, empty silence.

"What did you say?" he breathed.

He lit up the cell with his glow, but the sisters had flattened against opposing walls with catlike smiles.

"What did you say!" he shouted.

"Bush banana poo the panda!" sang Alpa.

The three Mistrals danced like hags around a cauldron. *"Bush banana poo the panda!"*

Tedros slammed the bars, yanking at the door, trying to get inside. *"WHAT DID YOU SAY!"*

But the three sisters just hopped and sniggered as Tedros ripped at their door the way he had his father's sword until at last he showed his teeth through the bars—

"I'm going to *kill* the Snake," he vowed. "And then I'm going to kill *you.*"

He raged down the hall and up the stairs. Breathing fire, Tedros threw his weight against the stone door—

It didn't move.

"Kei!"

He wasn't waiting to build an army. He wasn't waiting for

summits or wizards to be a king. He wasn't waiting for anything anymore. He'd ride to the Four Point right now and find this Snake.

Blood pumping, Tedros pummeled the door, drowning out the cackles from the dungeons below.

Tonight the Lion would roar.

17

The Map Room

S ophie should have been thinking about the Snake.
The Snake that had Arthur's blood. The Snake that had terrorized the Woods. The Snake that had killed their friend and would kill them next.

And yet, she couldn't stop thinking about hydrangeas.

"The whole castle's crawling with them," she whispered to Agatha, nodding at the thousands of pom-pom-shaped flowers in pink, purple, and yellow blanketing every inch of Castle Jolie. "I loathe hydrangeas, Aggie. They look like human brains. Just being around them makes me faint—"

"*Shhh!*"

Agatha snapped,

then kept on whispering to Nicola.

Sophie stewed as the chain gang pulled her along, deeper into the royal castle, the young pirate named Thiago with the tattoos around his eyes leading them on foot. The other pirates had remained outside the castle on their horses, sneering down at the crew as they shambled through the open doors like dead men walking to the gallows. Sophie watched the boys deliver each kid a demeaning kick in the bum—Hester, Anadil, Dot, Hort, Bogden, Willam. . . . But when it came Sophie's turn, sunburnt Wesley simply smirked and gave her a frightening little *hisssss*.

Which made it all the more foolish that with the Snake moments away, Sophie was offended by flowers. But it wasn't really the hydrangeas that were bothering her, though she did hate everything about this castle: its birthday-cake colors, its cloying, candy-cane scent, its treacly portraits of the royal children frolicking with dogs, and its endless loop of music, playing Jaunt Jolie's annoyingly catchy anthem through flowered walls (*"Tipple Top, Joy and Jaunt / Come and Be Jolie!"*). No, the real reason Sophie was annoyed was because she'd just saved everyone's noses in the pavilion with her brave performance and no one seemed to care—especially Agatha and Nicola, who kept whispering to each other like Flopsy and Mopsy.

Sophie couldn't fault Agatha for having another friend. Aggie was perfectly free to consort with whoever she pleased, including a first-year Reader with a bad attitude.

So why, then, did Sophie feel so upset?

She'd been so distracted by her reunion with Agatha and

all the action of their new quest that she hadn't noticed a creeping emptiness returning—the same emptiness that had made her impatient with her students at school, increasingly bored with her Dean's duties, and eager to comb Camelot's tabloids for sordid rumors about its new king.

And yet, Sophie hadn't been able to put a finger on *why* she felt this way.

She was happy being Dean, wasn't she? That was the Ever After she'd worked so hard to find and at the end of this quest she'd go right back to it, just like Agatha would go back to a wedding and a crown. Yet unlike Agatha, Sophie would have no one by her side . . . well, at least not the way that Agatha had Tedros.

But that was *fine* with her. Truly. She might flirt with delectable Everboys at parties and ogle a few of her own sultry Neverboys during school assemblies, but she'd learned her lesson with Tedros and Rafal. No boy could ever really understand her. She was too strong and empowered and . . . *complicated*. Boys always wanted her to change and she didn't want to change. Not when she'd finally figured herself out. She'd be far better off staying out of that swamp for a long, long time.

No, the only person Sophie needed was Agatha. Agatha understood her. Agatha balanced her. Agatha didn't expect her to change. Which is why Sophie had been so happy these past few days with her best friend back in her life. But seeing Agatha confide in this Nicola girl the way Agatha had once confided in her made Sophie realize how fragile this happiness was.

It was ironic, really. Agatha would have been happy living in Gavaldon forever with Sophie. But it was Sophie who had been determined to leave and find her own life.

Now it was Agatha who had her own life.

A life that didn't depend on Sophie anymore.

She heard Nicola whisper her name and Sophie promptly goosed Agatha with her knee: "Are you two *talking* about me?"

Agatha scowled. "We're talking about our plan to fight the Snake!"

"So now I'm not good enough to help you plan?"

"I'll tell you the plan if you're *quiet*," Nicola said.

"See how she talks to me?" Sophie mewled to Agatha.

"Because you're acting like a mopstick," Agatha scolded.

"You ungrateful Brutus. Not one word about how clever I was out there defusing those vile men, not one word of appreciation—"

"Sorry, we've been busy planning how not to *die*—"

"I remember when instead of gossiping about me with first years, it was me and you who made plans!"

"You *are* the plan, you idiot!"

"*What?*" Sophie blurted loudly.

The chain yanked to a halt. Slowly the two girls looked up to see Thiago glaring daggers at them from the head of the line.

Dark silence fell over the hall, punctured by gay sounds of singing: "*Tipple Top, Joy and Jaunt*—"

The pirate stabbed his sword into a flowered wall and the music squawked and petered out. He gave the girls a last glower of warning and the death march resumed.

Agatha and Nicola stared Sophie down.

Sophie reddened. If she was indeed the team's plan to fight the Snake, now she'd have to do it without knowing what the plan was.

Steeling herself, she followed the line into the Royal Keep, the king and queen's private residence, as evidenced by the preponderance of children's bedrooms, cozy sitting rooms, and opulent bathrooms. Sophie peeked in, unnerved by an unmade bed, an open wine bottle in one of the sitting rooms, a wooden toothbrush askew by the sink. Signs of life but no one living there.

At the front of the line, Hester coughed in surprise, snagging the chain.

Sophie followed her eyes, as did everyone else—

The library was coming into view, a two-floor yellow-and-pink rotunda cased in glass. Inside the library, three giant steel cages hung from the high ceiling, each packed to the brim with maids, guards, stewards, and members of the royal family. Two shirtless teen pirates, one thin and dark, the other hoggish with pig-colored skin, were perched on the railing of the second floor. They took turns kicking the cages as hard as they could and watched them swing back and forth, tossing all the people inside like marbles while they screamed and cried, though Sophie couldn't hear any of it through the thick glass.

The pirates looked bored.

As one of them punted a cage, Sophie saw the King of Jaunt Jolie tumbling inside it, his royal robes slashed and stained, his crown-points speared with rotted fruit, as he tried to grip onto two bawling boys—the same little boys Sophie had seen playing with the dog in the foyer painting. (The dog was cowering beneath a woman's blue gown in another cage, anticipating the next kick.)

The line pulled Sophie forward and the library started to recede from view. Through the glass she met the eyes of the king, who spotted her as his cage stopped swinging. His eyes watered as he clasped his hands, appealing to her for help, his tear-stained boys tucked at his sides. Sophie could only gawk back like a tourist in a sadistic museum being pulled to the next display.

This man's wife has been killed for satchels of gold, she thought, sickly. *Were these his boys?* Sophie felt her own eyes grow wet. *His now-motherless boys?* Sophie thought of Honora's two young sons, just like these, who her father, Stefan, loved so much—

Agatha elbowed her and Sophie saw her best friend nodding subtly at the next cage about to be kicked. The one with the dog cowering beneath the woman in the blue gown. Only now Sophie got a good look at the woman's petrified face and gasped. It was the same face they'd seen on that poster in the pavilion.

The one stamped EXECUTED.

The Queen of Jaunt Jolie was *alive?*

Astonished, Sophie and Agatha watched the queen try valiantly to reach through her cage bars and touch her children and husband as their cage swung past—

The chain jerked Sophie and Agatha forward and the library was out of sight.

Dragged ahead, Sophie thought back to the Lady of the Lake, who'd looked just as tortured as the Queen of Jaunt Jolie. The Snake could have killed the sorceress in Avalon, but instead he'd drained her magic and left her feckless and afraid. He could have killed this queen too, but instead he peddled *news* of her death. And he could have left Avalon without a trace, but instead he'd left that map in Chaddick's hands to taunt them. . . .

He's always one step ahead. Like Evelyn Sader and Rafal used to be, Sophie thought. *And this one plays games too. Just like them.*

An unsettling thought crossed her mind. *But why? If he has Arthur's blood . . . if he thinks he can pull Excalibur . . . why play games?*

Sophie held her breath. *Was it really Camelot's crown the Snake was after? Or was he after something else? Something . . . more?*

The line halted in front of her and Sophie broke from her trance to see golden double doors at the end of the hall.

They opened magically, revealing a room Sophie couldn't quite make out from this far back in line.

Suddenly her cuffs split open. So did Agatha's, and the piece of chain between them levitated into the air, turning black and shiny like an eel before it flew off into the room, vanishing from view.

"You two," Thiago said, pointing a grubby fingernail at them. "Come here."

Sophie and Agatha clasped each other's hands.

The tattooed pirate gestured ahead with his sword, directing the two girls through the gold doors. Holding hands tighter, Sophie and Agatha stepped out of line and entered the room. They looked back at the pirate and the rest of their friends still chained in the hall, gaping through the doorway.

"He's waiting," Thiago said darkly.

Agatha swiveled to Nicola, eyes wide—

The door slammed shut, leaving Sophie and Agatha inside alone.

Neither girl moved.

"All that planning with your new friend . . . ," said Sophie softly. "And here we are. You and me. Like always."

Agatha didn't answer.

They peered around warily, expecting a trap.

"No one's here," Agatha said, letting Sophie's hand go.

The first thing Sophie noticed about the room is that it was enormous—as vast and high as one of the ballrooms in the School for Good and Evil, lined with tall pillars. There were no doors, no windows, and no furniture, except for a long black stone table at the rear of the room.

The second thing Sophie noticed was that the room was *green*. Whereas most of Jaunt Jolie featured Easter-egg hues, here the carpet, pillars, and walls were a deep, luminous emerald, textured with shiny, snakelike scales. The torches on the walls crackled with green flames. Sophie knew this color well: it was the color of her own eyes as well as the color of Rafal's old school that had sought to turn her Good classmates Evil. But here it felt out of place, as if they'd passed through a portal into another realm.

There was something that *wasn't* green, though, Sophie realized, looking upwards.

Six parchment maps floated in rows above the center of the room, each as big as a flag.

"It's a Map Room," said Agatha, moving towards them.

"A what?" said Sophie.

"Tedros showed me Camelot's on our first night in the castle. It was where his father used to meet with his Round Table. It had floating maps of neighboring kingdoms just like this. Tedros couldn't wait to hold meetings there with his knights . . . but he never got the chance."

Sophie saw sadness in her friend's eyes, but there was no time for that now. "Do you recognize any of the maps, at least? I don't see labels on them," she said, gripping one by its corner and holding it while it tried to sail off like a balloon. "This one looks like Avalon. See, here's the sea around the kingdom and the big gates and the lake—"

Her throat closed up. *"Aggie."*

The map had a three-dimensional toy figurine positioned on top of the lake. The same exact figurine they'd seen on her and Professor Dovey's enchanted maps.

The figurine was labeled CHADDICK, his name crossed out.

Stomach fluttering, Sophie let go of the map and rushed to catch hold of the next. More figurines inched across black, rocky terrain: RAVAN . . . ARACHNE . . . DRAX . . . . Agatha grabbed on to a map with clear-colored mountains: KIKO . . . GISELLE . . . HIRO . . . Another with purple hills had VEX . . . BRONE . . . MONA . . .

"They're our Quest Maps," said Sophie, instinctively touching the gold vial on her neck to make sure it was still there.

"No wonder he knows our names and faces and could see us coming. No wonder the quests are going badly," Agatha said breathlessly, watching KIKO's figurine inch across the map. "Sophie, he can track all our moves! That's how he sent thugs to every kingdom and sabotaged their quests!"

"But I thought Kiko's and Vex's teams were missing!" said Sophie.

"Not missing. Just not responding to Dovey's messages," said Agatha, glancing between maps. "But why do all the teams seem to be moving in the same direction?"

Sophie jumped up and snagged the next map, spotting a peanut-shaped shoreline, a pavilion on a hill, and a pastel-colored castle. "Here's Jaunt Jolie," she said, spotting figurines labeled SOPHIE and AGATHA against the castle, while HESTER, ANADIL, DOT, BOGDEN, NICOLA, and HORT were moving out the back of the castle in a single-file line through what looked like the royal gardens.

"The pirates are taking them somewhere," Sophie said.

Her eyes flared. On the opposite side of the castle, far from the pirates and the captive crew, she saw three more blue-labeled names on the map lurking in a forest: BEATRIX . . . REENA . . . MILLICENT . . .

"*Sophie*," Agatha choked.

Sophie spun around.

Agatha was holding on to the maps with KIKO's and VEX's teams, one with each hand, both threatening to tug her off the ground. Gritting her teeth, she muscled them like puzzle pieces next to the one Sophie was holding.

"Look at where they're going," said Agatha.

For a moment, Sophie didn't understand. Then she saw it. The missing quest teams were each headed towards a corner of their maps. So was RAVAN's team. So was the crew of the *Igraine*.

Four teams.

Four corners.

All meeting at the same point, a short distance from where SOPHIE's and AGATHA's figurines stood now.

"The Four Point," said Agatha. "They're all going to the Four Point." She looked at Sophie. "Which means the Snake's thugs didn't just sabotage their quests. They must have kidnapped them too. That's why they aren't responding to Dovey. Because all of them are in the Snake's hands."

The two girls slowly raised their eyes to the only map left, floating over their heads.

TEDROS, alone in Camelot.

Agatha stiffened.

"We don't even know if these maps are *real*," Sophie argued quickly. "Dovey said only the Storian can make a Quest Map. How can the Snake have the Storian's maps? This could be more hocus-pocus to scare us, just like he lied about killing the queen—"

But Agatha wasn't paying attention anymore. "Listen," she said.

A soft scratching sound filled the room, like a cat clawing at a window.

It was coming from the black stone table against the back wall.

The two girls approached, their shoes padding on the green carpet. . . .

A gold-covered book lay open on the table. Hovering above, a magical pen drew on a blank page: a painting of the two girls as they were right now, gazing at a black pen drawing in a storybook.

The book on the table looked just like the one in the School Master's tower that held their new fairy tale. And the pen floating over it drew in the same bold colors and clean lines as the Storian.

Only this pen didn't *look* like the Storian, Sophie thought, peering closer. It was black, for one thing, not silver. And it wasn't steel like the Storian; it was flexible and eel-like, as if made out of sticky black goo, contorting with every stroke. It looked a lot like the piece of chain that had magically released her and Agatha before it flew into this room. Plus, the pen didn't have those strange symbols carved into its side either. Instead, it seemed to be covered in . . . scales.

Beneath the painting of the two girls, it wrote a caption:

"One of them would die today. But which one?"

Sophie saw the horror in Agatha's face.

"It's lying, Aggie. It's not the real story. It's not the Storian—"

But Agatha was dead white, her eyes darting around the room. "This is how it happened before."

"What?"

"He wanted us to find this, Sophie. . . . Just like we did then . . ."

"You're not making any sense—"

"This is how we met the School Master. We found the pen and book on the table. The pen was drawing a picture of us that looked exactly like this one. Sophie, don't you remember?" Agatha backed away from the storybook. "We were alone in a strange room just like this. We were standing just like this. The Storian began our fairy tale in front of our eyes and then we heard the School Master say behind us—"

"It must suspect a good ending," a voice echoed.

The two girls froze.

The voice came from behind them.

18

AGATHA

The Pen That Writes the Truth

Agatha gripped Sophie's palm.

The voice was low and crisp.

Definitely a man's.

Holding tight, the two girls turned.

At first Agatha couldn't see anyone, the Map Room as quiet and
deserted as when they came in.

Then she saw him.

He was camouflaged into a
pillar, hanging upside down, his
body covered in the same shiny
green scales as the rest of the
room. His pose was like a
lizard's: legs in a crouch, his
torso flat against the column,
with one hand outstretched and

cupping the stone. Agatha could only make him out because of the whites of his unblinking eyes, glaring right at her, ice blue at the center.

Sophie squeezed Agatha harder.

Agatha knew why.

Rafal had those eyes.

He slithered down the column, his scales undulating along green stone like a snake through grass, his eyes never leaving the girls. As his hands touched the floor and he rose to stand, the scales on his body magically turned black, becoming snug black armor from neck to toe. He had Rafal's long and lean body, like a teenager's rather than a man's, muscles throbbing against his supple, skintight suit. His face, however, stayed green, his features obscured by the smooth, thick scales that shrouded his face like the School Master's mask.

As Agatha watched him come closer, her heart jumped.

The scales on his face and body were *moving*.

They rippled in gooey, wave-like ribbons that looked strangely similar to the pen writing in the storybook on the table. Only now there were hundreds of these scaly strips, like a mass of eels, crisscrossing up and down, right and left, as if his body was made out of them.

From the way Sophie was crushing Agatha's hand, it was clear she was seeing this too.

"Rafal?" Sophie whispered.

He circled them quietly, his well-built chest rising and falling with his breath, his scales gleaming in the green torchlight, until he spoke again.

"Once upon a time, two girls wanted to find their way home. That was how your fairy tale began. All along, the pen sensed a good ending. Why else would it choose two Readers to become legends?" His blue eyes sparkled through his mask. "And what an ending it was. One girl becomes Good's next queen. The other becomes Evil's future. And the boy they each loved becomes Camelot's Lion."

He sounds like Rafal too, Agatha thought. But how? The School Master was dead, his corpse shattered to ash by Tedros' sword—

Her muscles locked. *Unless the sword being stuck in the stone reversed the spell . . . Unless Tedros failing his test brought Rafal back . . . Can a sword do that?*

"But that's not how your story ends," he said, his tone sharpening. He looked at Sophie. "You're not Evil's future." He looked at Agatha. "You're not Good's next queen." He looked up at the map with TEDROS' name. "And he's not Camelot's Lion."

He continued to circle. "You won't believe me, of course. Because you trust the Storian. The pen that gave you a happy ending. The pen you think tells the truth."

His shoulder grazed Agatha's arm and she felt the eels on his body squiggle across her skin. She swallowed a scream.

"But just as there are two sides with Good and Evil, with Boys and Girls, with Old and New . . . there are also two sides to the Truth. And until now, there's only been one pen. A pen that says *I* am the Snake come into the Woods; *I* am the Snake here to take down the Lion . . . and *you* are the ones here to stop me."

He approached the black pen dangling over its painting of the girls.

"But what if there was a new pen? A pen that told a *different* truth?"

The storybook rose into the air, tilting towards Agatha and Sophie. It began to flip backwards through pages, the captions beneath the paintings lit up in green glow.

Agatha's heart fluttered as she saw a painting of Tedros, safe and sound, gathered with Merlin, Professor Dovey, Lancelot, and Guinevere at a dining table. But then she saw the caption—

Back at Camelot, the Snake plotted with his henchmen to keep his throne.

"The Snake?" Agatha blurted. *"Tedros?"*

"Henchmen?" Sophie said.

But the book had flipped back to a painting of Agatha and Sophie dragged through the pirates' pavilion on a chain—

The two girls were led towards the castle to meet the Lion.

"You're not the Lion—" Agatha fought.

Only there were more paintings of Tedros and more captions—

The Snake tried again and again to pull King Arthur's sword, failing every time. . . .

The Snake stood by and did nothing as kingdoms in the Woods appealed for his help. . . .

The Snake was a coward, so he let his princess take over his quest. . . .

But now the book returned to the very first page of its fairy tale. The painting of Chaddick dead on Avalon's shore, precisely matching the image the Storian had drawn in its book.

Except the caption was different—

Once upon a time, a Lion made its way into the Woods. Its plan was simple: take down the Snake.

The book snapped closed with a thundercrack, jolting the two girls, before it plopped onto the table.

"It's lies," Agatha spat. "All of it. That's the side you're on. Truth versus Lies. That's what this story is about. And *you're* the liar. Look at you! *You're* the Snake—"

"You of all people should know better than to judge by looks," said the Snake. "But if you listened closely, I've already told you how this story will end. With your fairy tale shattered and the real story laid bare. With everything you thought true turned *untrue*."

"But Tedros is the Lion! You're the villain here," Agatha retorted. "You have the whole story backwards—"

"Says *your* pen. Mine says differently," the Snake spoke calmly, using his finger like a wand and lifting the scaly black pen into the air over the stone table. Silvery smoke trailed out of its tip, playing out scenes in front of the girls. "Your pen says *Cinderella* is about a kind girl rescued from her wicked family; my pen says *Cinderella* is about a clever dowager trying to save her daughters from poverty, only to see an intruder steal the life she planned for them. Your pen says *Peter Pan* is about a hero who saves his friends from a lethal pirate; my pen says *Peter Pan* is about a brave, hook-handed captain who defends himself against the children who mutilated him. Your pen says *Rapunzel* is about a fair maiden seeking to escape her cruel mother; my pen says *Rapunzel* is about a witch promised a child as repayment for a crime, only to see a man violate the terms of agreement. . . ."

The ghostly smoke curled into the silhouette of a silver mask, blue eyes blinking beneath.

"And while your pen says *The Tale of Sophie and Agatha* is about two girls battling an Evil School Master . . ."

The pen's phantom mask turned green—

"My pen says it's about a young man's soul traveling through generations, who finally found True Love with a girl . . . only to learn it was a *Lie*."

The smoke dissipated, revealing the green-masked man behind it, his gaze on Sophie.

"I-i-it's not possible," Sophie sputtered. "You can't be back—"

But from the way Agatha saw her looking at him, Sophie seemed to have no doubt he was.

"It all comes down to this. Your pen thinks I'm the Snake.

My pen thinks I'm the Lion. So which pen is right?" he asked. "Yours that writes Lies?" He glared at the two girls, his black, scaly pen spinning over his black, scaly hand. . . .

"Or mine that writes the *Truth*?"

Instantly all the scales of his body broke apart into a thousand eels, lifting off him like puzzle pieces and suspending in midair, so that for a moment his head was separated from this fractured body. The slimy eels squirmed as they floated, with no visible heads or tails, each one identical to the Snake's pen, which now hovered right above where his heart should be. But most startling of all were their squeals, high-pitched and knifing like the sound of amplified rats, growing louder and louder until Agatha and Sophie both cowered, shielding their ears—

In a flash, the eels went quiet and flew back into formation, rebuilding his shiny black suit.

The pen had become part of him.

The Snake loomed over the girls. "We'll see which is right in The End, won't we?"

From the way his eyes shimmered, Agatha knew he was smiling.

She could see Sophie's face change: there was something here Sophie didn't recognize . . . something that didn't match up with her once-Evil prince. . . .

"Who are you?" Sophie breathed.

Agatha felt it too. The School Master had been Good's greatest nemesis. But the School Master believed in the Storian. The School Master believed in its Truth. Or at least the same Truth they did. This Snake saw Lies as the Truth and

Truth as Lies. For a second, Agatha was back at school, trying to reconcile two sides that once seemed so clear and were now blurring into one. . . .

Out of the corner of her eye, she saw the open book, lying on the table, the painting of her and Sophie lit by green torchlight—

One of them would die today. But which one?

More Lies?

Or was it the Truth?

Danger shot up Agatha's spine.

Get out of this room.

Get out of this room now.

But how? She could feel a word flitting through her mind like a fly, trying to get her attention. She caught it—

Plan.

"And yet you wear a *mask*," Agatha challenged. "For one who speaks the 'Truth,' hiding your identity is rather suspicious. Unless, of course, your face is so terrible you want no one to see it."

"I'm afraid that's *you*," the Snake threw back. "The girl who wears the mask of a queen."

Agatha didn't flinch, sticking to Nicola's plan. "We can understand why you'd hide your face, of course. The Lady of the Lake showed it to Sophie. The lake waters are magic. Preserved your reflection. Sophie saw it. Said you're the ugliest man she's ever seen—"

The Snake's eyes flicked to Sophie.

Sophie gawked at Agatha, as if she might be betraying her to save her own skin. But then Sophie saw her friend's expression. Just like that, Sophie understood.

"Agatha's right," Sophie confirmed, pivoting to the Snake. "The Lady of the Lake said that's why you forced her to kiss you. That's why you drained her of magic and left her a hag. Because you like to punish beautiful girls who don't want to be with you—"

"*Lies*," the Snake hissed.

"No more Lies than your *Truths*," said Agatha.

"Which means there's only one way to prove the real Truth," Sophie egged on. "Show us your face. Show us what you showed her."

He took this in, staring at her, and then began to circle, closer than before. Agatha could see his chiseled muscles cutting against the thin scales of his suit. She could smell him now: a cool, minty scent she hadn't expected, like a forest after a snowstorm. She could see Sophie stiffen slightly, smelling it too. Because he didn't smell like Rafal did. He smelled more like . . . Tedros.

"Your friend Chaddick thought he knew things about me," said the Snake, passing behind them. "Girls at school must have enjoyed him. Such lovely thick hair and big gray eyes. And not just handsome, but sharp too. Sharper than you two and your boyfriend at least. He put together all the clues. He found the answers that are lying right under your nose . . . Such a pity. If only he'd just gone back to his king and told him what he'd found. If only he hadn't tried to be a hero. But he thought he had a way to trap me. He thought he had the perfect plan. . . ." The Snake curved past Agatha's shoulder and moved in front of the girls. "The last thing he saw as he died on the shore was the sorceress supposed to protect him kissing the one who'd killed him. And the last thing he heard was her telling me how beautiful I am, just like a king named Arthur who once had my blood." He glowered at Sophie. "*That's* what became of dear Chaddick's plan."

Agatha could see Sophie's eyes dart to her. Rafal's ego could be stoked, his attentions diverted. But this Snake was onto them. And their plan.

"At least Chaddick wasn't a *coward*," Agatha intervened, quickly changing tactics. "If it's true you have King Arthur's blood, then show us your face. Otherwise it's just another Lie—"

Eels shot off the Snake's body like ropes, shackling Agatha to a pillar. Before Agatha could scream, a last eel gagged her, sticky scales twisting against her tongue.

Sophie paled in horror, her whole body shaking.

"Sweet things, aren't they?" the Snake said, caressing the eel in Agatha's mouth. "My little scims."

The Snake skulked towards her. Sophie retreated until her back flattened against the column next to Agatha, who flailed under the scims.

"I see why boys love you, Sophie," he cooed, trapping her against the pillar. "I see why so many want you as their own. Everything about you is . . . sumptuous."

He stroked her cheek, scales against skin. Sophie shivered, breath shallowing. Agatha could feel Sophie's hand move along the stone, trying to find hers.

"That was Rafal's weakness, wasn't it?" the Snake said, curling closer. "Kissing beautiful girls."

Sophie's clammy palm found Agatha's beneath her binds. Agatha held it tight, while trying to break free—

"And I too had the same weakness for someone in your story. Someone I called a friend," the Snake said to Sophie, pressing against her. "Someone kinder than me . . . Someone gentler than me . . . Someone who never went quite far *enough*." He gazed into Sophie's scared eyes. "Do you know who it was?"

Sophie choked out a word: "Me?"

The Snake laughed. "No, not you."

His long tongue licked at her lips. . . .

"Aric."

Agatha gasped, thrashing wildly against her binds. But two scims blindfolded her, lashing across her eyes. . . . Another squeezed her throat so hard she started to black out. . . .

She heard scims shriek with bloodcurdling madness, then Sophie screaming like she'd never screamed before.

Something ripped Sophie's hand from hers.

Agatha lunged blindly to find it—

Darkness pulled her under like a sheet.

19

Four Point

A scream tore through the royal garden.

"*Sophie*," Hort choked, taking off towards the castle, barechested and bellowing—

But he'd forgotten he had six prisoners cuffed to him and they all went tumbling down into brilliant flowers, Hort included, like friends playing Ring Around the Rosie.

Nicola groaned, gashed badly by a pink rosebush, thorns still stuck in her

skin. She looked to Hort for help, but he was up and running again, trying to pull the other bodies towards the castle. "The Snake has her! Sophie needs me—"

A force held him back, keeping him running in place, slipping and sliding on flower petals.

Furious, he swung around to see Thiago stepping on the chain while sunburnt Wesley puffed on a cigar beside him.

"Thought the Snake killed 'em already," Wesley groused.

"Took the two girls. Rest comin' to the Four Point," said Thiago, studying Hort with his tattooed eyes.

"Four Point?" Wesley raised his brows. "Should be quite a show, then."

The pirates snickered before they each curled the chain around their boots and yanked it, sending the kids swinging to their feet and stumbling forward.

As they trudged through the hot, humid gardens, Hort kept peeping back at the castle.

"Hey, why does that pirate keep giving you strange looks?" Dot whispered in front of him.

Hort looked up and saw Thiago eyeing him again as he muttered something to Wesley.

Hort tried to keep his face in shadow.

"You know him, don't you?" Dot said.

"Shhh," Hort whispered. "He's Smee's son. I recognize him from a Pirate Parley that Dad took me to in Neverland."

"Smee? Captain Hook's henchman? You're *friends* with his son?" Dot retorted. "Then why are we chained up here like dogs—"

"Because I *killed* Smee, you fool."

Dot stared at him.

"Last year during the war against Rafal," Hort whispered. "Granted it was Smee's zombie, but even so. If he recognizes me, we're dead meat. Luckily Thiago hasn't seen me for a few years and I've buffed up and changed my hair, but not enough that he won't figure it out if we don't stop *talking* about it."

Hort looked back anxiously at the castle again—

"Hort, sweetie. We're well aware the Snake has Sophie," Dot simpered. "We all heard the scream and we're scared for her. Well, not really her, since she's horrible, but Agatha at least, since she's the only one who can command our ship and get us out of here. Meanwhile, we've been taken captive by pirates, are being marched to our doom, and this chain not only won't turn into chocolate, but I'm also pretty sure we saw a piece of it turn into an *eel* back there and fly away. So if I were you, I'd stop worrying about rescuing Sophie and use those lovely buffed-up muscles of yours to rescue *us*."

"I thought weasel and Sophie were old news," said Anadil in front of Dot.

"Left 'new news' crying with thorns in her bum," said Hester in front of her.

Hort glanced back at Nicola, who averted her eyes. Hort sighed gloomily. Here he thought he'd moved on to a girl who was smart and pretty and normal, a girl who actually liked him for his weird, scuzzy self, and then when it came time to show her he liked her too . . .

He'd picked You-Know-Who instead.

Again.

He forced himself to think of other things, like why they were heading to the Four Point . . . or how that piece of chain had turned into a flying eel . . . or where Beatrix's quest team was. . . .

But Sophie's wail still echoed in his head.

Is the Snake torturing her?

Will I ever see her again?

Is she . . . dead?

He whirled around, but the castle was obscured by colorful groves, which seemed to have sprouted up around him. He squinted over lilac hedges—

"Would she rescue you?" Dot asked, staring at him again.

Hort frowned. "Um, I don't think that matters—"

"Would Nicola rescue you?" Dot asked.

Hort blinked.

"It does matter, then," said Dot, archly.

She turned back around.

Hort's eyes widened as a tree sprinkled white petals on his hair like wedding rice. *It's that simple, isn't it?* If he stopped being an idiot, he could have a girlfriend right now. A *real* girlfriend kinder than Sophie and more attentive and definitely less psycho . . . a girlfriend he could take to Halloween haunts and go swimming in the school pool with and dance with at No-Balls and collect fresh beetles to lay on his dad's grave every Sunday . . .

"Wait, the Four Point is *Camelot's* land," he whispered to Dot suddenly. "Isn't that what the beaver said? There's a chapter about it in *A Student's History of the Woods* too. . . . It's a memorial to King Arthur. No one is allowed there, Good *or* Evil. . . ."

"Didn't learn much in history, to be honest," Dot whispered back. "First Sader dies teaching it and then his sister takes over and teaches us the *wrong* history and then *she* dies and then the School Master takes over and then *he* dies and now you're teaching history, which means *you'll* probably die soon, especially since the Storian didn't include you on our quest to begin with." Dot pursed her lips. "Goodness. I really shouldn't think out loud."

"Forget all that," Hort said, frowning. "If no one's allowed on Camelot's land, why are they taking us there?"

"Because then Camelot's *king* will have to rescue us," Hester cut in, glaring back at them. "A king whose sword is stuck in a *stone*."

"Tedros without his sword . . . ," said Dot. "Doesn't inspire confidence, does it?"

"We need to escape *now*," Hester demanded. "And by 'we,' I mean the whole crew, Agatha, Sophie, and Beatrix's team included. Questers stick together at all costs."

"Can't you turn into a man-wolf and bust us out of here?" Anadil said, swiveling to Hort.

"I can't wolfify with my hands like this; I need to point my glow at my chest," said Hort. "What about your rats?"

"Thugs got them too," Anadil moped.

Hort peered over her shoulder to see her three pets trapped in a chain link, heads squeezed through the loop and tiny feet dangling, like a rat version of an iron maiden.

Meanwhile, Hester's demon jangled its chains as if to pre-empt the question.

"So we got nothing," said Hort.

"Except the word 'wolfify,'" Dot wisped, eyeing his sweaty chest. "So sensual."

Hort was stonefaced.

"We need to talk to Nicola," Dot added, clearing her throat. "She saved our life twice. Maybe she can do it again."

Everyone looked at Hester for approval, Anadil included.

Hester grimaced. "Fine."

They glanced back at Nicola, concealed behind Willam and Bogden, who were still twittering. From what Hort could see of her, Nicola was gazing off glassily into the gardens.

"How can I talk to her from here?" Hort asked Dot.

"Send a message through us," a voice said.

Hort turned to see Willam eavesdropping.

"We've been trying to come up with our own plan to help us all escape," said Willam, red hair glinting in the sun. "I can't do magic and neither can Bogden because he says he doesn't have a fingerglow yet. But we figured out we're both good at fortune telling. Oh, and playing bongos."

"Helpful. Ask Nicola what we should do, then," said Hort.

Willam whispered to Bogden, who whispered to Nicola.

Nicola suddenly looked alert, meeting Hort's eyes for a half-second, before she whispered to Bogden, who whispered to Willam, who swiveled to Hort—

"She says this is like the story *Uncle Miyazaki*. If we can't bust off the chain, we all have to work as one unit. Like a snake, with Hester at the head and Nicola at the tail. That is, if Hort still remembers who Nicola is. She told me I had to say that verbatim and make sure everyone heard."

Hester, Dot, Anadil, Willam, and Bogden glowered at Hort.

"Well, tell her that if we get out of this alive, I'll take her on a date to Dumpy's Dumpling House," Hort promised.

Willam whispered to Bogden, who whispered to Nicola, who sent her reply up the chain—

"She says Sophie can't come on the date and that it can't be at a place called Dumpy's," said Willam.

"Beauty and the Feast in Sherwood Forest is exquisite," Dot offered. "Robin Hood took me there once. I didn't tell Daddy."

Hort gave her a strange look before turning to Willam. "Tell her she has a deal. First date. Somewhere romantic. Just me and her," he said, smiling, which Willam was about to pass down the chain, but Nicola had gleaned the message because she was smiling too.

"Glad you have your love life sorted since we're about to *die*," Hester snarled. "How are we supposed to work like one unit when there's seven of us on this chain, including two first years and an *altar boy*—"

But the pirates were watching now, clearly listening, and Hester went mum.

Thiago gave Hort another knife-sharp look before murmuring to Wesley.

Ornate gates lay ahead, made of blue-and-white porcelain,

marking the end of royal property. Though the gates were unlatched with plenty of room to pass through, Wesley kicked them ajar with his silver-tipped boot, shattering the bottom of a gate. Doves scattered from the trees above.

Dad was a pirate and never acted like these goons, Hort thought. That's because he and his dad had gone to school, where they'd learned that even though Good and Evil were eternal enemies, the two sides were in balance. The two sides had *respect*.

Except the Snake and his minions had no respect for Good *or* Evil. They attacked both sides the same.

A troubling thought dawned on Hort. If the Snake didn't have respect for either side, what did he have respect for? And what would happen if he gained control of Camelot? You'd have a king of the most powerful realm in the land of Good and Evil who spat in the face of both.

What would happen to the Storian? he thought, chest pounding. *What would happen to the Woods?*

The broken gate creaked behind him, reminding him of Sophie's scream. Goose bumps peppered his skin. For all they knew, Sophie and Agatha were dead by now. . . .

Sooty clouds seeped into the sky, veiling the sun, and a damp cool wind snaked into the garden with a soggy, moldy smell. Hort could see the path widening ahead, the trees and clover growing sparser around it.

He heard something now, drifting in on the wind. A dark rumble, like an elephant shaking the earth.

"What is that?" Hort whispered.

It was getting louder now, slashes of high-pitched noise piercing the thunderous roll.

"Whatever it is, it doesn't sound good," Willam said behind him.

The young pirates peeked back and grinned.

The path was gone entirely now, the forest thinning out to open grass that craned steeply uphill, with the ominous buzz coming from beyond it. Hort followed his fellow prisoners up the slope, his legs burning, pushing the limits of fatigue. He could hear Dot panting and Bogden's puny wheezes, but no one flagged, the amplifying rumbles propelling them forward. Hort's heart beat faster, surging blood into his muscles, begging him to run and get his friends out of here as fast as he could. But there was no escape from what was coming. It was time to find out the Evil they faced.

Soon they were at the crest, sopping with sweat. Thiago and Wesley fell back with leering smiles, ceding way for their captives to see what lay down below.

The seven crew members huddled together in a ball, the chain folding around their bodies. They peered over the hill.

Hort instantly felt sick.

From his vantage point, he could see four kingdoms in the distance converge on a plot of land in the middle, about 100 yards wide and 50 yards long. From the east, he glimpsed the midnight-blue castle and rising pink moon of his home kingdom, Bloodbrook; from the south, the green peapods of Kingdom Kyrgios; from the north, the kingdom of Ravenbow, with its steaming rivers of blood and towers made of bone;

from the west, the outlying vales of Jaunt Jolie, awash in Easter-egg colors. All four kingdoms smashed up against the Four Point, sealed off by four walls made of frozen water, jagged and brittle, as if a waterfall had frozen midflow. The iced walls were at least fifty feet high over the Four Point, shivering with sonic roars.

But now Hort saw what was making the noise.

Bodies.

Thousands and thousands of them—and not just human: dwarves, giants, trolls, dwarves, fairies, nymphs, goblins, and more—assailing the frozen walls from every direction, screaming and kicking and battering them with weapons, revolting against what was inside.

Slowly, Hort's eyes lifted.

Inside the Four Point, a colossal gallows loomed beneath a pink-and-gray sky like an open-air theater. Dozens of nooses hung from beams above the high wooden platform, arranged in three distinct rows.

Only the nooses weren't made out of ropes, Hort realized, as they gleamed in the few scraps of sun coming through the clouds. They were made of thick black scales and instantly familiar. Because they reminded him of . . . *eels.*

That wasn't the worst part, though.

The worst part was that the second and third rows of nooses were already filled, the prisoners' heads slipped through the scaly black loops and their feet planted firmly on trapdoors beneath them. The moment the trapdoors opened, each person would fall through and be hanged.

High above the prisoners, Camelot's flag fluttered from a pole speared through the stage.

Heart racing, Hort tried to see past the empty first row of nooses to the faces of the prisoners in the second and third rows, but the darkening sky had left most of them in shadow—

"Isn't that the King of Jaunt Jolie?" Dot said.

As Hort's eyes adjusted, he made out the king's sullied robes and broken crown. In the nooses next to him were his two young boys and his queen—a queen that the Snake had already declared dead.

"Get everyone to *think* she's dead and then kill her in front of them," Hester murmured. "Make them grieve twice. What better way to scare people?"

"Not even Granny would have thought of that and she was the White Witch," said Anadil, unnerved.

Panicked citizens of Jaunt Jolie bashed against the iced walls in their pastel-colored clothes, screaming and begging for their leaders to be saved, for the young princes to be spared. . . .

As they listened to these pleas, Hort felt his fellow crew members instinctively huddle closer.

"Wait, that's the king of Bloodbrook!" he said, recognizing the great gray man-wolf who led his home kingdom, noosed up in the second row. Citizens of Bloodbrook, including dozens of man-wolves, beat the walls with weapons and tried to ram them down.

"Walls are still holding," said Hester. "Even with the Lady of the Lake powerless, whatever charm she put on the waterfalls hasn't broken yet."

"But if the walls are holding, how'd the prisoners get *inside*?" Dot asked.

Hester looked at her.

"Hester," said Anadil.

Hester tracked her gaze to a black-haired man in a noose with gold flakes in his long beard and hair.

"Pea-man," said Dot, remembering the Grand Vizier they'd interviewed to be School Master.

Ravenbow too had its queen strung up and its people rushing the frozen walls, desperate to set her free.

Once upon a time, leaders of Good and Evil fought over this piece of land.

Now they'd be killed on it together.

But there were no guards on the stage, Hort realized . . . no pirates or henchmen or executioners . . .

Dot was right. How had the leaders been captured?

And who was going to hang them?

"Hort?"

He turned and saw Nicola nestled in next to him.

"The first row," she said.

Hort followed her eyes to the empty nooses, black scales shining.

"There's seven of them," said Nicola, trembling. "And there's seven of us."

Everyone stared at her, overhearing—then at each other, then at Hester. But even the fearless witch looked afraid. So did her demon.

Nicola's eyes welled up. "I want to go home, Hort," she

whispered. "I want to see Pa."

Gone was the cool, unflappable girl, replaced by a first-year Reader far away from her real life.

It only made Hort want to protect her more. The way Nicola had protected him and their crew.

Then, out of the corner of his eye, he saw the spot where the two pirates had just been—

"They're gone!" Hort blurted, spinning to the group. "The pirates aren't here. There's no one guarding us! We have to run—we have to run *now*—"

A boy's scream came from the valley, rising over the roar: *"HELP!"*

Hort stopped cold.

Another scream echoed, this time a girl's: *"PLEASE HELP US!"*

Hort's face went white and he saw the three witches gaping at him with the same expression.

Slowly they looked back down at the gallows.

Not at the empty first row or the second filled with royal leaders . . . but at the third row, which they couldn't quite see. The row where the screams had come from. Screams that made Hort's stomach flip.

Because one scream had been Kiko's.

And the other scream was Ravan's.

"He has our classmates," Hort rasped, making out Mona's green skin . . . Brone's bald head and hulking frame. . . .

"Hey, guys," said Nicola—

"We're not leaving our friends down there," said Hester,

fear burning to anger. "Questers defend each other, no matter what. We have to help them."

"But how can we get over the walls if we're chained up?" Anadil asked.

"And how can we get through the crowd?" said Hort.

"*Guys*," Nicola said.

All eyes went to her.

"They're *gone*," said Nicola.

"We know the pirates are gone," Hort said, impatient, "that's why we need to go right no—"

But Nicola wasn't looking at where the pirates had been.

She was looking at the nooses.

The front row of them.

All missing.

"Huh? Where did they g—" Hort started.

Then he gasped.

So did everyone else, the chain of teenagers suddenly lurching backwards, each of them tripping over their feet—

Because scaly nooses were flying towards them, over the valley, over the crowd, like bats out of hell.

No one had time to scream.

The eels lashed around their necks like vises and ripped the crew into the air, bodies still chained in a line. Hort bucked madly, feeling Nicola choking beside him, but the nooses just squeezed harder, draining their breath, before all at once, the eels dragged the prisoners down towards the gallows, seven prey quivering before the kill.

20

The Lion and the Snake

S ophie awoke to the smell of roses.

She opened her eyes, feeling their petals drizzle down her back. A single wine-red bloom lay cupped in the lap of her baby-blue dress. Her body was moving, magically coasting past bushes and flower beds as if pushed by a strong wind. White leaves and florets fluttered from trees overhead like an enchanted snow.

I'm in a dream, she thought, her eyes still on the rose in her lap, its lush folds sparkling under a pink sunset.

Not only because she was magically gliding through a garden under someone else's power, but because the rose matched the one Tedros had thrown into the crowd on the first day of school, hunting for the girl who would be his princess . . . a rose Agatha had caught just like this . . . the happy ending to a fairy tale that hadn't yet begun. . . .

But now the rose was in Sophie's lap, which meant it *must* be a dream, for this rose wasn't meant for her. If there was one lesson the whole world learned from her fairy tale, it was certainly that.

Unless it isn't Tedros' rose at all, Sophie thought. *Unless someone else threw it and I caught it, just like Agatha caught her prince's. Which means this is a new fairy tale and this time I won't end up alone. There's someone else in this story . . . someone just for me. . . .*

Sophie looked up, curious . . . fearful . . . hopeful. . . .

Her face changed.

It was no dream.

Agatha glided beside her, bound, blindfolded, and gagged by the Snake's slimy, scaly scims. Not only that, but the entire back of her best friend's body was *covered* in scims like a coat of armor, from the dome of her hair, down to her calves, down to the soles of her shoes, not a shred of clothes or skin left bare. With high-pitched gurgles, like a chorus of helium-voiced rats, the scims pushed Agatha along, twitching and waggling, as she writhed blindly under her binds.

Sophie grew aware of the drizzling feeling on her back again . . . the one she'd dreamily ascribed to falling flowers. . . .

Dread rising, she peeked over her own shoulder and saw that she too was coated in thick, gooey scims, all the way down to her dainty slippers. Fear bolted her spine straight, upending the rose, which fell to the ground and smashed under her feet. A scream stalled in her throat.

"Aggie," she wheezed. "What do we—"

But Agatha shook her head sharply and Sophie read the gesture at once: *He's listening.*

Sophie's eyes darted around, looking for the Snake in the garden.

Where is he?

The scims were moving her faster now, through blue-and-white gates and up a steep grassy slope. Sophie looked at Agatha, who was unable to see or talk, her friend's body helpless to the scims. A swell of panic crashed over her. Sophie liked to pretend the two of them were a team, but in truth, it was always Agatha who took charge, Agatha who kept her safe. No matter how much of a witch Sophie could be, she was Agatha's princess, riding behind her on her white horse. Maybe that's why Agatha had been drawn to Nicola as a friend. Because she wasn't a spinning top like Sophie. Because with Sophie, Agatha always had to take the reins of the story when it counted.

Only now the roles were reversed, with Agatha left helpless. Which meant for once, it was Sophie who had the reins.

She tried to remember what had happened in the Map Room. Slowly it all came back to her . . . the Quest Map with their classmates' names . . . the storybook that called Tedros a Snake and the Snake a Lion . . . the new pen he vowed would shatter their fairy tale forever. . . .

All of these were pieces of a bigger plan, the Snake said. A plan Chaddick had figured out.

It's why he'd had to die.

The Snake wasn't Rafal. That much was clear.

And yet, he seemed to *know* her, Agatha, and Tedros intimately . . . as if he'd come from inside their storybook. . . .

Something had happened in that story. Something that made him want revenge.

So who was he, then?

Terror attacks.

Arthur's blood.

Tedros' crown.

All of it was connected. How?

Aric.

He'd been friends with Aric, he said. Close friends.

But Aric was dead, slain during the School Master's war . . . so the Snake and Aric had to have been friends *before* that. . . .

Could the Snake have been a student at school?

She pictured the Snake's long, youthful body . . . his lean, perfect muscles . . . his glacial blue eyes. . . .

Or was it someone Aric met before school?

Sophie's forehead throbbed. *Think harder.*

But all she could think about was the Snake pinning her against the pillar, with his minty Tedros scent, before he fractured into a thousand eels, which came flying towards her. . . .

That's when Sophie had passed out.

Now these same eels were plastered across hers and Agatha's backs, wheeling them around like corpses. Sophie felt faint once more, but she forced herself to stay conscious.

The scims pushed the two girls down the hill, through a gathering mist, the fading sun infusing it with a bruised-purple glow. Over the scims' loud burbles, Sophie heard dark rumbling ahead. But she couldn't see anything but thick, gray fog. . . .

Sophie coughed.

Not fog. Smoke.

Only now it was clearing and Sophie's eyes flared wide—

The scims drove them smack into a screaming mob, brandishing fiery torches and weapons under a darkening sky. The crowd spread as far as Sophie could see in every direction, converging from four different kingdoms around a walled-off plot of land.

The Four Point, Sophie thought. It's where her quest mates were headed on the Snake's Quest Map. Now she and Agatha were heading there too.

Sophie spotted Camelot's flag flying high above the Four Point.

Chills ran down her spine.

The Snake was bringing them all there for a reason.

Even so, the Four Point was still a hundred yards off with at least a thousand bodies in the way—

The scims paid no mind, barreling straight for the jagged-ice walls and thrusting the two girls into the crowd with reckless force. Sophie ducked her head, jammed between men and trolls, children and centaurs, scims gripping her tighter and tighter. She could hear the crowd as she squeezed through—

"King Tedros is on his way with his knights," a horned ogre said to his family.

"But I thought Camelot had no knights anymore," said his lumpy ogre daughter.

"Then he'll fight single-handedly," his humpbacked mother assured. "He's King Arthur's son."

"A useless king, that's what he is," groused her surly son. "Don't even have Excalibur."

"Watch your mouth, boy. Heard folk say they saw him riding down Glass Mountain," a pastel-dressed man cut in. "He'll be here soon—"

"And he'll make whoever's responsible for this *pay*," growled a troll.

Sophie's head jerked up. If they were all waiting for Tedros to save them . . .

That means they're on our side!

This whole crowd was on their side, Good *and* Evil! Everyone knew Agatha was Tedros' princess and Sophie his friend. Everyone knew their fairy tale—

She swiveled her head left and right, frantically making eye contact with the ogres and everyone else near her. But as the scims rammed her and Agatha through the crowd, no one seemed to notice. Confused, Sophie started bucking against her binds, knocking hard into people and creatures, who whirled around, peering angrily, but then went back to surging towards the walls.

Undaunted, Sophie cried out: "Help! Someone help us!"

A few people glanced in her direction, perplexed.

Sophie tried harder. "We need help! It's us, Sophie and Aga—"

A scim gagged her.

Can't anyone see us? Sophie thought, flailing wildly. *They're acting like we're—*

She stiffened.

The scims on her and Agatha's backs.

They were made of snake scales.

Which meant . . .

We're invisible.

Snakeskin was the one fabric that could hide its wearers, given the right hex. Sophie had used it for her own devilish designs at school; indeed, her famous snakeskin cape now hung inside the Exhibition of Evil, cased in a special gallery dedicated to her and Agatha's fairy tale. But now the Snake was cheekily ambushing her with snakeskin as if to turn her own fairy tale on its head. . . .

They were almost at the frozen walls. Just as Sophie could glimpse through them as to what lay inside, the scims yanked her and Agatha into the air, flying them up and over the walls, their backs caressing the Camelot flag flying over the Four Point. Embers of sun blinded her before they extinguished in the horizon, and it was only as she descended that Sophie could see what lay beneath her, illuminated by the crowd's torch flames. . . .

Gallows.

Sophie lost her breath, scanning three rows of prisoners to be hanged, their nooses made of oily black scims. The first row had Hester, Anadil, Dot, Hort, and the rest of her crew mates, still chained together, hands cuffed behind their backs. . . . In the second row, leaders of Ever and Never kingdoms were strung up by the neck, which had drawn the raging crowd, desperate to save them. . . . But it was the third row that startled Sophie the most, loaded with fourth years from the School for Good and Evil, kidnapped from their quests. These captives gazed fearfully into the crowd, unable to see Sophie or Agatha descending to the stage in front of them. Ravan looked gaunt, his once-flowing black hair crudely shaved; Mona's green skin was littered with bruises; Vex was missing a chunk of his pointy right ear; Kiko cried to herself, burn marks on her arms. More classmates teetered on trapdoors near them, all injured in one way or another: Brone . . . Giselle . . . Drax. . . .

The last light in the sky went dark as the scims parachuted Sophie towards the wooden platform, Agatha floating down next to her. Their feet touched the stage—

Instantly the scims scattered off them, stripping them of their invisibility and revealing them to the mob.

The crowd froze in shock.

Agatha spun around, finally able to see. She took in the stunned prisoners, her eyes assessing the scene like a panther's, her fingertip glowing gold. "The Snake . . . Where is he?"

Sophie scanned the stage, her fingertip glowing pink. "I don't see him!"

A buzz swept through the crowd, hopeful and intense—

"IT'S TEDROS' FRIENDS!" someone cried.

"THAT MEANS HE'S HERE!" shouted another.

"WE'RE SAVED!"

"Hurry up, you nitwits!" Hester barked at Sophie from the front row, demon strung up next to her. "Cut us loose!"

"No, the children first!" the King of Jaunt Jolie said—

Sophie was about to sprint for his young princes, but then she saw Agatha hadn't moved, her friend's eyes wide and pinned ahead.

Slowly Sophie turned to see the scims reassembling at the front of the stage, globbing and sticking to each other at lightning speed, until they'd reformed the Snake, his mask glimmering green in the mob's torchlight.

It's why Agatha had silenced her in the garden.

The Snake had been with them all along. Split up into scims on their backs, waiting for the moment to reunite.

Now the Snake's cold blue gaze crept across the crowd, which was silent as a tomb. "For thousands of years, you thought your pen told you the *Truth*," he said, voice resounding. "The pen of Good and Evil. The pen whose stories you have believed without the slightest doubt. And what does that pen tell you now? It tells you I am the one who attacks your kingdoms. It tells you I am Evil. That I am the enemy." The Snake paused. "But what if I tell you everything you think is Truth is *Lies*?"

His eyes moved to the flag flying over them. "You won't believe me, of course. No one will. Not even your greatest heroes," he said, glancing at Sophie and Agatha.

"You think a Lion is your only hope. You think only a Lion can save you. *All* of you. That's what Camelot promised. A Lion who can destroy Evil like me. A Lion with King Arthur's *blood*."

He looked back down at the people. "You wait for this Lion named Tedros. You wait for him to answer your prayers. Yet here we are on the Lion's land . . . with the Lion's princess . . . with the Lion's friends . . . with the rulers who call on the Lion to lead. . . . Everyone but the Lion *himself*," he mocked. "He stays in his castle while your kingdoms burn. He stays in his castle while his friends die. He stays in his castle like a coward."

He turned to the crowd. "Say it with me. 'Cowardly. Little. Lion.'"

Nobody made a sound.

The Snake stabbed out his finger and the noose around the youngest prince of Jaunt Jolie strangled him. The prince choked, legs twitching.

The crowd screamed in horror—

"*Say it with me*," the Snake hissed. "Cowardly. Little. Lion."

"Cowardly Little Lion!" the crowd shouted.

"So he can hear you from his castle in the sky," the Snake demanded.

"Cowardly Little Lion!" the crowd yelled louder.

"*He can't hear you!*" the Snake lashed.

"*COWARDLY LITTLE LION!*" the crowd thundered, shuddering the land.

The Snake dropped his finger and the prince's noose

relaxed, the young child wheezing for breath. His mother and father crumbled into sobs.

"Cowardly Little Lion indeed," said the Snake.

His eyes flicked to Sophie and Agatha. "Well, then. Let's see if he comes out of his *cage*."

He whirled to the mob and with a wave of his hand, snuffed out the sea of torches.

The stage plunged into darkness.

In the vast, empty night, two dozen nooses glowed green, fluorescing like electric eels, lighting up the prisoners with heads looped through.

At the front of the stage, Sophie and Agatha faced off against the Snake, awash in the gallows' alien green haze.

Beyond the iced walls, the crowd was hushed in the dark, like an audience in wait of a play. Sophie could see them looking back anxiously, searching for any sign of Tedros.

"Perhaps we shouldn't write off the Lion so soon. By now he knows of your predicament," the Snake said to the girls, the edge coming off his voice. "I'll give him ten more seconds to show his face."

Neither Sophie nor Agatha moved.

"Aren't you going to help your friends?" the Snake said serenely. "1 . . . 2 . . ."

"*Go!*" Kiko shrieked.

Sophie twirled to Agatha. "I'll take front row."

"He's lying, Sophie," Agatha breathed—

"3 . . . ," said the Snake.

Sophie took off, shooting the back nooses with her pink glow. Agatha unleashed her gold glow at the front row's.

"It's not working!" Sophie shouted—

"Magic won't break it!" said Dot.

"Try something else!" said Anadil, her three rats dangling from tiny nooses next to her.

"4 . . . 5 . . ."

"Break the wood!" Nicola cried, eyeing the beams over their heads.

Agatha and Sophie both fired at them—

The beams only turned thicker and stronger.

"6 . . ."

"Hurry!" Hester bellowed.

Sophie magically sealed the trapdoors around her feet, but the doors grew weaker, threatening to break.

"Spells are backfiring!" Hort said.

"7 . . . 8 . . ."

Sophie shot the frozen walls with her glow, hoping to shatter them and let the crowd storm in—

Nothing.

"9 . . ."

Agatha climbed the beams and tried to undo the nooses by hand. They shocked her like lightning and she fell to the platform—

"*10*," said the Snake.

The two girls turned to him, panting.

"And still no Lion . . . ," the Snake tutted. "So now the *real* show begins."

He opened his palm and a pack of playing cards appeared with a tuft of smoke. He spread them out in his fingers, revealing some of their faces—

Not card faces, Sophie realized. *Actual* faces. For each of the cards had a prisoner painted on it: Dot . . . Bogden . . . Nicola . . . the King of Bloodbrook . . .

"Each of you takes a turn picking a card," the Snake said to Sophie and Agatha. "Whoever you pick, their door drops."

The crowd drew a breath, cocking towards the horizon like panicked chickens. Surely Tedros would stop this. Surely he would slay this villain the way King Arthur had slain many before. . . .

"Why are you doing this?" Agatha rasped.

The Snake's eyes glittered like gems. "Ask my *father*."

He held out the deck. "Pick."

Sophie looked at Agatha, paralyzed.

Agatha slackened, her cheeks bright red.

Then she picked the first card, the back of it painted with the Snake's crest.

Her hands shook as she turned the card over.

The face on it was Kiko's.

The door under Kiko's feet dropped open but Agatha was already diving, snagging her friend by the legs and pulling her back onto the platform so she couldn't fall through.

It happened so fast that the crowd didn't make a sound.

Agatha stayed on her knees, hugging Kiko's calves with all of her strength, as Kiko hung from the noose at an angle. If Agatha let her go, her friend would drop and break her neck.

Which meant both of them were trapped in their position.

"Don't leave me," Sophie heard Kiko whimper.

"I won't," Agatha assured.

"Bad things happen when you leave me," Kiko said. "Bad things happen to all of us."

"Your turn," a voice said.

Sophie looked up to see the Snake glaring at her.

He held out the deck of cards.

There was a flatness in his eyes, a ruthless insistence on the rules of the game as if he knew precisely how it would end.

"Pick," he said.

Sophie did.

The card was Nicola's.

Across the platform, Nicola's trapdoor opened.

In a flash, Sophie sprinted across the stage and tackled the first year just before she fell through, shoving her to the side of the opening and holding her by the ankles.

Sophie looked up and saw Nicola goggling at her. Agatha too.

"Guess we're friends now," Sophie said to Nicola.

With no sign of Tedros, the crowd revolted, battering the walls with renewed force—

Suddenly, thirty young pirates broke through the crowd, seizing the hardest protestors from behind, swords to their necks. The rest of the mob went quiet with fear.

"It seems we have a dilemma . . . ," the Snake continued, watching the two girls in opposite corners, clutching their friends. "Because someone has to pick *next*."

Neither girl budged.

The terrified crowd glanced between them and the Snake.

"Ah, I see," the Snake said. "It seems you're both a bit tied up. Well, then."

He held out the deck in his open palm.

"*I'll* pick."

He turned the first card over.

Hort.

Sophie and Agatha whirled to each other. Either one of them had to let go of their friend or Hort would hang.

"Go!" Nicola said to Sophie.

"No! Stay!" Hort cried.

Tears fogged Sophie's eyes. She couldn't watch Hort die—

His trapdoor opened. The noose around his neck yanked tight.

Sophie and Nicola screamed—

Instantly, the rest of the prisoners in the row kicked their legs out, using the chain cuffed across them to swing like a five-headed dragon: Hester, Anadil, Willam, Bogden, and finally Dot, who thrust her legs and caught Hort's backside with her shins before he fell through the door. With every ounce of strength, she held him up by the tailbone, their bodies planked at right angles, like trapeze performers midflight.

Sophie buckled in relief, briefly losing grip of Nicola but catching her just in time.

Hort was dripping sweat, rope burns around his neck.

"Thanks, Dot," he croaked.

"Don't thank me, thank *Uncle Miyazaki*," Dot panted,

smiling over at Nicola. She looked back at Hort. "Though I'll take a date too if you're offering."

Hort coughed.

The Snake watched all of this, his body still, his green mask obscuring any reaction, except for his winnowing blue eyes.

"So much for the *rules* of the game," he said.

With a flourish, he flung the cards into the air, dozens of painted faces glinting in green glow as they fluttered to the stage.

Sophie locked eyes with Agatha, their hearts stopped.

Every trapdoor started to magically open, all the prisoners about to drop through.

The crowd reeled, preparing for mass carnage—

Suddenly fire-tipped arrows bombed down from the sky, just missing the Snake and igniting the wooden platform.

The Snake swiveled, taken by surprise, the gallows doors still half-open.

In the distance, the mob parted a path as two figures in buckskin tunics blazed through, astride a red-spotted deer: a blond shooting arrows from a bow as someone behind, dark-skinned with long brown hair, lit arrows on fire with her purple fingerglow. They were being chased by at least fifty bellowing pirates with swords and spears, trying to catch up with the sprinting deer. Sophie recognized the riders at once—

"Beatrix and Reena," Sophie marveled.

And the deer was . . .

"*Millicent*," Agatha realized.

More of Beatrix's arrows rained over the wall, aimed at the Snake—

He split into a thousand squealing scims, dispersing like leeches to elude them.

Reenergized, the crowd came to Beatrix's and Reena's defense, rushing headlong at the pirates, while onstage flames from the missed arrows started to spread.

Agatha whirled to Sophie. "Fire kills the scims! Just like fire killed Rafal's zombies!"

She grabbed one of Beatrix's missed arrows and lit Kiko's noose, searing away the shrieking eel and setting her classmate free.

Kiko blubbered: "I thought I was going to die and then I would see my beautiful Tristan up there in heaven and I would say—"

"*Kiko!*" Agatha said, glaring at all the prisoners still hanging.

"Good point," said Kiko.

Like a rabbit, Kiko dashed across the blazing stage, grabbing arrows out of the wood and lighting the scaly nooses on fire along with the chains between prisoners, starting with Nicola's.

"I have no idea who you are, but Sophie doesn't help *anyone* unless they're important," Kiko cheeped, before burning through Nicola's cuffs, which let Sophie drop the first year to the stage, grab one of Kiko's arrows, and start helping the others in the row, while Agatha took the second and third rows.

"Hurry, Sophie!" Agatha cried, as she freed the young princes of Jaunt Jolie. "The fire is spreading!"

Sophie ran to Hort first. But out of the side of her eye, she glimpsed Beatrix and Reena outside the iced walls, cornered by the pair of young pirates they'd seen kicking cages in Castle Jolie. The boys had stripped the Evergirls of their bows and arrows and were aiming the arrows back at their heads. Beatrix and Reena leapt off Millicent and hewed together, confronting the pirates with lit fingers. . . .

"Man-wolf. *Now*," Sophie ordered Hort as she freed him.

"Aye-aye, Captain," Hort said, lighting his fingerglow and bursting out of his breeches a mighty, hairy beast, before scaling the Camelot flagpole in a single bound and bellyflopping onto the pirates with a howl.

As Kiko, Nicola, and the other freed prisoners helped burn away more nooses, Sophie felt Agatha seize her from behind.

"Whole stage will collapse!" Agatha said, covering her mouth from the smoke. "We have to get everyone out of here!"

Sophie squinted up at the high walls that sealed them into the Four Point, while the war against the pirates raged beyond them. "But how can we get them over *that*?"

"Leave it to me," Hester grunted, prying between the girls, fingerglow lit. The tattooed demon on her neck engorged with blood, turning redder, redder, until it tore out of its chains and flew off her skin, swelling to three-dimensional life. Mumbling hissy gibberish, it began snatching prisoners from the stage, three at a time, starting with kings and queens, and ferrying them over the walls and to the ground beyond, where throngs of citizens shielded them and spirited them back towards their kingdoms.

"Move faster, Hester!" Agatha cried as the witch directed the demon with her glow from inside the Four Point. "Stage is burning up!"

"And I'm *on* the stage so believe me when I say I'm moving as fast as I can!" Hester berated.

Eyes watering from the smoke, Sophie weaved around the fires, intending to free Mona and Brone next—

But now she saw Hort's man-wolf slammed up against the glass wall in front of her by tattooed Thiago, who'd pinned the tip of his pirate blade against Hort's hairy belly.

"Knew I'd seen yer grubby lil' face before," Thiago seethed. "Scourie's son. Bragged ye'd be the first man-wolf pirate at Hook's Parley years ago. Took a blood oath to help us fight the Lost Boys. Instead ye turn round and kill Hook's captain like yer Pan's stooge. Ye killed my *father*." He dug his blade into Hort's stomach, drawing drops of blood. "Shoulda bragged ye'd be the first *fink*."

"I did what any true man would have, unlike your lot," Hort growled in pain. "You kill for money. You follow a leader with no soul. You're the *real* Lost Boys."

Thiago cut him deeper. "Bleats a pirate who killed one of 'is own."

"What I killed wasn't your father," Hort insisted.

"Tell yerself all the lies ye want," Thiago snarled. "But this I know fer sure. The thing I'm about to kill is *you*."

He gripped the sword hilt to run Hort through, but Hort

grabbed the blade by the tip and muscled it away from his stomach, the steel slicing into his hand. Before Thiago could react, Hort slapped him across the head as hard as he could with his big, hairy palm. The pirate wheeled wildly, swinging his sword and biting it into Hort's bicep, spattering the frozen wall with blood and obscuring Sophie's view.

Spinning around, Sophie saw Hester's demon had rescued nearly all the prisoners from the stage, with only her, Agatha, Hester, Anadil, and Dot left. On the battlefield, Willam, Bogden, Beatrix, Reena, and Nicola were fighting pirates with weapons flung at them by fleeing citizens—

Hester's demon swooped to rescue Sophie, his beady eyes flashing: *"Lookie missie witchie fishie!"*

"No, take the witches!" Sophie said, ducking his grab. "You three! Go help Hort!"

The witches gaped at Sophie, then at Agatha, as if they didn't trust Sophie could possibly be deferring her own rescue.

"*Go!*" Agatha cried.

Immediately the three witches hooked on to the demon's claws and flew up and over the walls. As he streaked down, Hester's demon attacked Thiago, blasting red firebolts from the demon's mouth, while Anadil's rats grew twenty feet tall and crashed into the fray, rampaging through pirates as the three witches rode on the rats' backs, shooting stun spells right and left.

Onstage, Sophie and Agatha were the only two left behind, pushed to the edge by the fires.

"Aggie, we don't have time for the demon to come back,"

Sophie said. "It's spreading too fast!"

"Maybe this'll work," said Agatha, thrusting her glowing fingertip into the air. Heavy rain started falling over the Four Point, dousing the blaze. It was one of Agatha's trusty spells from her first year at school—

Then, all of a sudden, the fires seemed to grow stronger in the rain . . . the orange flames turning a glowing emerald green. . . .

Agatha's eyes bulged. "What in the—"

But now there was something falling towards them, straight out of the sky: a deer bounding over the wall, hooftip glowing red, and landing on the stage, which half crumbled like a giant sinkhole, before the deer recovered, lurching for the two girls.

"Come on! Get on my back!" Millicent said.

Sophie and Agatha leapt onto her, just as the gallows imploded in the green flames. Millicent sprinted for the walls, her legs tensing with power, about to magically propel over the barrier—

Something slammed into Sophie and Agatha like harpoons, bashing them off the deer's back and pinning them into opposing walls.

Scims.

They glued down the girls' wrists and legs and spread them against the inside of the glass, like mice caught in a trap.

Petrified, Sophie swung her head towards Agatha, the two of them struggling against the scaly black eels.

At the center of the stage, the Snake reformed again, rising out of the green bonfire like a phoenix.

Millicent charged for him, hurdling over the holes in the stage.

The Snake calmly peeled one of the scims off his chest, which rolled up in his palm like a tiny tube. Instantly it turned to shiny black steel, razor sharp at both ends.

Millicent leapt, hooves aimed at his chest, poised to crush him—

The Snake hurled the scim at her, spearing the deer in the heart. She fell down dead and burnt up in the green flames.

Outside the walls, the students saw Millicent fall and stopped fighting, paralyzed in horror. The pirates seized them at once, knives and swords to their throats. With a pirate's dagger to her own neck, Hester stalled her demon, as did Anadil her rats, afraid to cost any more friends their lives. Hort gnashed his teeth, feeling Thiago's sword point on his spine, poised to slice him open. Nicola, Bogden, Dot, and Willam were all trapped by pirates, along with the rest of the questing Evers and Nevers.

Onstage, the Snake was circled in green flames like a ringmaster. His eyes shifted between Sophie and Agatha, pressed against the glass on either side of him, as if he was deciding which girl to handle first.

Instead, he pulled two scims off his body, one in each hand, letting them morph into steel black blades.

Slowly he raised both arms, extended outwards, each blade aimed at a girl's heart.

This was how I died, Sophie thought. Rafal had killed her with a shot to the heart before Agatha had woken her with true love's kiss.

But this time there would be no kiss.

Because her true love was about to die with her.

The Snake gripped the blades and coiled to throw—

A roar exploded through the land.

So full and deep it shook the earth.

The Snake stilled, the green flames cooling around him.

Sophie and Agatha gaped at each other.

Again came the roar, this time louder than before, shattering the iced wall between the two girls. Jagged shards rained over the Snake, who turned away, shielding himself.

As he looked back up, so did Sophie, craning her head to see through the wall.

Someone was coming towards the stage.

Galloping through the crowd on a white horse, his body tall and muscular, in a dark blue jacket with a brilliant gold pattern, dark blue riding pants, and gold-lined boots.

He was wearing a mask.

A mask of gold that glimmered in the moonlight and shrouded his face.

The mask of a Lion.

As his horse accelerated towards the stage, the lion-masked figure rose, feet sturdy in the stirrups, and climbed to stand on the horse's back, the reins in his hands. Then he lowered into a crouch, balanced on the horse's hide as if surfing a wave, and just as the horse started to buck him off, he jumped from the animal, sailing through the air like a ball from a cannon, through the busted ice wall, and onto the gallows stage. As he stood to full height, he thrust out his finger like a wand, lighting the tip up with hot gold glow and illuminating the stage.

Sophie saw Agatha's eyes widen.

Only one person they knew had that glow.

A glow that matched his true love's.

Tedros.

The crowd exploded with cheers.

The Lion had come.

Across the stage, Sophie saw Agatha stop resisting her scims. All this time, Agatha had tried to fight Tedros' battles on his behalf, but now he'd come to wrest back control of his quest from his princess. Sophie could see Agatha sigh with exhaustion and relief, as if at last, her fairy tale with Tedros was back on track, their Ever After salvaged from the ashes. Slowly Agatha looked up and met the Lion's aqua-blue eyes. Camelot's princess smiled, even though she was squashed against a wall like a fly in a spider's web . . . even though there was a deadly villain still on the stage. . . .

Sophie knew that smile.

It was the smile of love.

The Lion and the Snake faced off on a charred heap of ruins, all that remained of the stage. They circled each other inside a ring of dying green flames.

"This is Camelot's land," said the Lion in his low, strapping voice.

"To which I have a rightful claim," the Snake returned, chilly and sure.

His opponent peered through his lion mask. "And what gives you that right?"

"My birth," said the Snake, casting shadows in the green light. "I am the true heir to Camelot's throne. I am King Arthur's eldest *son*."

This last word snapped over the quiet crowd like a whip-crack.

Sophie's stomach dropped.

Son.

Son?

She locked eyes with Agatha, both of them stupefied.

Even the pirates looked stunned, still clutching their prisoners.

But the Lion held his ground. "There is no son but Tedros of Camelot. The one true king."

"And yet Excalibur remains in a stone," the Snake said. "Until I free it, that is, and prove the throne is mine."

"You will never touch Excalibur as long as I'm alive," the Lion vowed.

The Snake's eyes sparkled. "So it is written. So it is *done*."

He tore scims off his body, which turned to steel in his hands, before hurling them at the Lion's chest. The Lion deflected them with gold rays from his finger, then scooped up a handful of jagged ice from the shattered walls and whizzed it at the Snake. The shards shot into his flank, shearing away scims and embedding in youthful, snow-white skin beneath that started oozing blood. The Snake stumbled back, surprised, and crashed through a hole in the stage.

Taking advantage, the Lion glanced between Sophie and Agatha and dashed for Agatha. He grabbed a piece of smoking wood off the stage and burnt the scims off her, careful not to burn her too.

"Tedros," Agatha breathed.

Across the stage, Sophie watched them together, feeling her own heart fill up. For Tedros to risk his life and be this courageous when his people needed it most . . . He wasn't just a prince. He was every inch a king. Any residue of Sophie's envy drained away, replaced by gratitude and admiration. She'd give him and his queen the best wedding two friends could ask for.

The Lion freed Agatha and gazed into her big brown eyes.

"Go," he said. "Before the rogue comes back."

"No," Agatha said firmly. "We're a team now. We're fighting him togeth—"

The Lion pointed his gold glow and sent her flying way up the flagpole. Camelot's flag magically came loose and tied around her waist, lashing her to the pole and out of the Snake's reach.

"Get me down!" Agatha yelled.

The Lion winked at her and stormed back into battle—

The Snake rushed him headfirst, smashing the Lion against the pole, before the Lion delivered a vicious kick to his thigh, scattering a few scims and revealing more of the Snake's milk-white flesh. The two masked men launched at each other, firing spells and scims, shattering two more frozen walls, the remainder of the stage collapsing under their every step, until they were on the final piece of the gallows, a small square of scorched wood. With their bodies jammed together, they could no longer rely on magic and the two set on each other with their fists, trying to knock the other off the platform and into the fiery pit below.

As the Lion clocked the Snake, a scim crawled out of a hole and snagged the Lion by the ankle, yanking him towards the edge of the stage. The Lion swiveled and stomped on the scim, crushing it. But now the Snake came from behind, hands out, about to push the Lion off the stage and face-first into the blaze below—

Sophie screamed.

The Lion whirled just in time, belting the Snake with all of his might, who staggered backwards and plummeted off the stage, landing in the fire and dispersing to a thousand shrieking scims. Wounded, the scims glowed green and rose shakily into the air, forming a massive phantom cobra in the sky. It hissed at the Lion with the promise of vengeance before spraying into the night, terrible shrieks echoing.

Covered in blood and bruises, the Lion stood on what was left of the stage, gold mask glistening in the moonlight, his chest heaving.

Slowly he raised his head to the boy pirates clutching prisoners in the field.

The Lion roared.

Pirates dropped their weapons and ran.

Students and citizens let out a raucous cry, the Four Point reclaimed and the Snake beaten back.

"LONG LIVE KING TEDROS!" someone shouted.

"LONG LIVE THE KING!" said another.

As Nicola climbed the flagpole to bring Agatha down,

Hort and Dot kneeled to comfort Reena and Beatrix, who were sobbing over their lost best friend. Hester and the witches hurried to the sides of the other Evers and Nevers, many of who'd been wounded in their battle against the pirates.

Indeed, the questers were so quick to help each other that none of them noticed that inside the billows of smoke coming off the stage Sophie was still trapped on the lone wall standing.

But the Lion had.

He strode over the misty crumbles of stage until at last he reached her, his jacket ripped open and sweat soaking his light blue shirt. He burnt her scims away and squashed them under his boot, leaving a puddle of black goo. Then he looked at Sophie through his mask.

"Thank you," he said. "If you hadn't screamed to warn me, I'd be dead."

"Can't have you dying yet, Teddy," Sophie sighed, rubbing at her sore wrists. "I'm your wedding planner."

"Are you?" he said.

His eyes reflected mischief, like a hall of mirrors.

Something flooded inside Sophie. Something hot and stormy in the deepest swells of her heart.

It was something she'd never felt with a prince.

Slowly she reached up and pulled the mask off the Lion's face.

Sophie staggered back.

It wasn't Tedros.

The boy had tanned skin the color of amber and copper-brown hair cropped close to his head like a soldier's helmet. He had a strong brow bone, a long, straight nose, sensual lips, and thick dark brows that ran flat over his eyes like two streaks of paint. Beads of sweat dotted his coat of brown stubble and his eyes seemed to change colors with the intensity of his stare, from blue to hazel and all the shades in between.

He looked her age. Perhaps a bit older.

One thing was for sure, though. She'd never seen such a beautiful boy in her life, masculine, sultry, and smelling of salt and sand, as if he'd been dewed from the mouth of a desert flower.

"Who are you?" she choked.

"A humble servant of Camelot," he said, calm and commanding. "Come to protect the king and his princess."

Sophie shook her head. "But . . . but . . ."

"I suppose that isn't the whole truth," said the boy. "My loyalty is to Camelot and I will fight until my dying breath to make sure the rightful king weds his rightful queen. But I've also come to find someone else along the way. Someone I saw in a storybook and haven't been able to stop thinking about since. Someone who in my quest to protect Camelot . . . perhaps I can protect too."

"Who?" Sophie asked, confused.

From inside his shirt, the boy pulled a red rose.

"The girl who's already protected me," he whispered.

He leaned in and kissed her, slowly and deeply, his hands taking her by the waist. Sophie heard herself gasp, his breath filling her mouth, her body lighting up in his grip. She closed her eyes, lost in the softness of his lips, his hot-spice scent, and the impossibility of this moment in the wake of all that had come before. . . .

His lips slipped off hers.

She opened her eyes and the Lion was gone.

Sophie stood there in the fading smoke, her heart throttling.

A delusion.

A dream.

<u>*Something.*</u>

But then she felt a drizzle on her neck.

She raised her fingers and pulled down the perfect red rose, dripping with his sweat, that he'd slid into her hair as he kissed her.

But that wasn't all that the Lion had left behind.

Because across the stage, as the last smoke cleared, she saw a girl wrapped in Camelot's flag watching her . . . her pale, big-eyed face as shell-shocked as Sophie's had been once upon a time, when another red rose had dropped into their story just like this. . . .

A rose from a boy who was never supposed to be in their story at all.

PART II

21

TEDROS

Allies and Enemies

He dreamed of his father again.

Staring at Tedros through harsh, peacock-blue eyes.

But this time, King Arthur was taller than he'd been in real life. As tall as the statue of him that Tedros had desecrated.

They met on the rooftop of the Blue Tower under gold night clouds. Tedros was in pajama shorts, no shirt, and his feet were bare and wet. He looked down and saw the roof was flooded with water an inch thick, mirroring formless clouds. Only the clouds had a different shape in the water's reflection. They looked like lions.

His father wore the crimson robes in which he was buried, his bearded face ruddy and fresh, the way Tedros remembered him in the prime of his reign. Camelot's crown glistened on Arthur's head and Tedros found himself reaching up to make sure his own crown was still there.

It wasn't.

"They say he's your son," Tedros accused. "They say you know who he is."

Arthur grew taller.

"Who is he!" Tedros shouted.

Higher and higher Arthur grew, reaching for the clouds.

"TELL ME THE TRUTH!" Tedros cried.

King Arthur roared, shaking the earth with his fury.

He bent down like a giant and glared into his son's eyes.

"*Unbury me,*" he said.

Then the clouds pounced down and devoured Arthur into the night.

Tedros woke in a pool of sweat on a cold floor.

He pried open his eyes and saw he was at the top of the dungeon staircase, curled up in front of the stone door.

How could I fall asleep!

He had to get to the Four Point. He had to find this Snake *now*—

"KEI!" he screamed, pounding on the door again.

But the dream had felt so real, his father's roar reverberating through him.

For months, he'd been haunted by his dad, but this was the

first time he'd been given an order from the grave.

An order that didn't make sense. How could there be answers in a heap of bones and dust? All he was left with was the riddle of a dream.

But what happened with the advisors wasn't a dream.

They'd hinted that the Snake was his father's son.

Which meant he'd be Tedros' *brother*.

Impossible.

He would have known. Someone would have told him. His mother. His father. *Anyone.* No secret like that could be kept for so long.

"*KEI!*" Tedros blared, bludgeoning the door.

Faint shouts echoed beyond it, as if they were miles away.

He'd attacked the door for hours last night, shouting himself hoarse, waiting for someone to open it. It didn't make any sense: his guard, Kei, had left through the very same door—

Tedros' heart stopped. *Unless Kei locked me in.*

He thought back to their heartfelt conversation on these stairs.

Why would Kei seal me in the dungeons?

An oily dread coated Tedros' throat.

Did Gremlaine give Kei her key before she left?

Have Kei and Gremlaine been working with the advisors all along?

Tedros' blood went hot.

What were they doing while I was trapped?

He battered the stone with renewed force—

Shouts amplified outside the door, as if multiple voices were yelling at once.

Tedros flattened onto his stomach and put his ear to the razor-thin slit at the bottom.

"*Tedros!*" the voices called.

"Get me out!" he yelled.

"*KEY!*"

Immediately Tedros fumbled his key ring from his pocket and pried the black key off it. He tried to slide it under the door, but it got stuck beneath the thick slab of stone. Tedros pressed his little finger through the crack, trying to flick the key to his rescuers. No luck. He put his mouth to the opening and tried to blow the key across—

A piece of wire surged through the slit, stabbing his chin. Startled, Tedros watched the wire hook the top of the key and scrape it out the other end. The lock snapped and the door pulled open, revealing the shadows of Lancelot and Guinevere.

"You know how long I've been in there!" Tedros spat, storming past them. "Find Kei and lock him in the jail until I return! I'm riding to the Four Point right now—"

"Snake attacked the Four Point last night," said Lancelot.

Tedros whirled, midstride.

"Almost killed the leaders of the four kingdoms," Lancelot snarled, "along with Agatha, Sophie, and more than twenty other questers from your school while they were waiting for *you* to arrive."

Tedros spluttered: "Wait. Agatha was at the—"

"You should have been there! I don't care what the old wizard said! Should have just gone myself when I got word we were attacked!" Lancelot seethed. "But then we couldn't find you—we've spent hours pounding on that door, with no idea if you were inside or hurt or—"

"Dead!" Guinevere cut in, relief boiling to anger. "Do you know what you put us through!"

"Is Agatha okay?" Tedros asked, paling.

"I told you not to go into the dungeon without me! I told you to ride with me to the Four Point and be a *king*!" Lancelot harped. "Your father would have listened to me and not that old wizard! Your father would have trusted me! But you had to do things *your* way—"

"*Is Agatha okay!*" Tedros demanded.

"Your classmates, your fellow rulers, your princess could all be dead because of *your* carelessness, Tedros!" Lancelot flayed. "Luckily, someone *else* came to their rescue."

Tedros felt like he'd been slammed over the head. "What? Who!"

"Ask the leaders that were saved," said the knight, pulling Guinevere away. "They're all *here*."

Five minutes later, Tedros sat at the Round Table in the Map Room, surrounded by twenty Good and Evil leaders.

"So let me get this straight," said Tedros, crown askew and smelling like dungeon. "The Snake staged an execution at the Four Point to bait me into fighting him. A Snake who says he is my father's son and Camelot's rightful king. And then a Lion shows up in a mask and defeats him in battle." Tedros leaned forward. "A Lion who is *not* me?"

The onslaught came from every direction—

"The Snake says he's Arthur's eldest *son!*" cried the King of Jaunt Jolie.

"He says he can pull Excalibur! That he's the true heir!" added the Fairy Queen of Gillikin.

"Is that why Excalibur is stuck in the stone? Because it's waiting for *him*, not you?" the Ice Giant of Frostplains asked.

"Even if he *is* the true heir, you can't let him get near that sword!" the Queen of Jaunt Jolie gasped.

"Nearly killed my dear friend and her little boys!" said the Duchess of Glass Mountain, touching the queen with her translucent hand. "If he pulls the sword and becomes king, nothing will stop him from murdering us all!"

"If my sons had died because you failed to intervene—" the Queen of Jaunt Jolie said to Tedros, before she broke down.

"Thank goodness for that Lion chap," said the eight-armed Queen of Ooty. "He beat the Snake off!"

"And here we thought *you* were the Lion," the King of Bloodbrook growled at Tedros, swatting his paw at the floating maps that kept bumping into his head.

"For weeks, we've begged you to intervene," said the Queen of Ravenbow. "Instead, many of us were almost hanged on Camelot land while the king sits at home!"

"Though, according to the Snake, you may not be king *at all*," noted the Vizier of Kyrgios, stroking his gold-flecked beard.

Tedros was about to implode. They were all right: he'd ignored them . . . he'd failed them . . . he'd let the Snake go unchallenged . . . but not because he'd been sitting on his bum and eating cake. Ever since he stepped foot in this castle, he'd tried to make the right decisions: from encouraging the people to forgive his mother and Lance at his coronation . . . to prioritizing Camelot's problems over those of other realms . . . to staying behind and serving his kingdom while Agatha went into the Woods. . . . Even last night, he was sure he'd chosen the right course. He'd followed Merlin's and Dovey's advice. He'd met with the advisors, trying to get answers. He'd done *precisely* what a king should do! And it had led him right into a trap: a trap that nearly killed his princess, killed his friends, and made him look like a coward.

His whole life he'd thought being king was about doing Good.

But now that he was king, Good kept leading him astray.

Tedros could see Lancelot standing with his mother near the door. He'd told them to stay away from this meeting—that it was too dangerous revealing themselves when there was a bounty on their heads. But Guinevere hadn't listened, insisting her son might need her. Nor had Lance, who was glowering at him, clearly still miffed and surely enjoying the sight of the young king spit-roasted by half the Woods' leaders.

"If the Snake pulls Excalibur, we're dead!" the Empress of Putsi pressured.

"How could Arthur have a secret son!" the Duke of Hamelin demanded.

"How do we find this Lion! He's the one we need!" urged the Queen of Jaunt Jolie.

Tedros tried to quell his rage, spewing in all directions. He needed to think.

Last night, those three shrews had warned him what was coming.

"At the Four Point, the real story begins."

Somehow, they'd plotted with the Snake from prison to trap Tedros last night while the Snake attacked Tedros' princess, his friends, and his allies.

What must have Agatha thought, waiting at the gallows for him to come?

And who was this Lion who had saved her?

All he'd gleaned is that it was a boy his age who'd fought off the villain, then promptly disappeared. No one knew who he was. He'd asked no reward for his efforts. He hadn't been seen since.

So who could he be, then? In Agatha and Sophie's world, beyond the Woods, heroes came out of nowhere, riding in on white horses to save fair maidens from Evil. But not here. Heroes had motives in the Woods. Heroes had a history. And this hero seemed to have *neither.* He certainly hadn't come at Tedros' behest. So why would he risk his life to save a bunch of strangers? Had he been rejected from the School for Good and was trying to get his name in a fairy tale? Had he read about his and Agatha's troubles and was making a move on his queen?

Don't be a Never, always seeing the worst, Tedros thought bitterly. *Maybe he's just like you, trying to do Good in this world.*

But no matter how much he told himself to be grateful, Tedros hated this boy for playing the part *he* should have played. For trying to do Good and actually succeeding. For showing him up like a fool. How was he supposed to prove himself the rightful king when there was a Snake in the Woods saying he wasn't king and now an impostor Lion doing *his* job? He could feel his anger stoking again like wildfire while more voices shot at him from around the table, sharp as arrows, heckling and questioning—

"Are you king or not?"

"Who is this Lion!"

"If you won't fight the Snake, he will!"

"*Be quiet*," said Tedros.

No one listened.

Tedros shot his gold fingerglow over their heads like a firework, scorching a hole through all the maps.

"I SAID *BE QUIET*," Tedros roared.

The whole table fell silent.

"Thought there was a ban on magic at Camelot," Putsi's empress peeped.

A map smacked her in the head.

"Listen to me and listen clearly. The Snake is *lying*," Tedros declared. "He says he's King Arthur's eldest son and rightful heir. If that were true, my father would have to have had a child before I was born. But my father was with my mother from the time he was a boy at school until he married her and she gave birth to me. It's impossible my father would have another son. First of all, he loved my mother devotedly and would never betray her. Second, he would have never kept a secret like that from the woman he married nor from the son he groomed to be king. Whatever became of my father in his last years, he was

a Good man—and an honest one. All of you know that to be
true. It's why your kingdoms turned to him to lead whenever
Good and Evil faced a common threat. But there is more evi-
dence that the Snake is lying. For instance, who would be the
mother of this supposed heir? Certainly not *my* mother. And
any other woman who'd have borne King Arthur's son would
have shouted it from the rooftops for gold or fame alone. And
lastly, would a son of King Arthur—the king who fought to
protect all of you—be out wreaking havoc and murdering my
friends? This Snake is not my father's son. This Snake is not
my father's heir. *He cannot pull Excalibur.*" His eyes went to
Guinevere near the door. "Right, Mother?"

The entire table turned to her.

Guinevere blinked back. "Of course."

The group murmured agreement. Tedros tried to feel
relief, but then he saw his mother's eyes shift to the floor, her
throat bobbing.

Should have asked your mousy old mum, the advisors had
said. *She knows everything, no matter how dumb she plays. . . .*

But now Tedros could hear the Ice Giant and the King of
Bloodbrook murmuring over whether there was still a reward
for his mother's and Lance's heads. . . .

Tedros glared daggers at them. "This Snake is a lying mon-
grel and yet he's managed to divide us right at the moment
when we need each other most. Good and Evil may be at
eternal war, but we must also come together when our world
faces an outside threat—something my father understood and
fought for. We cannot let the Snake tear us apart. We must join

as allies, build an army that I will command, and destroy him once and for—"

The door flew open, almost knocking Guinevere and Lancelot over, and a hawk and a horned owl whizzed into the room, spearing more holes in the maps, each bird carrying a scroll in its beak. The hawk dropped its scroll into the hands of the King of Foxwood and the owl dropped its message to the Prince of Mahadeva, both of whom opened them quickly.

"'*Snake and his band of trolls broke into castle, took your daughter hostage*,'" the Foxwood king read, eyes wide. "'*Lion arrived and freed her. Trolls executed. Snake on the loose.*'"

"'*Snake's werewolves fed three guards to the man-eating hills*,'" the Mahadeva prince read from his scroll. "*Lion saved the rest.*"

A sparrow zipped through the door and dropped a note in the King of Camelot's lap.

Tedros opened it.

"'*Snake knows I'm on his tail. He's coming for Camelot. Will try and take your kingdom by force. We must meet immediately and prepare for war. Name your time and place*,'" he read out loud. "Signed, '*Your Loyal Knight.*'"

Tedros stared at it, speechless.

"You ask us to build an army for you," said the King of Bloodbrook. "When perhaps it's the Lion who deserves such an army."

Tedros shook his head. "So-called 'Lion,' you mean. Because he's lying too. I haven't appointed any knights. My only knight is dead—"

"Well, then this boy surely took it upon himself to replace

him," said the King of Jaunt Jolie. "Your father had his best knight defending his banner in the Woods. For a good while at least." He glanced sourly at Lancelot, then back at the king. "In times like these, you need an ally you can trust. An ally like this Lion, who has already proven himself."

"I don't even know who he *is*," Tedros persisted.

"Then I'll ride out with a full envoy to meet the Lion as he asks," said the Duchess of Glass Mountain.

"I will ride with you," said the Queen of Ravenbow. "We should meet the one who's fighting the Snake."

"The one doing a *king*'s job. Count me and my knights in too," said the King of Foxwood—

"*I'll* go," said Tedros.

The leaders turned to him.

"What all of you say is true," Tedros said, regaining his composure. "Whoever this so-called Lion is, he's saved my princess and friends in the name of Camelot and is calling himself my knight. But he asked *me* to meet him—no one else—and I will oblige. The rest of you will stay here in the castle and make plans for battle. If the Snake is coming for Camelot soon, we must be ready to fight him."

Lancelot stepped forward. "Your Highness, you won't be safe in the Woods alone. You don't even know where the Snake is. He could ambush you with his army. It's too risky—"

"More risky to let this Snake spread lies and depend on a *stranger* to stop him. A stranger we know nothing about," said Tedros. "When we were arguing about the Four Point, you were the one who told me to leave the castle and do my job as a king. Well, I'm taking your advice, Sir Lancelot. I'll go meet this Lion and if he is indeed a loyal ally to our cause, I'll bring him to fight in our army. I'll ride into the Woods tonight."

"Then you'll take me with you," said Lancelot.

"No," Tedros ordered, for his mother's sake. "You are needed here—"

"A king must have a knight. You will take Lancelot," said Guinevere's voice.

Tedros and Lancelot both spun to her, surprised.

"Lancelot was your father's best knight and champion. Taking Lance is what your father would have done and it's what you must do too," said Guinevere, standing tall.

Whatever tension was in her face had been replaced with a firm resolve, leaving no room for negotiation.

"I can't leave you here alone, Mother. Not without him," Tedros said, still stunned. In moments like this, she'd always chosen to protect Lancelot over her son. She'd always chosen to protect their love first.

Guinevere turned to the leaders. "While the king and his knight ride into the Woods, I'll work with your kingdoms to build an army. This boy who calls himself the Lion is surely right. If the Snake's attacks in the Woods are failing, he will come for Camelot with a vengeance. And he'll do it *soon* to rob us of time to regain our strength. It doesn't matter anymore what the king did or didn't do at the Four Point. If Camelot falls to the Snake, he will not summon councils or build alliances or solicit your opinions. He has no respect for diplomacy, legitimacy, or the Truth. Many of you saw this firsthand when he tried to murder you and your families. That is just an inkling of what could lie in store for us all. If Camelot falls, then so will all of your realms. From here on out, we are either allies or enemies, and if we are enemies, Good and Evil are *both* doomed. Choose now."

Rulers mumbled to each other, giving her suspicious looks, but Guinevere cut them off. "As for your feelings about me, I was once a king's wife. I know how to execute the work of a queen." She looked right at the King of Bloodbrook and the Ice Giant of Frostplains. "And if the bounty on my head is worth more than the safety of your people, then by all means, strike the first blow."

Neither of the Never leaders said a word. The rest of the table gazed at Guinevere with fresh eyes, as did her son, who knew all too well how easy it was to misjudge her. The only sounds in the room were the impatient tweets of the Lion's sparrow, waiting for a reply to take back to his sender.

"Then it's decided," said Tedros, turning to his colleagues. "I will ride to meet this 'Lion' and the rest of you will remain at Camelot to prepare for war. My stewards will show you to your rooms. Summit dismissed."

The leaders dispersed, giving both the king and his mother small nods as they left. Tedros tucked the Lion's sparrow messenger into his pocket and sewed up the holes in the floating maps with his fingerglow before he glanced up and saw that the room had emptied, save for his mother and Lancelot, embracing in the corner.

Tedros came up behind them. "Thank you for helping me.

Both of you. When it came to protecting the kingdom, I know how much my father trusted you as his knight, Sir Lancelot. It's time I did the same. You are now my knight too."

Lancelot met the young king's gaze. "We ride tonight, Your Highness."

Guinevere lifted her head from Lancelot's arms, her eyes red and scared, looking between her son and her true love.

"Bring him back safe," she said.

Tedros didn't know who she was talking about.

And he didn't ask.

Tedros blew gently on the black ink until it was dry. He'd rewritten the scroll a few times to make sure his handwriting looked especially regal.

SHERWOOD FOREST TOMORROW
6:00 P.M.
AT MARIAN'S ARROW
PASSWORD IS: "LITTLE JOHN"

—KING TEDROS OF CAMELOT

A cool breeze sifted into his bedroom through the open balcony door. Tedros rolled up the parchment, stamped a wax seal of Camelot's crest, and tucked the message into the sparrow's feet. He fed the tiny courier a scrap of toast, and leaning out the balcony, he sent it flying into violet evening.

Sherwood Forest was the only possible place to meet this so-called Lion. For one thing, it was less than a day's ride from Camelot. But more importantly, the Forest was a secure stronghold guarded by Robin Hood and his Merry Men, its routes so dense that the Snake or his minions couldn't possibly attack there. Luckily, Tedros' father had a long-standing alliance with Robin Hood, so the king and the Lion could convene safely—and privately—at Marian's Arrow, where the door was password protected and where everyone knew the only rule of the pub: what happens inside *stays* inside.

Standing at the balcony, Tedros watched the twilight cast shadows on the Pool Garden. King Arthur hadn't wanted his bedroom smelling of flowers, so he'd had the royal gardens ripped up and replaced with a landscape of reflecting pools, some small, some big, in a variety of shapes, with a maze of paths swirling around them. Tedros could remember running about as a boy in wet shorts, hopping in and out of pools, chasing his mother, who was always one step ahead of him.

The king took a deep breath, his first after the fever of the day. When the unexpected summit was over, he'd managed a quick bath and wolfed down a dinner of steak, broccoli, and sweet potatoes, pounding down double portions so he'd be ready for the ride to come. His stewards were preparing the horses with Lancelot and packing bags of provisions; Agatha's maids, who'd been acting like headless chickens without Lady Gremlaine or Agatha to direct them, were put to work cleaning swords.

Tedros was about to close his balcony door when he noticed

a shadow sitting out on the stone bench by the biggest reflecting pool. He stepped out on the terrace and walked down the steps, passing a guard stationed at the entrance. In the dark, he could hardly see the thin path around the pools.

"Hello," he said, coming up behind the shadow.

His mother smiled up at him, barefoot on the bench.

"When are you leaving?" she asked.

"Soon," said Tedros, sitting beside her.

"Did you—"

"Eat? Believe it or not, if you don't worry about me eating, I will still do it. And in sufficient quantities over the past six months to make the cooks despise me as much as the guards do. Which is . . . a lot."

His mother sighed. "They weren't especially fond of you as a child either."

"Thanks, Mother," said Tedros.

They both looked at each other and cracked up.

Slowly their laughter trailed off.

"I wish I'd been here instead of hiding with Merlin and Lance these past months," said Guinevere. "The reason I came back to Camelot in the first place was to *stop* hiding after all these years. To help you be king. I can't imagine how hard it's been for you."

"I've gotten used to not having parents, to be honest," Tedros said.

His mother sat quietly, watching the wind sweep across the pools.

"When I'm gone, keep your eye on the guards," said Tedros.

"No one can find Kei. The guard who locked me in. The other guards say they've never even heard of anyone by that name. But I don't know what's Truth and Lies anymore. Nor do I know who to trust. If anyone tries to kill you for the bounty, you'll have nobody to help you."

"The price on my head is the furthest thing from my mind right now," his mother said, dipping her foot in the pool. "But I've learned my lessons about trust. When I was queen, I snuck out of the castle every night for months to see Lance. I had to figure out which guards would keep my secret. In the end, I chose the wrong one. That's how your father found out."

Tedros glanced at her, surprised. It was the first time she'd ever talked so honestly about deceiving his father.

"Sometimes I worry about whether you know who to trust, though," said Guinevere. "You seemed to have grown close to Lady Gremlaine while I was gone."

Tedros flinched. She was talking about that moment in the Hall of Kings when she, Merlin, and Dovey had returned. His mother's first image of her son after six months of being away was seeing him coddled by a woman she hated.

"I was surprised she was still in the castle," said Guinevere briskly. "I thought you were going to fire her after the coronation."

"I needed her, Mother," said Tedros, heating up. "The people were revolting, there was a bounty on your head, the kingdom was falling apart. . . . I needed someone who the people had faith in. Someone who could help me. No one was here—"

"Agatha was here for you. That wasn't enough?" said his mother.

"I was trying to protect her from all that. It's why I kept Lady Gremlaine in the castle," said Tedros, defensively. "When you were queen, you ran away with Lance and hid from the world. You abandoned your responsibilities for love. But I have to balance my responsibilities *with* love. That's what makes me different from you. Because what Agatha and I have . . . it isn't a mockery like whatever you had with Dad."

Guinevere exhaled as if he'd socked her in the chest.

"It wasn't a mockery," she said.

"It wasn't love. Let's agree on that," said Tedros. "If it were love, I wouldn't have spent my whole life trying to figure out what love *is*. I wouldn't wake up every day desperate to keep it now that I've found it. You can't fathom how alone I felt, knowing my mother's true love wasn't my father. And every day I'm not with Agatha, that loneliness comes back. Because she's the only person who has ever fought for me when I'm down. Everyone else just runs. You included."

His mother said nothing.

"If it makes you feel better, you were right about Gremlaine," Tedros mumbled. "Pretty sure she was conspiring with the advisors the whole time."

"I doubt that," his mother said softly, almost to herself. "As little as I care for Lady Gremlaine, she cared for the Mistral Sisters even less. If I hadn't fired her back when I was queen, she would have made sure Arthur never brought them into the castle. So we all paid a price for our mistakes in the end."

Tedros frowned, the plot he'd worked out in his head between Lady Gremlaine and those three hags suddenly growing fuzzy. . . .

"Do you know where she lives?" he asked. "Lady Gremlaine?"

Guinevere paused. "No."

It was pitch-dark now, save the torchlight coming from the windows of the castle behind them. Tedros could hardly see his mother's face anymore.

"Did the Mistrals tell you anything? About what they did with the money?" his mother asked.

"No. They hid it somewhere, though. That's for sure." Tedros hesitated, picking at his nails. "They did say you know more than you're letting on. That you're playing dumb."

His mother pulled her toes out of the pool and slipped both feet back into her slippers, about to leave.

Tedros grabbed her shoulder. "Why did you fire Lady Gremlaine? Please. I need to know."

Guinevere's shadow was very still. Finally she slackened, as if there was no running from this anymore. "She grew too close to your father, Tedros. This was before you were born. Gremlaine had always been in love with him—the whole *kingdom* knew that—so when he came back from school with me on his arm, she absolutely loathed me. To the point that I never drank from any glass she offered, fearing it was poisoned."

Tedros' eyes bulged. "She was in love with him? *Before* I was born? But then that means—"

"No, she did not have his child, Tedros," said Guinevere

testily, pulling away. "That's why I didn't want to talk about this. Because I knew you'd jump to conclusions. Do you really think I'd keep that secret from you? If I knew you had an elder *brother*? If I knew you weren't the rightful king? Your father would have told me. Arthur had his faults, but he was not a liar and he was not a cheat. Which is more than you might say about me. But this is the truth: you *are* king. No matter what any Snake says."

Tedros looked down, his crown sinking deeper on his head.

"It's time you knew the whole story," Guinevere continued. "I told Arthur to fire Gremlaine, but he wouldn't. Not that I was worried about Arthur betraying me. He was too honest a man and too in love with me to ever do anything like that. It's why I know the Snake is lying. Still, I didn't want to watch Lady Gremlaine continue fawning over him so openly. It was infuriating, for one thing, and for another, people were starting to talk. So I had her moved to the White Tower early in my reign so we would see as little of her as possible. Our paths rarely crossed that year you were born. Even with her out of sight, though, I could feel her lurking, always insinuating herself between your father and I. After you were born, I finally convinced Arthur to let me fire her. It wasn't easy. . . ."

His mother was still talking, but Tedros felt that slimy feeling in his throat again. "There's a strange guest room in the White Tower," he said, interrupting her. "It connects to Lady Gremlaine's old roo—"

"I'm aware," said Guinevere, anticipating him. "Your father had it built right after you were born to house a blind seer who painted your coronation portrait and wanted privacy during the week he was painting it. It adjoined to Lady Gremlaine's in case the seer needed her assistance." His mother paused. "Even so, there was something about that room I never liked. When the seer left, I made your father give me the only key to it. It's why you have the key on your ring instead of Lady Gremlaine. All of this means that your father never could have used that room while we were married, Tedros. So whatever theories you've conjured in your head, you can let go—"

"Then how did she get in that day?" Tedros asked.

Guinevere's shadow straightened. "Who?"

"Lady Gremlaine. I was trying to hide from the guards. I locked the door to that room, but somehow she got in. She pretended I hadn't locked it. But I *know* I did. She had a key. She had to have had a key."

Slowly Guinevere turned towards the castle, lit by its faint glow, the tightness in her face returning.

Tedros stared at her. "Mother, where does Lady Gremlaine live?"

Guinevere shook her head. "Nottingham. Tedros, stop. Nothing happened. You're confusing Lies with Truth," she said, turning to him. "Focus on finding—"

But her son was already gone, leaping between pools as he ran, like he'd done all those years ago as a child. . . .

Only this time he left his mother behind.

22

AGATHA

The Mysteries of a Name

"**H**ere comes the Prude Brigade," Sophie groaned, fresh-faced and glowy in a blue-and-gold caftan, her giant hoop earrings shimmering in the afternoon sun. "Just because he kissed me doesn't mean I have the faintest clue who he is."

"Because, really, who needs to know who they're kissing?" Agatha snapped next to her.

"Girls, let's focus on what's important," Professor Dovey frowned, her face magnified inside the bubble over the dining

table, wobbling from the ship's bumpy course. "The Snake is still at large and coming for Camelo—"

"Is it my fault your dear Teddy didn't show up to save us?" Sophie puffed in Agatha's direction. "Is it my fault your king is derelict in his duties? Don't blame me for being swept off my feet by a hero who actually knows how to do his job."

"We don't even know who he is! You don't even know his name!" Agatha blared.

"Does knowing Tedros' name make him any more competent or useful? No, it doesn't," Sophie said, inhaling her rose luxuriously. "Say what you want about your Lion but *this* Lion adores me, shows up on time, and smells like a red-blooded man."

"Right, because your nose for men is *so* reliable!" Agatha barked.

"Keep your voices down!" Professor Dovey said. "The last thing we need is word getting out that while the Woods is crumbling and a villain is on the loose, a Dean of our school is kissing nameless boys!"

"Less a Prude Brigade and more a Prude *Police*," Sophie murmured.

Agatha subtly turned her head towards the galley. With all the new questers rescued onto the *Igraine* after the Four Point battle, the ship's interior was chock-full. Luckily no one was listening to her and Sophie. Beatrix and Reena were sniffling and writing letters of condolence to Millicent's relatives, while Dot was at the window whispering to Agatha's courier crow, which had Camelot's official ring around its neck. Hester and

Anadil were tending to Kiko's burns, Vex's mangled ear, and ten other injured questers in a makeshift hospital; bandaged-up Hort was barking at the enchanted pot to make him a sandwich (it made broccoli instead); Nicola was studying Sophie's Quest Map (that Sophie had let Nicola borrow it at all was proof their friendship had come a long way); and through the bathroom door, Agatha could see Bogden and Willam poring over a round of tarot cards on the floor.

"Agatha's right. It matters *who* this boy is," said Professor Dovey. "Not just because we need him on our side, but also because we need to know what he wants—"

"I told you. He wants *me*," said Sophie, still fussing with her rose.

"A boy doing Good deeds to impress an *Evil* Dean?" Dovey said.

"Good boys love bad girls. Everyone *my* age knows that," Sophie bit back.

"If he's so Good, then why haven't I seen him before?" Dovey hounded. "It is a truth universally acknowledged that a boy in possession of a Good character must want to come to my school. Yet, despite the fact I review thousands of applications for prospective Evers each year, I've never seen this 'Lion' in my life. And I've had a good look at his face—"

The Dean seemed to move her ball because the field of view turned upside down, veering around Sophie's quarters in the School Master's tower, which the wolves were violently remodeling while Professor Manley supervised—thankfully Sophie didn't notice—before the crystal ball settled on the Storian's painting of a tan, copper-haired boy kissing Sophie.

Dovey turned the crystal ball back on herself. "I had the fairies copy the boy's image and without giving details, I asked all the teachers and students of *both* schools if they recognized him. No one has ever seen this boy before. Not a single person. Which, given his accomplishments and skills last night, seems rather *impossible*. There is something familiar in his face, though . . . something I can't quite put my finger on—"

She coughed hard, clutching her chest, upending the ball. As it resettled, Agatha noticed the black ridges under Dovey's eyes had grown deeper, her face seemingly older overnight.

"Professor, I know you want us to retrieve the rest of the quest teams," said Agatha, "but you don't sound well—"

"We can come back to school and help you," Sophie agreed, suddenly alert. "That's my quest as Dean—"

"No, your quest is to follow my orders. Besides, I'm fine, though my crystal ball is running out of time for today, so pay attention," Dovey insisted, her voice still shaky. "After what's happened with Millicent and Chaddick, I don't want any more students hurt. Find the remaining quest teams immediately, bring them onto the *Igraine*, and return them to the School for Good and Evil, where they'll be safe. Also, I've spoken to Guinevere. More of the Snake's attacks have been foiled by the Lion in Mahadeva and Foxwood. With the Lion on his tail, the Snake will surely storm Camelot and try to take it by force. If Camelot falls to the Snake, so will *all* the kingdoms of the Woods. Guinevere is working with Good and Evil leaders to quickly build an army to defend Camelot from the Snake and his mercenaries. Tedros, meanwhile, is riding out with Lancelot to meet the Lion tonight and find out who he is. If this Lion is indeed a loyal ally, he will be a crucial asset in fighting the Snake when he and his army assault the castle."

"Tedros is riding into the Woods?" Agatha asked, bolting straighter.

"The Lion is meeting him?" Sophie asked, perking up.

"*Where?*" the two girls overlapped, then glanced at each other, frowning.

"Sherwood Forest," said Professor Dovey. "It's the only safe space near Camelot where the Snake can't get to Tedros—"

"Mmm, not so safe anymore," said a voice.

Agatha, Sophie, and Dovey raised their heads.

Dot held up soggy parchment, stamped with the Sheriff of Nottingham's seal. "Since Agatha hasn't been using her courier crow, I sent Daddy a note after the Four Point telling him I was safe. He's sent back a letter saying those eely, snaky things were spotted around Nottingham last night. They haven't attacked anyone or done anything bad, but they're slipping in and out of people's houses as if they're searching for someone. If the Snake's in Nottingham, that's next to Sherwood Forest, where Tedros and the Lion are meeting."

Sophie blinked at her. "You eavesdropped on everything we were saying?"

"Eavesdropped? You were *yelling*," said Beatrix, looking up.

"About the Lion," said Anadil.

"And the kiss," said Nicola.

"And how you don't know his name," said Hort, stonefaced.

"Sophie kisses Rafal, Sophie kisses Tedros, now Sophie kisses Lion with No Name," said Kiko. "My mother said kiss too many boys and you turn into a snail."

"Preach," said Hester.

Sophie pursed her lips.

Dovey suddenly looked worried. "Scims in Nottingham? Girls, there were over a dozen Good and Evil leaders at the Camelot summit. All of them know Tedros and Lancelot are riding to meet the Lion in Sherwood Forest tonight. One of them could be a spy for the Snake. If so, the Snake might try to attack Tedros in Nottingham before he loses him in the Forest!" Dovey cast open her Quest Map, inspecting it. "Looks like Tedros is already close to the Nottingham border. A message won't reach him in time. And Merlin hasn't answered any of my letters so I don't even know where he is. If Tedros is ambushed, it'll fall on Lancelot alone to protect him!" She swiveled to the girls. "But your crew has the advantage of numbers. It's our only option. You must find him before he meets the Lion and warn him he may have been betrayed—"

"We'll set our course to Nottingham at once," said Agatha nervously.

"We can't let him be attacked!" Dovey pressed.

"We'll save the Lion like he saved us—" Sophie breathed.

"She means *Tedros*, you idiot!" Agatha shot back.

"Right. Of course," said Sophie tightly.

"Get to Nottingham, girls! *Quickly!*" said Dovey, the image of her face starting to fade. "Keep Tedros safe and bring him to

Camelot. You must not fail! My crystal ball resets at midnight, so I'll—"

She vanished midsentence like a ghost.

"Really, that crystal ball is a menace," said Sophie.

Agatha whirled towards her. "We need to talk—"

Sophie was already standing. "We'll do a nice catch-up over tea and those vile chocolate cookies you love," she said, hustling away. "But you need to set the ship's course and Kiko is desperate to speak to me, so it'll have to be another time. . . ."

Tedros riding into the Woods . . . Tedros meeting the Lion . . . the Snake looking for him . . .

Agatha's heart hammered as she hurried onto the deck and gripped the captain's wheel. She had to get to Tedros before the Snake did—

"*Fly to Nottingham!*" Agatha commanded.

The ship rocked backwards, knocking her off her feet.

She heard screams from the galley as the *Igraine* pulled out of the sea, the ivory sails catching the wind, and launched straight upwards, like a balloon cut from its string, soaring up, up, up, until it leveled off, surrounded by puffy sunlit clouds. The *Igraine* pivoted west, as if setting its course, and zoomed into the horizon with smooth, comfortable speed.

Agatha lumbered off the floor, hearing groans and shouts inside the ship.

"You could have warned us!" someone hollered.

"Good job, Captain!" heckled someone else.

Agatha ignored them, watching the *Igraine* plow out of

the cloud tunnel and into open sky. She should go and check on her crew—that was the Good thing to do—but her nerves were frayed, her body exhausted, and all she could think about was finding her prince.

A sense of déjà vu swept over her. Because last night she was sure she'd *found* her prince. When that masked Lion freed her, she'd felt so relieved and protected, back in her true love's arms. But it wasn't her true love and instead she'd watched the boy she thought was hers . . . kiss *Sophie*.

The shock of the Lion pulling off his mask and not being Tedros had left her reeling. Yet instead of being thankful to this so-called Lion or comforted that he'd saved them when Tedros hadn't, Agatha wanted nothing to do with him. *Why?* Why wasn't she happy that Sophie had found a new romance and their team a new ally? Why was her blood boiling as if this boy were a villain instead of a friend?

Was it because Sophie was back to her old princessey self, mooning over boys she barely knew? No . . . that wasn't it. Sophie hadn't sought out this Lion like she'd once sought out a prince. This boy had dropped into their story and kissed *her* out of the blue.

Maybe that's what was irritating her: that some boy would kiss her best friend as his reward for a Good deed. No . . . that wasn't it either. Most Everboys claimed to do Good for Good's sake, but in the end, let's face it: it was usually to get a girl.

No, deep down, Agatha knew what was really bothering her.

It was that Sophie was right.

The Lion had done Tedros' job: not just last night, but now the Lion was heading off the Snake in other kingdoms. He'd swooped in like a hero and beat back the enemy, like *she'd* tried to—only, unlike her, he'd actually succeeded.

He'd been Tedros' champion better than she'd ever be.

What would Tedros think of this boy who so effortlessly did what he hadn't done? What she couldn't do either? What must Tedros be thinking, going to meet him?

That it's time he act like a king, the voice inside her retorted. *But it's too late.*

No, it's not, Agatha fired back. *He is king. And I'll help him prove it.*

Once she and Tedros were reunited, everything would be fixed. They'd fight the Snake at each other's side just like they'd once fought Rafal. They'd be a team again, stronger together than apart.

And as for this Lion . . . well, he could fight with them too.

Because having three people in your story always works out well, the voice inside her said.

Agatha squashed it.

Just get to Tedros, she told herself.

"Where are we going to land?" a voice asked. "Nottingham's landlocked."

Agatha turned to see Nicola striding purposefully onto the deck, the necklace with Sophie's gold vial dangling off her fingers.

"We'll figure it out when we get there," said Agatha. "Sorry about the takeoff. Everyone okay?"

"Willam puked again and we had to put him down for a nap, which he probably needs since he keeps insisting that he can use tarot cards to communicate with the dead. Meanwhile, Bogden's creepily sidling up to people and asking everyone if they saw the Lion's face and whether he's handsome, as if that matters. Think those two had a little too much lemonade at lunch. Rest of the crew is fine, though a bunch of them are too injured from their quests to come ashore in Nottingham; we'll have to leave them on the ship. But forget all that," said Nicola, breathless. "I found something. . . ."

She opened the gold vial on the necklace and poured out its contents, forming the magical Quest Map.

"See anything different?" Nicola asked.

Agatha peered at the Quest Map and its fourth-year figurines, spread across the kingdoms. At first, her eyes went to Chaddick and Millicent, both crossed out and dripping with blood.

Tedros, meanwhile, was streaking out of Camelot, and was only a short distance from Nottingham, the gateway into Sherwood Forest. His name was red, the way it had been since the first time Agatha had seen the map. The names aboard the *Igraine* were red too, including Agatha and Sophie, which was no surprise, since the Snake was still at large—

Agatha's eyes widened.

"Hold on," she said. "Why aren't these teams red?"

She pointed at Gronk's quest team in Mahadeva . . . Flavia's team in Foxwood . . .

"More of the Snake's attacks have been foiled by the Lion in

Mahadeva and Foxwood." . . . That's what Dovey had said in the dining room.

There was another team turning blue now, before her very eyes . . . JACOB's group in Pifflepaff Hills, a kingdom west of Mahadeva and Foxwood . . . a kingdom adjacent to Nottingham. . . .

"Look closer," said Nicola.

Agatha saw it and gasped.

A figurine separating from JACOB's quest team, headed towards Nottingham.

A figurine in a Lion mask.

But that wasn't all.

There was a name beneath it.

RHIAN.

"His name is . . . Rhian?" Agatha breathed.

"That's what you're focused on? His name?" said Nicola. "Not the fact this Lion boy has suddenly appeared on our school's *Quest Map?*"

Agatha goggled at her, understanding. "But that means he's a student at the School for Good and Evil. . . . That means he's a fourth year. . . ."

"If there was a fourth year in your class named Rhian, wouldn't you know who he is? Wouldn't everyone on this ship?" Nicola asked. "Hort and I asked the whole crew. No one's heard that name before."

"But how else could he be on the Quest Map if he's not a student at the school?" said Agatha.

"Well, whoever he is, the Storian recognizes him. Plus, he's

fixing students' quests," said Nicola, watching RHIAN streak
away from JACOB's team, which finished turning blue. "Are you
sure you've never heard the name before?"

Agatha shook her head, stumped. "'Rhian' means nothing
to me. Nothing at all."

"Well, maybe it'll mean something to his new girlfriend,"
said Nicola.

Both of them looked towards the galley, hearing lovedrunk
humming from a cabin below.

Agatha thumped on the door.

"Pretend to be talking to me!" she heard Sophie whisper
inside. "Maybe she'll go away!"

"But we don't even like each other!" Kiko protested.

"Shhh! Just talk!"

"About what! Willam was going to read my tarot cards—
he said he could communicate with Tristan from beyond and
then you grabbed me and told me you had to show me something in your room—"

"Tristan? Sounds lovely. Tell me about him," Sophie simpered.

"He's dead!"

Agatha kicked in the door. "Get out, Kiko."

"She kidnapped me!" Kiko peeped, fluttering away.

Sophie backed against her bed frame, sheets wrapped pro-
tectively around her, the Lion's rose in her hair. "I know you're
mad he kissed me, Aggie—"

"Tedros is about to meet this Lion, and the Snake may

be about to kill them both. I'm not mad about kisses. I want *answers*," said Agatha, occupying the edge of the king-sized bed. She scanned the aggressively masculine chamber with a leopard-skin rug, dark wood finishes, and old maritime relics, which now smelled of sweet lavender and was crammed with Sophie's dresses, beauty creams, and vast array of shoes. It was supposed to be the captain's quarters, but both Agatha and Sophie knew from the moment they saw it that even if Agatha was captain of this ship, it was Sophie who would be staying here.

"Tell me what he said to you," Agatha ordered.

"It's private," Sophie snipped.

"Well, so is *my* room, so how about I move you in with Hort?"

"You wouldn't dare."

"Wonder what he sleeps in since you stole his frog pajamas."

Sophie threw a pillow at her. It missed.

"Look, he said he knows about me from our fairy tale and hasn't been able to stop thinking about me," Sophie boasted, tightening her ponytail. "He came to protect me."

"And that's all?" said Agatha.

Sophie hesitated.

"Maybe Beatrix has room in her bed," said Agatha.

"And they call *me* the witch," Sophie retorted. "He also said he's a humble servant of Camelot, come to protect its king and his princess, and that he would fight until his dying breath to make sure the rightful king weds his rightful queen. Happy?"

Agatha stared at her. "He said that?"

Sophie picked at a loose thread in her caftan. "He wants to be Lancelot to Tedros' Arthur. He wants to see you and Teddy married. That's why he really came to save us, okay? Because of you and Teddy. Everything is always about you and Teddy. I'm just the girl he has a crush on at the moment." Sophie balled her knees to her chest. "There could be a thousand other girls like me, for all I know, Aggie. A thousand other roses in a thousand other kingdoms. One for his every Good deed."

Agatha could see the anxious pink spots on Sophie's cheeks . . . the way she was curling into herself like she used to their first year at school, whenever Sophie talked about her future prince. . . .

"You really like him, don't you?" Agatha said, surprised.

Sophie sighed. "I'm completely happy on my own. I don't need a boy, so don't make it sound like I do. Nor do I believe in love at first sight anymore or even true love for that matter. Not after Teddy and Rafal taught me that loving any boy only leads to them disappointing you once you realize that they're boring or immature or an axe murderer. But this boy came out of nowhere when I least expected it and even though he didn't say we'd meet again, I keep thinking about how nice it'd be to have a proper date where he picks me up and I wear my furs and boots and we dine on *coq au vin* so I can ask what his father does for a living and what he does when he's not saving people and why he liked me in our fairy tale when I behaved quite badly most of the time, but . . ." She sank into the pillows. "I can't *really* like him. I don't even know his name."

"Rhian," said Agatha.

Sophie bolted back up. *"What?"*

"His name is Rhian."

Agatha drew Sophie's vial from her pocket and deployed the Quest Map. Sophie followed Agatha's fingertip to the Lion-masked figurine, riding towards Nottingham. Sophie turned sickly pale—

"That can't be his name!"

"So you *have* heard it," said Agatha, eyes flaring.

"Professor Sader mentioned that name once," Sophie said quickly. "Rhian was the name of Rafal's twin brother!"

"The School Master's brother? The Good one?" said Agatha. "He's . . ."

". . . *alive?*" Sophie said.

The two girls gaped at each other.

"Impossible," said Agatha. "We saw the Good School Master's ghost take over Professor Sader's body our first year. They both were destroyed. Professor Sader *and* Rhian. *Forever.*"

"Unless Rhian's ghost came back somehow and took a younger form," said Sophie. "Like Rafal."

"But Rhian *can't* come back. Just like Rafal can't come back," said Agatha, shaking her head. "Not even the strongest magic could do that."

"So maybe this Rhian is the Good School Master's son? Dads name their sons after them, don't they? Narcissistic ones at least."

"His *son?* If the Good School Master had a son, don't you think we would have known about it before now? Wouldn't he have helped us fight *Rafal?*"

Sophie shook her head. "So it's just a coincidence."

"Must be . . . ," said Agatha skeptically.

"*Igraine landing! Nottingham ahead!*" Nicola's voice echoed above.

"Hurry! Rhian and Tedros are meeting soon. We need to find Tedros—" said Agatha, yanking Sophie off the bed.

"And I need to find out who this Rhian is that's going around kissing girls and not writing them the next day," Sophie puffed.

"*After* we help Tedros," Agatha growled.

The *Igraine* hit land with an earth-shaking crash—

Agatha seized Sophie in her arms, hugging her tight as debris and clothes and shoes showered over them and the ship tremored until, at last, the room went quiet and still again. They could hear the commands and bootsteps of crew preparing to disembark.

"Come on," said Agatha, pulling Sophie towards the door.

"Aggie?"

Agatha turned.

"Maybe it'll all work out. You with Teddy, me with Rhian, whoever he is. Our own versions of Arthur and Lancelot, with Camelot great again," Sophie breathed hopefully. "What if that's our Ever After? What if that's our perfect ending?"

"Well, for one thing, Arthur and Lancelot finished with Lance betraying Arthur and Arthur wanting him dead," said Agatha, dragging Sophie behind her. "And if there's one thing I know, Sophie . . . it's that you and I don't get to have perfect endings."

23

THE COVEN

The Sheriff's Daughter

When it came time to land, the *Igraine* didn't have a port to dock in and its captain was below deck, so the ship made its own decision and thumped down in front of Nottingham Prison, crushing a statue of a fat, bearded Sheriff beneath its hull.

A few pigeons scattered.

No sounds came from the jail.

"Daddy won't be happy," said Dot, blinking over the rail.

Hester took in the deserted scene. "Where is everyone? You'd think flying ships land here every day."

"Jail's pretty empty," Dot explained. "Daddy and his men are so focused looking for Robin Hood that anyone else they put in there usually escapes."

"Good Sheriff," said Anadil, her rats snickering.

"He's caught Robin before. He'll catch him again," Dot defended. "When he caught Robin, Dad was so happy. He told me I was pretty, bought me cakes and dresses, and didn't have a care in the world. But then when Robin escaped . . ."

Her eyes clouded over.

"But *how* did Robin escape?" Anadil pushed.

"Oh, look! Bertie!" Dot said, waving over the rail. "Hi, Bertie!"

She beamed down at a filthy old man who'd rushed out the door of the jail to check on the commotion. He had no shirt, his pants were falling down, and he was sucking on a lit cigar.

"Any Robin sightings lately?" Dot asked cheerily.

The old man cursed at her and went back inside.

Dot smiled. "He's such a good friend."

A few minutes later, the crew gathered before their captain on sandy dirt, the *Igraine* in shadow behind them. A soft rain fell, the cloudy glow over Nottingham draining fast. Still, they could see downhill to the quiet village below, bounded on the north side by the rich greenery of Sherwood Forest.

"Tedros and Lancelot are heading towards Sherwood Forest to meet the Lion," said Agatha. "According to the Quest Map, Tedros will soon reach Nottingham on his way there. But scims were spotted here in Nottingham last night. Surely it's because the Snake sees a chance to attack Tedros before he gets to Sherwood Forest, where the Snake can't follow him inside. Sophie and I will use the Quest Map to find Tedros before the Snake does—"

"And the Lion," Sophie chimed in. "We'll look for him too."

Agatha glared at her. Sophie pursed her lips.

"The rest of you search Nottingham for scims," Agatha continued. "If the Sheriff spotted those eels last night, that means the Snake is here somewhere. If you find him, cast your glow into the sky as a signal. Don't try to fight him on your own." Agatha scanned the group. "Understood?"

The questers dispersed. Ravan's team went with Vex's to explore the hill around the jail. Beatrix, Reena, and Kiko teamed up to search the area bordering Sherwood Forest. Bogden and Willam took the Nottingham school, Hort and Nicola headed towards the outer cottages, and Hester and Anadil followed Dot into the center of town.

"Daddy will know where the scims were. We have to get to my house," said Dot as they passed a billboard with a flattering painting of the beefy Sheriff chasing an ogrish-looking Robin Hood, about to snare him in a big, gray sack. The sign read: "WELCOME TO NOTTINGHAM, LAND OF LAW AND ORDER." "Can't wait for you to meet Daddy. I've told him all about you."

"Since when are you so chipper about 'Daddy'?" Anadil scorned. "The way you talk about him, calling you a failure and a loser, he sounds like a demeaning, belittling mope. And that's coming from *me*."

"Well, he appreciates me more now," said Dot cryptically.

Hester tuned out whenever Dot talked about her dysfunctional relationship with her father. (She had no patience for parental issues, which she thought most kids used as an excuse for mediocrity and avoiding real responsibility). Instead, she was unnerved by how dead this town was as she took in the square's empty streets, stagnant fountain, and closed shopfronts.

"Um, sorry this isn't Ravenswood or Bloodbrook, with bird-bone temples and man-wolf raves," Dot said, seeing her face. "It's Robin's fault, to be honest. Robbed all the rich people to give to the poor, so the rich people left. But then the poor got rich from all Robin's stealing, so then he started robbing from them and they left too. So the only people here are neither rich nor poor and there ain't too many of those in this world. So yeah . . . it's a sleepy town."

"This isn't sleepy. This is *zombie*," said Hester.

"No thugs running around wreaking havoc either," said Anadil. "If the Snake's here, where are the attacks?"

A spooked villager rushed towards them, carrying an axe.

"Get inside, you fools! Eely things flyin' around all last night! They're huntin' for someone!" he spat, blowing past them. "If you're idling about, they might come back!"

The witches watched him flurry towards the cottage lanes.

Hester frowned. "At least we know why the streets are empty."

"Hold on. Last night? Dot's father said the scims were looking for someone last night too," Anadil pointed out. "*Last night*. Long before Tedros even left his castle. So the Snake can't have been looking for Tedros. He must be looking for someone *else* in Nottingham."

"Someone he wants to kill?" said Hester.

"Or it could be someone he needs," said Anadil.

"Someone he needs in order to take Camelot . . . ," Hester mulled.

"You're soooo overestimating this town," Dot quipped.

Anadil's eyes roamed the clear sky. "Well, we've been here a while and haven't seen a thing. So either the scims gave up . . . or they found who they're looking for."

Hester noticed the news and sundries shop they were passing, the Sheriff's Blotter, covered in WANTED posters of Robin Hood, which had a cartoon of an executioner chopping off his head. In the window, Hester glimpsed the latest edition of the *Royal Rot*—

BANISHED FROM CAMELOT?
LADY GREMLAINE SPOTTED
IN HOMETOWN OF NOTTINGHAM!

Isn't that Agatha's steward? Hester thought. The one she'd complained about? It was suspicious that she'd be back in Nottingham just when Camelot needed her most . . . but then again, the *Royal Rot* claimed that Agatha and Sophie were secretly sisters, which was the most preposterous thing Hester had ever heard. Still, she'd ask Agatha about Gremlaine just in case. . . .

But now Hester was distracted by the row of local Nottingham newspapers next to the *Rot*—

FOUR-POINT REPORT! SHERIFF OF NOTTINGHAM SAYS DAUGHTER WAS THE TRUE "LION"!

DOT THE HERO! READ HER EXCLUSIVE LETTER TO DADDY INSIDE!

"I'M SO PROUD OF MY DAUGHTER!" SHERIFF BOASTS

"Dot, honey . . . ?" Hester said.

"Mmmm?"

"In your letter, what did you tell your dad about the Four Point?" Hester asked sweetly.

"Um, you know . . . that we won," Dot said, eating a chocolate WANTED poster. "We should hurry. It's getting dark."

More WANTED posters of Robin Hood decorated the shuttered shopfronts: Sheriff's Coffee, a cozy café selling drinks like "Frothy Marian" and the "Sheriff's Special Blend"; the Headless Robin, a souvenir shop selling Sheriff and Robin masks and fake Sheriff badges, plus replicas of the famous gray sack the Sheriff had used to catch Robin and parade him through town; Books and Badges, with books about Robin and the Sheriff prominently displayed in the window. . . .

And one about *Dot*, Hester realized, peering closer.

THE SHERIFF'S DAUGHTER:
Dot, Robin, and the Woods' Most Famous Escape

Hester narrowed her eyes. "Dot, what happened exactly between you and Robin Hood?"

"You're full of questions today, aren't you?" Dot snapped, swiveling—

"*Watch out!*" Anadil yelped.

Hester and Dot whirled to see a scim whiz over their heads.

In a flash, the three witches took off after it, hightailing down the street and around a corner to follow it—

They crashed right into Sophie and Agatha, the five of them toppling to the ground.

By the time they found their feet, the scim was gone.

"Where'd it go?" Hester asked, breathless.

"You saw it too?" Agatha said, pulling Sophie forward and calling back to the witches, "We'll take the east lanes. You girls take west!"

The three witches sprinted away from them into the next row of cottages. Anadil tore up a rosebed, Hester kicked aside a bicycle, Dot peeked inside mailboxes.

Hester snarled: "Dot, you spitwad, it's not going to be in a mailbo—"

The scim flew out of the box right into Dot's mouth, then shot back out, rocketing past the witches, down the street, and under the door of a big gray cottage at the end.

"I take that back," said Hester, hurtling towards the cottage, as Anadil raced after her, the two witches shooting their glow into the sky to signal the others. Sophie and Agatha's glow flared from the next street, acknowledging the witches'—

But Dot still hadn't budged, rooted by the mailbox, her eyes on the house where the scim had gone.

"*Daddy,*" she gasped.

Dot burst into the house.

"Daddy? Where are yo—"

A meaty arm slung Dot against the wall.

"*Don't move,*" a deep voice said.

Dot lifted her eyes to see her father holding her back with his big, hairy hand. The Sheriff was tall with a bushy black beard, a greasy mane of hair, and a bloated belly that hung over his belt, jangling with his jail keys. But his dark, stony eyes weren't on his daughter. They were on the scim floating in the foyer of the dimly lit house. The scim was lethally sharp at both ends, one end pointing at Dot and the Sheriff, the other at Anadil and Hester, who were plastered against another wall.

"Tell us how to kill it, Dot," the Sheriff demanded quietly. "Tell us what you did before."

Dot swallowed, feeling Hester and Anadil staring at her, her friends cornered beneath the Sheriff's famous gray sack, hooked on a wall.

Anadil's red eyes flicked back to the scim. "Use your demon," she whispered to her friend.

"Not unless I have to," Hester whispered back. "If my demon dies, *I* die."

The Sheriff squeezed his daughter harder. "Dot, *hurry . . .*"

The front door flung open—

Sophie and Agatha busted in, fingertips lit, only to see the scim pivot in their direction, deadly tip glowing. The girls stumbled back to a wall, tripping over shoes, old newspapers, balled-up underpants, and dirty dishes.

"What do we do?" Sophie breathed.

"Nothing stupid," said Agatha, shielding her.

The scim spun between the pairs of captives like the arrow on a game wheel, as if deciding who to kill first: Dot and her father, Sophie and Agatha, Hester and Anadil. . . .

All of them looked at each other, thinking the same thing: there were six of them and one scim. If they worked together, surely they could take it down.

But perhaps the scim sensed these thoughts, for suddenly, through the open window, more scims silently floated into the room, joining the first.

Two . . .

Then four . . .

Then six.

Each one turned razor sharp and pointed at a prisoner's heart.

"Dot, what are you *waiting* for! Do what you did at the Four Point!" the Sheriff hissed, fingers digging into her. Dot winced under her father's grip.

"What is he talking about?" Sophie blurted.

"She saved all of you there!" the Sheriff shot back. "She beat the Snake single-handedly! Why isn't she doing it now!"

Dot's face was blotchy, her eyes ignoring her father and fixed on the scim pointing at her. "We need to send a signal to the rest of the crew," she said shakily. "We need to tell them not to come here."

On cue, Anadil's rats skittered out of her pocket, crawling down their master's leg and shuttling for the door—

The door crashed open, sending the rats flying, as Beatrix, Reena, Ravan, Nicola, and Hort barreled in together. They saw the scims and scattered with shrieks and shouts to the walls.

Five more scims breezed through the window, each turning knife-sharp and taking its place in front of a student. Three smaller scims coasted in and set aim at Anadil's rats.

But still . . . none of the eels attacked.

"What are they waiting for?" Sophie said, watching the scaly ribbons hover patiently in front of their victims.

The Sheriff's eyes were widening, his hand slowly loosening on his daughter. "It's not true, is it? You didn't save anyone at the Four Point. . . . You made it all up. . . ."

Dot's nose started running. "I—I—I just wanted you to like me again. I wrote you letters from school, asking you to forgive me. I missed you so much. But you wouldn't even answer them—"

"Because you're a *curse*," her father snarled. "You helped Robin Hood *escape*. You sided with my Nemesis over your own family. And now when I finally think you've redeemed yourself, when I can look the people in the eye and tell them you've made something of your life . . . you humiliate me *again*?" The Sheriff burned red, nostrils flaring. "I thought at that school they'd teach you some sense, but instead it's made you more stupid and delusional than you already were! Only reason you got into that school in the first place was because I did a favor for the School Master. Yeah, you didn't know that, did you?

Came to me with something he needed and in return, he took you off my hands. Plus, he enchanted my catching sack so that if I ever catch Robin again with it, this time there's nothing you can do to foul it up! Robin would be still in jail if it weren't for you! I'd be a legend in the Woods! But then you stole my keys and snuck them to him, all because you wanted to be his friend. As if anyone could ever be *your* friend! Should have known your letter was all lies. Was there anything true in there about you beating the Snake? About you being the real Lion? Even one word?"

Dot didn't answer.

The Sheriff bared his teeth at her. "You ugly, disgusting *pig.*"

He raised his hand to strike her—

Hester's demon slammed into him, bashing the Sheriff in the groin with its horns. Before it could gore him again, a scim ripped through the demon's claw, pinning the demon to the ceiling.

The Sheriff crumpled to the floor, wailing high-pitched noises. Hester gasped, buckling against the wall, as if the wind had been crushed out of her, her skin turning white. Overhead, her red-skinned demon bleated in pain.

"H-H-Hester, you okay?" Agatha sputtered.

But Hester wasn't listening, her eyes bloodshot and still fixed on the Sheriff.

"Too bad for you, your daughter *has* friends," she said.

"Lots of friends," Anadil seethed.

"And if you ever touch Dot, you ever speak to her like that

again, those friends will tear out your throat," said Hester. "We will kill her own father to protect her and we won't feel an ounce of guilt. You don't know us. You don't know what we're capable of."

"And you don't know the truth about your daughter either," said Anadil, red glare slashing through the Sheriff. "She isn't an embarrassment or ugly or any of the other *lies* you dump on her. She's a miracle. You know why? Because she came from stock like you and is still the best friend anyone could ask for."

Dot's face flooded with tears, her whole body quivering.

The Sheriff sobbed in pain behind the couch.

Dot shook her head, panicking. "You shouldn't have hurt Daddy—it was my fault—I shouldn't have lied—"

Agatha moved to comfort her, but the scim aimed at Agatha jerked as if to strike, and Sophie snagged her back.

"Nothing stupid, remember?" Sophie said.

"We can't wait here like sitting ducks," said Hort, shirking from his scim. "We have to *do* something—"

"Our fingerglows don't work against scims. . . . We have no weapons . . . ," said Beatrix.

The crew looked at Nicola for ideas, but she seemed to be in a trance, her narrowed eyes roaming the scene. . . .

"What is it, Nic?" said Agatha.

"The scims were looking for someone," said the first year. "And now they've lured us here. They lured *all* of us here. But if they're looking for one of us, why haven't they attacked? They're using us as bait. To find who they're really looking for. This whole thing is another one of the Snake's traps—"

The door smashed open, this time ripping off its hinges.

Tedros stood in the threshold, his black hooded coat silhouetted in evening light. His eyes were watery and red, his face flushed.

He spotted Anadil and Hester first. "Agatha's glow! I saw it! Where is sh—"

But now he glimpsed the Sheriff of Nottingham crumpled on the floor . . . the demon impaled on the ceiling . . . his classmates fixed to the walls . . . the scims aimed at their hearts.

Then Sophie.

Then Agatha.

But before he could move towards his princess, the nearly twenty scims moved first, turning swiftly from their chosen targets and all pointing in Tedros' direction.

"*No*," he breathed.

With a deafening scream, the scims flew for his head.

Tedros dove as the scims ripped past him, tearing open a wall. A split second later, they ripped back out, aiming at the king once more. But Tedros was as strong as he was nimble, ducking under furniture and hurling chairs and lamps and kitchen pots at the scims, which obliterated everything he threw in their direction.

"Get out of the house!" he commanded his classmates. "*Now!*"

Ravan, Hort, Beatrix, Reena, and Nicola fled through the open door.

Agatha instinctively surged towards Tedros, but Sophie blocked her.

"I have to help him!" Agatha cried.

"By getting cut up into a thousand pieces? You don't have anything to fight with!" Sophie blistered.

But now the scims had the upper hand on Tedros, spreading out and coming at him from different angles, forcing him against the windowsill—

"He doesn't even have Excalibur! He can't fight them with his bare hands!" Agatha panicked, struggling in Sophie's grip. "Where's Lancelot? Lance was supposed to be here helping him—"

"There's only one way to help now!" said Hester, grabbing Sophie. "The Lion! We have to find him!"

Agatha spun to Sophie. "Use your map!"

Suddenly alert, Sophie emptied the vial on her neck, unfurling the Quest Map. . . .

The scims had Tedros checkmated, trapped against the windowsill with no other move to make. They glittered brighter, each aiming at a different part of his body—

"There he is . . . ," Sophie said, tracking RHIAN's name. "He's close to us. . . . Getting closer. And closer even . . . wait a second . . ."

The scims launched for Tedros—

A flash of gold blasted through the window, crossing in front of Tedros' body. Scims slammed into the solid gold of a Lion's mask as its wearer swung two torches like swords, lighting eels on fire—

The boy landed on his feet, pulling off his Lion mask.

"Here, Your Highness!" Rhian said, tossing Tedros a torch.

Tedros caught it. He stared open-mouthed at the boy who'd just saved his life: tan and copper-haired, his lean, muscular frame clad in a blue-and-gold suit. . . .

Then the scims came stabbing at them again.

"At my wing!" Tedros ordered Rhian, launching at the eels with his torch.

Rhian obeyed straightaway, flanking the king as the two boys swept their torches in perfect sync, burning through scims, which fell to the ground shrieking.

Agatha broke from Sophie, sprinting to help them—

"Stay back!" Tedros and Rhian yelled at once.

Agatha stalled midrun. She, Sophie, and the three witches watched wide-eyed as Tedros and his new knight teamed effortlessly, twin swordsmen, calling out moves to each other as they dispatched the scaly ribbons.

"Feint left!" Tedros shouted.

"Parry right!" Rhian called back.

Hester could see the awe on Agatha's face, watching Tedros join forces with someone his equal. At school, Chaddick had always been Tedros' sidekick, but he could never truly keep up with the prince. Now Agatha was seeing what it was like for Tedros to finally have a teammate to rely on. This whole time, Agatha had thought *she* was that teammate, but now she realized that as much as he loved her, Tedros needed someone else— someone who wasn't his girlfriend, just like Agatha needed Sophie, even when she had Tedros. Just like Hester needed Anadil and Dot. Because there were all kinds of needs that one person couldn't possibly provide; it's why the bond between two boys was as distinct and mysterious as the bond between two girls. And it's why Agatha had misread Tedros so fundamentally these past six months, when she'd felt so alone and unneeded. Because it had nothing to do with Tedros needing his princess . . . and everything to do with him needing a knight.

Meanwhile, the scims didn't leave a scratch on either boy, the two of them so melded and ruthless in destroying them that they began wordlessly anticipating each other's moves like silent dancers. And it was only when the last scim fell that Tedros and Rhian finally bent over with relief and turned to their audience.

"Hi," Tedros said to Agatha.

"Hi," Agatha said, breathless.

Sophie and Rhian exchanged grins.

But then more scims came.

Hundreds of them, swarming through the window, glittering green instead of black. They funneled like a tornado and spewed a gust of wind that snuffed out the boys' torches and knocked the king and his knight into a corner. Before they could recover, the scims cycloned faster, building into a black, scaly suit, then a shimmering green mask, reforming the Snake himself. His suit had several holes in it, where scales had been ripped away, revealing milk-white flesh, gashed and bloodied, as if the killed scims from his recent defeats had left both his armor and body vulnerable.

The Snake's cold gaze settled on the boys, trapped in the corner. All the remaining scims on his body turned instantly to spikes, their tips shining fatally. The Snake's emerald eyes darkened with purpose. . . .

Then he charged.

Rhian and Tedros both yelled—

A bag swallowed the Snake's head, yanking him backwards, before engulfing the rest of his body.

Stunned, the Snake slashed and kicked from inside it, but he couldn't get out. Nor could any sound he was making be heard through the sack's gray fabric, as if he were a dove trapped in a magician's hat.

Tedros and Rhian lifted their heads to see Dot pull the sack tight, sealing the Snake inside.

"Daddy said the School Master enchanted it," she shrugged. "Figured it was worth a shot."

Curled up on the floor, the Sheriff gaped in disbelief.

So did Sophie, Agatha, Anadil, and Hester against the wall.

"Guess his fake pen didn't see that coming," Sophie said, watching the Snake thrash inside the bag.

"Don't think anyone did," said Anadil, as her three rats sniffed around it, giving Dot flabbergasted looks. "I thought spells don't work on the Snake."

"Rafal's spells weren't ordinary spells, apparently," said Hester, prowling towards the Sheriff—

"No, please! Don't kill me!" he choked.

Hester snapped the jail keys off his belt, before holding them out to his daughter.

"Help Robin escape all you want. But this one *can't* escape," said Hester. "Deal?"

Dot smiled, her hand clasping Hester's tight for a moment

before she took the key. "Deal."

"Then let's get this Snake to jail," said Hester as Dot and Anadil dragged the sack towards the door.

"Guess the scims were looking for Tedros after all," Hester heard Dot say.

"But it still doesn't make any sense," Anadil insisted. "I told you in the square. They had to be looking for someone *else* last night. . . ."

Hester moved to help them but she stopped at the door, watching Tedros approach his new copper-haired friend, the boy's stubble sparkling with sweat.

"Thank you," said Tedros.

"Don't think I need this anymore, Your Highness," said his knight, handing Tedros his Lion mask. He bowed to his king. "My name is Rhian."

"You mean *Sir* Rhian," said Tedros.

His knight's steely gaze softened, a blush rising on his amber cheeks.

But now his king had seen his princess out of the corner of his eye. Without a word, he swept towards her, lifted her off the ground, and kissed her like it was the very first time. Agatha kissed him back harder, until they both ran out of breath.

"No more going at things alone," she said. "No more spending time apart."

"That goes both ways," said Tedros. He kissed his princess again.

Meanwhile, Sophie had cozied up to Rhian, who still looked dazed from his exchange with Tedros.

"So now the Lion has a name," she cooed, holding out a kerchief from inside her dress.

He took it and wiped his forehead, his blue-green eyes gazing fervently at her. "And a lady-in-waiting, I hope."

Sophie touched his chest. "A lady who is waiting for you to ask her on a real date . . ."

But Rhian wasn't listening. He was looking past her, at Tedros. The king's expression had slowly changed, as if the triumph of the moment had worn off, giving way to cold reality.

"Teddy, what is it?" Agatha asked.

The king was breathing shallowly now, unable to get words out.

"Your Highness, are you okay?" Rhian said, rushing to his side, almost pushing Agatha out of the way.

He seemed to smell something on Tedros, because he put his nose to the king's neck and then quickly pulled off Tedros' jacket—

Tedros was drenched in blood.

"You're hurt!" Agatha cried.

"No." Rhian put his hands on Tedros' shirt, feeling beneath it. "There's no wound. It's not his blood."

Agatha and Sophie stared at him.

"Whose blood is it?" said Agatha.

Her prince didn't look at her.

Agatha's face changed.

"Tedros . . . ," she rasped. "Where's Lancelot?"

Slowly Tedros lifted his eyes.

That's when he started to cry.

24

Sides of a Story

A few hours earlier, Tedros had been riding with his father's knight across sun-drenched hills.

The two had made good time through the night, moving east from Camelot through the outskirts of Pifflepaff Hills, before curving north towards Nottingham.

They'd traveled in silence, each in a long, black coat, with hoods shadowing their faces, so that even the few riders they encountered hurried past, avoiding eye contact, no doubt thinking they were minions of the Snake.

At night, the Endless Woods usually left Tedros tense and

on edge, especially with WANTED posters of Lance's and his mother's faces coming in and out of the dark at him, tacked to trees as he passed. But the young king was distracted by the sheer freedom of being on open land. It was the first time in *six months* that he'd left the castle. He hadn't realized how claustrophobic he'd been, sealed inside that crumbling compound, no matter how vast it was. Nor had he realized how relieved he would feel to be away from Excalibur taunting him at all hours of the day, despite having to replace his hallowed sword with a middling blade he'd scrounged from the Armory. And though he could sense the tension inside him building, as if a storm was coming, he felt unshackled out here, more capable and kingly than he ever did in that castle—even when he and Lance galloped through Camelot's slum cities spattered with graffiti and effigies denigrating his reign . . . even when they skirted the shells of towns ravaged by the Snake's attacks . . . even when his conversation with his mother kept pulsing in his head. . . .

"*She grew too close to your father, Tedros. . . .*"

"*. . . always insinuating herself between your father and I . . .*"

"*There was something about that room I never liked. . . .*"

All through the ride, Lancelot's black horse stayed neck and neck with Tedros' blue-gray one, though the king rode at a reckless pace, not stopping once to eat or sleep. Tedros kept glancing over at his knight, but Lance was always there, right beside him, his face as placid as Tedros' was clenched.

And indeed, as they reached the outskirts of Nottingham, it was Tedros who finally halted first, his back hurting, stomach aching, and bladder bursting. He almost fell out of the saddle, darting behind a shrubby tree, while Lancelot opened a bag and laid out a late breakfast of smoked salmon, toasted bread, and fresh pears.

"How much longer to Nottingham?" Tedros asked impatiently when he sat, lumping salmon between pieces of bread and scarfing it down.

"You're not due in Sherwood Forest until six," said Lancelot, watching Tedros stuff more food in his mouth. "No need to give yourself indigestion."

"I have business in Nottingham first," said Tedros.

The knight snorted. "No one has business in Nottingham."

"I need to see Lady Gremlaine."

"Thought we were rid of that woman."

"I have questions to ask her."

"About what?"

Tedros glared at the knight. "Nothing that concerns you."

Lancelot took his time putting salmon on his toast. "You're right. None of my business if you think your steward had a child with your father."

Tedros stopped eating, mouth full.

"You don't think I've thought it too? For a half-second, at least," said Lancelot. "You not pulling Excalibur. Guinevere hating that woman. The Snake saying he's Arthur's son. All the clues are there."

"And yet . . . ?" Tedros said.

"They don't add up. You didn't know your father when he was young. When he came to the School for Good, he was

shy, anxious, and a newly crowned king. No matter how popular he became or how much muscle he built or how cocky he
might have acted, he was always that same Arthur inside, asking why he was chosen to pull Excalibur over everyone else in
the Woods. It was Arthur's greatest strength: he relentlessly
questioned himself and wanted the brutal Truth. It's why
he chose me as a best friend, a greasy, pockmarked lout who
would tell him that Truth instead of all the refined Everboys
who'd lie and say whatever he wanted to hear. And it's why he
chose Gwen over all the other girls who just wanted him for
his crown."

"But Mother said Lady Gremlaine was in love with him—"
Tedros argued.

"Doesn't matter. Arthur followed his heart," the knight
returned, pawing at his unruly curls. "He was too faithful
to the Truth to sneak around with this Gremlaine creature.
Gwen and I were the ones who traded in Lies. Not Arthur.
Whoever this Snake is . . . he's not your father's son."

"I want to make sure of it," Tedros pressed. "I want to hear
it from her mouth—"

Lancelot put down his food. "Sometimes the last person
you should ask for the Truth is the one who knows it."

"What do you mean?"

"Just because Lady Gremlaine knows the Truth doesn't
mean she'll *tell* the Truth. Look at your own father. Every girl
at school was in love with Arthur. Every single one. They all
wanted to be his queen. But not Guinevere. That didn't stop

him from loving her, of course. Still, he *knew* she didn't love him, even if she never revealed this Truth to him herself. But I did: I told Arthur that Gwen didn't love him, because it was obvious to both of us that she was in love with me. Yet, no matter how much Arthur valued the Truth, in this one case, the Truth wasn't good enough for him. He thought Camelot *needed* Guinevere. He thought having her as queen would make him a better king. It didn't matter that she didn't love him. If he could *bend* this Truth through sheer force of will . . . it would mean all his doubts about his being chosen king were wrong. That he deserved to be Good's leader because he knew how to put Good first." The knight gazed squarely at Tedros. "That's how I know for sure there was nothing between your father and Lady Gremlaine. Because King Arthur staked everything on his love for Guinevere. *Everything.* And it's why he lost everything when she left."

Tedros shook his head, riling up. "But that's *your* side of the story. It's the side you tell yourself to feel better about taking my mother away from my father. It's the side that makes my father look like the villain. But what if there's another side? What if Arthur knew you and my mother were secretly seeing each other and so he took revenge with Lady Gremlaine? Or what if my father sensed my mother didn't love him and began to fall in love with his steward instead? Or what if my father made one bad decision . . . had one bad night—"

"All of these are possible," said the knight. "But beware trying to bend the Truth to fit your story instead of facing it head-on. That was your father's mistake. And that's how a Snake becomes a Lion and a Lion becomes a Snake. Because the more you bend the Truth to fit a story, the more it turns into Lies without you even realizing it."

"Says the one who traded in Lies," Tedros replied.

Lancelot went quiet.

"After a successful battle or war, it is tradition for a king to exchange gifts with his best knight in front of the kingdom," he said. "Arthur and I always gave each other the same gifts. I kneeled before Arthur's queen and kissed her hand in tribute. And in return, Arthur offered me anything on earth a king could provide a man."

"What did you ask for?" Tedros said.

"Always the same. Nothing at all," said Lancelot. "I'd already taken from him everything a man could take. My gift was meant to tell him that."

He looked at Arthur's son. "Is it really a Lie if someone is unwilling to see the Truth?"

Now it was Tedros who fell silent.

Lancelot cleaned up the remains of their food and drank from his water jug. "I spoke to a few of the leaders in the castle as the guards took them to their rooms. They mentioned something about the Snake having a powerful suit of armor made out of living eels—'scims,' he calls them. They think that there's a connection between these scims and the Snake's life force. That there's magic in his blood. But they also say the scims can be killed. Kill enough of them and you can penetrate the Snake's flesh."

"So he's just as mortal as you and me, then," said Tedros, looking Lance in the eye. "See, he's someone's son after all."

"Well, then seeing as this Snake and his minions are still on the loose, if anyone asks who you are while we're in Nottingham, you're someone's son too," said the knight, pulling the young king to his feet.

"Whose?" Tedros asked, confused.

Lancelot grinned as he walked towards the horses. *"Mine."*

Soon they reached the entrance point to Nottingham: an imposing, sooty, black-brick jail at the top of a hill and a gleaming bronze statue of the Sheriff in front of it.

"The Land of Law and Order," Lancelot muttered, eyeing the WELCOME sign down the slope, with a cartoon of the Sheriff chasing Robin Hood. "Any kingdom that promises Law and Order surely has neither."

From the hillcrest, Lancelot could see the lush outskirts of Sherwood Forest a mile north and steered his horse towards it—

"This way," Tedros corrected, riding his horse away from the Forest and towards the center of town.

"Don't be a fool. The second we cross into Sherwood Forest, we'll be safe for the night," Lancelot scolded, nosing his horse next to the king's. "We left Camelot so that you could meet the Lion boy. And that's the *only* reason we left."

"We still have two hours until I have to be at Marian's Arrow."

"Do you even know where Gremlaine lives?"

"I'll ask someone."

"We haven't seen a soul."

"I'll figure it out—"

"It's an unnecessary risk, Tedros."

"It's something I have to *do*." Tedros held firm.

Lancelot exhaled.

It was midafternoon in Nottingham, but there wasn't a person to be found in the square, the only sound the out-of-rhythm *clop* of the two men's horses. Lancelot peered around at the closed shops and empty streets.

"No animals," he said. "First sign of trouble."

Tedros wasn't listening. He'd spotted something in the window of the Sheriff's Blotter: a copy of the latest *Royal Rot*, with a headline about Lady Gremlaine above the fold. He couldn't read the full article from outside the window, so he punched in the corner of the glass pane and pulled the paper out.

"So much for Law and Order," mumbled Lancelot.

Tedros scanned the story—

> Has Lady Gremlaine been fired from Camelot for a second time? Fifteen years ago, King Arthur's once-steward was exiled from the castle by Guinevere (rumor has it for being too chummy with the king, which both Lady Gremlaine and Guinevere have vehemently denied). But in an ironic twist, Guinevere's son Tedros—our so-called new "King"—latched on to Lady Gremlaine as his own steward, just like his father

once did. However, the last two nights, Lady Gremlaine has been seen in her hometown of Nottingham by numerous observers. Said Bertie, an attendant at the Nottingham Prison: "No one's been in the house at 246 Morgause Street for several years now, but neighbors sayin' that haughty woman's back."

We asked Bertie: Could she be in Nottingham to visit family?

"She ain't got no family here," Bertie replied.

What about a vacation?

"No one vacations in Nottingham except stupid tourists thinking they might see Robin Hood."

So what's Bertie's conclusion?

"She ran afoul of the king and came back to lick her wounds. Good place to hide your face, Nottingham. No one's gonna find ya here except nosy neighbors."

And the *Royal Rot*, of course. Stay tuned as we pursue an exclusive interview with the "King's" (disgraced?) steward.

Tedros folded up the newspaper, thrust it back through the window, and used his fingerglow to repair the glass. "Come on," he said, hopping onto his horse. "We need to find Morgause Street."

A booming crash echoed in the distance.

King and knight swiveled to see a plume of smoke and dust rising at the top of the hill near the jail, though they couldn't see what had caused it.

"Something's wrong. . . . Let's get to the Forest," Lance urged.

"Ten minutes. That's all I need. Then you can feast at Marian's Arrow while I meet this 'Lion' fellow and tell him in no uncertain terms that I already *have* a knight," said Tedros, riding towards the cottage lanes.

"Happy to let him have the job if he wants it," Lancelot growled, following him.

But Tedros was already amongst the houses, shifting and squinting in his saddle to make out the streets around him: Oldherde Court . . . Magpie Grove . . . Marian Mews. . . . He could see people peeping through curtains from inside their cottages; they all had the same spooked expressions, their eyes tracking him. He pulled his hood farther over his head.

"They think we're the Snake's men," said Tedros. "They're waiting for us to attack them."

"Or waiting for something to attack *us*," said his knight. "Something they know is out here that we don't."

Tedros met his eyes, a flicker of doubt passing over the king's face. "Look! There it is!" he exclaimed suddenly, spying the sign for Morgause Street over Lance's shoulder. "Gremlaine's house is that wa—"

A gleaming black blur flew under Lance's horse, and the animal bucked in surprise, neighing wildly, almost throwing the knight off. Tedros whirled around, following the gleam . . . but it was gone.

"What was it?" Lance panted, trying to soothe his horse.

Tedros scanned the clear crossroads. "Must have been a bat

or a crow. Come on," he said, pulling his horse towards the lane ahead. But his horse wouldn't move, tugging his head in the other direction. Lancelot's horse oriented the same way.

"They want us to get to the Forest," the knight said.

Tedros dismounted and jogged towards Morgause Street, leaving Lancelot and the horses behind.

Rounding the corner, he tracked the street numbers: 232 . . . 240 . . . 244 . . . until he found a two-floor white cottage with "246" above the door in peeling red paint.

This is Gremlaine's?

The front garden was dead and overgrown with bristly weeds. The cottage's white panels were spotted with mildew and bird droppings. Both windows were cracked, with tiny holes in them, as if they'd been shot through with marbles. In leaving Camelot, Lady Gremlaine had traded a ramshackle castle for an even more run-down house.

As Tedros approached the front door, he noticed the welcome mat: an embroidered needlepoint of young King Arthur with a halo over his head and the words stitched beneath him in golden thread—

THE ONCE AND FUTURE KING

He'd seen these before, sold cheaply in Camelot's street markets. They were popular with the poorest citizens of the kingdom, who'd lionized the lofty king, and with zealots who saw Tedros' father not as a man, but as an immortal saint who would one day return from death to reclaim his kingdom.

But Lady Gremlaine? She didn't fit into either category. She worked for his father. She was Arthur's friend. Even if she did secretly love him, having this in front of her house felt like something other than love. Something creepier. It made Tedros' stomach lurch.

He caught a whiff of powdered rose at the door. Quickly he put his hand on the knocker, but then he smelled the rosy scent overtaken by a hot, sweaty musk. Tedros turned, frowning.

"Where you go, I go," groused Lancelot, sword gleaming on his belt.

Tedros turned back and knocked hard on the door.

No one answered.

"Glad that's settled," said the knight, starting to drag him away—

Tedros unsheathed his sword, aimed the hilt against the door lock, and smashed it.

"Few months as king and you've gone vigilante," Lancelot marveled.

Tedros shoved the door open and went inside the house, Lancelot hewing close to him.

"Did you stalk my father like this too?" Tedros sniped.

"Mmmhm. Didn't smell as nice as you, though. You know, with the number of baths you take, it's a wonder you get any work as king done at all—"

Tedros stopped in front of him. "Lance . . ."

The knight looked up and stiffened.

Lady Gremlaine's house had been ravaged: the furniture

upended and slashed open; closet doors splintered and rugs frayed; lampshades ripped apart, their glass bases shattered; books shredded, pages showered around like confetti.

"Who would do this?" Tedros asked, stupefied. "It's like an army shot the place through with arrows."

Lancelot studied a pillow speared with holes, the stuffing spilling out, then squinted around the room. "Only there aren't any arrows *here*."

Glancing inside a closet, Tedros found a safebox, broken open and dumped on the floor. He sifted through the wreckage: first, some old clippings from the *Camelot Courier*, the top one announcing his father's coronation, with a portrait of Arthur accepting the crown and a young Lady Gremlaine smiling to the side of the stage, while another clipping featured a picture of a young Arthur and young Gremlaine sitting together, with the caption: *"King and his steward hard at work in the early days of his reign."* There was also a copy of the *Royal Rot*, with the headline: *"GUINEVERE WHO? How Lady Gremlaine Is the Real Secret to King Arthur's Success!"* Tedros flung it aside, noticing a ledger beneath it with a handwritten label:

Camelot Beautiful

Tedros opened the ledger, only to see all its pages blank . . . except for a business card clipped to the last one:

Albemarle
Licensed Manager
BANK OF PUTSI

But there was something stuck to the back of the ledger, Tedros realized—a stack of letters, banded together, addressed to Lady Gremlaine. He peeled them off the ledger and flipped through the stack, his eyes widening.

All of the letters were in his father's handwriting.

"Tedros, look at this," Lancelot's voice said.

Tedros shoved the letters in his coat along with the business card and moved out of the closet to find his knight inspecting the wall. Black marks streaked across it, with a strange wet sheen. Tedros scraped his hand across the marks, then peered closely at his fingertips. Shiny black debris like sequins had embedded in his skin.

"Snake scales . . . ," said Lancelot ominously.

Tedros thought of that black blur he saw in the street. . . .

Something rustled upstairs.

The two men stared at each other.

"Lady Gremlaine?" Tedros called out.

No answer.

Warily, Tedros ascended the staircase, Lancelot behind him.

On the second floor, they found more of the scaly black

marks on the hallway walls and on a square hatch built into the ceiling, presumably a portal to the attic.

More rustling came from the room at the end of the hall.

"Lady Gremlaine, are you here?' Tedros called again, inching forward. Lancelot drew his sword behind him.

Together, they turned the corner into a bedchamber that had been pulverized as ruthlessly as the downstairs rooms. The mattress had been flung off its frame, the white sheets sliced to ribbons, the pillows gutted of feathers.

A blue-green butterfly rustled feverishly against the window, trying to find a way out.

Tedros' shoulders relaxed. He looked at Lancelot, hunching over the bed.

"What is it?" Tedros asked.

His knight held up a torn strip of white sheet.

A big splotch of blood had soaked it through.

Fresh blood.

"Lady Gremlaine?" Tedros hollered.

Lancelot checked closets; Tedros searched under the bed and behind furniture. But there were no other bloodstains or signs that his steward was in this house—

Tedros' boot caught on something sticky.

He looked down at a glob of black goo, beaten to a pulp.

A shadow came over him and he swiveled to see Lance looming over his shoulder.

"It's one of those 'scims,' isn't it? The things the Snake is made of," Tedros asked. "It's why all the villagers must be hiding. The Snake was here."

"And from the looks of it, Lady Gremlaine had her way with the the scim he sent for her," said Lancelot, before glancing back at the bed. "Though judging from that blood, it may have had its way with her first."

"But her body isn't here. That means she's still alive, wherever she is."

"Or lying in a ditch with her throat cut," said Lancelot. He nudged at the dead scim with his boot. "Doubt this thing came alone. If the Snake wants to kill Lady Gremlaine, he'll find her."

"But it doesn't make any sense," Tedros said, shaking his head. "If Lady Gremlaine is the Snake's mother, why would he want to kill her?"

A sharp squeal came from the first floor, like a teakettle at full steam.

Lancelot pulled his sword, eyeing Tedros. "Stay here."

The knight crept back down the stairs.

Blade at the ready, Tedros waited at the top of the twisting steps. He couldn't see where the knight had gone.

"Lance?" he said.

No answer.

Tedros had a bad feeling in his gut . . . a feeling that told him to follow Lancelot. . . .

Gripping his sword harder, he started to descend—

Something wet dripped on his face.

Tedros smeared it off and looked at his hand.

Blood.

He craned up and saw more droplets of blood leaking from the edges of the hatch built into the ceiling.

"Lance?" he bellowed down the stairs.

Still nothing.

Tedros dragged the frayed mattress out of the bedroom and shoved it into the hall. Standing on its edge, he sheathed his sword and reached up for the hatch's handle, but his fingers couldn't catch it. He jumped a few times, but he still fell short. Finally, he took a running start, rebounded off the mattress, and grabbed hold of the hatch with both hands, yanking it open. He hung from the handle, kicking his legs midair as he muscled his hands onto the sides of the floor above him, pulling himself through—

A heavy weight slammed him in the head.

Before he could scream, it slammed him again.

Gasping in shock, he felt cold hands seize him by the neck and drag the last of his body into the attic.

Tedros wished he'd blacked out, so he didn't have to feel this kind of pain, as if his head had been cracked open like an egg and the yolk set on fire. Curled up on the floor, he ran his hand down the back of his hair, expecting a mass of blood or brains, but instead found a swollen lump at the ridge of his skull.

He pried open his eyes to watery slits and saw a blurred vision of Lady Gremlaine standing in an attic, her turban gone, her dark brown hair long and wild, her makeup spattered, and the shoulder of her lavender robes drenched in blood. There was terror in her eyes.

Something else too.

Madness, Tedros thought.

His gaze moved to her hand.

She was holding a hammer.

The flat side was coated with black, scaly goo.

"V-v-voices. I heard voices—" she stammered. "I didn't know it was you. . . . You can't be here—he'll find you—"

"Who will?" Tedros said, struggling to his knees. His head was throbbing so hard he couldn't think.

"His scims are l-l-looking for me. One already did this," said Lady Gremlaine, touching her bloody shoulder. "I killed it and I hid, so they'd think I escaped. But now you're here. . . . They'll find me. . . . He'll come back—"

"The Snake?" Tedros steadied against the only window for support, the glass so dirty and stained he couldn't see out of it. "Why is the Snake looking for you?"

But Lady Gremlaine was haunted now, her gaze glassy and unfocused. "I read the papers. . . . I knew about the attacks . . . but I didn't know it was all connected . . . not until he came for me. . . . I'd taken care of it. . . . It was in the past . . . buried and forgotten. . . ."

Tedros' heart stopped, his eyes locked on her. "He's your son, isn't he? The Snake is my *father's* son. Is that why Excalibur is trapped in the stone?"

Lady Gremlaine didn't answer, looking everywhere but at him.

"*Can he pull Excalibur!*" Tedros demanded.

Tears spilled down his steward's face. "I was so jealous . . . ," she whispered. "That your mother would have his child and I wouldn't . . . And then when I had my chance. . . ." She clutched her throat, choking out a sob. "I did something terrible. Before you were born. Something your father never knew. But I'd fixed it. . . . I'd made sure the boy would never be found. . . . He'd grow up never knowing who he was. . . . I told no one. How could he know! How could he find out! It's impossible—" Her voice faltered and she folded into herself, dropping the hammer to the floor. "I told so many Lies to protect the Truth. . . ."

"*CAN HE PULL EXCALIBUR!*" Tedros yelled.

Lady Gremlaine looked up at him, her face ghost-white. She started to answer—

The window shattered behind Tedros and he lunged to the ground as three scims crashed in and ripped through Lady Gremlaine's chest. Tedros had no time to think or move to her dead body—the scims were already coming for him. He scrambled for the hatch on his knees, flinging it open and diving through just as the scims grazed his legs; he reached up and slammed the hatch shut, hearing the eels bash against the door, squealing violently, as Tedros free-fell onto the mattress below.

Down the stairs he fled, slipping on newspapers and lampshades and pillow stuffing, trying to stay on his feet as he surged towards the front door—

"Lance! Where are you!"

I should have listened to him. . . . This was all a mistake. . . .

They had to get to the horses, Tedros thought, bursting through the door. They had to ride to the Forest *now*—

He stopped dead.

Lancelot stood in the front yard, surrounded by a hundred scims, swirling around him like a moving cage. His sword had been stripped from him, held over his head by the scims, out of his reach.

The knight's face was pale, his lips trembling.

It was the first time Tedros had ever seen Sir Lancelot afraid.

Slowly the scims congealed into the Snake, his green mask glinting in the last of daylight, the scims on his body slithering and hissing. He took hold of Lancelot's sword and held it to the knight's neck.

The Snake raised his eyes to Tedros.

"Hello, Brother," he said.

Tedros couldn't breathe. "Listen to me. It's me you want. Not him. Please . . . let's finish this once and for all."

"This?" The Snake glared hatefully at the king. "*This* is just the beginning."

He slashed Lancelot's throat.

"*No!*" Tedros screamed.

The Snake fractured into scims and flew away, letting the knight's bloody sword clink to the street.

Tedros sprinted to Lancelot, catching him as he fell. Blood gushed from the knight's neck. Tedros ripped off Lance's shirt to seal the wound, the knight's blood soaking through Tedros' black coat.

"I'm . . . fine . . . ," Lance wheezed. "I'll . . . live. . . ."

"Why you—" Tedros sobbed, holding the knight in his arms. "Why not me—it's me he wants—"

Overhead, glowing sparks flew into the sky and Tedros whirled to see them coming from the next street.

He recognized the glow colors: Hester's . . . Dot's. . . .

Then more.

Sophie's . . .

Agatha's.

Lancelot saw it too.

"Go," the knight whispered. "He'll . . . hurt her. . . ."

"No, I won't leave you," Tedros fought. "I'll find help—I'll get you home—"

Lancelot smiled peacefully. "I'll be here . . . right here when you return. . . ."

"No—please—"

"*Kill him*, Tedros . . . for me. For Camelot."

Tedros hugged Lancelot with all his might, unable to let go. "This is my fault. I should have never brought you here."

"Our story brought us here for a reason. Agatha needs you, Tedros. Like Gwen needed me," the knight whispered.

Tedros choked up.

"*Go*," said Lancelot. "Before it's too late."

With a cry, Tedros released him and ran into the streets, trying not to look back.

He'll live . . . , he told himself, smearing tears. *He'll live. . . .*

But inside, the young king knew the truth.

25

Date Night in Sherwood Forest

Agatha stood at the edge of a high, domed treehouse, lit by blue and purple lanterns, gazing out at the labyrinth of other colorfully lit treehouses, connected to hers via bridges, swings, and ropes. She could see into each of these

houses, watching her fellow crew members rest after Sir Lancelot's and Lady Gremlaine's burials, either taking naps, quietly talking, or slipping in to shower in the private barrels that hung off each house. But Agatha just stood there, unable to move or even cry, having shed all her tears at the funeral.

It was only seven o'clock, a full night ahead.

And yet, it felt like an ending.

"Not quite a castle, I'm afraid," said a voice below her.

Agatha glanced down at a shadow climbing the tree, wearing a green coat and a brown cap speared with a green feather. He paused on the branch below the door and looked up at her, his face coming into the light.

"But still . . . it's home," said the man.

He was as old as Sophie's father, but he had a baby face, with clean-shaven pink skin, save a red-brown tuft beneath his lip that matched his mop of wavy hair.

"Better than a castle, to be honest," said Agatha, holding down a fresh wave of tears. "Especially when we're about to go back to that castle with a Good man gone."

"Might seem that way, but men like Sir Lancelot never really are gone," said the stranger. "He's a legend. And legends grow bigger with time. Or at least that's what I tell myself these days whenever I meet young ones like you who have no idea who I am."

"Even the dimmest Readers know who Robin Hood is," Agatha said, forcing a smile.

"And even the dimmest heroes know *The Tale of Sophie and Agatha*," said Robin Hood. "Though I do wish we could have met under better circumstances."

Agatha felt the stone lid on her emotions crumble. She smeared at her wet eyes. "Guinevere . . . What will she do . . ."

From his rucksack, Robin pulled a metal flask. "Gold-leaf tea. Cures every ailment, including a crap day and crap days to come," he said, holding it out. "Dot just helped me make a fresh brew. Made with real gold that I rob from rich, miserable people who don't even know what gold is good for."

Agatha took a big swig. "Tastes like . . . chocolate," she sniffled.

"Like I said: Dot helped me make it," Robin sighed. "Mind if I come in? Marian insists she left an earring and better I find it than have her looking for it herself."

"By all means," said Agatha, mustering composure as he swung through the door. "I can't thank you enough for letting us stay here."

"We knew all about the Snake and that business at the Four Point, but there's a reason I ain't in the League of Thirteen. We Merry Men keep our noses out of other kingdoms' affairs and they stay outta ours in return—especially since we've started raiding rich folks beyond Nottingham," said Robin, scavenging near a wall decorated with newspaper clippings touting his various robberies and escapes. "But then I got the message from Dot via a crow with Camelot's official ring around its neck. That got my attention. Oh look, found it—" He held up a pearl earring. "Actually, this ain't hers," he mumbled, and started searching inside leather quivers filled with arrows. "Sherwood Forest ain't the most welcoming to strangers, especially a crew with a bunch of Nevers, but we'll do anything for Camelot and for Dot. Camelot because King Arthur once saved us from a villain called the Green Knight. And Dot because . . . well, Dot's like a daughter. Her dad will say that's a lie. That I just used her to escape jail. But her dad's about as fit to be a dad as I'm fit to be a husband. That's what I tell Marian at least." He winked at Agatha. "Jackpot!" He glided past her and picked a gold earring out of the gap between two wooden planks on a wall. "This is definitely it . . . maybe."

"Where will you and your men sleep tonight?" Agatha asked. "We've put you out of your houses—"

"Ha! Don't you worry about us. Pity the lad who sleeps too often in his own bed. We'll go to the Arrow and see where the night takes us . . . ," said Robin, smelling dirty shirts in the hamper until he found one clean enough to wear. He crumpled it into his pocket. "And don't you worry about that Snake either. He's still cooped up in the Sheriff's magic catching sack and locked in a jail cell, while three of my men sit in front of that cell the whole night, armed with bows. Sheriff's in the clinic—won't be walkin' for a few days—and with the Sheriff gone, it was easy to pay Bertie off to skip town. Dot has the only key to that jail and she's here in the Forest, with zero chance to mess things up, because let's face it: Dot has that capability. To keep her occupied, I arranged a date between her and the newest member of the Merry Men, who is clean as a whistle and about her age, so tonight she and the rest of you can kick back and relax. Then tomorrow, you and your lot will return to Camelot and argue with the other rulers of the

Woods over who gets to cut off the reptile's head." He looked back at Agatha. "I'd go with one of the Never kings if I were you. Good at executions."

He jaunted towards the door. "I'm serious about kicking back, though. Go enjoy Sherwood Forest. Hell of a lot better than Nottingham. I'll be at the Arrow if you need me—"

"Robin?"

"Mmm?" he said, turning.

"You sure it's safe here?" Agatha said, her eyes puffy and red, looking out at the open treehouses glowing in the middle of a dark Forest. "I know it is, of course. . . . It's just after the last few days . . ."

Robin Hood put his fingers in his mouth and whistled. Trap nets exploded from every direction, swooping down between houses, along with snapping bear traps, booby-trapped tree trunks, ricocheting swords, and a hailstorm of arrows, slicing through the darkness and embedding in doors. Spooked crew members looked out their windows. Hort stirred from a nap.

"False alarm!" Robin called.

Everyone grumbled and went back to what they were doing.

Robin smiled at Agatha. "Go. Enjoy the night. Sometimes when things get too dark, we need help remembering why life's worth living."

"I don't think I can," Agatha rasped. "Not tonight."

"Don't do it for you, pumpkin," Robin said. "Do it for *him*."

Agatha followed his eyes out the window to the hill where she and the crew had just returned from, moonlight casting down on a row of graves . . .

And a boy in a blood-soaked shirt, standing in front of the newest ones.

Lancelot and Lady Gremlaine had been buried at sunset, when Sherwood Forest had the humid, heavy scent of a jungle. But now that it was dark, Agatha's route back to the gravesite felt new, as if the Forest only came alive at night. Fairy girls in green dresses and fluorescing pink wings poked their heads out of tree holes, tittering: *"That's Sophie's friend!" "Oooh, we love Sophie!" "Who's Sophie?" "The one with pretty clothes!" "Didn't Sophie kill fairies?" "I heard the Storian got that part wrong!"* A trollcat bobbed his head out of branches to see what the commotion was about and sneezed, scattering the fairies. Agatha, meanwhile, almost stepped on a forest gnome, who was livid at first, then recognized her, chanting, "AGATA, AGATA," and holding out a pint-sized notebook for her to autograph before his frumpy wife pulled him back into his hole.

Agatha sighed, relieved that for once her fairy tale's fame hadn't resulted in sleazy tabloid headlines or someone trying to kill her. Two dragon birds, one red, one orange, breathed fire as she passed, scorching a mouse they'd caught, then chittered happily in her direction as they ate it. A family of sparklefrogs burped the Camelot anthem in salute and a fat mongoose leapt out of a log, mouth full of butterflies, and pipped, "Uma friend!"

Slowly Agatha's body relaxed in the thicket's muggy warmth, the trauma of the last few hours melting away. Even in the most beautiful stretches of the Endless Woods, there was always an undercurrent of danger. But here in Sherwood Forest, Robin and his Merry Men had created their own magical Woods within the Woods, untouched by the politics of the Ever-Never world. In fact, given he was at once a thief, a philanderer, and a champion of the poor, Agatha wasn't even sure if Robin himself was Good or Evil . . . and Robin probably liked it that way.

As she approached the hill, Agatha glimpsed Tedros' silhouette and felt a swell of love. Robin was right: no matter how much sadness or pain she felt, Tedros was feeling it a thousand times worse. Her prince needed her.

She crested towards the gravesite, coming up behind Tedros—and stopped.

He wasn't alone.

Without really knowing why, Agatha ducked behind a tree so she could overhear.

"I used to make-believe I was Sir Lancelot when I was little," Rhian was saying, barefoot and freshly bathed in a black cut-off shirt and beige breeches. "Riding alongside your father and slaying the Green Knight. Imagining that I was standing before the people after a triumphant battle, exchanging gifts with the king. I ruined a lot of pillows jabbing at them with wooden spoons, pretending they were enemies of King Arthur. . . . I dreamed of serving Camelot one day, just like Sir Lancelot did."

"Lots of boys did. And still do," said Tedros, his blood-spattered shirt unbuttoned in the heat. "Had a guard at the castle recently who dreamed of serving Camelot too . . . only to then betray it."

"Serving is much harder than the work of dreaming," said Rhian. "I just wish my own service didn't have to take the place of Sir Lancelot's."

A few fairies settled in Tedros' hair, clearly listening in. By their light, Agatha could see the new knight was taller than the king and darker in complexion, though not as pumped with muscle. Still, with his cropped hair, high forehead, and sculpted jaw, he seemed sturdier than Tedros. More intense.

"You really think the Snake is your brother?" Rhian asked. "That he's your father's son?"

"Lady Gremlaine never said it for sure. But she said she'd done something terrible, something she'd hidden from Arthur and the world," said Tedros. "Plus, the Snake called me 'Brother.' He vowed he can pull Excalibur. And Lady Gremlaine never denied it. And yet, if he can pull Excalibur from the stone . . . that would mean he's truly my father's son. Would my father's son try to kill his own brother? Would he really murder Lancelot? His father's best friend and knight?"

"A friend and knight who betrayed your father. A knight with your father's price on his head," said Rhian warily. "Maybe the Snake is taking revenge in your father's name. If Dot hadn't captured him, your mother might very well have been next."

Tedros stiffened. "All this time, I thought King Arthur's son could never be a villain like the Snake. I never considered he could be a villain *because* he's Arthur's son." He looked at

Rhian. "So it is possible, then. The Snake might be Camelot's real king."

"Don't fear, sire. The Snake is in prison where he belongs. When you return, you will try your hand at Excalibur again. And this time, I'm sure it will give you the answer you deserve," said Rhian warmly. "In the meantime, you have a kingdom to take care of. A wedding to plan." He paused. "And a mother to be there for."

Tedros looked at him, his mouth quivering. "I'm dreading going back, Rhian."

"Tedros—"

"You don't understand. I hated Lancelot after he took my mother away. I *wanted* him to die. But in the end, I learned to love him like my own dad. My mother won't be able to live without him. Lance was her whole life. And to watch her stand there at my wedding alone . . . I can't do it. I just can't. I don't know why she made Lancelot come with me into the Woods. I'm not enough for her—"

"Yes, you are," said Rhian. "You said it yourself. She knew the risks of sending Lancelot into the Woods. But you're worth those risks to her. Or she wouldn't have made Lancelot go with you."

Tedros sniffled, dabbing at his eyes quickly. "So you don't just save kings' lives, you talk sense into them too."

"All part of a knight's work."

"Is dying part of a knight's work too?" said Tedros morosely. "Because every knight I have ends up dead."

"I'll take my chances," said Rhian. "My duty as a knight is

to protect you, with all the risks that incurs."

Tedros looked at him, wiping his nose with his shirt. "Where were you when I was at school? You could have saved me from . . . you know . . . *girls*."

Rhian laughed.

Behind the tree, Agatha spied on them, conflicted. On the one hand, she was so relieved Tedros had someone to talk to after such a terrible loss. On the other hand, she was envious that he wasn't sharing these feelings with her. She couldn't remember a time when he'd been this open with her during the last six months. Or ever.

"Seriously, how could the School Master not take you?" Tedros asked.

"Beats me," said Rhian. "I'm from Foxwood, which sends more boys to the School for Good than any other Ever kingdom. And I tried to be a Good boy growing up. But on kidnapping day, I didn't get a Flowerground ticket. Sometimes I think my mother hid it. She never wanted me to go to that school. But I also wonder if I'd be here today if I'd been in your class at the School for Good. Out in the Woods, I could prove myself to you by being there when it mattered: fighting the Snake at the Four Point or riding across the Ever and Never lands, beating back the Snake's thugs, and saving your friends' quests. At school, I would have just been another Everboy trying to curry your favor. At school, there's no real way to prove that you can be a good knight."

"Or a good king," said Tedros.

"Or a good son," sighed Rhian.

Tedros raised a brow.

"From what I know of your story, we have a lot in common," Rhian explained. "My father died too. My relationship with my mother is . . . difficult. And when neither parent is a comfort, you live haunted by their shadows instead of finding your way out from under them. But hearing *The Tale of Sophie and Agatha* showed me a path. Camelot has a divine duty to unite the Woods in times of crisis. That's why I idolized your father over mine. His power transcended Good and Evil and made both sides look to him as a leader. Maybe he didn't always use this power the way he should have, but he was more than a king. He was a *legend*. And that's why I'm here to help you. Because I realized it's my destiny to make sure the one true king rules Camelot and that you and your queen earn your rightful place."

Tedros took this in, silent for a moment. "So you risk your life . . . you risk your name . . . you put everything on the line . . . for *me*?"

"For you. And for Camelot." The young knight cracked a smile. "And for Sophie."

Tedros burst out laughing. "Now we have the truth! Be a knight to me and my queen and you can snake your way to the queen's best friend! Of all the girls in the Woods . . . *Sophie*!" He thumped Rhian on the back. "Godspeed, friend. You'll learn your lesson in time."

"Unlike you, I know how to handle her," Rhian ragged, tripping him.

"Only one way to handle her. Hide in a cave until she's gone," said Tedros, booting him in the behind.

Both boys bent over, cracking up; fairies careened out of the young king's hair.

Tedros' laughter ebbed. His expression changed. "Fitting, isn't it? Lancelot dies and you appear," he said quietly. "As much as I loved Chaddick, I wasn't bonded to him like my father was to Lance. I never had that kind of knight. I never had a brother. At least not one I knew about. Perhaps I resented Sophie so much because of how close she was with Agatha. And I never had something like that with a boy—or at least nothing that ever lasted. Maybe because I never could fully trust one after what happened between my father and Lance. . . . But you're different than all the rest. It feels like I finally have my own Lance."

Rhian smiled. "A Lance that isn't after your girl."

The two boys gazed at each other.

"Want to get dinner?" Tedros asked. "I'm famished and Marian's Arrow has a back room that actually serves decent food—"

Rhian grinned. "If it was any other night . . ."

"You dog! You have a date with Sophie!" Tedros said.

"At Beauty and the Feast. Dot helped me use Camelot's courier crow to make reservations before I came here to check on you. Turns out Dot's heading there for a date too."

"Beauty and the Feast! Where a piece of bread costs more than a new carriage? Where a cook once killed himself because he served a gold-truffle-coated steak two shades overdone?"

"Have to make an impression, don't I? Bring Agatha. We can all sit together."

"First things first, I'd rather go on a date with *Hort* than sit at dinner with Sophie. Plus, getting Agatha to go to Beauty and the Feast would be like trying to get a cat to swim. She'd spend the whole meal ridiculing the place. Besides, we shouldn't be wasting what little money Camelot has. You and I can do dinner another time. Especially since you'll be my knight at Camelot for a long while to come." Tedros hesitated. "If you want to come home with me, that is."

Rhian locked eyes with the king. "I wouldn't have it any other way." He put his hand on Tedros' shoulder. "And if you need someone to stand by you when you first see your mother . . ."

"Thank you, Sir Rhian . . . but I'll have Agatha with me," said Tedros softly.

Rhian straightened. "Of course, Your Highness."

"You better go get changed for dinner," said Tedros, buttoning his shirt. "They won't let you in looking like you're going to the gym. Or Sophie won't, at least. . . ."

The knight rocked back on his heels. "Trust me. I'll be taming that girl long before she tames me. Should we walk back?"

"Think I'll stay out here a bit longer," said the king.

"See you later, then."

"See you later."

The two boys parted. Tedros watched Rhian go.

He stood at Lancelot's grave for a long moment, fairies detonating around him, before he turned to leave—

"Hey," he said, surprised.

Agatha treaded uphill towards him. "Was worrying where you were. I'm starving."

"I was about to head back," said Tedros.

"Everything okay?"

"Yeah. Why?"

"You were gone awhile."

"Lost track of time. You know, just thinking a bit . . ."

"By yourself?"

Tedros batted at a fairy hovering around his ear. "I need a shower. If you wait for me, we can grab a quick dinner at the Arrow," he said, jogging past Agatha—

"Tedros?"

He stopped and turned.

"Can we go somewhere else for dinner?" Agatha asked. "Somewhere, you know . . . nice."

Tedros stared at her. *"Nice?"*

Less than an hour later, Agatha and Tedros arrived at a boxy cottage deep in the Forest, with dark-green brick walls and a terra-cotta rooftop. Dressed in a tight red dress that wasn't her own and standing next to Tedros, who wore a borrowed blue tuxedo with a gold bowtie, Agatha blinked skeptically at the dumpy-looking house.

"I put on a dress . . . for *this*?" she said.

Tedros knocked on the door.

A slit opened and two dark eyes glared through. "Reservation time?" said an oily voice.

Tedros steeled himself. "We don't have reservations."

The slit slammed shut and high-pitched cackles echoed behind it.

Tedros knocked again.

The slit reopened. "Reservation ti— Oh. *You*. Surely you know that Beauty and the Feast is both the most sought-after meal in the Endless Woods as well as the recipient of 'Best Restaurant' from the Everwood Gastronomical Society for the last 265 years straight. Even with the Snake crippling the Woods, we haven't lost a *single* reservation. Reservations that must be made months, if not *years*, in advance, though we made an exception tonight for Sophie of Woods Beyond, a diva, icon, goddess, and personal hero of mine, and her date, a gorgeous new knight of Camelot—all of which is to say, we do not have room for stragglers off the street. So please take you and your poorly tailored clothing and vacate the premises before I call the dogs."

The slit slid closed.

Agatha knocked.

The eyes reappeared, about to combust—

"I'm Sophie's best friend," said Agatha.

"I'm the King of Camelot," said Tedros.

"And I'm the Queen of Bazoo," the slimy voice said.

"No. *Really*," said Tedros, staring hard at him.

The eyes looked at him. Then at Agatha.

"*Mamasita!*" the voice gasped.

The door flew open and a man appeared, his skin caked in bronzer, his thick, black toupee crowned with gold feathers, and his tall, lithe body wrapped in what appeared to be a fur kimono.

"Welcome, welcome, welcome!" he said, seizing Agatha by one arm and Tedros by the other and dragging both through the door into the restaurant, whirling with color and motion. "I'm Masha Mahaprada, Master of Dining and Chief Visionary Officer of Beauty and the Feast! Tonight's theme is '*Through the Looking Glass*: Our Bodies, Our Food, Ourselves. . . .'"

Agatha scanned the place, wide-eyed. Tablecloths made of peacock feathers lay across gold-legged tables, heaped with chicken liver fondue, samphire tempura, pheasant wing confit, crab escabeche, vegetable towers, and chocolate water- falls. . . . Evers and Nevers dined in proximity, clad in the most lavish outfits—luminescent dresses, swan-feather hats, sequined saris, crog-skin suits, stymph-bone jewelry (even the trolls were dressed up)—with any enmity between Good and Evil transcended by the shared experience of an extraor- dinary meal. Red foxes in crisp black tuxedos took orders, magic carpets brought and cleared plates, and hummingbirds swooped in and swept away breadcrumbs. Mini-chandeliers over tables dripped magical gold at the start of each course while fireworks exploded upon the completion of desserts, and a neon cricket symphony surfed the restaurant on discs of white-chocolate ganache, playing a love serenade.

"Now a few simple rules of dining," Masha confided,

clutching Agatha and Tedros tightly.

A chorus of lovebirds, each a different color of the rainbow, landed on Agatha's and Tedros' shoulders and sang a jingly song—

> *Beauty and the Feast*
> *Beauty and the Feeeeast*
> *Where boys bring girls to give them rings*
> *And a kiss or two at leeeeast*
>
> *Girls, wear your best dresses*
> *Let the boys take all your stresses*
> *They'll order for you and make all of you*
> *Feel like the very best princesses*
>
> *Girls, don't talk too loudly*
> *Boys, don't talk too brashly*
> *And both of you—this includes me too —*
> *No politics, they're <u>ghastly</u>*
>
> *So enjoy your meal*
> *Please try the veal*
> *Don't slurp or burp or splash or gnash*
> *And most important of alllllllll . . .*
> *ALWAYS PAY IN CASH!*

Tedros and Agatha looked at each other.

"It's very . . . sexist," said Agatha.

"It's very . . . expensive," said Tedros.

"Sherwood Forest, darling. Chi chi chi chi chi!" said Masha, pulling them ahead.

Agatha held her breath, soaking in the spectacle. At one table, a boy and girl kissed over a smoking chocolate volcano, shrouding them in red mist, before it erupted with strawberry mousse. At another, two giants shared an appropriate-sized mountain of rabbit and fennel linguini, while at a side table, two old fairy godmothers waved their wands to extinguish a crepe that had been over-flambéed.

"Agatha!" said a girl's voice.

Agatha turned to see Dot rushing towards her in a sparkly, flower-print dress. "We just finished eating and are headed to the Arrow! Oh, Tedros, you look so handsome and you know I never say that, because I don't want to blow up your ego since it's already past capacity. Eek, there goes my date," she said, pointing to a tall boy in a brown cap ahead of her, already opening the front door. "Meet us at the Arrow later!"

Dot hurried off as Masha propelled Tedros and Agatha forward. "Come, my loves, I'll show you your table. . . ."

Agatha noticed Tedros squint back at the front door, frowning.

"What is it?" she said.

"That boy she was with," said Tedros.

"Is your place as the Fairest One of All threatened?"

"Pssh, no . . . I mean, that's not what I meant. . . ."

But now they had to part ways to let two waiters hurry

through, toting a pepper-roasted goat on a spit—

"I'll put you at the second-best table, right next to Sophie and her knight, so you can all be together," said Masha, taking hold of them again. "I was saving it for myself in the hopes that I could join Sophie for dessert, but you, of course, have priority. . . ."

Tedros, still peeking back at the front door, suddenly whipped his head forward. "Wait. Next to Sophie? No no no no no—"

But it was too late. Sophie and Rhian were already up and out of their seats as they saw their friends coming towards them, with Rhian in his blue-and-gold suit, freshly cleaned, and Sophie perfectly matched in a shimmering blue-and-gold gown.

"Aggie, darling! Who knew you even ate in restaurants," Sophie teased, kissing her on both cheeks. "And you're wearing a dress! And lipstick! Without my help! We really are in a fairy tale. Oh, you look marvelous, darling! I messaged Brone to bring my dress all the way from the ship to the Forest, even though the poor thing has a broken leg. But I just had to wear Camelot colors alongside Camelot's newest knight—" She finally glanced at Tedros. "Oh. Hello, Teddy."

Tedros barely smiled. "Hi," he said before quickly turning to Rhian.

Sophie nuzzled up to Agatha. "Aggie, isn't Rhian a *hunk*? I can see why Teddy wants him as a knight. With Rhian behind him, he'll look a bit more *regal*, won't he? Don't give me that look. You know I love you both. While we're on the subject, we should talk about the wedding. It's only a few weeks away and now I have a *date*! But let's focus on you. For the cake, I'm thinking . . ."

Agatha tuned out, trying to hear Tedros and Rhian next to her.

"How'd you get your suit so clean?" Tedros was saying to him.

"Fairies! Moment I took my shirt off, they came fluttering into my treehouse, offering to help," Rhian chuckled. "Boy crazy, that lot . . ." The knight saw Agatha watching them. "Hi, I'm not sure we've really met," he said to Agatha, cutting off Sophie midsentence. "I'm Rhian."

"Sorry, we didn't mean to intrude on your date," Agatha said self-consciously.

"Not at all. Let's pull our tables together," Rhian insisted, about to bridge the gap between them. "We just finished ordering—"

"No, a little distance is just fine," said Tedros, pushing Agatha into a seat and jumping into one of his own. "Please, don't let us distract you."

"Won't even notice you're there," Sophie said tartly to Tedros, before winking at Agatha and sitting back down.

Tedros reclined into his chair and exhaled. Before Agatha could speak, a handsome fox appeared with two menus. Agatha read hers in the chandelier light . . .

BEAUTY
and the
FEAST

Special Menu for Sophie & Friends

APPETIZER SAMPLER

Sophie's Dewy Skin Cold Soup:
Pureed sea cucumber infused with fairy-churned
sparkle butter and egg-white fireworks

followed by

Callis' Forest Herb Salad: Kyrgios pea shoots, enchanted mushrooms,
and a poached golden goose egg with magic-bean dressing

followed by

Wish Fish Crudo: Delicate mermaid pearls and royal lily pads swirled
with jellied sunshine and served in a pirate treasure chalice

followed by

Doom Room Dumplings: Savage Sea urchin shells stuffed with
white-swan gold caviar and peacock egg-cream

CHOICE OF ENTREE:

1. *"Edgar and Essa" Duo of Lamb:* Emerald-dusted
lamb shank embossed with foamed pixie's breath
and a mahogany-smoked lamb pillow with
a wood-nymph essence reduction

2. Agatha's Gold Fingerglow Fondue:
Sumptuous yak cheese aged in a siren's cave,
melted and served with spheres of stardust cream and
okra foam meringues, in a levitating leprechaun gold pot

3. Dean Dovey's Deconstructed Chicken Pot Pie:
An arrangement of silk-fed roast chicken cubes dipped in
rainbow glow and topped with moon-glimmer gravy

DESSERT SAMPLER

Evers' Snow Ball Mousse: Ethereal clouds of white chocolate
enriched with opal tapioca, topped with Frostplains crystal snow tuiles

followed by

Hester's Gingerbread House Brûlée: Altazarra buttercream pudding crusted
with petrified blood orange and sprinkled with eau de white rose

followed by

No-Ball Dancing Jelly: Bewitched hazelnut gelatin mold
with a princess-pea granita and sweetened dragon-fire beads

FLAT PRICE:
20 gold pieces per person

"Lucky Robin gave us some of his gold," Tedros murmured, patting a satchel in his coat pocket.

"Lucky Robin's house had one of Marian's old dresses that fit me and that the vendor at Sherwood Suits recognized you or else we'd be eating in a pub somewhere off a menu I could actually understand," said Agatha.

They both looked up and snickered.

Silence lingered, each of them waiting for the other to continue the conversation.

In the void, Agatha could hear Rhian and Sophie talking—

"My name is on your map?" Rhian asked, surprised.

"Yes! The Quest Map made by the Storian," said Sophie. "But that's only possible if you're a *student* at the School for Good and Evil."

Rhian chewed on his lip. "Maybe my mother hid my Flowerground ticket after all."

"Rhian is a beautiful name, by the way," said Sophie, as their fox waiter brought a basket of buttermilk bread. "Where did you get it from?"

"My father named me."

"After the Good School Master? The one Rafal killed in the Great War? That's what his twin brother was named."

"Was it?" Rhian laughed, biting into a roll. "Better change my name, then. A bit too much to live up to. Sophie fits you perfectly, though." He winked at her.

"Not sure that's a compliment, but I'll certainly take it as one," she said archly.

Agatha noticed Tedros listening too, but now their waiter reappeared.

"I'll have the chicken," said Agatha.

"I'll have the lamb," said Tedros.

The fox took their menus and glided away.

Agatha smiled at Tedros, trying to reset.

"Feels like our first date," she said shyly.

"Most of our relationship has taken place in times of war," said Tedros. "We're still figuring out how to do peace."

More awkward silence.

"You've been through a lot today. More than any of us," said Agatha, trying to force the same intimacy she'd seen between him and Rhian. "Do you want to talk about it?"

Tedros put his hand through the gold drops from the chandelier, which magically passed through his palm. "I'd rather talk about other things. Like why you didn't write me when you promised you would."

"I didn't want you to worry about me," Agatha sighed. "If you knew what we were dealing with on our quest, you'd have panicked."

"I see," said Tedros, not looking at her.

"But my point is you can confide in me, Tedros. I don't want to repeat the mistakes of the past six months. You can tell me things. Anything. About how you're feeling. Don't try to protect me—"

"Says the girl who wouldn't pick up a pen to tell me how she was feeling because she was trying to protect *me*," said

Tedros, his gaze settling on her again. "And then you wonder why I don't tell you things."

Agatha didn't know what to say.

"I'm going to the bathroom," Tedros said, getting up.

Agatha fidgeted with the tablecloth as he left. In the silence, she could hear Rhian and Sophie again.

"I was talking to Hester and Anadil after the burial," said Sophie, nibbling around the edge of a roll. "I suggested you might be a good candidate for School Master. We need a new one, as you know—"

"School Master!" Rhian nearly spewed his cider. "So I can fly you in and out of my tower like Rafal did? So you can replay your fairy-tale fantasy with someone slightly less murderous and far less qualified?"

"No!" Sophie said, offended. "I think—or *we* think—you'd be perfect for the job. You'd still have to interview with Professor Dovey, of course, but given my popularity with the students, I'm sure my opinion would have more weight—"

"Not interested," said Rhian. "In the position, that is. Still interested in you." He flashed a smile and Sophie blushed. "But I have a job now for the rest of my life. At Tedros' side."

"I know," said Sophie sincerely. "But I have a job too. One that isn't at Camelot, where you and Teddy will be."

"Are you happy being Dean?"

"I'm good at it," said Sophie. "It's what I was meant to do."

"But are you happy?"

"I'd be happier if you were School Master."

Rhian smiled. "I don't want us to be apart. You'll just have to visit Camelot often. It's less than a day's journey."

"If only it was that simple. Teddy wouldn't even let me in the castle to plan his own wedding, let alone 'visit often.' Plus, to be honest, I think he feels a bit insecure around me. . . ." Sophie checked to make sure Agatha wasn't listening. (Agatha dropped her napkin and pretended to be looking for it.) ". . . given how poorly Teddy's reign started versus how successful I've been as Dean, I mean," Sophie said to Rhian, softer. "Catching the Snake will help Teddy's reputation, of course. But I just don't think he'll ever feel comfortable around me. Too much history. And maybe . . . well, I shouldn't say it. . . . It doesn't even make sense. . . ."

"Tell me," said Rhian.

Sophie again glanced at Agatha, who was watching the cricket symphony intently. Sophie leaned towards her knight. "I think deep down, Teddy knows I'd make a better king than he would."

"Ah," said Rhian. "King Sophie . . ."

The knight cracked up.

So did Sophie. "I told you it was silly—"

"Your story promised you'd be a handful, but I had no idea."

Sophie stopped laughing. "I ruined it, didn't I. . . . I shouldn't have said anything. . . . I should have faked being nice and bashful like all the other girls you date—"

"I like you even better now, if that's what you're asking," said Rhian.

Sophie stared at him, speechless for once.

"Come back with me to Camelot," said Rhian. "Just for a few days. It'll give you and Tedros a chance to thaw before you go back to school. Once he sees me with you on his home turf, he'll realize it's the perfect ending. That you and him don't have to be at odds. The four of us can be true friends, regardless of where we are."

Sophie considered this. "But my students . . ."

"I'm sure the other Dean can handle things. Just a few days. The school will still be there when you get back."

"You really think we can have a perfect ending?" Sophie asked.

"You deserve it. Anyone who says you can't isn't telling you the Truth," said Rhian.

Sophie took him in . . . then turned to Agatha. "What do you think, Aggie?" she asked, her green eyes twinkling as if she knew her friend had been listening all along.

Agatha startled in her chair. "What? Oh. Um—"

"What does Agatha think about what?" Tedros asked as he sat back down.

Agatha, Sophie, and Rhian spun to him—

"*Nothing*," they said.

Foxes circled the tables.

The first course had arrived.

After dinner, they walked through the darkest part of the Forest towards Marian's Arrow, the four of them together.

Agatha had her arm hooked in Tedros' as Rhian and Sophie cuddled on the sandy path ahead of them.

"I'm going to burst out of these clothes," said Tedros with a burp.

"I've never eaten so much in my life," Agatha moaned, feet shuffling lazily. "Even Sophie had dessert. *Sophie*. She ate all three!"

"What do you mean, 'all three'? All *six*! She ate mine too!" Rhian called out, pecking Sophie on the cheek.

"I don't care if I have to do yoga in a steam room for eight hours tomorrow and juice fast for the rest of my life . . . ," Sophie said, wobbly-legged and food-drunk in Rhian's arms. "It was *worth* it."

"And that is how a witch is felled," Tedros whispered to Agatha. "Gourmet dining."

Agatha nuzzled into his chest as they watched Sophie and Rhian kissing intensely.

"I remember when we were like that," Agatha sighed.

"What do you mean 'were'?" said Tedros, sweeping her up in his arms and kissing her as he carried her.

"Oh, put me down," said Agatha.

"You told me to put you down when I carried you at school and then you fainted and Sophie turned into Satan and we almost died," said Tedros, clasping her tighter. "So request denied."

Agatha relaxed in his arms. "I love you, Tedros."

"I love you, Agatha."

"You love me even though sometimes I try to control things too much?" she said.

"You love me even though sometimes I try to shield you too much?" he said.

"You love me even though I don't write you when I'm supposed to?" she said.

"Well, it's not like you write Sophie either," said Tedros.

Agatha laughed.

"No more Snake to worry about. The Woods safe again. Our allies back on our side," said Tedros. "And soon we'll be king and queen. Husband and wife."

"We'll be as good in peace as we are in war," said Agatha.

"We already are," he said, kissing her again.

"Does anyone actually know where we're going?" Rhian's voice hollered.

Tedros lifted his lips off Agatha's. "Oh, for God's sake, Rhian. How hard is it to follow a *path*?"

They were totally lost, it turned out, but no one seemed to care, with Tedros now whispering to Rhian at the fore, and Sophie canoodling with Agatha behind them. Fairy lights flickered occasionally over their heads as if to assure them they were perfectly safe, despite the fact the emerald Forest had turned inkblack and they could hardly see each other's shadows anymore.

When a silent moment finally came, it was the king who broke it.

"If Sophie wants to come stay at Camelot for a few days, it's fine," said Tedros.

"There's my man," Rhian crowed, slinging an arm around him.

Sophie and Agatha goggled at each other.

"Provided she does all the wedding planning and stays locked in the dungeon," Tedros said, half-joking.

"Will Rhian be locked in the dungeon with me?" Sophie asked.

The four of them burst into laughter.

"Speaking of witches . . . ," said Tedros.

Far off the side of the path, Agatha could see a small fire burning in a dug-out pit. At its edge, Hester and Anadil leaned against each other, speaking softly as they roasted marshmallows and ate them off sticks. Neither noticed the group.

"Should we go say hi?" Tedros whispered.

Sophie and Agatha swiveled to him at the same time. *"No."*

Sophie smiled at Agatha knowingly.

"Let them be," said Sophie.

The witches weren't the only ones taking sanctuary in the Forest. As the foursome went on, they spotted a tent made out of a bedsheet, surrounded by melting wax candles, lighting up two shadows inside the tent, kissing and giggling.

"Now *this* we have to see," Sophie said.

She sashayed into the thicket and pulled open the tent—

Hort and Nicola tumbled out.

"I told you I heard someone!" Nicola said.

"Hiya," Hort beamed, seeing Agatha, Tedros, and Rhian first. "Robin told us you guys went to Beauty and the Feast. I wanted to take Nic there for our first date, but I don't have the money, so I made a picnic inste—"

He saw Sophie. But Hort didn't look the slightest bit embarrassed or aggrieved. "Um, you guys going to the Arrow?"

"We're on our way right now," said Sophie. "Want to join us?"

"Maybe we'll meet you there," said Hort.

Sophie smiled at him. "No pressure." She turned to his new girlfriend. "Oh, and Nicola, I used one of Robin's best crows to send a message to your father in Gavaldon and let him know you'll be home for Christmas."

Nicola goggled at her. "Y-y-you did?"

"Didn't tell him you'd *stay* home, of course. In case something compels you to come back to the Woods," she said, winking at Hort.

Hort smiled at Sophie and squired Nicola into his tent.

"That was so nice of her," the group heard Nicola saying.

"Nice of her, indeed," said Agatha to Sophie as they retook the path.

"Everyone deserves to be happy in The End," said Sophie, almost singing it. "Including little weasels."

By the time they reached Marian's Arrow, it was well past midnight. In their dresses and suits, they traipsed through a silent fernfield to get to the rusty barn, painted with a cartoon of a young Robin Hood in his green jacket kissing Maid Marian in a white pinafore. From both of their mouths came a speech bubble that read:

LEAVE ALL YE TROUBLES BEHIND

A beady-eyed vulture peered down at them, perched over the door, eating what looked like a deep-fried rat.

"Password?" he asked throatily.

"Little John," said Tedros.

"Proceed," said the vulture, sprinkling ratcrumbs.

Agatha pushed open the steel door.

A wave of noise crashed over them as Agatha looked around a place that was half seedy pub and half country jamboree. Harried waitresses in tight Sheriff's uniforms scampered about, some taking orders, others dive-bombing food to the tables, sloshing ginger beer, cheeseballs, and pig-skins on customers' heads. In the center of the Arrow, a throng of customers square-danced while two billy goats fiddled on their hind legs beneath a massive porcelain statue of Maid Marian, tall as a giant, that blew bubbles if you deposited a silver piece. Everywhere Agatha looked, she glimpsed men wearing brown caps speared with colored feathers, each one of them flirting with someone. But she couldn't see Robin himself anywhere.

Tedros came back from the bar with four tall mugs of cider—

"Look, there's Hood!" he said.

Agatha spun to see the famous rogue standing atop the bar, a woman under each arm who was *not* Marian, and raising a mug to the crowd.

"Let us toast first to my Merry Men, for livening these Woods and spoiling its women!" The crowd cheered and the men in brown caps around the pub took a collective bow. Robin grinned down at Agatha, Tedros, Sophie, and Rhian. "Let us also toast to the questers of the School for Good and Evil for fighting a battle that not many are willing to fight and protecting kingdoms that most of you come to our Forest to escape!" Another cheer. "Let us also toast to Maid Marian, for being my true love since my own school days and for letting me name this place in her honor, and most importantly . . . for being at home asleep!" Perhaps the loudest cheer of all. "And let us toast the girl who deserves our greatest thanks on this day and always . . . for her courage, her kindness, and her heart. *To Dot!*"

"*To Dot!*" the crowd roared.

"*To Dot!*" said Tedros, clashing mugs with Agatha, Sophie, and Rhian.

"But where *is* Dot?" said Sophie.

Then Agatha saw her, slumped over a table in the corner.

"Oh my God," she said, breaking from Tedros and sprinting to Dot's side.

"Dot, are you okay?" she breathed.

"*Beauty and the Feast . . . Beauty and the Feeeeassssst . . . ,*" Dot warbled, looking up, eyes red and squinty, clutching a mug. "*Where boys bring girls to give them rings—*"

"What is this?" Agatha demanded, snatching the mug out of her hand. "What are you drinking?"

"Chocolate millllk," Dot mumbled. "What I alllllways drink at the Arrrrroooo—"

Rhian rushed in and seized the mug, sniffing it. He dumped the remainder on the table and watched it curdle. "Sleeping Willow seed," he said, eyeing Agatha. "The milk was doctored."

"He got me my millllllk . . . Best date everrrrrr," Dot slurred.

"Who's he?" said Tedros intensely, kneeling at her side.

"Kissss meee, Teddy," Dot piffled, slumping over.

Tedros hoisted her up like a child and sat her on the table. He looked into her pouty face. "Dot. Who's '*he*'."

"My date . . . ," she said, yawning. "Went to the bathroom a few hours ago . . . He'll be back any second. . . ."

Tedros went white. "The boy I saw at the restaurant?"

"You thought you recognized him—" said Agatha, seeing Tedros' face.

"Kei doesn't like Teddy," said Dot, poking at Tedros' muscles. "Kei wanted to see Daddy's keys . . . said he'd give me a kiss for each one I showed him . . . Look how many kisses I got. . . ." Dot dug into her dress and thrust her keys into the air like a trophy—

Dot screamed.

The whole Arrow screeched to a stop: the music, the dancing, the beer.

Because the key ring Dot was holding had no keys left.

⟨⟨⟩⟩

By the time they made it to the jail, blood spilled out its doors like a river.

The cell door was ajar, the magic sack inside shredded to threads and scattered about the stone floor like snakes.

And guarding the cell were three Merry Men, with eyes wide open, their hearts speared through with their own arrows.

26

TEDROS

Questions of a King

This meeting will come to order!" Tedros declared, standing in front of the captain's wheel of the *Igraine* as it flew through the pink-and-purple dawn sky. He looked down at the gathered crew, still in their clothes from the night before and sitting cross-legged on the deck. "I won't waste words, as Professor Dovey's crystal ball does not give us much time with her—"

"Indeed," said the Dean, from a

watery bubble hovering next to Tedros' head, her office a mess in the background. "The Snake is on the loose after escaping Nottingham, and though neither he nor his scims have yet to be sighted, he will surely come for Camelot, for Excalibur, and for the king. We must protect all three. Judging from my Quest Map, your ship will arrive at Camelot in an hour and we need to be clear on the plan—"

"Now as to the details of this plan—" Tedros cut in.

"Tedros, I think it's best if I handle—"

The king turned to the Dean. "We may be your students, but this is my kingdom that we're about to land in. So are you leading this meeting or am I?"

Professor Dovey pursed her lips. "Proceed."

Tedros scanned the crew: Rhian watching him intently; Sophie fixed on Rhian and nuzzling his arm; Hort, Nicola, Hester, Anadil, Beatrix, Reena, Kiko, Willam, and Bogden. (The rest of the students they'd left at a clinic in Nottingham, so they could recuperate from their injuries sustained at the Four Point.)

"Where's Agatha?" he heard Kiko whisper to Sophie.

"Taking care of Dot in her room," Sophie whispered back. "Dot's too afraid to show her face."

"She should be," Hort grumbled.

"First of all, this is not Dot's fault," Tedros admonished the group. "The boy named Kei of Foxwood arrived in Sherwood Forest just a few days ago, hounding Robin for a chance to join his Merry Men. Robin ignored Kei at first, but when Kei expressed an interest in the Sheriff's daughter, Robin saw a chance to make Dot happy. He told Kei to take Dot on a date she'd remember and then *maybe* he'd consider him for his men. Little did he know Kei was in league with the Snake the whole time. So please. What happened last night was an accident. Be kind to Dot."

"Challenging," groused Hester.

"Impossible, honestly," Anadil mumbled, rats grumbling too.

"As soon as we land in Camelot, we'll divide into two teams to fight the Snake," Tedros forged on. "One team will be with me and Agatha at Camelot Castle. The other team will be with Rhian and Sophie in Camelot City."

"I told you he wouldn't let me in the castle," Sophie murmured to Rhian.

Tedros ignored her. "My team will be responsible for securing the royal grounds. You will work with Agatha and me to fortify the towers, protect Excalibur, and lay traps for the Snake's army. Rhian's team will be responsible for helping my mother and our Ever and Never allies to recruit an army to fight the Snake's. Professor Dovey has been in touch with Guinevere—" Tedros' face changed. He looked up at the Dean in her bubble. "And she's, um, aware of everything that happened last night?"

Professor Dovey paused. "Yes, she is."

Tedros swallowed, lost in thought.

The Good Dean quickly took over. "Ever since the Four Point, Guinevere has led Camelot's allies in building a unified army of Good and Evil. Recruitment is currently taking place in Maker's Market, the main thoroughfare of Camelot City. Rhian's team will join this effort and conduct loyalty tests to ensure none of the Snake's allies make it into our ranks, like Kei of Foxwood did. . . ."

Kei's name snapped Tedros out of his daze. He glanced at the Dean, thankful she'd stepped in, his stomach still queasy at the thought of his mother learning that Lance was dead. Yet as he studied Dovey closer, the Dean looked haggard, as if she hadn't been sleeping.

". . . Those working on Rhian's team must be cautious, for the Snake's minions may have already seeped into Camelot City," the Good Dean was saying, stifling a cough. "But before the king assigns you to your teams, I have a few questions for our new knight." Her eyes locked on Rhian.

"At your service, Professor Dovey," said the copper-haired boy, immediately rising to his feet.

"What kingdom are you from, Rhian?" she asked.

"Foxwood."

"Your parents' names?"

"Levya and Rosamund. My father is deceased."

"Siblings?"

"Two younger brothers. Stad and Gilderoy."

"Address?"

"62 Stropshire Lane in Foxwood."

"Thank you," said Professor Dovey, scribbling this all down, before looking up at him. "You see, I'm afraid there is no record of a Rhian in our files for prospective students to either the School for Good or the School for Evil."

"Perhaps I did not qualify to be a prospective student, then?" said Rhian.

"*All* children in the Woods and Woods Beyond between the ages of twelve and fifteen qualify to be prospective students and thus have a file at the school," Professor Dovey clipped.

"Then it must be an oversight, surely," said Rhian, scratching his stubble. "I will be seventeen next month. I would have been in Tedros' class."

"If it is an oversight, then why is your name on my Quest Map?" the Good Dean pressed. "Why is your name recognized by the Storian?"

"Because the Storian made a mistake by not including him in our class and now is atoning for it," Sophie snapped, standing up next to her knight.

"I understand your reservations, Professor Dovey. I would have the same ones," said Rhian, his attention still on the Dean. "I've come to serve Camelot. To protect its king. I cannot speak to the mysteries of the Storian or the admissions process at your school. But if you have doubts about my loyalty, then I will return to Foxwood at once."

"No one has doubts about your loyalty," said Tedros, glaring at Dovey.

"Doubts about your loyalty? No," said the Dean. "In reporting this fairy tale as it unfolds, the Storian has showed me what kind of knight you are, Rhian. You've saved Tedros' life. You've saved all of my students' lives, along with numerous kingdoms under threat, from Foxwood to Mahadeva to Nottingham. Your loyalty to Tedros, to his friends, and to Good is unquestioned. What I question is why this loyalty has not come to my attention before *now*. But perhaps that is something that only the Storian and our previous School Master have the answers to and, unfortunately, neither is capable of giving them. One last question, however." She peered into Rhian's eyes. "About your intentions towards Sophie—"

"Oh, for God's sake, Clarissa!" Sophie scorched.

"Let me answer," Rhian said firmly. "Go on, Professor."

Professor Dovey gave him a keen once-over. "Do you find it strange for a knight of Good to take a Dean of Evil as his lady?"

"No more strange than a princess of Good like Agatha to have a Dean of Evil like Sophie as her best friend. Or a Dean of Good like you to have had a Dean of Evil like Lady Lesso as your best friend," Rhian answered. "Good and Evil are no longer as irreconcilable in our world as they once were. Something we have to give Sophie quite a bit of credit for. But to be perfectly honest, I wouldn't have wanted the Sophie that came to your school her first year. That Sophie was Evil in the most self-serving way. There was little to attract someone like me, who wants to do Good in this world. But I don't see that Sophie anymore. Her soul may still skew toward Evil, but now her Evil serves the greater Good. It's what I most admire about her. She can change people's minds. She knows how to *lead*. I think we can all agree on that, Professor. Even more, I think we can all say that she deserves to find real love. Wouldn't you?"

Sophie's eyes had turned to stars.

The Dean of Good smiled warmly. "I look forward to meeting you in person, Sir Rhian," she said, before looking at the king. "Tedros, I leave it to you to divide the teams."

As Rhian and Sophie sat, Hort leaned over to Nicola: "Watch, Tedros won't pick me for his team because he thinks I'm a loser."

"Well, at least we'll be together, then, 'cause he doesn't even know my name," said Nicola.

"On my team, it's Agatha, Hort, Nicola, Kiko, Bogden, and Willam," said Tedros. "On Rhian's team, it's Sophie, Hester, Anadil, Dot, Beatrix, and Reena."

Hort and Nicola blinked, surprised.

"Any questions?" Tedros asked.

"Why are all the boys on your team?" said Reena.

"Because Rhian is all the man a team needs," Sophie vamped.

"Next question," said Tedros, staring Sophie down.

"How big is the Snake's army?" said Beatrix.

"We don't know," said Tedros. "But judging from the chaos he caused across the Woods and his ability to pay for loyalty, we can expect a sizable force."

"Can Merlin help us like he did against Rafal and his zombies?" asked Kiko.

"Merlin is missing," said Professor Dovey gravely. "All I can hope right now is that he is still *alive*."

Tedros tensed, sensing the genuine fear in the Dean's face—

"You say we have to build an army, but do the people even *want* to fight for Tedros?" Beatrix asked, raising her hand.

"From the news we read, it doesn't seem like you have much support from other kingdoms after you left them to deal with the Snake on their own. Or from the people of Camelot, for that matter. Rhian might have saved half the Woods single-handedly . . . but are those people going to rally behind *you*?"

Tedros went bright red. "Um, look . . ."

"Tedros is the *king*," Rhian lashed, spinning to Beatrix. "The king of the Woods' greatest kingdom. And it is our duty to show the people of Camelot and beyond what loyalty to the king looks like. Anyone unable to fulfill that duty is welcome to jump off the boat right now."

Beatrix shirked under his hot blue-green eyes. "Sheesh. Just asking," she muttered.

Tedros gave Rhian a grateful nod. "Any other questions?"

No one spoke.

"Meeting dismissed," said Tedros. "Get yourselves some-thing to eat or go down for a nap, because as soon as we land, our work begins."

He looked up at the Dean, who was already starting to fade. "When can you make it to Camelot, Professor?"

"As soon as I can," the Dean said vaguely.

Her bubble vanished while the crew leapt to their feet and headed towards the galley. Tedros saw Nicola walking with Rhian. "Sophie was asking whether you have any psycho ex-girlfriends from school she should worry about," said Nicola.

"Mmm, given I went to a school for boys, psycho ex-girl-friends aren't a problem," Rhian laughed. "Anything else she's concerned about?"

"Just that you're too Good to be true. Surely there's *something* wrong with you."

"I bite my nails, snore if I eat too close to bedtime, have a birthmark on my bum, and can be a bit temperamental."

"Real dealbreakers," said Nicola, smirking.

Tedros made a face. Last he'd heard, Sophie and Nicola were barely friends. And now Sophie was sending her to check up on Rhian?

"Teddy?"

Tedros turned to see Sophie next to him.

"I didn't mean to suggest you aren't as good or as manly as Rhian," she said. "I was just being stupid—"

"I know, Sophie."

She touched his shoulder. "Will you be okay?"

The way she left her hand there, Tedros knew this had nothing to do with what she'd said about Rhian and everything to do with his having to face his mother soon.

"I have to be," he said.

"I know you and I have had our . . . issues. But I'm here for you," said Sophie, quiet and heartfelt. "Please know I mean that."

Their eyes met and for a moment, Tedros forgot everything that had happened between them.

He cleared his throat. "I better go check on Agatha," he said, heading towards the galley.

Tedros paused. "Sophie?"

He turned to her.

"Rhian's my knight. He saved our quests. He saved Ever

and Never kingdoms from the Snake. You don't have to hunt for flaws or dig up dirt on him," he said.

Sophie stared at him quizzically. "Um, I know that," she said. "Since when do you give me love advice?"

Tedros smiled. "Since I started believing in perfect endings."

Then he hustled inside, leaving Sophie wide-eyed behind him.

By the time Tedros took a bath and had his turn at the enchanted pot—he asked it for meatloaf and broccoli and it'd given him pancakes instead—the *Igraine* was starting its descent towards Camelot.

Hair wet, mouth full, he knocked on Dot's door.

Agatha peeked out. "I'll meet you on deck in a minute," she whispered.

"Starboard deck, where we can be alone," said Tedros.

Agatha nodded and closed the door.

Tedros could hear Dot's muffled wails: "It's not just that I let the Snake loose or that everyone thinks I'm horrible or that if anything happens to Tedros it'll be my fault. . . . The worst part is I'll never kiss a boy agaiiiinnn!"

"Yes, you will," said Agatha's voice. "You'll get over this—"

"That's not what I mean. I mean what other boy will ever kiss me? Kei was my first kiss! And he only kissed me because he wanted to get my keeyyysss. . . ."

"Dot, love is more than finding a boy to kiss."

"You only say that 'cause you get to kiss Tedros all day longgggg!"

"And we still have our problems, like everyone else," said Agatha patiently. "But if it'll make you feel better, you're welcome to kiss Tedros as much as you like."

Tedros sighed.

As he waited in the starboard corridor, elbows on a railing, he watched the sky turn gray, dark clouds spiraling around the ship. Tedros tried to steel himself, preparing for the war ahead, but he could feel a current of nausea underneath his forced calm. Everything about the Snake terrified him. His ruthlessness. His coldness. The way he'd slashed Lance without mercy.

But it was more than that.

Rafal was Evil, but Evil in a way that Tedros understood. Rafal wanted Sophie. Rafal wanted a love so Evil it would destroy Good forever.

But what did this Snake want? To rule Camelot? *Why?*

Is that what he was really after? Or was the Snake after something more?

What scared Tedros the most was that he still didn't know the answer.

The ship broke through a wall of clouds, giving him his first view of Camelot City. The king's eyes bulged. Massive lines of people streamed through Maker's Market. It looked like some kind of holiday parade, with men, women, children, and mogrifs packing every street. But as Tedros tracked the lines, he saw where they led: the gates of Camelot Park, where huge signs flashed "ARMY RECRUITMENT: EVERS" and "ARMY RECRUITMENT: NEVERS." The moment the crowd caught sight of the *Igraine* above, they let out a roaring cheer as the ship zipped past the city and out over the Savage Sea, curving back around towards Camelot Castle and the royal docks.

"Further proof that no one should ever listen to Beatrix," said a comforting voice.

Agatha nestled up to him. "Because from what I just saw, the people are certainly on your side."

"In times of crisis, the Woods needs a leader," said Tedros. "Maybe they finally realized that no matter how many mistakes I make, I will always be there to protect them and fight for them and put my life on the line for them, just like my father."

"Or they're afraid the Snake's going to kill them and you're their only hope," smiled Agatha.

"That too," said Tedros.

"Though according to the Snake, *he's* actually the Lion. And *you're* the Snake," said Agatha.

"What?"

"When he captured us in Jaunt Jolie, he had a Storian of his own—a *fake* Storian—that tells the fairy tales from his point of view. And in his version of the story, he's the Lion and rightful king and you're the usurping Snake. He claims all of this will only end when everything we think is true is proven 'untrue.'"

Tedros thought about this. "So when Lies become Truth and Truth becomes Lies."

"Which is impossible, because the Woods knows this Snake

now. They will never confuse him for a Lion," said Agatha. "He's the villain of this story. And you're their hero. That's why they're cheering for you."

"And it's why I cannot let them down," said Tedros.

He held her tightly as the castle came into view, a light rain starting to fall.

"Dot doing okay?" he asked. "Or do I need to kiss her back to her senses?"

"I was hoping you'd overhear that. She'll be fine. By the time I left, she was turning her tears to chocolate and eating them."

"Gross."

The ship floated down in front of the castle. Tedros spotted Excalibur in the Blue Tower balcony, now guarded by five men and also sealed off in a huge, thick glass lockbox. Clearly his mother was taking no chances.

The moment the *Igraine* hit the water, surfing to the docks, the crew bounded to their positions, led by Rhian, lashing the ship to the pier as Hort dropped anchor.

From the railing, Tedros and Agatha watched the knight gather his group on the east dock.

"My team, follow me," said Rhian, leading Hester, Anadil, Beatrix, and Reena away in the rain, with Dot scurrying and sniffling behind.

"Our turn," said Tedros, taking Agatha's hand, about to summon his team—

The king froze, squinting over the railing. Agatha followed his eyes.

There was a woman at the end of the west dock.

She wore all white, her hair the same ghostly color, wet from the rain.

"The Lady of the Lake?" Agatha breathed as she and Tedros moved closer—

Only now they could see the woman's face.

Tedros squeezed Agatha's hand. "Take our group and go," he ordered.

"Let me come with—"

Tedros kissed her gently. "Go. I'll see you inside."

Agatha nodded. She gathered Hort, Nicola, Kiko, Willam, and Bogden and herded them down the east dock and into the castle.

Tedros came off the ship alone and faced the woman in white.

A key made of glass dangled from a chain around her neck.

"The Snake will have to kill me to get this key," said Guinevere. "He won't touch Excalibur as long as I'm alive."

"I'm sorry, Mother," Tedros rasped, trying to quell his emotion.

"My hair changed color the moment I heard the news," said Guinevere. "And yet, I haven't been able to cry."

"He loved you so much," said her son, his voice breaking. "In a way Dad never could. You were everything to Lance. He said it to me as he . . . as he . . ."

Guinevere pulled him into her arms. "He loved you too, Tedros. Like his own son. Even if he wasn't always sure how to show it."

"Why did he kill Lance? Why not me?" Tedros breathed, rain falling on his face.

"Remember what Merlin said," his mother whispered. "He wants to break you. To take away everything you love so you'll be too weak to fight back. But you have to fight back, Tedros. You have to stay strong. Both of us do."

She tilted his chin towards her.

Tedros looked into his mother's fiery eyes.

"We can't let that monster *win*," said Guinevere.

Tedros swept through the White Tower, his crown back on his head, peering at a map of the castle grounds in one hand and a ledger accounting for all of Camelot's weapons in the other. He crossed through the staff dining hall, now turned into a war room, where Chef Silkima and her cooks were filling giant barrels with cooking oil.

"How many barrels, Silkima?" Tedros asked, without stopping.

"Sixty-four, sire."

"And they'll detonate easily?"

"At first flame, sire."

The young king strode out of the hall and saw Hort in the corridor, helplessly surrounded by heaps of broken and rusted weapons: maces, spears, axes, swords—

"This is a holy mess," said Hort.

"Which is why I wanted a Hort on my team to fix it," said Tedros.

"Aye-aye, sire," said Hort.

Tedros veered into the next hall, where Kiko was standing with a beefy, shirtless guard amidst piles of mismatched pieces of armor that Kiko was trying to fit back together. Tedros raised his brows.

"I told him that if I could watch him put the armor *on*, then maybe I'd see how it all goes," Kiko defended.

Tedros shoved past them and peeked into the stewards' common room, where two maids were trying to repair a mound of splintered bows and arrows. He glimpsed a few newspapers spread out on a table. On top was the *Jaunt Jolie Journal*—

KING TEDROS' CREW BUNGLES SNAKE CAPTURE! LANCELOT DEAD! SNAKE ON THE LOOSE!

Tedros flung it aside to see the latest *Camelot Courier*—

SNAKE EYES CAMELOT! IS THE LION OUR ONLY HOPE?

Tedros lifted it up to see the *Royal Rot* underneath, a huge portrait of Rhian and Sophie on its front page—

DREAMY LION IN LOVE WITH TEDROS' EX-FLAME?

Tedros rolled his eyes, hurrying back into the hall. Agatha accosted him, Reaper at her heels.

"Guinevere and I met with the Treasury Master. Good news is the leaders of our allied kingdoms are contributing weapons, armor, and men to our army. Bad news is they're only doing this on the condition that the 'Lion' lead that army instead of you, since a) he saved so many of their kingdoms from the Snake, and b) they blame you for losing the Snake last night, since Dot is your friend."

"And is there a reason these leaders won't tell me this to my face?" Tedros asked, frowning.

"When they found out the Lion was in town, they went gaggling out of the castle to try and meet him. Dragged your mother with them."

"Whatever," Tedros growled. "Let them think Rhian is leading the army. He's my knight. His loyalty is to me, not them."

"How else can I help?" Agatha pressed.

"Check on Rhian's team in Maker's Market. I'm worried the Snake or his thugs will find their way in, especially if my mother's down there," said Tedros. "If you see anything, shoot your glow into the sky. Don't try and fight them yourselves. Deal?"

"Deal," said Agatha, hurrying away.

"Agatha?"

She turned.

"We are good in war, aren't we?" said Tedros.

"I'll ask Sophie if she can do a war-themed wedding, then," said Agatha dryly.

They split in opposite directions, with Tedros heading down a hall, searching for the remainder of his team—

He tripped over Willam and Bogden, who were dealing tarot cards on the carpet.

"You can't be serious," Tedros said, scowling.

"We're saving your kingdom. See, look," Bogden peeped, holding up a Five of Wands. "Be wary of gifts."

"If I'd known I'd get stuck with two astrology-obsessed monkeys, I would have put you on Rhian's team!"

"Tarot cards aren't astrology," said Willam.

"Where's Nicola?" Tedros asked, tempted to give both of them a beating.

"She said she saw stars and was following them into the bathroom," said Bogden.

"Is this more astrology crap?" Tedros barked.

"No, she literally found stars in the hallway and was following them into the bathroom next to Lady Gremlaine's old room," said Willam, his eyes still on the cards. "Hmm. Definitely be wary of gifts."

Tedros had no clue what Willam was talking about, but he couldn't deal with these two nitwits anymore, nor did he want a random first year hovering around his father's old guest room.

He hastened through the second floor towards the bathroom—

Tedros stopped short.

A white star glowed on the carpet in front of him.

Merlin's white star.

Tedros lifted his eyes.

More stars lined the hallway, leading up to the closed bathroom door.

Tedros knocked on it. "Nicola?"

No answer.

He turned the knob. "Nicola, you in here?"

The bathroom was empty, the opposing doors to Lady Gremlaine's room and the guest room both shut.

But the trail of stars continued, tracking right to the edge of the guest room door.

Tedros pulled it open, revealing the dim, airless chamber.

Nicola wasn't inside.

More lit stars dotted the carpet like breadcrumbs, pointing to the bed in the corner.

He followed them until he was standing over the mattress, where a single star lay on top of its sheets, blinking with white light.

Tedros waited for something to happen.

The star kept flashing at him.

Instinctively, the young king found himself climbing into the stiff bed and sliding under the stale beige sheets. Except the sheets felt oddly thicker than they looked, layered underneath with a heavy blanket that felt soft against Tedros' skin, made of some kind of wool or . . .

Velvet.

Tedros' heart jumped.

He yanked the blanket over his head, seeing the glint of silver-sewn stars in the darkness.

The next thing he knew he was falling.

As he crawled across the cloud, he saw Merlin seated next to Nicola at its edge, framed against the purple sky, the wizard and first year sharing a chocolate-chunk cookie. Nicola had Merlin's hat in her hand and was petting it like a dog, the hat purring softly under her palm.

"Yes, don't worry, Professor Dovey knows I'm alive," the wizard was telling her. "Or she will soon, at least. I've sent her a note ordering her to remain at school and let Tedros handle affairs at Camelot. After what happened to Lancelot, I don't want Clarissa to put herself in harm's way. Especially when she isn't at her best."

"Is she ill?" Tedros asked.

Merlin turned and saw the young king. "No, she's not ill," said the wizard. "Nicola and I were having a nice chat. She happened to come across the trail I left for you, and being a clever little Reader, she found her way to me first." Merlin saw Tedros' blank expression. "I'm assuming you two know each other?"

"Yeah," said Nicola. "Not really," said Tedros at the same time.

"I see," said Merlin.

"Can we talk alone?" Tedros pressed the wizard.

"Don't mind me. I'm just on your team," said Nicola, standing up.

"Sorry if I don't have time for pleasantries. I'm trying to

keep all of us alive," Tedros retorted.

"So am I, but whatever," the first year mumbled. "Everyone else is different in real life than they are in books, but you're pretty much spot-on." She returned the hat to the wizard. "I'll see you soon, Merlin—"

"How am I in books?" said Tedros, frowning.

Nicola threw him a glance. "High-handed and overemotional."

Merlin's hat whistled.

"Thanks in advance for that favor, Merlin," Nicola said.

Cookie in hand, she cannonballed over the edge of the cloud and vanished into the purple night.

Tedros settled next to Merlin, shoving the hat away.

"She wanted a favor?" Tedros asked sourly.

"Suggested I check on a student's records from school," said the wizard.

"Rhian's? Dovey already checked on Rhian—"

"No. Not his. Nicola really is a sharp young girl. I can see why the Storian included her in your—"

"Lancelot is dead, Merlin," Tedros cut in, cheeks reddening. "The Snake is coming. War is coming. And you're sitting here on a cloud, entertaining irrelevant favors from first years. Where have you been!"

"The answer to that question is always the same, my boy. I've been trying to *help* you. And when I leave at the close of this conversation, an exit to which you will no doubt take great offense, I hope you'll remember that."

"You're leaving? *Now?*"

"Whatever you think I should be doing, Tedros, please believe me when I say that whatever I *am* doing will prove far more beneficial to your future."

"Which is what, exactly!"

"I cannot tell you," said Merlin.

Tedros let out a roar, which resounded through the Celestium, then faded to silence.

"I will not live forever, Tedros. There is still a bounty on my head. Nor am I immortal or extending my life with leprechaun blood, regardless of what those peons at the *Royal Rot* write," said Merlin. "My work with your father remains unfinished. I must carry it through with you until I am dead or the work is done."

"When will the work be done?" Tedros asked.

"On the day I look to you for wisdom instead of you looking to me," said Merlin.

"Better invest in leprechaun blood, then," said Tedros.

"I am well aware we are running out of time," said Merlin. "You and me both. The Snake is coming for you. And I'm afraid I have little to offer in the way of help."

"'Little.' Not 'nothing,'" said Tedros hopefully.

"Indeed. On the way here, I stopped in Avalon to see the Lady of the Lake."

Tedros straightened. "Did she really give up her powers for the Snake? Did she really . . . *kiss* him?"

"She wouldn't see me, which makes me think she did," Merlin replied. "She sent me a note through her waters, however, which said that if I promised to never return to her castle,

I could ask her one and only one question and she would answer it honestly. Since she was quite clear about not seeing me, I accepted her offer."

"What did you ask her?"

"Whether Excalibur has a message for you," said the wizard.

"*That's* what you asked the Lady of the Lake? Not what the Snake's face looks like or who he is or how we beat him or if he's really my father's son?" Tedros said, aggrieved. He stared at his mentor. "Well? What was her answer, then? What was Excalibur's message?"

Merlin pulled a crinkled scrap of paper from his robes and handed it to him. Tedros looked down at its light, ethereal script:

Unbury Me

"Rather cryptic, but at least it's something," Merlin sighed. "Though the more I think about it, the less I—" He suddenly noticed Tedros' expression. "What is it?"

"My father. He said it in my dream," said Tedros anxiously. "The same message. '*Unbury me.*'"

Merlin pulled at his beard. "Do you have any idea what it means?"

"Looking to me for wisdom already? You'll be sorely disappointed," said Tedros. "What's strange, though, is both my father and Excalibur had the same message. It can't be literal, then. If I could unbury Excalibur from the stone, I would. And my father can't possibly want me digging up his grave. So there must be something that connects my father and the sword . . . something hidden that I have to figure out. . . ."

"And you must figure it out soon, Tedros," Merlin pressured. "Your father and the Lady of the Lake are trying to help you. *'Unbury me.'* Those two words are the key. You must find out what they mean. Before it's too late."

"But why more riddles?" Tedros asked, frustrated. "Why can't they just tell me?"

"Perhaps answering that riddle is as much a part of your coronation test as pulling the sword," the wizard replied. "I'm assuming you haven't tried your hand at Excalibur since you've returned to the castle?"

"No. Not until the Snake is dead. I won't feel like a king until then."

The wizard gazed deeply at him. "You've come a long way from the boy who sat upon this cloud only recently, insisting you were a king by birthright. That there was no quest to be had in putting a crown that you already deserved upon your head."

"Doesn't feel like I've come a long way," Tedros replied glumly. "Snake is still loose. Lance is dead."

"Let me ask you a question," said Merlin. "When you looked into the Snake's eyes, did you see a brother?"

"No. I saw pure darkness," said Tedros. "Loathing and fury like I've never witnessed before. Not even in Rafal or Aric or Evelyn Sader or . . . *anyone.* How could someone hate me so much? *Why?*"

"And yet he didn't kill you."

Tedros looked at him. "Maybe he wants to kill me in pieces. By killing everyone I love first. By murdering everyone I'm supposed to protect. By shoving my failures in my face."

"Is he succeeding?" Merlin asked.

The young king didn't answer. Finally, he looked at the wizard. "If I didn't have Rhian, I don't know what I'd do."

Merlin smiled. "Ah. Nicola was telling me about this Rhian boy, who's saved your lives and showed so much courage and skill. I'm not surprised, really. Foxwood boys are exceedingly well-trained. Ask him what house he was in at the Foxwood School for Boys. My old friend Brunhilde was the Housemaster of Arbed House at that school. Though he certainly won't have been in her house—"

Tedros didn't have time for diversions. "Listen, Agatha said something to me. That the Snake has a fake Storian. A pen that writes the story from his point of view, where he is the Lion and I am the Snake. The Snake said our Ever After isn't real. That our fairy tale wouldn't really end until everything that is true becomes 'untrue.' But that's impossible. No one would believe *I'm* the Snake and *he's* the Lion. Not after what he's done."

Merlin considered this. "If there's one thing I've learned in my long life, it's that every villain thinks they're the hero of their own story. And yet it's curious that the Snake focuses on undoing the Truth as his ultimate goal. That's the lesson of *The Lion and the Snake* after all."

"What do you mean?"

"Think about the original tale. The Snake said that under

his reign, the Eagle would be free from his rule. Meanwhile, the Lion said that under his reign, the Eagle would have to obey him. So the Eagle naturally chooses the Snake to be king," said Merlin. "The Snake believes he's told the Eagle the Truth. He didn't try to subject him to his rule, after all. He only tried to kill him. The Lion, on the other hand, believes the Snake has told a *Lie*—for how could the Eagle be free if the Snake tried to murder it the very same night? So what's the true moral of the tale? Both the Lion and the Snake believe they are king. Both lay claim to the Truth. It just depends on who is telling the story. And it appears the Snake in *your* fairy tale thinks his version is as right and as true as yours. Only he forgets there is a third party in the story . . . a third party whose loyalty decides the fate of the king. A third party who can make all the difference between who lives and who dies at the end of this fairy tale."

"The Eagle," said Tedros.

"And as the Lion, you've found your Eagle in Rhian. A knight standing by the rightful king," said Merlin. "Which leaves us with one question that you would do well to consider while I'm gone. The Snake thinks *he's* the Lion, right?"

The wizard locked eyes with Tedros.

"So who's *his* Eagle?"

He swept the cloud from under Tedros like a cape and the young king went tumbling down into the stars.

"Who's his Eagle. . . . Who's his Eagle. . . ," Tedros murmured. *"Who's the Snake's Eagle. . . ."*

"Tedros?"

His eyes fluttered open.

"It's me."

He stirred in bed to see Agatha at the door of the guest room.

"What time is it?" he said, jolting upright.

"They're about to serve lunch," she said.

Tedros sighed with relief. "I've only been asleep a little while, then." He noticed the purple cape was gone from beneath the sheets. He looked up at Agatha. "I was with Merlin in the Celestium. He'd visited the Lady of the—" He suddenly noticed his princess's face, tense and unsettled. "What is it?"

"I just got back from Maker's Market," she said evenly.

"And?"

"I think you should come and make sure you're happy with how army recruitment's going."

Tedros frowned. "But Rhian's there. He should be handling it—"

"He *is* handling it," said Agatha. "I just think you should—"

Nicola barreled through the door. "*The Snake*," she gasped.

Instantly Tedros leapt out of bed, sprinting with Agatha after Nicola into the hallway and through the passage to the Blue Tower. They rushed into the dining room, past the full lunch spread, to the balcony, where all of Tedros' team and the maids and cooks were pressed against the stone rail, staring up into the dark, storming sky.

Green scims flew over Camelot, forming a giant phantom snake like a beacon, its head rearing through dark clouds.

Screams resounded from the city and market, where the people could see it too.

The snake glowed like lightning.

"*Tonight*," it hissed, echoing across the realm. "*Midnight.*"

Then it broke into a thousand eels and went screaming into the rain.

27

The King's Speech

A few hours earlier, Sophie and Rhian had been riding together in a carriage towards Maker's Market, while the rest of Rhian's team trailed in carriages behind.

"Filthy walls, dusty windows, weeds in the front garden . . . and then that hideous rope bridge we had to walk across to get to the carriages . . . I thought Camelot was supposed to be inspiring," said Sophie, wiping mud off her heels with Rhian's handkerchief. "You'd think in six months, Teddy and Agatha could raise enough money to at least

give the *appearance* of a new regime."

Rhian leaned back, muscles tight against his blue-and-gold coat. "Perhaps the money they raised went to things that actually matter."

"Appearances *do* matter, Rhian," said Sophie, smoothing a businesslike blue pantsuit she'd picked for the occasion. "How do you think I remade Evil at school? By dumping all that doom and gloom and helping both Evers and Nevers see Evil in a new light. Then again, I had the advantage of using magic in my renovations, and magic is apparently banned at Camelot Castle per a dead king's orders." She tapped a finger to her lip. "Truth is, if I were Aggie, the first thing I would do is wipe out all trappings of Arthur's legacy, which haunts that place like a ghost, and bring Camelot into a new era. Granted, that's hard to do when Arthur's son is king and Aggie's soon-to-be husband, but . . . I'm only thinking of what's good for the people rather than what's good for Teddy."

Rhian watched her, rain pattering against the windows. "Anything else, King Sophie?"

Sophie sighed. "I suppose this is proof that my soul is Evil, isn't it?"

"Not necessarily. But given the Snake is coming to kill us, you've chosen a peculiar time to start planning your reign," Rhian said with a wink. "Once we get to the Market, we need to stay alert. We can't let the Snake's thugs infiltrate our army."

A buzz grew outside the carriage, and Sophie and Rhian looked out opposite windows to see the streets packed with people at the base of the hill.

"I still don't understand how Teddy expects us to march in and put together a functional army from this *mob*," said Sophie as the carriage wove down the slope. "For one thing, they're all from different kingdoms. For another, we don't have the slightest idea of their skills or abilities. Plus, it's not like Tedros has any authority over them. He can't even free Excalibur. He's *barely* King of Camelot, let alone King of the Woods. And if he doesn't have authority over them then his knight and ex-girlfriend certainly won't either."

"Authority comes from doing your job," said Rhian, his flat, dark brows pulling in. "That's where Tedros and I differ, perhaps."

Sophie noticed a group of teenage boys walking along the streets towards the Market. Two of them wore gold-foil Lion masks that looked just like Rhian's old mask.

She turned to the knight. "What do you mean that's where you and Tedros differ?"

"No knight should speak thoughts of his king without that king present," said Rhian.

"Would you speak these thoughts to Tedros directly?"

"Certainly."

"Then he won't have issue with you speaking them to me," said Sophie. "Especially after he told me that he thinks you and I are a 'perfect ending.'"

"Did he?" Rhian smiled, mulling this over. "Well, here's what I'd say to him. Tedros believes it's Arthur's sword that gives him authority. That being Arthur's son is all he needs to be king. But that's what's made him vulnerable to the Snake in the first place. The moment the Snake claimed he was Arthur's son, Tedros fell into the trap of fighting the Snake's claim instead of fighting the real war: the war for the people's hearts. Think about that story *The Lion and the Snake*. The Snake may have become king by playing a game of Truth and Lies. But the Lion didn't play that game. The Lion became king by saving people. The Lion became king by *action*. That's what Tedros keeps missing." Rhian's eyes sparkled like a sunlit ocean. "Because in the end, it's not Arthur's sword that gives a king his authority. It's a king's authority that earns him that sword."

Sophie was quietly watching him.

"Then again, everything Tedros has done has led to me being here with you in this moment . . . so maybe the story is working exactly as it should," said the knight, gazing at her.

"Depends on how it ends," Sophie said friskily.

The carriage rocked along the bumpy road.

Suddenly they were kissing, Rhian gripping her hard, Sophie's hands on his waist, the feel of his heartbeat against hers as their lips slid over each other's—

Over Rhian's shoulder, Sophie glimpsed three teenaged girls through the window, wrapped in a white flag with a Lion symbol.

Sophie pulled away from her knight.

"What is it?" Rhian asked.

"Turn around," said Sophie.

Rhian swiveled and jumped, his head hitting the ceiling—

Through the window, he saw a thousand images of his own face.

Evers and Nevers jammed the streets of Maker's Market, hoisting banners and posters and flags with paintings of Rhian. A group of young men in the Ever recruitment line flashed green Gillikin jackets that read "SONS OF THE LION" on their backs, as a parade of young girls from Kyrgios flaunted pea-green sashes that said "LION'S ARMY." In the Never line, a clan of man-wolves from Bloodbrook wore gold Lion masks, while street vendors sold everything from Lion shirts to Lion sparklers to chocolate Lions to fuzzy Lion slippers. Everywhere Sophie and Rhian looked they saw men, women, and children from all over the Woods, dressed in their various kingdoms' colors, with Lion tattoos painted on their arms and chests, bellowing songs and chants:

> *He kills the scims*
> *He'll kill the Snake*
> *The Woods was doomed*
> *Until the Lion did wake!*

> *To Camelot he comes*
> *To our king he swore*
> *Now we join the fight*
> *To watch him roar!*

Ogres, dwarves, and goblins mixed in the lines, as did mogrified bucks and bulls with Lion-insignia collars, while fairies and nymphs floated above the crowd with glittery Lion patterns on their wings.

Speechless, Rhian rolled down his window to get a better look. Instantly people in the crowd spotted him and rushed his carriage—

"You saved my nephew at the Four Point!" said a man in Jaunt Jolie's royal uniform, a Lion shaved into the side of his head.

"Woulda been fed to the man-eating hills if it weren't for you!" said a one-eyed girl in Mahadeva's guard jacket.

"Trolls left my village as soon as you appeared!" crowed a strapping young boy in a Foxwood school uniform.

"Fires stopped in Glass Mountain too!" said a nymph with translucent skin.

"Same with the attacks in Ravenbow! Snake's scared of the Lion!" said a dark-dressed boy wearing a Lion necklace.

"We're here to fight with you!" said a girl from the Lion's Army, hanging on Rhian's window.

"We're here to fight *for* you!" said a Son of the Lion.

More Evers and Nevers thronged the carriage as the driver tried to whip the horses on, but the crowd blocked them and the two carriages behind.

"*LION! LION! LION!*" they shouted.

Sophie and Rhian exchanged baffled looks.

Without warning, Sophie opened the carriage door—

"Sophie, no!" Rhian barked.

But the moment Sophie emerged, the people let out a huge cheer.

"She's with the Lion!" a girl cried.

"The rumors were true! He's Sophie's prince!" said her friend.

"Sophie's with Camelot now!" a boy hollered.

Lost in a daze, Sophie scanned the thousands of people and creatures and animals, Good and Evil, cheering for her and Rhian as rain soaked her hair. She could see Beatrix, Reena, and the three witches gaping through the windows of their respective carriages, just as bewildered by the sight of the Woods rallying around Evil's Dean and her new love.

"SOPHIE! SOPHIE! SOPHIE!"

Sophie closed her eyes and soaked up the sound of her name. Ever since Rafal died, she'd been happy with a Dean's life. She'd been happy on her own. That was the Ever After she'd fought so hard to find.

But then Rhian had come into her story. And for the first time, Sophie began to wonder if she was meant for more.

Much more.

She climbed up onto the side of the carriage and waved to the crowd—

"Hello, my loves! I'm here! I'm here for you all!"

"SOPHIE! SOPHIE! SOPHIE!" they roared.

She felt Rhian's hand clasp her arm and she stepped down, cozying up to his broad chest, drinking in the Woods-wide worship and the breathless, red-hot feeling of fresh, new love.

"Isn't it amazing?" she gasped.

"Sophie."

"Yes, my prince?" she said, gazing up at him.

Rhian eyed her sternly. "We need to get to work."

Stripped to wet shirtsleeves, Rhian huddled with his rain-soaked team behind the gates to Camelot Park.

"We're looking for two things. Loyalty to Camelot and loyalty to Tedros. That's all. Anyone who passes the loyalty test qualifies to fight," he said, raising his voice over the chants of his and Sophie's names. "When the Snake comes, we need our army to stop him outside the castle perimeter. *Before* he crosses the drawbridge. These soldiers will be our first line of defense, so we need as many as we can get. But they must pass the loyalty test first." He held out his hand. "Ready?"

Sophie, Hester, Anadil, Dot, Beatrix, and Reena put their hands on his.

"Ready!" they said.

The gates opened. Selection began.

The process was simple. Rhian took charge of the Evers line with Beatrix and Reena; Sophie helmed the Nevers line with Hester and Anadil. As each candidate came forward, the respective teams tested them:

1. *Do you believe Camelot is the leader of the Woods?*
2. *Do you believe King Tedros is a good king?*
3. *Are you willing to die to protect Camelot and King Tedros?*

If they passed the test, then they were sent to Dot, who stamped them with her fingerglow and ushered them to the

Town Hall inside Camelot Park, where they'd be fitted with armor and weapons.

If they didn't pass, then they were denied entry and sent home.

At first, progress was slow.

For one thing, the leaders of the allied kingdoms came flurrying down the hill amidst a cavalcade of carriages, camels, elephants, magic carpets, and other modes of royal transport, Guinevere trailing behind, with each foreign leader determined to have a private audience with the Lion. Sophie thoroughly enjoyed this impromptu summit, staying close to Rhian and greeting Ever and Never kings and queens, while they kissed her hand and complimented her pantsuit ("If I'd have known this was a royal occasion, I would have dressed the part!" Sophie wisped). One by one, the leaders gave Rhian gifts for saving their kingdoms: a medal of honor from Foxwood, a mother-of-pearl wristwatch from Malabar Hills, a ruby-hilted dagger from Ravenbow, a diamond monocle from Glass Mountain. . . .

"We've informed Tedros and his mother that *you* must command the army," the King of Jaunt Jolie told Rhian quietly, so Guinevere wouldn't hear. "With you in charge, we know we'll win."

"You've shown yourself to be a leader," the Ice Giant of Frostplains confided. "We only feel comfortable in your hands."

"And with a face like that, you're made to be a hero," added the Empress of Putsi, admiring Rhian's torso through his wet shirt.

Rhian gritted his teeth politely, looking eager to get back to work.

Even Guinevere herself couldn't stop thanking him for saving her son in Nottingham, emotion nearly overtaking her, before she remembered Rhian and his charges had a job to do and she whisked the leaders into the Town Hall to make sure that the deliveries of weapons and armor from their respective kingdoms had arrived.

But just as Rhian and his team tried to push on, Agatha rode up, hidden beneath a hooded cloak, looking unnerved by the crowd.

"Aggie, isn't it wonderful? They *love* him," Sophie said, helping Agatha from her horse.

"And it seems they love you too," said Agatha tightly, hearing chants of Sophie's name.

"Who would have thought that a Dean of Evil would have to come to *Camelot* for respect?" Sophie marveled. "At school, kids pound on my office night and day, complaining about rankings or feigning some pustulous disease or asking inane questions, treating me like a maid or a tour guide, never once taking the time to appreciate how lucky they are to be talking to a real-life fairy-tale hero in the first place. But here . . . well, just look at all this! I'm going to revel in it while I can—" She saw Agatha's face. "Oh, don't be greedy, darling. Not everything in life can be about you and Teddy. You'll get more attention than you can handle at your wedding."

"I'm not worried about attention, Sophie," said Agatha,

facing her dead-on. "I'm worried about Tedros ending up like Lancelot."

Sophie's smile vanished. "I know that, Aggie," she said sincerely. "So am I. And we're doing the best we can to protect him."

She carried on interviewing, but she felt oddly self-conscious with her best friend watching from beneath her black hood like the grim reaper. But Agatha didn't stay long and when she left, Sophie sighed with relief.

"She's right, you know," said a voice.

Sophie turned to see Rhian in the other line.

"A knight shouldn't overshadow his king," he said.

"Oh please. You and Tedros are a *team*. It doesn't matter," Sophie dismissed.

"You don't get it," said Rhian. "People weren't cheering for Lancelot when Arthur was around, were they?"

He went back to work.

Sophie tugged at her wet hair. Her knight had a point. Tedros' ego *was* delicate, especially after all that had happened these past six months. But it's not like Agatha would mention what she'd seen to Tedros. Aggie might be relentlessly honest, but she wasn't stupid. Being a good queen meant propping up your king when he needed it, not seeding more doubts.

Then again Agatha wasn't queen yet. And massaging boys' egos . . . well, it wasn't her friend's strong suit.

But she didn't have time to obsess over Agatha's love life yet again. She had a job to do. A job that was remarkably difficult,

Sophie realized, as she and the witches tested more Nevers, including a shifty-looking dwarf.

"And you believe Tedros is a good king?" Sophie asked.

"As good as his father," the dwarf said in a basso voice.

"And how good was that?" said Anadil.

"About as good as one might expect," said the dwarf.

"Which is how good?" Hester pushed.

"Depends on your definition of 'good,'" the dwarf said.

They didn't give him a stamp.

But that was the rare interview where they got to talking about Tedros at all. Most of their tests went like this:

SOPHIE: Do you believe Camelot is the leader of the Woods?

NEVER: I believe the Lion is the leader of the Woods so if he's at Camelot then yeah, Camelot is the leader of the Woods.

Or:

HESTER: Do you believe Tedros is a good king?

NEVER: Not until he brought in the Lion I didn't.

Or:

ANADIL: Are you willing to die to protect King Tedros?

NEVER: Tedros? Ain't heard of 'im. I'm 'ere for a Lion.

Sophie glanced over at Rhian's group.

"So you *swear* your loyalty to King Tedros?" Beatrix tested a seven-foot nymph with hot-pink lips.

"I swear my loyalty to the Lion," said the nymph airily.

"But do you swear your loyalty to Tedros too?" said Rhian.

"Only as much as the Lion swears his loyalty to Tedros," said the nymph.

"But I *am* the Lion," said Rhian.

"Then you should be the one answering these questions, not me," said the nymph.

Rhian frowned, but Beatrix approved the nymph anyway. "Loyal enough," she murmured. "If we limit ourselves to Tedros fans, *I* wouldn't even qualify."

Sophie hurried off to use the toilet in the Hall and returned to find the witches bickering.

"What happened?" Sophie asked.

"Ani and Hester just let in a pirate!" Dot said.

"No, we didn't," Hester snapped. "You don't think Ani and I know how to give a loyalty test? We spent the last six months interviewing School Masters!"

"So did I! I'm on your quest, remember?" Dot retorted. "I saw his face—it was Wesley, the sunburnt one from Jaunt Jolie—he had peeling flesh around his eyes—"

"You're just paranoid after what happened with Kei," Anadil growled.

Dot appealed to Sophie. "I saw him. I swear!"

"I just came from the Hall," said Sophie skeptically.

"Certainly didn't see a sunburnt pirate—"

"Because he already has a stamp!" said Dot. "He's probably sneaking into the castle as we speak!"

Sophie could see Dot about to cry. "Look, if you're that sure, let's at least check the Hall again. . . ."

A blast of thunder came over their heads, dark clouds assembling in curious formation.

The girls looked up, startled.

That's when the Snake came with a message.

Before the Snake's warning, there'd been a rowdy, aimless pace to the recruitment, as if the prospect of war with the Snake was itself a phantom. As if by building an army to fight him, it would never have to actually be used.

After the Snake's message, things changed.

The chants quieted, an edgy silence falling over the Market. The witches stopped bickering. Sophie stopped checking on Rhian or worrying about her rain-streaked makeup. Tests moved faster. Lines whittled down. The Town Hall filled up with new soldiers.

There were only seven hours until midnight.

Evers and Nevers took their loyalty tests with grim resolve, mustering nice words about Tedros in order to win their spot behind the Lion. Sophie noticed the new soldiers giving Rhian awed stares as they received their stamps, knowing that it wasn't just their loyalty to the Lion being tested but the Lion's loyalty to them, for now both Good and Evil had put their lives—and those of their families and kingdoms—in the knight's hands.

Even Sophie found herself gazing into each candidate's eyes with will and strength, silently reassuring them as if she were their queen. Indeed, the longer the testing went, the more Sophie began to forget this was Tedros' kingdom and Tedros' army and began to see it as hers and Rhian's. . . .

A boy appeared next to her in a gold Lion mask.

"They love you," he said, his pure blue eyes roaming the crowd. He looked over at Rhian. "Both of you."

"Tedros?" Sophie said, stunned. She glanced back to see Agatha in her black hood, arms folded, standing in front of a horse.

"Found Rhian's old mask in my bag before I rode down with Agatha. Didn't want to distract the crowd from your work," Tedros said. "Though it seems like I wouldn't be the main attraction anyway."

Rhian paled slightly when he saw the king.

"Y-y-your Highness," he said—

"I'm under no illusions of my own popularity compared to yours, Sir Rhian," Tedros said, putting his hand on his friend's shoulder. "You're the one who saved their kingdoms. You're the one who saved me. Their loyalty to you will only be an asset." The king's eyes hardened through his mask. "As long as you grant me one request."

"Anything, Your Highness," said Rhian.

"*I* kill the Snake tonight," Tedros commanded. "No one else. Understood?"

"Understood," said Rhian.

"Good. We need to start moving soldiers to the castle.

Snake's coming in four hours," said Tedros. "Meet me in the Hall so I can address the army. Move quickly, please."

He walked towards the Hall.

"Look who's decided to be a king," Hester murmured.

"While wearing his knight's mask," mumbled Anadil.

"Why did you bring him here?" Sophie hissed, accosting Agatha.

"He's the *king*," Agatha retorted. "He has a right to address his soldiers."

"The leaders want Rhian to command the army—"

"Rhian fights for *Tedros*. And so does any army of Camelot."

"Don't be stupid, Agatha! The last thing we need is tension between him and Rhian!"

"Well, maybe Rhian shouldn't grandstand so much!"

"Grandstand! He's been nothing but humble and loyal!"

"Then why is he pretending to be the Lion, riding around wearing a lion mask? *Tedros* is the Lion!"

"Is it Rhian's fault he saved everyone? Is it his fault the other leaders trust him over Teddy? Is it his fault everyone here came for *him*?"

"Oh please. You just love to see Tedros humiliated."

"So now Rhian's successes are *my* fault? Is Tedros' insecurity my fault too?"

"No, it's mine," said a voice.

The girls turned to see Rhian, red-faced.

"I told you, Sophie. It's a mistake for them to pin their hopes on me," said the knight. "I'm not the king. Tedros is. And now *he* will lead them."

He turned to Agatha. "To the Hall to hear the king?"

Agatha smiled. "To the Hall to hear the king."

The group dismissed the rest of the crowds by shooting sparks into the sky—"THANK YOU!" read Beatrix's message to the Evers; "GO HOME" read Hester's to the Nevers—and together, they sealed the gates to Camelot Park and went into Town Hall together to listen to Tedros' speech.

The Hall thrummed with life, like a seaship off to war. More than a thousand new soldiers crammed inside on the dusty marble tile, lit by oil lamps overhead, which flickered every time a moth burnt in their flames. Men, women, creatures, and mogrifs were fitted with armor and weapons as leaders from the various kingdoms supervised from the stage and Guinevere made the rounds to check their stamps, her newly white hair slick from the rain.

Sophie and Agatha found Tedros standing in a corner in his Lion mask.

"Ready to inspire your army?" Agatha said eagerly.

Tedros blinked through his mask.

"Do you know what you're going to say?" Agatha prodded.

Tedros didn't answer, his eyes on the allied leaders.

"Tedros?"

"Stop badgering me," he said, glaring at Agatha.

Sophie saw Agatha peek at her for support.

"If you're nervous, Rhian can address them," Sophie said to Tedros.

"*No*," said Agatha, giving Sophie a death stare.

"What is it?" Rhian said, arriving.

"Nothing," Tedros replied sharply. "I'm doing it. It's just . . . I had a flashback to the coronation. That's all."

He headed towards the stage.

Sophie turned to Agatha. "Was the coronation that bad?"

Agatha gave her a look that more than answered her question.

"He'll be great," Rhian assured, seeing their faces. "He's a king. This is what kings *do*."

As soon as Tedros stepped before his army in a Lion mask, the soldiers exploded into cheers—

"LION! LION! LION!"

Tedros took off the mask.

Soldiers hushed, staring at him.

The Hall was silent.

Agatha started clapping loudly and so did Rhian, before the crowd joined in with stiff applause for the king.

It ebbed quickly and Tedros was again standing in front of a quiet room.

"Hi. Hello. Welcome to Camelot," said Tedros, his voice scratchy. "Thank you for your service. It's my honor to have you—"

Someone fumbled a sword and it clanged to the ground.

Tedros cleared his throat. "It's my honor to have you fight by my side. At midnight the Snake will come and we must be ready. I am hereby rescinding my father's ban on magic at the castle, since the Snake himself will surely not abide by it. My father would have no doubt done the same. To get to the castle, the Snake's army will have to climb over Camelot's outer gates . . . then cross the broken drawbridge from the cliffs to the royal grounds. We will be magically fortifying the outer gates so no scims can fly over it. All of you will be positioned inside these outer gates to prevent the Snake's army from using the drawbridge or the temporary rope bridge to get to the castle. My team, meanwhile, will be positioned inside the castle courtyard to protect both the castle and Excalibur. As a last barrier, barrels of boiling oil will be placed atop the towers to ensure none of the Snake's army can get inside the castle. . . ."

Agatha whispered to Sophie: "He's rushing, but he's doing okay, isn't he?"

But he wasn't doing okay and both girls knew it. The crowd was listless, rocking back on their heels, fidgeting with their armor and weapons.

"His army will be made up of pirates, trolls, and other paid mercenaries," Tedros went on. "Paid loyalties cannot compete with your genuine commitment to our cause. . . ."

Sophie could see the allied leaders murmuring to each other, shielding their mouths with their hands. So were the witches, while Anadil's rats toyed with a dead butterfly. Guinevere glanced back at Agatha, looking nervous.

Sophie whispered to Agatha: "A king is supposed to rally his army, Aggie, not bore them with details and put them to sleep! This isn't a speech for Class Captain or some school challenge! He has to boil their blood! He has to fire them up! This lot is the only thing between the Snake and all of us dying!"

Agatha bit her nails, no longer pretending that this was going well.

In front of them a dwarf yawned.

Tedros kept talking: "Because of the magical barrier, no scims can pass Camelot's outer gates. Which means the Snake's army is his only weapon against us—"

An ogre in Bloodbrook armor raised his hand. "What's the Lion gotta say?"

Tedros stopped talking.

A thousand soldiers turned away from him and looked to his knight.

Rhian retreated into the shadows.

Sophie could see Tedros taking in the sight of his allies and soldiers, hungry to hear from his knight instead of him, many of them adorned with Lion masks, Lion tattoos, and Lion shirts.

Sophie could see it in Tedros' face. The way they were all looking at his knight . . . it was almost as if the king wasn't there.

"Rhian," said Tedros finally. "Would you like to speak?"

The crowd stirred, woken from their sleep.

"Rhian! Rhian! Rhian!" the Sons of the Lion sang.

Others whistled and shouted, "Speech! Speech!"

Rhian scowled, waving this off—

But then Agatha squeezed his arm.

Princess and knight locked eyes.

"Please," she said. "Help him."

In that moment, Rhian's face changed.

"As you wish, milady," he said softly.

With a deep breath, the knight took the stage and the king fell back, offering Rhian a weak smile.

Rhian stepped cautiously into the spotlight.

The crowd went quiet—a new quiet, as if the air had somehow turned kinetic.

The tan, amber-skinned boy gazed down at his shoes for a moment. Then he looked up, his copper hair shining in the lamplight, his sharp-boned face radiant and calm.

"What is a king?" he said. "To some a figurehead. To some a throne in a castle far above the kingdom where the work is actually done. To many a stuffed shirt or a man of privilege who expects you to fight for him without knowing of your struggles, your toils, and your pain. But not to me. To me, a king is a lighthouse. A guide who can cast his glow across his kingdom and bring every last one of us out of the shadows. A beacon who we can look up to when the world seems lost. A bridge who can unite us when our differences seem too stark to reconcile. Tonight, we need a king who is all of those things. A king who can look each of you in the eye and make you feel that you won't just fight for him or his kingdom, but you'll fight for our way of life. Because tonight, we join forces to take on a Snake: not just because he's attacked our families and our kingdoms, not just because he's sabotaged the rules and order of our world, not just because he's too scared to show his face . . . but because he dared us to come together, Good and Evil, and bring forth a hero. A hero that will stand up to him and destroy him like the coward that he is. A hero that will plunge into battle and make sure he has the last blow. That sordid, slippery little Snake looked us in the eyes and dared us to sire a king. And tonight, that king will have his vengeance."

Rhian held up his fist. "To King Tedros!"

"To King Tedros!" the crowd roared, weapons raised, before erupting in warmongering cheers and chants.

Tedros stared at Rhian dumbly from the shadows.

Agatha looked at Sophie with the same expression.

Sophie smiled, her cheeks glowing. "Now *that*, my darling, was a speech."

An hour before midnight, Tedros' team and Rhian's team reunited in the Blue Tower Dining Room over a simple buffet of grilled chicken, cabbage salad, wild rice, and chocolate ice cream. All of them were in chainmail armor that Kiko had scavenged and cleaned and they carried the weapons from the Armory that Hort had repaired.

From the dining room windows, they could see the torches of Camelot's new army in the distance, lighting up the night sky, as the thousand-plus soldiers barricaded the broken draw-bridge within the outer gates.

Tedros took his place at the front of the dining room, the metal of his armor gleaming under a chandelier, Lancelot's old sword on his belt.

Everyone stopped eating to listen to the king.

"Professor Dovey will arrive soon to place a magical bar-rier over Camelot's outer gates. Which means the only way the Snake can get in is if his army gets past ours. Given our size and strength, that *will* not happen," he said, trying hard to sound regal after the events in the Hall. "Here's your assignments. Hort, Beatrix, Reena, Kiko: you'll be on guard with the soldiers in front of the drawbridge. Hester, Anadil, Dot: you'll patrol the rope bridge to make sure nothing gets across. Willam and Bogden: you'll man the barrels of hot oil atop the towers. Rhian and Sophie: you'll be the first line of defense in front of the castle doors. Agatha and myself will protect Excalibur. Everyone know where they're supposed to be? Finish eating, then get to your posts."

The room set into motion.

Sophie piddled half of a chicken breast and a bit of cabbage onto her plate. She hesitated, then added a teaspoon of ice cream.

"Ice cream? You must think we're going to die," said Tedros, sliding next to her with three hunks of chicken and a mound of rice on his plate.

"You and I might die, but Sophie won't," Rhian piped in, having finished eating. "No way will I let anything happen to my girl. Even if she does send her little friends to check up on me."

"What?" Sophie asked, confused.

"Don't play coy. I know you have Nicola sussing out my ex-girlfriends," said Rhian.

Mystified, Sophie looked at Tedros.

"Don't look at me. I heard Nicola too," said the king.

Sophie remembered what Tedros had said to her back on the ship: *"You don't have to hunt for flaws or dig up dirt on him. . . ."*

"Well, if there are any demented ex-girlfriends, Nicola certainly hasn't mentioned them to me," Sophie puffed, hanging on Rhian's arm. "So you better come clean before I become a knight's lady."

"A knight's lady," Rhian mused, fingering ice cream off her plate into his mouth. "Such a downgrade from Evil's queen."

"Then you better find a way to make me feel like a queen," said Sophie archly.

"Oh, I have some ideas," Rhian said, dotting ice cream on her nose.

"You're good at talking, aren't you?" Sophie said.

"Don't I know it," Tedros said flatly. "Made me look like the opening act in front of my army."

"On the contrary, I'd say he honored you and everything you're fighting for," said Agatha, joining them, a mountain of ice cream on her plate.

"I know," said Tedros, forcing a smile. "It's why I assigned him to guard the castle doors. If the Snake manages to get onto the grounds, I know Rhian will stop him. As long as I get to kill the Snake myself like Rhian promised."

"You have my word," said Rhian firmly.

The two boys kept talking, while Agatha pulled Sophie aside.

"What's wrong with Dot?" Agatha asked.

Sophie spotted Dot alone in the corner, separate from Hester and Anadil, sulkily turning her chocolate ice cream to extra-extra chocolate.

"Thinks Hester and Ani let a pirate through during loyalty

tests, which is ridiculous, given those two are suspicious of *every-thing*," said Sophie. "But after what happened with her dad and Kei, I think Dot's just looking for a way to feel useful."

Agatha sighed. "Let me talk to her."

As her friend left, Sophie could hear Tedros and Rhian—

"Where's your mother?" said Rhian.

"Waiting for Dovey at the outer gates," said Tedros. "Leaders of the other kingdoms are out there with her. They want to fight alongside their soldiers. I still think you and I should do the same instead of manning the castle."

"And if the Snake gets *past* the soldiers, then what?" said Rhian.

"No way his army gets past ours. They're paid mercenaries. Our soldiers fight for a cause," said Tedros.

"Regardless, you and I need to protect the castle and Excalibur. We're Camelot's last stand," said Rhian.

Tedros looked at him. Then he glanced away. "It's strange when a king trusts his knight's judgment more than his own," he said.

"You don't mean that," said Rhian.

Tedros didn't answer. He moved food around on his plate. "By the way . . . what house were you in at that Foxwood school?"

"Arbed House," said Rhian. "Why do you ask?"

"Figured if Sophie is digging up dirt on you, I should too," said Tedros, grinning.

"Hey, Sophie—" said Nicola, jolting Sophie back to attention. "I wanted to thank you for sending a letter to my Pa. Even if something happens to me tonight, at least he'll know I was thinking of him."

"Of course. I am still your Dean after all, even if you're no longer in my school," said Sophie, eyeing the first year hawkishly. "Though I might have to send another letter to your father telling him that you're snooping on the Dean's boyfriend and pretending that I asked you to do it."

Nicola didn't flinch. "I wanted to check something. That's why I lied to Rhian and said what I said. But I was wrong."

"Wrong about what?"

"It's nothing. If I was right, Merlin would have come back already."

Sophie frowned. "What does Merlin have to do with this?"

Nicola didn't answer, watching Willam and Bogden pass in front of Rhian and Tedros as they got more food.

"Hey, Bogden. Should I still be wary of gifts?" Tedros asked.

Willam and Bogden both turned around.

"Very wary," said Bogden.

"If you value your life, that is," said Willam.

"But he has a wedding coming," said Rhian, nudging Tedros. "He's going to get a lot of gifts."

"Maybe we should put 'No Gifts' on the invitation," Tedros said, nudging Rhian back.

"Ignore them," Willam murmured to Bogden, pushing him along. "My brother told me to stay away from Tedros."

"Your brother?" Tedros said, still laughing. "Who's your brother?"

Willam didn't answer.

"Can I ask you a question?" Nicola said, turning to Sophie. "Do you find the Snake's attacks . . . *odd?*"

"Odd?" Sophie said. "What do you mean?"

"In storybooks, Evil's advantage is that it attacks and Good has to defend. That's the number one rule of Good and Evil. So Evil usually does everything it can to make sure its attacks are a surprise," said Nicola. "But the Snake always seems to tell us when he's attacking. We knew he was going to attack the Four Point. We knew he was going to attack Nottingham. We know when he's going to attack tonight. I mean, what villain gives you a *time* when he's coming for you?"

Sophie pondered this. "Maybe it's his way of making sure he gets to fight Tedros himself."

"Maybe," said Nicola. "But it seems strange somehow . . . artificial, even. Like he's setting something up."

Sophie peered at her, mind churning—

Professor Dovey suddenly swept into the dining room, her hair a mess, her face tired and gaunt, and a bag on her arm.

"I came as soon as I could," she said to Tedros. "I did what you asked—I cast a barrier over the outer gates so the scims can't fly in. It's a spell the School Master showed Lesso and me to seal the school in a crisis. If Rafal's sealing of the Sheriff's sack worked on the Snake, then the barrier is guaranteed to work too—" She coughed, clutching at her throat. "Sorry . . . I'm feeling a bit . . ."

"Professor Dovey, you shouldn't be here!" Nicola said, running up to her. "Merlin sent you a note telling you not to come!"

"And Tedros sent me a note saying he needed me," Good's Dean countered, turning to the king. "What else can I do to hel—"

Her knees buckled, her body starting to slump. Instantly, Tedros seized her waist and propped her up. Sophie and Agatha sprinted to help him.

"I'm okay—I just . . . I just need to sit down—" Professor Dovey stammered.

"I'll take her into my room," said Agatha, grabbing her from Tedros.

"I'll come with you," said Sophie, taking one of Dovey's arms.

"I'll come too—" Tedros started.

"*No*," Agatha said to him. "Get the others in position."

Sophie noticed her friend's voice was unusually harsh, but Agatha's focus stayed on Good's Dean, helping her towards the queen's chamber at the end of the hall.

As soon as Professor Dovey was safely inside, Agatha closed the door. "Tedros should never have sent for you," she said, laying the Dean on the bed. "And you should have stayed at school like Merlin told you to, Professor."

"When Camelot's king calls for me, I will always be there," Professor Dovey rasped, hacking another cough. "It's this crystal ball. . . . I've told Merlin I can't handle it alone. . . ." She pointed at her bag, half-open. Through the flap, Sophie could see the top of the glowing orb. "I brought it here in case something happens to me."

"Nothing will happen to you," said Sophie, feeling the

Dean's forehead. "You just have a slight fever. That's all."

"But no more using this ball until you're better," Agatha said, taking the Dean's bag and slinging it onto her arm.

In the hallway, the clock struck a quarter hour. 11:45. Fifteen minutes left.

"And until you're better, you're to stay here and rest," said Sophie. "Don't move from this room."

"That's an order, Professor," said Agatha—

But Professor Dovey was already snuffling softly, fast asleep.

Sophie blew out the lamp and closed the door.

The two girls slipped onto the Blue Tower balcony, only a short distance from Excalibur, still protected by the glass lockbox, while the fleet of guards usually manning it had been dispatched to the perimeter with the army.

"I'm worried about Dovey," said Agatha, tucking the Dean's bag in a corner of the balcony.

"You heard her. It's that crystal ball. Whatever she's been doing with it clearly drains her," said Sophie. "Just keep it away from her and she'll get better—"

"Tedros *knew* she was ill. He could see it when she appeared on the ship. Why would he make her come all the way here in the dead of night? Why would he risk Professor Dovey's life?" Agatha harped. "And then that rambling speech in the Hall . . . and going to see Lady Gremlaine instead of taking Lance into Sherwood Forest, where Lance would have been safe . . . and everything that happened at the coronation . . ." Agatha shook her head, a sad look clouding her face. "Maybe you're right about him."

Sophie stared at her. "Right about what?"

"Don't make me say it. I know full well you doubt him as a king," said Agatha. "I believe in Tedros. I really do. I defend him as much as I can. His quest for glory was to be a true king to Camelot. And I want him to succeed. But sometimes . . . sometimes he just doesn't *think* like a king. Or act like one. And the fact I'm saying this when my quest was to be his queen . . . well, maybe I'm failing my quest too."

Her focus moved back to Sophie, who'd gone stiff as a board. For a moment, she thought her friend was shocked at her confession—but then she noticed Sophie's eyes. They weren't looking at her. They were looking past her.

Slowly Agatha turned.

"It's five minutes until midnight," said Tedros, shadowed under the balcony. "Sophie, you should be with Rhian."

"Of course," Sophie said, giving Agatha a nervous glance before hurrying away.

But Sophie didn't go to Rhian like she was supposed to. She hid behind the balcony wall and peeked around the edge. . . .

Agatha and Tedros stood together in silence, Excalibur hovering above their heads. In the distance, they could see Dovey's magical barrier glinting green in the moonlight over the outer gates. Behind the gates, Camelot's army walled off the drawbridge, while the three witches patrolled the temporary rope bridge. Beneath Agatha and Tedros, Rhian waited in the courtyard, right in front of the castle doors.

"I'm sorry, Tedros," said Agatha, holding back tears. "I just was worried about Dovey and I got frustrated. I shouldn't have sai—"

"You're right," said the king.

Agatha looked at him.

Tedros met her eyes clearly. "It's why you tried to take over my quest. It's why you're always jumping in to help me. Let's face it, Agatha. You don't think I'm a good king. And the truth is . . . you're right. Everything you said about me is right."

Agatha reached out, searching for words. "Tedros—I . . . I . . ."

Shouts rose from the outer gates.

Agatha and Tedros turned sharply. So did Sophie.

There was movement on the rope bridge . . . shadows barreling towards the three witches in charge of defending it . . .

Then suddenly, Anadil, Hester, and Dot were fleeing back across it, onto the castle grounds, along with a crush of soldiers jamming onto the rope bridge, which swayed and teetered under their weight.

Tedros' eyes flared. He sprinted past Sophie, calling for Rhian, Agatha chasing behind him—

Sophie ran out onto the balcony and watched the rope bridge snap between the gates and the courtyard, sending dozens of soldiers plunging into the Savage Sea below.

Booms echoed nearby from the broken drawbridge, sealed between the gates.

CRACK! CRACK! CRACK!

The drawbridge smashed open, battered down by desperate soldiers, who stampeded across its splintered planks towards the castle. Sophie could see Reena, Beatrix, Hort, Guinevere, and panicked leaders of allied kingdoms bolting into the courtyard, along with the rest of Tedros' army—

Sophie gasped.

Because now she could see what everyone was running from.

Scims were stabbing the army from behind, razor-sharp at both ends, impaling bodies and then whipping around and spearing them through the front, like killing machines. They moved so quickly and brutally, each one with a life of its own, that the soldiers didn't stand a chance. They fled in droves as scims slashed through Camelot's defense, before the eels started veering sharply towards the castle.

Shell-shocked, Sophie looked up at Dovey's shield over the outer gates . . . completely *intact*.

In a flash, Sophie was scrambling down the stairs, as soldiers' screams tore through the courtyard, along with the scims' searing shrieks—

It's impossible, she thought. *The barrier over the gates . . . He couldn't get through. . . . He was supposed to need an army. . . .*

Which left only one explanation.

He didn't need an army.

Because he didn't need to get through the gates.

Sophie's heart thundered.

The Snake had been inside all along.

28

The Princess and the King

T̶edros met her eyes.

"And the truth is . . . you're right," he'd said. "Everything you said about me is right."

Agatha struggled under his gaze, searching for words.

But a warning pounded in her head.

"I've already told you how this story will end. With your fairy tale shattered . . . With everything you thought true turned untrue . . ."

Six months ago, she and Tedros thought their story *had* ended. They'd been off to Camelot Castle, destined to restore it to glory as queen and king. Good had won, Evil vanquished, with the success of their quests a foregone conclusion.

But now they were atop that castle, admitting they *hadn't* won after all. That their quests to be that glorious king and queen had failed, no matter how much they loved each other. The End wasn't The End at all . . . but the beginning of something thornier, twistier, where every truth about her and Tedros' love story suddenly seemed untrue, just like the Snake had promised.

Was this the final crack in her and Tedros' fairy tale? A fairy tale that would shatter forever?

Were the Snake's Lies really the Truth?

Agatha looked at her prince. "Tedros . . . I . . . I . . ."

Shouts exploded near the outer gates.

It happened so fast.

Drawbridge smashing down . . . the witches fleeing across the bridge . . . the scims stabbing soldiers from behind, before the eels turned and flew towards the castle . . .

"RHIAN!" Tedros yelled as he dashed from the balcony and down the stairwell to find his knight, while Agatha chased him, her heart slamming.

"Dovey's barrier—it's still intact—" she called out. "He was inside the gates all along!"

"*RHIAN!*" Tedros yelled again, leaping down stairs as he drew Lance's sword from his belt.

How did the Snake get in? Agatha thought, trying to keep up with her prince.

But there was no time to think. She and Tedros dashed

out of the archway and into the courtyard, only to see a slew of scims shoot for their heads—

Someone tackled Tedros and Agatha to the ground, making the scims miss, before the eels circled around and savagely killed a dwarf right in front of them.

Agatha lifted her head from the dirt as Rhian grabbed her and Tedros and pulled them both into an archway behind a stone pillar, where Sophie was already hiding.

Across from them, Hester, Anadil, and Dot crouched behind a second column, with Beatrix, Reena, Nicola, and Hort's man-wolf behind a third. Reena had a gash in her thigh, her shield dented. Hort let out a growl of pain as he ripped a spasming scim out of his calf muscle and crushed it in his hairy palm.

Agatha peeked out from the pillar to see the once-quiet field in front of the castle turned into a deathzone, with soldiers trampling each other across muddy grass, desperately seeking cover in the dark while scims stabbed them left and right. A Son of the Lion took a scim to the arm a few yards in front of Agatha before one of his friends yanked him behind a bush.

"They're going to find us. *All* of us," Beatrix said, watching scims easily take down a giant before they went off to search for fresh prey.

"We have to kill as many as we can," Rhian urged. "The scims are his armor. We can strip it away. Kill enough of them and he's nothing but flesh and blood."

"We need fire! It's the only way to kill them!" said Agatha.

"Where will we get enough fire to kill that many scims?" Sophie retorted.

Tedros jolted straight. "From *oil*."

He spun to Rhian. "Cover me."

Rhian took Reena's shield and blocked Tedros as the two boys moved towards the courtyard. As soon as Tedros was out from under the archway, he tilted his head upwards and whistled between two fingers—

Bogden and Willam peeped over the edge of a Blue Tower balcony, their bodies hidden behind a fortress of barrels.

"Use the oil!" Tedros called as Rhian smashed scims away.

"How?" said Bogden.

"*How?*" Tedros barked.

"No one told us!" said Willam.

Tedros seethed. "It's *oil*! Just take it and—"

Rhian snatched Tedros by the arm and flung him back behind the pillar.

"Why'd you do that!" Tedros berated, starting to get up again—

He froze still.

Four scims peeked around the side of the pillar at him, Agatha, Sophie, and Rhian. Their sharp, eyeless tips squiggled with glee, before they looked past the king's group and saw Hester's and Hort's teams across the archway. The scims murmured high-pitched gurgles, taking in the bounty of flesh. They hewed together like a single arrow, drifting between targets, as if they couldn't decide who to kill first. . . .

Then they flew at Tedros.

"Tedros, move!" Agatha gasped, shoving him left just as Rhian shoved him right, trapping Tedros straight in the scims' path—

A gush of amber liquid suddenly slopped down from above, drenching the eels and splashing to the ground.

The scims looked up, startled. So did Tedros.

Bogden and Willam gaped down between pillars. "Bogden thought we're supposed to pour it," said Willam.

Tedros groaned.

But now the oil-soaked scims had turned back to the king, their lethal tips glowing green. They slashed towards him—

Tedros lunged forward with his gold fingerglow just as the scims hit his chest, and with a lion's roar, he swiped his fingertip across them, setting the eels aflame.

Instantly the scims detonated into a fireball, shrieking and sizzling before they crumbled into dirt.

Anadil's three rats set upon them, scarfing them up like they were crisped bacon.

The entire group slumped with relief.

Rhian squeezed Tedros' shoulder. "Good thinking, Your Highness."

Tedros glanced at Agatha. "Occasionally I can think like a king."

Agatha flinched. "Tedros—"

"Sorry to interrupt your drama but we're still about to die," Sophie said as more scims shot through a seven-foot nymph in front of them. Somewhere Kiko screamed. "Tedros might have killed a few scims, but how do we kill the rest!"

"Brains," said Hester, eyeing Anadil.

"Talent," said Anadil, eyeing Hester.

The witches turned to Sophie. "Neither of which you have," said Anadil. She snapped her fingers and her three black rats hopped onto her shoulders.

"Rats?" Sophie sniped as Anadil whispered to her pets. "That's what's supposed to save us—"

Anadil's red eyes sliced through her. *"Watch."*

The rats jumped off her shoulders and cannonballed into the puddle of oil like pigs into mud, slathering every inch of their fur, gulping up mouthfuls of it and hissing gleefully. . . .

Then they took off, scrambling up soldiers' bodies and onto their heads. They whipped their rat tails and sprayed oil onto any scims within reach, before leaping to the next soldier's head like a landing pad, dousing eels as they flew. Like stealth trapeze artists, they swung across the battlefield, twirling and tumbling and shaking out their fur to make sure every scim got a flick of oil, careful not to wet the soldiers. Agatha's eyes tried to keep up with them in the night sky, ping-ponging in and out of torchlight like kamikaze fairies. Locked in battle with Camelot's army, the scims didn't notice three tiny furballs silently crisscrossing the air above as they executed spiral death drops and aerial dives, squeezing every last drop of oil from their bodies onto eels and spraying them with whatever they'd gargled in their mouths . . . until at last, their work was done and they collapsed exhausted and reeking in their master's lap.

Agatha and the rest of the group blinked at the rats.

"Now what?" Sophie said, unimpressed.

Hester glared. "Now it's *my* turn."

With a searing cry, the demon on Hester's neck flew off her skin, grazing Sophie's cheek as he whizzed towards the battlefield, inflating to red-skinned, full-blooded life. Conjuring glowing firebolts from his mouth, he hurled them at unsuspecting scims, igniting the oil and combusting the eels to ashes.

Soldiers ducked in shock as flame-bombs exploded all around them like a fireworks show, scims' screams multiplying until they were all Agatha could hear.

Rhian and Tedros looked at each other, then whirled to the group—

"*Let's go!*" said Tedros.

The crew charged into battle behind the king and knight, who hacked at flaming scims with their swords. Bleeding and struggling with a limp, Hort's man-wolf snatched scims out of the air and let out savage roars as he tore the eels apart. Sophie slit blazing scims open with a dagger she'd swiped off the ground; Beatrix and Reena shot them through with bows and arrows; Hester and Anadil ran to help Kiko, tormented by a burning scim that had yet to die, while Nicola wielded Reena's dented shield like a frying pan at her father's pub and smashed scims to pieces. . . .

But Agatha still hadn't moved from the archway. She'd never fought without magic nor used a sword before. She didn't have Tedros' strength or Rhian's skills or Sophie's Evil.

But neither did Nicola or Hort or Dot.

They had something else to fight with, she realized, her heart thumping like a war-drum. The same thing that had fueled her in every war against Evil.

Her friends.

She grabbed a pickaxe from a fallen dwarf and stormed into the fight, chopping scims out of the air and spinning round to bludgeon more. Burning scims came from every direction like falling comets, streaking at Good's future queen. Over and over she took them down with vicious yells, spraying the air with firedust, until Agatha was bent over and heaving, with no more scims to kill. Slowly she rose, her axe over her shoulder, her face smeared with ooze, her hair matted to her head. The rest of the group gathered at her side, looking out at a field awash in bodies and mist. Wounded soldiers stirred; others looked out from their hiding places, stunned to still be alive.

Agatha turned to Tedros, who stood by Rhian's side, their arms on each other's shoulders, gazing blearily into the distance. . . .

Then the king and knight went rigid.

Agatha followed their eyes.

Out of the smoke and embers came the Snake, his suit of scims shredded from top to bottom, revealing the young, mortal flesh of his pale chest and legs. Blood and bruises covered his milk-white skin, his body weakened by the death of his armor. But the Snake lived, moving towards them with clear purpose, his emerald eyes honed in on Tedros through his green mask, still intact.

He stopped ten feet from the king.

Excalibur shimmered in its lockbox above their heads.

"Hello, Brother," said the Snake.

"I'm not your brother," Tedros spat, lit up with rage. "I'm the Lion who kills the Snake. I'm the king who will bring your head to my people. I'm the *real* king."

"Are you?" said the Snake, his stare hard and cold. "Time will tell."

Tedros stepped forward. "You're out of time."

The king stripped off his armor, revealing his bare, golden chest. He threw Lancelot's sword aside.

"No magic. No weapons," he said. "We end this tonight."

"Tedros, no!" Agatha said, seizing his arm.

He pushed her away, glowering at the Snake. "You and me."

The Snake stepped forward, torchlight casting shadows on his rippled torso.

"You and me," said the Snake.

"Witches, mark it," Tedros ordered.

Anadil's rats sprinted around the two boys, dripping oil. Hester's demon set the ring aflame.

"He doesn't fight fair—" Agatha insisted to Tedros.

Tedros didn't listen.

"On your signal," he said to the Snake.

"Younger brother first," the Snake cooed.

Tedros gnashed his teeth. *"Now."*

They launched at each other like gorillas, chests slamming, before Tedros gripped the Snake by the neck and bashed him face-first to the ground inside the ring of fire. The king punched him in the head, Tedros' fist crunching loudly against the Snake's green scales, connecting with the flesh beneath it.

The Snake struggled onto his side, then stabbed out his leg, hitting Tedros' sternum and knocking him backwards, dangerously close to the flaming ring.

Agatha clasped Rhian's arm. "You have to help him—"

Rhian didn't move. "I made a promise," he said. "This is his fight."

The Snake lunged forward and clobbered the king, clawing at Tedros' face, opening up bloody scratches. Tedros swung his arm around his opponent's throat, driving him into the ground, before the Snake thrust his hips and kneed Tedros in the gut, taking the king down.

Agatha watched in horror as Tedros weathered blows from the deadly villain, while her friends looked on anxiously from outside the ring. Together, they could destroy the Snake. They outnumbered him ten to one! It didn't matter what Tedros wanted. Not when he might die.

She lurched towards the ring, about to bound over the low flames—

Rhian snagged her back.

"*His* fight," he said.

The two were on top of each other now, wrestling for dominance, Tedros hammering at the Snake's chest as the Snake lay flat on him, squeezing the king's throat. The Snake strangled Tedros harder and the king started to choke, his punches weakening. The Snake took advantage, slamming Tedros in the face with his fist, swelling the king's eye and opening up a spigot of blood. Tedros writhed, struggling to free himself from the Snake's deathgrip—

"No!" Agatha cried, trying to break from Rhian's grasp—

The king turned blue, wheezing for his last breaths. . . .

Tedros shoved his palm onto the Snake's face and with a stifled cry, he muscled the green-mask backwards, the king grunting desperately, about to pass out, until at last Tedros managed just enough space between their bodies. . . .

He jammed his boot against the Snake's ribs and crushed him as hard as he could.

The Snake toppled backwards and fell close to the flames—

In a flash, Tedros was on him, gasping for breath, punching the Snake again and again.

"That's for Chaddick," he said, belting him.

"That's for Lancelot," he said, walloping him harder.

"That's for Lady Gremlaine."

"That's for the Lady of the Lake."

Blood seeped through the scales of the Snake's mask, his body listless.

"That's for *me*," said Tedros, delivering the hardest punch of all.

He stopped to take a breath—

The Snake kicked him in the chest, sending Tedros flying out of the ring, his bare back grazing the flames and searing red.

Tedros landed in dirt, bloodied, bruised, and burned.

Agatha rushed to his side.

"Tedros—"

He was still breathing.

Slowly he lifted his muddy head and looked past his

princess to the Snake in the ring. The green-masked villain hadn't moved, still flat on his back, surrounded in a pool of blood.

Agatha remembered Chaddick posed the same way in a painting. The first page of a fairy tale that was now about to end.

"Come and kill me, little boy," the Snake rasped. "Come and kill your brother."

Tedros staggered up, but his legs buckled and he fell back. He tried again—

Agatha stopped him.

"Let . . . me go . . . Agatha," he panted, blood streaming.

"He'll kill you!" said his princess.

Tedros struggled against her, but she held him down. "This is . . . my . . . *quest*," he snarled. "Let me . . . finish it."

"Stay down. You're losing too much blood," Agatha said—

She saw the Snake's body shift, starting to rise once more.

Agatha locked eyes with Tedros' knight.

"Rhian," she said firmly.

The knight didn't move.

"I have to kill him," said Tedros, pushing against his princess.

Agatha held him down, her gaze on the knight.

Still Rhian didn't budge.

"This isn't a choice, Rhian. I'm ordering you," said Agatha sharply. "I'm ordering you as your *queen*."

This time Rhian blinked.

"As you wish, milady," the knight said.

Tedros glanced between them, suddenly understanding.

"No! I'm the king. . . . He's *mine*. . . ." Tedros fought—

But Rhian was already walking into the ring.

The copper-haired boy slammed the Snake back down to the ground and put his foot on the Snake's pallid chest.

"By order of the queen, I sentence you to die," said Rhian.

The Snake quivered under his boot—

Rhian bent over, took the Snake's head in both hands, and wrenched it hard, snapping his neck.

The Snake jerked one final time . . . then went still.

Fires cooled around the ring. Smoke blew across the Snake's dead body.

Tedros slumped limply in Agatha's arms.

Dazed soldiers converged on the courtyard littered with wounded bodies and scims. The allied leaders emerged from the gatehouse, along with Guinevere, to see the king and knight still alive and the Snake dead.

The depleted army unleashed a cry of victory. Over their heads, Willam and Bogden rang the bell in the Blue Tower, which echoed down to the city, where bells tolled in response and a cheer resounded, signaling that the people of Camelot knew the Snake had been killed.

Here in the field, the cheers fell away as everyone realized Tedros was still on the ground. Together they circled the wounded king.

Rhian kneeled beside Agatha, helping her hold Tedros' body.

But the king's eyes stayed on his princess.

"He was mine. . . . He was mine . . . ," Tedros breathed, again and again.

Agatha touched his face. "You're still alive, Tedros. That's what matters. It could have been a trick." She held him closer. "I was protecting you."

Tedros resisted. "But you didn't protect me. You held me back. You always hold me back," he said, looking right at her. "You don't have faith in me, Agatha. You stop me from being a king. Don't you see?"

He blinked through blood and tears.

"The only trick is *you*."

The words hit Agatha like a stone. Her hands let go of him, ceding his body to the knight.

That is where the princess and the king ended.

Because the people of Camelot were already flooding through the gates, expecting a celebration.

By sunrise, the royal grounds were filled with Evers and Nevers from all over the Woods, eager to see the dead Snake and the Lion who killed him.

Still filthy and covered in blood and ooze, Agatha crouched behind a pillar near the balcony to eavesdrop on the people beneath.

"So-called King ain't so-called anymore, ain't he?" said a man proudly. "Beat the Snake with 'is bare fists."

"Lion killed him, though," said his friend.

"King already beat him to nothin'."

"Lion finished him. All that matters."

Agatha stopped listening.

She rose to her feet and looked back into the castle's sitting room across the hall, where Sophie and Rhian were treating Tedros' wounds.

"This is going to hurt," said Rhian, standing over Tedros, who was shirtless and facedown on the couch, his back red-hot from the burns.

Tedros bit into a pillow and his knight spread salve on his skin while Sophie held the king down. Tedros let out a stifled roar, his teeth tearing the pillow to feathers, before his yells muted to groans and he let his two friends wrap him with gauze.

Agatha watched Sophie and Rhian take care of Tedros the way she should be.

"Something must be wrong when Good's greatest helper isn't helping," said a voice.

She turned to see Guinevere next to her, dressed all in white, watching her son with Sophie and Rhian.

"I think I've helped Tedros enough for now," Agatha said softly.

"You did what you had to do, Agatha. You kept my son alive."

"And yet he hates me for it," said Agatha, tears flowing.

"Because the Snake was *his* to kill," said Guinevere. "Not for his own pride. But for his people. Tedros needed to be the king, no matter the cost, even to the end if need be. You took that from him."

"But I didn't want him to end up like Lancelot," Agatha

argued, smearing at her eyes. "I didn't want him to die. Surely you understand that!"

"More than you can ever imagine," said Guinevere starkly. "I didn't want Lancelot to die, Agatha. Of course I didn't. And yet I asked him to go into the Woods with Tedros, knowing he might."

Agatha shook her head. "But you just said I did what I had to do. . . . So which is it? Which is more important? Keeping Tedros alive or letting him be a king when he might die for it?"

Guinevere smiled sadly. "Welcome to being a queen."

She touched Agatha's shoulder and walked inside.

A short while later, Agatha returned to the sitting room, bathed and dressed in a black gown, with Professor Dovey's bag on her arm.

Tedros stood in front of the mirror, adjusting his father's old coronation robes while Rhian changed into his blue-and-gold suit.

"God, this thing smells even worse than the first time I wore it," said Tedros, fussing with the collar, clearly trying not to look at his battered face in the reflection.

"It's just for a short while," said Agatha.

The king glanced at his princess in the mirror. "You sound like my mother," he said coolly.

He went back to Rhian. "You're sure you tried to get the Snake's mask off? There's no way to see who he *is?*"

"The scims are both his armor and part of him somehow,"

Rhian answered. "He sent the scims on his body to fight us, but the ones that make up his mask can't be dislodged. His face is melded with them. Hard to tell where the magic begins and the human ends."

"Well, as long as both the magic and human are dead," said Tedros. He stared hard at Rhian. "Since *you're* the one who killed him."

"As I was ordered, Your Highness," Rhian said stiffly, his eyes darting to the future queen. "My men will present his body to the people at the ceremony."

Agatha waited for Tedros to say something to her.

He didn't even look in her direction.

"Why are you lurking?" Sophie said to Agatha, sidling next to her at the back of the room.

Agatha frowned at Sophie's shimmering pink princess dress. "I thought you were done with pink."

Sophie eyed Agatha's black one. "Pot. Kettle," she said. "Oh come now, Aggie. I know I said I don't wear pink anymore, but surely even a girl like me is allowed to *feel* like a princess. For one day, at least."

"He certainly is a prince," Agatha murmured, watching Rhian put cream on a gash near Tedros' eyebrow.

Sophie tapped the bag on her friend's shoulder. "Dovey's crystal ball?"

"Found it untouched where I left it, thank goodness. Did Dovey really sleep through the entire battle?"

"I think we're lucky she woke up at all this morning, given what she looked like last night," said Sophie soberly. "Dovey claimed it's that ball that's been sapping her strength. Whatever you do, keep it away from her."

"Where is she?"

"Getting the crew ready for the celebration. Dovey insists the Nevers be as presentable as the Evers in deference to the king. Which is taking some work, to say the least."

Agatha snorted half-heartedly. Sophie rested an arm on her shoulder as they watched the boys.

"Will we exchange gifts in front of the people?" Rhian was asking Tedros. "As king and knight, I mean?"

"We won our battle, didn't we?" said Tedros. "Besides, can't deny a boy who grew up jabbing pillows with spoons and rehearsing for this moment his whole life. With all that preparation, your gift better be a good one."

"My gift I know you'll like," said Rhian thoughtfully. "It's your gift I'm concerned about."

"Very funny," Tedros said, elbowing him.

"Tedros?" Sophie asked.

The king turned.

"Are you going to try to pull Excalibur again?" she said. "At the celebration, I mean?"

Tedros considered this for a long moment. "The Snake is dead. The people of Camelot are happy. The Woods are safe once more. Excalibur will have its day," he said. "Just not today."

He smiled warmly at Sophie and Rhian . . . then at Agatha.

"See, darling?" Sophie whispered to Agatha. "You two are going to be okay. Everything is going to be okay."

Agatha didn't answer.

Because from the way Tedros smiled at her, Agatha was thinking very much the opposite.

The door flew open and Merlin shambled in, his slippers muddy, his cape tattered, and his hat slashed and full of holes.

He took in the scene and grinned, revealing three teeth missing where there'd been teeth before.

"Ah. Just in time," said the wizard.

"Presenting King Tedros and his royal court!" a courtier announced.

The crowd unleashed a roar as Tedros and Rhian emerged onto the Blue Tower balcony, followed by Agatha, Sophie, Guinevere, and Merlin. Tedros and Rhian took their places in front of the archway with Excalibur trapped in its stone, while Agatha and the others stood off to the side behind them. Agatha could see from the crowd's dress and colors that it was composed overwhelmingly of citizens from beyond Camelot, many wearing Lion masks, holding Lion banners, chanting, "LION! LION! LION!"

Tedros raised Rhian's fist in his and they soaked in the ovation together.

Agatha made sure to stand next to Merlin, accidentally smacking him with Dovey's bag as she did.

"That crystal ball shouldn't be in your hands, Agatha," said the wizard.

"Well, it shouldn't be in Professor Dovey's hands either, with what it's done to her."

"Then swear to me it will stay in your hands and no one else's, until you return it to her," Merlin said, glaring.

"Fine," said Agatha.

"Swear it!" Merlin demanded.

"I swear! Happy now?" Agatha said, exasperated. "Where have you been? You look terrible."

"I've always appreciated your candor, Agatha," the wizard replied dryly. "I wish I could be as candid about my own travels, but the perils I've endured have served little purpose. It appears the king has found a happy ending all on his own."

Agatha watched Tedros and his knight wearing matching smiles and waving to the people.

"Though maybe *your* ending is the one I should be concerned about," the wizard said.

Agatha saw Merlin's blue eyes peering at her suspiciously. She looked away.

Sophie touched her from the other side. "Look at them, Aggie," she said, watching Tedros and Rhian hand in hand. "Who knew two boys could be best friends like us?"

Agatha mustered a smile.

"You sure you're okay?" Sophie said, studying her.

Thankfully that's when Tedros started his speech.

"Today I stand here as your king on a proud day for Camelot and a proud day for the Woods," he said, amplified by one of Merlin's white stars. "Under siege by a villain who threatened our way of life, we came together to stop him: Camelot and the Woods, Good and Evil, Ever and Never. Not just with our army built from my kingdom and yours, but also with a loyal group of friends at my side. Friends whose fairy tale the Storian is writing as we speak. And when that tale ends at the close of this celebration, the pen will have told the story of a team of peers who gave up their own quests for glory to set off on a bigger and more dangerous one. A team who not only succeeded in that quest, but achieved a glory bigger than any one of them might have attained on their own. People of Camelot, People of the Woods: I present to you, Dean Clarissa Dovey of the School for Good, and the crew of the *Igraine*!"

Professor Dovey came out onto the balcony to a hearty greeting from the masses, looking rested, refreshed, and more like her old self. At her side were Beatrix, Reena, and Kiko in three of Guinevere's old gowns, along with Willam and Bogden, hair combed and smartly dressed in starched shirts that Dovey must have borrowed from Tedros' closet. Together, they took their place behind Agatha, Sophie, Guinevere, and Merlin.

Tedros waited for the last three members of the crew to emerge.

The archway stayed empty, Excalibur glinting silently from its glass box overhead.

Professor Dovey pulled her wand from her pocket and shot a spell through the archway. A collective yelp echoed, followed by Hester, Anadil, and Dot shuffling onto the balcony in pastel-colored dresses, their hair curled and primped like poodles'.

Agatha gaped at them.

"Dovey said it was a condition for us to go back to our old quest and look for a School Master," Hester mumbled.

Tedros cleared his throat, returning to the crowd. "Whenever my father had a great victory in battle, he invited the people onto the grounds of the castle to share in that victory. Just as he once brought back the body of the Green Knight for all of you to see, today we, too, have proof that a terrible villain will never harm our Woods again."

The crowd stirred with anticipation.

"Behold," Tedros declared, "the Snake is *dead*!"

Four guards in full knight's armor and helmets marched through the archway at Rhian's direction, carrying the Snake's body on a plank.

The crowd erupted in its biggest cheer yet, as Tedros and Rhian took the plank and raised the Snake's blood-spattered corpse over the balcony for all the Woods to see.

Agatha saw Rhian make eye contact with Sophie, giving her a loving wink. Tedros, meanwhile, kept his focus on the crowd, not even glancing Agatha's way.

All the while, Agatha could hear the witches behind her.

"Difference between Evers and Nevers is we don't showboat for applause," Anadil grumbled.

"Because what we care about is getting the work *done*," said Hester. "Can't wait to get back to School Master interviews."

"You sure we can't convince Rhian to be School Master?" said Dot. "Look at how he is with Sophie. They definitely don't want to be apart."

"Dot's right. Long-distance relationships never work. Plus he'd have a lot more power as a School Master than as a knight," said Anadil. "Besides, I can't think of a better candidate, Hester. Can you?"

"He's already proven he can bring Good and Evil together," Dot appealed to Hester. "Dovey loves him. And Sophie listens to him. Around him, she's calmer, nicer, and less of a lunatic. What more could you ask for in a School Master?"

For once, Hester didn't argue with them. "Maybe we're at the end of our quest after all," she said finally.

"Does this mean I have to go back to teaching history?" said Hort.

"Does this mean I have to go back to being a first year?" said Nicola.

The group snickered.

"Dovey's assigning my team a new quest to be a peacekeeping force near the Four Point," said Kiko.

"Dovey's sending me and Reena to help rebuild Jaunt Jolie after what the pirates did to it," said Beatrix.

"It'll be strange not being all together anymore," said Hort. "Coming on this quest felt like school again. Only this time I actually liked you guys."

"We'll all be at Agatha's and Tedros' wedding, won't we?" said Nicola.

"That we will," said Hester.

Silence ensued and Agatha could feel the group's eyes on her, while she pretended not to be listening.

Sophie had certainly been listening, though, because she squeezed Agatha's wrist and whispered to her: "As long as they're not in any of the wedding portraits."

Agatha gave her a look.

"I'm your wedding planner," said Sophie. "Clarissa might have made them all look like wet farm animals, but you can be assured I'll be dressing them *myself*."

In front of the girls, the guards reclaimed the Snake's body from the king and knight and held it off to the side as the ceremony continued.

"And now for our final tradition that comes at the end of every victory. The exchange of gifts between king and knight," Tedros announced to the people. "In so many of his battles, my father fought alongside his greatest knight, Sir Lancelot du Lac. Lancelot was killed at the hands of the Snake, but his legend will live on." He looked at his mother. "Not only in the hearts of those who loved him most, but also in the spirit of a new knight. I have a Lancelot of my own in Rhian of Foxwood, a knight who will fight with me for the rest of my life. I may be the Lion of Camelot and your king, but Rhian is *my* Lion and thus has earned the name as well. Rhian, please address the people you so bravely serve."

"*LION! LION! LION!*" the people bellowed.

Tedros put Merlin's white star under Rhian's suit collar, so his voice could be heard.

"I do hope Rhian gives Tedros something suitable," Sophie whispered to Agatha. "You can always judge a man by his gifts."

Rhian stepped to the balcony. "It is no easy feat to think of a gift for King Tedros of Camelot. So as inspiration, I looked to the gift that Sir Lancelot always gave King Arthur at the close of a winning battle. The knight would kneel before a lady of Arthur's court and offer his tribute to her. As I stand before Arthur's son, I, too, would like to offer my tribute to a lady of his court."

He turned towards Agatha and sank to one knee.

Agatha blushed.

"Oh, Aggie," Sophie breathed. "How chivalrous—"

"Sophie," Rhian said, his eyes shifting to her. "Will you step forward?"

Sophie glanced at Agatha, surprised. Tedros looked equally confused.

"Go," Agatha whispered.

Sophie obeyed and stepped towards the knight.

Rhian looked up at her, his face warm in the sunlight.

"Sophie of Woods Beyond . . ."

He opened his palm, revealing a glittering diamond ring.

"Will you marry me?" the knight asked.

Agatha and Tedros drew the same stunned breath. Merlin and Professor Dovey exchanged wide stares, as did the group of students behind them.

The crowd had gone completely still.

But no one was as shocked as Sophie, who had turned the color of a rose, unable to move.

Then, a light rushed into her cheeks, the moment dawning on her, and she leapt into his arms—

"Yes," she gasped. "A thousand times, yes!"

In an instant, she was off the ground, as Rhian picked her

up off her feet and kissed her passionately.

"I love you, Sophie," he whispered.

"I love you too, Rhian," she said, wiping tears. She shook her head, still in a stupor, and looked out at the crowd. *"We're getting married!"* she shrieked.

A single hurrah shattered the silence. Then like a wave of love, the mob let loose an adoring cheer, chanting Sophie's and Rhian's names as they kissed again and again. . . .

Tedros stepped back between Agatha and Merlin, baffled.

"Lancelot always gave his gift to the king's *queen*. A tribute to the queen is a tribute to the king. That's the point," Tedros said to the wizard. "But Sophie isn't the queen. Agatha is."

Merlin frowned slightly. "Well, not yet."

"I suppose he just wanted to surprise us," said Tedros, trying to shrug it off. But still he seemed unsettled.

Even so, Agatha felt a tinge of relief, hearing Tedros reaffirm her place as his queen. The relief was followed by guilt that she was obsessing over her own relationship when her best friend had just gotten *engaged*.

She saw Sophie make eye contact with her and give her a sheepish, blissful smile as Rhian fit the ring on her finger.

Agatha tried to mirror the same smile back.

"Did you happen to ask what house at school Rhian was in?" Merlin asked Tedros casually.

"Arbed House," said Tedros, looking at him.

Merlin lowered his glasses. "Arbed House? Are you sure?"

"Think so. Why?"

"Arbed House is where parents in Foxwood send children they want to *hide* from the School Master. Children they believe are Evil, despite growing up in Good families. And not just Evil. So Evil they're a threat to the Woods. So Evil they're too dangerous to be trained as villains. For a large fee, Dean Brunhilde magically conceals them from the School Master so he never comes to know of their existence. While every other child in the Woods has a file at the School for Good and Evil, these children's files as prospective students simply disappear. Brunhilde never tells the Arbed students this, of course; she does her best to turn their souls Good. Meanwhile, the students never learn they were meant for great Evil all along."

"But Rhian doesn't have a drop of Evil in his body. He couldn't have been sent there," Tedros scoffed, watching the knight and Sophie still waving to the crowd. "Besides, Dovey checked him and his family out thoroughly. I must have misheard."

Merlin tugged at his beard, his jaw tensed, as if he was trying to find a solution when he didn't quite know the problem.

"By the way, whose file did Nicola want you to look at?" Tedros asked.

"Kei's," said the wizard. "She wanted to know if he and Rhian were in the same class at the Foxwood School for Boys. But there was no record of Rhian at the School for Boys at all. There was one for Kei, however. He was a student at Arbed House. And it seems he had an interesting roommate."

"Who?" said Tedros.

Merlin looked at him. "Aric."

"Lady Lesso's son? Kei was roommates with that creep?" said Tedros. "Figures."

Agatha listened to them, a prickly feeling slithering up her spine.

The Snake had been friends with Aric.

Close friends.

That's what he'd told her and Sophie.

And the Snake clearly knew Kei too, since Kei had acted as his henchman.

Was it just a coincidence that Kei and Aric were roommates?

Or is that how the Snake met them?

Agatha's heart pumped faster.

Had the Snake been in Arbed House too?

Nobody knew the Snake's name, after all. Without his name, there was no way to check his file. . . .

But *Rhian* had been in Arbed House. That's what he'd told Tedros.

So wouldn't Rhian have known Aric and Kei as well?

The knight's voice snapped her out of her thoughts: "Tedros, I believe it's your turn," said Rhian, grinning.

Tedros stepped forward and gave his knight a hug to congratulate him. He hugged Sophie too—

But Agatha wasn't watching them anymore. She was watching the armored guards lift the wooden plank with the Snake's dead body and carry it off the balcony, back into the castle. As they left through the archway bearing Excalibur, one of the guards glanced in Agatha's direction. His dark eyes met hers through the opening of his helmet . . . the flesh around them peeling from sunburns.

Agatha's muscles shot up with adrenaline.

Sunburn.

Dot.

Pirate.

In a flash, she was running after the guards. Sophie intercepted her: "Aren't you going to say congratulations?"—but Agatha was already shoving her aside, sprinting through the archway.

She chased them down the stairs as the guards looked back and saw her coming. Immediately they moved faster, shuttling the Snake's dead body to the ground floor and turning the corner into a hall that led from Blue Tower to White Tower—

Agatha jumped stairs, trying to catch up, as Dovey's bag and crystal ball banged hard against her arm. She could hear Tedros' voice resounding from the courtyard—

"My dear Rhian, I wish you and Sophie the best for your lives together," the king proclaimed. "And perhaps more than that, I wish for a double wedding."

The crowd laughed.

"But now it's my turn to give you a gift," said Tedros.

Agatha hurtled off the last steps and onto the ground floor, lunging forward after the guards. She hiked up her dress, slipping on the dusty marble, as she turned the corner into the hall, barreling towards the White Tower—

Agatha stopped cold.

In the middle of the hall lay the wooden plank the guards had been carrying.

The guards were gone.

So was the Snake's body.

Dread cut through her heart.

Slowly, Agatha looked up and saw the Snake standing at the end of the long, dark hall.

He leaned against the wall, barechested, his neck unbroken.

He watched her through his green mask.

Then he turned the corner and walked away.

Agatha stood there, frozen to the spot, blood pounding in her ears.

The Snake was alive.

Which meant Rhian hadn't killed him.

Which meant . . .

"What could I possibly gift a knight who has given more to me and my people than I could ever ask?" Tedros' voice echoed.

Panic hardened to clarity.

I have to get to Tedros, Agatha thought.

I have to get to Tedros now.

She ran back towards the staircase, then slid around the corner and saw a fleet of armored guards, at least twenty of them, walking up the steps towards the balcony. She was about to call out to them, thinking these guards were on Camelot's side—

Then she saw their boots beneath their steel armor.

Muddy, filthy, black.

With silver tips.

Pirate boots.

Agatha jerked behind the wall before they could spot her.

"My father felt the same way about Lancelot as I do about you," Tedros was saying. "And he too struggled to find a gift worthy of his knight."

I can't get to the balcony, Agatha thought, watching the guards head that way. *I have to get Tedros' attention from below it—*

As the last guards climbed the staircase, she scrambled across the ground floor, through one of the doors leading into the courtyard. She flung it open. Sunlight hit her hard as she charged right into the teeming crowd, jostling past men, women, and children.

"So my father offered Sir Lancelot the world instead," Tedros' voice boomed above her. "The same gift I give to you today, Rhian."

Agatha squeezed between bodies, whacking them with Dovey's bag to get them out of the way, trying to get far enough into the crowd that Tedros could see her.

The clues had been there all along.

The way Rhian had appeared on cue to save them each time the Snake attacked.

The way he had worn the mask of the Lion as if he was playing a part.

The way the terror in the Woods had stopped once the Lion appeared.

The way the Lion had become Tedros' new knight once the Snake killed the old ones.

The way the Snake had gotten into Camelot before the war had ever begun.

And most of all, that speech the Lion had given about the Snake in the Hall . . .

"He dared us to bring forth a hero. . . . He dared us to sire a king. . . ."

Agatha pushed people aside. Someone shoved her to the ground. But she kept moving—

"Who's his Eagle . . . ," Tedros had mumbled in his sleep. *"Who's his Eagle. . . . Who's the Snake's Eagle. . . ."*

Agatha knew the answer.

The Lion.

The Lion had been in league with the Snake from the beginning. The two of them playing both sides of a story, working towards the same goal.

But this Lion wasn't just the Snake's Eagle.

This Lion was the real Snake all along.

Agatha looked up. She was still too far under the balcony, out of Tedros' sightline.

"My dear Rhian," said Tedros' voice, "I offer you anything on this earth that a king can give a man."

Agatha sprung through bodies. She was almost there—

"I ask for only one thing," said Rhian's voice.

Agatha dove forward and spun around. She finally glimpsed Tedros high above her, smiling at Rhian, as if Tedros knew what Rhian was about to ask of him.

"I ask for the key around your mother's neck," said Rhian.

Tedros' smile erased. He looked utterly confused. "You want the *key?*"

"*Tedros!*" Agatha shouted.

He didn't hear her. She jammed through more bodies, trying to get closer to him—

But Guinevere had already stepped towards the knight. "He's asking to keep your sword safe, Tedros," she said to her son, before turning to Rhian. "You've saved my son again and again. Even when choosing your own gift, you think selflessly of him first when you could have asked for anything in the world. You are worthy of Lancelot's legacy." She took the necklace with the glass key from her own throat and held it towards Rhian. "And I can think of no one better to protect Excalibur than you, my child."

"No!" yelled Agatha—

Rhian took the key out of Guinevere's hands.

"*TEDROS!*" Agatha cried.

This time he heard her.

Tedros met her eyes from the balcony and for a moment had a cold expression, as if yet again she wasn't standing behind him where she should be . . . as if yet again she was coming between him and his duty as a king. . . .

But then he turned and saw Rhian in the archway, already slipping the key into the lockbox.

Tedros spun back to Agatha and, suddenly, he understood. So did Merlin and Guinevere, following the king's eyes to his princess in the crowd.

In a flash, Tedros leapt for his knight. So did Tedros' mother and the wizard, but it was too late—

Rhian seized Excalibur with both hands and pulled it smoothly, the blade sliding clean out of the stone without a sound. He turned to the crowd and thrust King Arthur's sword towards the sun, free at last, the rays of light spearing the steel and spraying across the balcony, blinding Tedros and his court.

For Agatha, everything slowed to half speed. No one seemed to be moving. Not the crowd. Not Tedros nor their friends, who stood there like statues, the sword's light streaked across them. Not Merlin, Guinevere, or Dovey, who each seemed unable to fathom the sight of a king's sword in a knight's hands. And not Sophie, who watched her betrothed brandishing the most powerful sword in the Woods, a dazed smile on her face, before that smile slowly vanished, her eyes moving to Agatha in the mob.

"*I* am the eldest son of King Arthur, raised in secret and returned to claim my throne," Rhian declared, his voice as sharp as a whip. "*I* am the true heir to the throne of Camelot. *I* am the one true king come to restore this kingdom to glory." He raised Excalibur to the people like a grail. "*I am your Lion!*"

For a moment, the Evers and Nevers of the Woods were quiet as a tomb, their stares shifting from Tedros to Rhian, caught between two kings.

Citizens of Camelot broke the silence first, reacting first with murmurs and boos. They grew louder, as they rallied to the defense of Arthur's son, a son they'd known since he was a child—

But then it came.

A unified roar from the masses around them.

Masses that outnumbered them, from kingdoms Good and Evil that Tedros had once ignored.

This was the ending they'd been waiting for. This was the Storian's justice. A king for all kingdoms. A fairy tale finally complete.

"*RHIAN THE KING! RHIAN THE KING!*" they bellowed, madly waving their Lion masks and signs.

All at once, the gallery of bodies behind Rhian surged into motion—

Agatha saw Guinevere grab Tedros, wresting him towards the archway. Dovey snatched Sophie by the wrist, pulling her after them, while Merlin herded the other students—

But now a fleet of twenty armored guards marched through the arch, blocking their entry to the castle.

Merlin waved his arm, about to fire a spell, but a guard clubbed him hard over the head with his fists, knocking the wizard to the ground. The other guards captured Guinevere, Dovey, and all the others, leaving only Tedros and Sophie untouched.

"Those loyal to the previous reign cannot be trusted. They've done enough harm to Camelot and will do no more," said King Rhian. "Take them to the dungeons!"

Tedros yelled, lunging for his friends, but a guard caught him, as the armored men towed Merlin's unconscious body and the others into the castle.

"As for you, Tedros of Camelot," Rhian said, leering at him.

"You may have grown up with our father, but I am his son in deeds and in action. I am more his son than you will ever be. Look at you. You ruled your kingdom as an illegal king, uncrowned, untrusted, unwanted. When Camelot wanted a True king, you offered a Lie. When the Woods asked for help, you turned your back. When the Four Point was attacked, you stayed at home. When the Snake had to die, you left it to me. You've let your castle rot, your people starve, and the Woods suffer. You are a fraud. A failure. An impostor wearing my crown. If I am the real Lion, then you are the real *Snake*."

"Rhian—" Tedros gasped from his guard's grip. "What are you doing—"

"What you could never do," Rhian said, his blue-green eyes tearing into him. "Being a *king*."

He turned to the crowd. "I hereby declare Tedros of Camelot an enemy of the kingdom and sentence him to death. Take him to the dungeons to await his execution," he thundered, as the guard tried to pull Tedros into the castle. "And find his so-called queen too!"

The crowd roared its approval, drowning out Camelot's dissenters, as Tedros struggled against his guard—

"DEATH TO TEDROS!" shouted one.

"GLORY TO RHIAN!" shouted another.

"GLORY TO THE WOODS!"

Two more guards emerged from the archway. Through one of the guard's helmets, Agatha could see familiar red tattoos around the eyes. They lashed Tedros' body in green metal chains.

All the while, Sophie couldn't move, her body shaking, her skin ghost-pale.

Finally Rhian set his eyes on her.

Sophie whirled towards the archway, but Rhian was on her, wrenching her close to him as he swiveled towards the crowd and raised Sophie's fist in his.

"Today, Camelot begins a new era of Truth over Lies, with a new king and a new princess, soon to be your queen," Rhian said, holding Sophie so tight her knuckles turned white. "All of you are invited to the royal wedding to take place one week from today!"

Run, Sophie! Agatha thought. *Run, now!*

But now she saw Sophie looking down at her, terror in her face, her body pivoting slightly so Agatha could see something.

The sword.

Rhian had its tip right against Sophie's spine.

Either she played the part of his princess or he'd split her open.

Someone grabbed Agatha's arm—

"She's here!" a toothless man croaked. "I found her! I found Tedros' queen!"

By the time anyone heard him, Agatha was already running.

She ripped through the gauntlet of bodies towards the castle gates, Dovey's bag slamming against her. She glanced back, spotting a dozen guards starting to plow through the crowd. Agatha ran and ran, over the broken drawbridge, down the carriage roads, now far out of the sight of the guards. But still she ran, until she was down the hill, catching her breath just long enough to look up at the sunlit castle, where guards took Tedros away as Rhian placed Camelot's crown upon his own head, Sophie still tight against him. And as a cloud passed over the sun, sending the scene into shadows, the last thing Agatha saw was a new king cast in a golden glow and the old one dragged into the dark by his twisted green chains . . .

The Snake become the Lion and the Lion become the Snake.